To Jo,

who guides and steadies me

Every question that can be answered must be answered or at least engaged.
Illogical thought processes must be challenged when they arise.
Wrong answers must be corrected.
Correct answers must be affirmed.

—From the Erudite faction manifesto

CHAPTER ONE

TRIS

I PACE IN our cell in Erudite headquarters, her words echoing in my mind: *My name will be Edith Prior, and there is much I am happy to forget.*

"So you've *never* seen her before? Not even in pictures?" Christina says, her wounded leg propped up on a pillow. She was shot during our desperate attempt to reveal the Edith Prior video to our city. At the time we had no idea what it would say, or that it would shatter the foundation we stand on, the factions, our identities. "Is she a grandmother or an aunt or something?"

"I told you, no," I say, turning when I reach the wall. "Prior is—was—my father's name, so it would have to be on his side of the family. But Edith is an Abnegation name, and my father's relatives must have been Erudite, so . . ."

"So she must be older," Cara says, leaning her head against the wall. From this angle she looks just like her brother, Will, my friend, the one I shot. Then she straightens, and the ghost of him is gone. "A few generations back. An ancestor."

"Ancestor." The word feels old inside me, like crumbling brick. I touch one wall of the cell as I turn around. The panel is cold and white.

My ancestor, and this is the inheritance she passed to me: freedom from the factions, and the knowledge that my Divergent identity is more important than I could have known. My existence is a signal that we need to leave this city and offer our help to whoever is outside it.

"I want to know," Cara says, running her hand over her face. "I need to know how long we've been here. Would you stop pacing for *one minute*?"

I stop in the middle of the cell and raise my eyebrows at her.

"Sorry," she mumbles.

"It's okay," Christina says. "We've been in here way too long."

It's been days since Evelyn mastered the chaos in the lobby of Erudite headquarters with a few short commands and had all the prisoners hustled away to cells on the third floor. A factionless woman came to doctor our wounds and distribute painkillers, and we've eaten and showered several times, but no one has told us what's going on outside. No matter how forcefully I've asked them.

"I thought Tobias would come by now," I say, dropping to the edge of my cot. "Where *is* he?"

"Maybe he's still angry that you lied to him and went behind his back to work with his father," Cara says.

I glare at her.

"Four wouldn't be that petty," Christina says, either to chastise Cara or to reassure me, I'm not sure. "Something's probably going on that's keeping him away. He told you to trust him."

In the chaos, when everyone was shouting and the factionless were trying to push us toward the staircase, I curled my fingers in the hem of his shirt so I wouldn't lose him. He took my wrists in his hands and pushed me away, and those were the words he said. *Trust me. Go where they tell you.*

"I'm trying," I say, and it's true. I'm trying to trust him. But every part of me, every fiber and every nerve, is straining toward freedom, not just from this cell but from the prison of the city beyond it.

I need to see what's outside the fence.

CHAPTER TWO

TOBIAS

I CAN'T WALK these hallways without remembering the days I spent as a prisoner here, barefoot, pain pulsing inside me every time I moved. And with that memory is another one, one of waiting for Beatrice Prior to go to her death, of my fists against the door, of her legs slung across Peter's arms when he told me she was just drugged.

I hate this place.

It isn't as clean as it was when it was the Erudite compound; now it is ravaged by war, bullet holes in the walls and the broken glass of shattered lightbulbs everywhere. I walk over dirty footprints and beneath flickering lights to her cell and I am admitted without question, because I bear the factionless symbol—an empty circle—on a black band around my arm and Evelyn's features on my face. Tobias Eaton was a shameful name, and now it is a powerful one.

Tris crouches on the ground inside, shoulder to shoulder with Christina and diagonal from Cara. My Tris should look pale and small—she *is* pale and small, after all—but instead the room is full of her.

Her round eyes find mine and she is on her feet, her arms wound tightly around my waist and her face against my chest.

I squeeze her shoulder with one hand and run my other hand over her hair, still surprised when her hair stops above her neck instead of below it. I was happy when she cut it, because it was hair for a warrior and not a girl, and I knew that was what she would need.

"How'd you get in?" she says in her low, clear voice.

"I'm Tobias Eaton," I say, and she laughs.

"Right. I keep forgetting." She pulls away just far enough to look at me. There is a wavering expression in her eyes, like she is a heap of leaves about to be scattered by the wind. "What's happening? What took you so long?"

She sounds desperate, pleading. For all the horrible memories this place carries for me, it carries more for her, the walk to her execution, her brother's betrayal, the fear serum. I have to get her out.

Cara looks up with interest. I feel uncomfortable, like I have shifted in my skin and it doesn't quite fit anymore. I hate having an audience.

"Evelyn has the city under lockdown," I say. "No one goes a step in any direction without her say-so. A few days ago she gave a speech about uniting against our oppressors, the people outside."

"Oppressors?" Christina says. She takes a vial from her pocket and dumps the contents into her mouth—painkillers for the bullet wound in her leg, I assume.

I slide my hands into my pockets. "Evelyn—and a lot of people, actually—think we shouldn't leave the city just to help a bunch of people who shoved us in here so they could use us later. They want to try to heal the city and solve our own problems instead of leaving to solve other people's. I'm paraphrasing, of course," I say. "I suspect that opinion is very convenient for my mother, because as long as we're all contained, she's in charge. The second we leave, she loses her hold."

"Great." Tris rolls her eyes. "Of course she would choose the most selfish route possible."

"She has a point." Christina wraps her fingers around the vial. "I'm not saying I don't want to leave the city and see what's out there, but we've got enough going on here. How are we supposed to help a bunch of people we've never met?"

Tris considers this, chewing on the inside of her cheek. "I don't know," she admits.

My watch reads three o'clock. I've been here too long—long enough to make Evelyn suspicious. I told her I came to break things off with Tris, that it wouldn't take much time. I'm not sure she believed me.

I say, "Listen, I mostly came to warn you—they're starting the trials for all the prisoners. They're going to put you all under truth serum, and if it works, you'll be convicted as traitors. I think we would all like to avoid that."

"Convicted as *traitors*?" Tris scowls. "How is revealing the truth to our entire city an act of betrayal?"

"It was an act of defiance against your leaders," I say. "Evelyn and her followers don't want to leave the city. They won't thank you for showing that video."

"They're just like Jeanine!" She makes a fitful gesture, like she wants to hit something but there's nothing available. "Ready to do anything to stifle the truth, and for what? To be kings of their tiny little world? It's ridiculous."

I don't want to say so, but part of me agrees with my mother. I don't owe the people outside this city anything, whether I am Divergent or not. I'm not sure I want to offer myself to them to solve humanity's problems, whatever that means.

But I do want to leave, in the desperate way that an

animal wants to escape a trap. Wild and rabid. Ready to gnaw through bone.

"Be that as it may," I say carefully, "if the truth serum works on you, you will be convicted."

"*If* it works?" says Cara, narrowing her eyes.

"Divergent," Tris says to her, pointing at her own head. "Remember?"

"That's fascinating." Cara tucks a stray hair back into the knot just above her neck. "But atypical. In my experience, most Divergent can't resist the truth serum. I wonder why you can."

"You and every other Erudite who ever stuck a needle in me," Tris snaps.

"Can we focus, please? I would like to avoid having to break you out of prison," I say. Suddenly desperate for comfort, I reach for Tris's hand, and she brings her fingers up to meet mine. We are not people who touch each other carelessly; every point of contact between us feels important, a rush of energy and relief.

"All right, all right," she says, gently now. "What did you have in mind?"

"I'll get Evelyn to let you testify first, of the three of you," I say. "All you have to do is come up with a lie that will exonerate both Christina and Cara, and then tell it under truth serum."

"What kind of lie would do that?"

"I thought I would leave that to you," I say. "Since you're the better liar."

I know as I'm saying the words that they hit a sore spot in both of us. She lied to me so many times. She promised me she wouldn't go to her death in the Erudite compound when Jeanine demanded the sacrifice of a Divergent, and then she did it anyway. She told me she would stay home during the Erudite attack, and then I found her in Erudite headquarters, working with my father. I understand why she did all those things, but that doesn't mean we aren't still broken.

"Yeah." She looks at her shoes. "Okay, I'll think of something."

I set my hand on her arm. "I'll talk to Evelyn about your trial. I'll try to make it soon."

"Thank you."

I feel the urge, familiar now, to wrench myself from my body and speak directly into her mind. It is the same urge, I realize, that makes me want to kiss her every time I see her, because even a sliver of distance between us is infuriating. Our fingers, loosely woven a moment ago, now clutch together, her palm tacky with moisture, mine rough in places where I have grabbed too many handles on too many moving trains. Now she looks pale and small, but her eyes make me think of wide-open skies that I have never actually seen, only dreamed of.

"If you're going to kiss, do me a favor and tell me so I can look away," says Christina.

"We are," Tris says. And we do.

I touch her cheek to slow the kiss down, holding her mouth on mine so I can feel every place where our lips touch and every place where they pull away. I savor the air we share in the second afterward and the slip of her nose across mine. I think of something to say, but it is too intimate, so I swallow it. A moment later I decide I don't care.

"I wish we were alone," I say as I back out of the cell.

She smiles. "I almost always wish that."

As I shut the door, I see Christina pretending to vomit, and Cara laughing, and Tris's hands hanging at her sides.

CHAPTER THREE

TRIS

"I THINK YOU'RE all idiots." My hands are curled in my lap like a sleeping child's. My body is heavy with truth serum. Sweat collects on my eyelids. "You should be thanking me, not questioning me."

"We should thank you for defying the instructions of your faction leaders? Thank you for trying to prevent one of your faction leaders from killing Jeanine Matthews? You behaved like a traitor." Evelyn Johnson spits the word like a snake. We are in the conference room in Erudite headquarters, where the trials have been taking place. I have now been a prisoner for at least a week.

I see Tobias, half-hidden in the shadows behind his mother. He has kept his eyes averted since I sat in the chair and they cut the strip of plastic binding my wrists together. For just for a moment, his eyes touch mine, and I know it's time to start lying.

It's easier now that I know I can do it. As easy as pushing the weight of the truth serum aside in my mind.

"I am not a traitor," I say. "At the time I believed that Marcus was working under Dauntless-factionless orders. Since I couldn't join the fight as a soldier, I was happy to help with something else."

"Why couldn't you be a soldier?" Fluorescent light glows behind Evelyn's hair. I can't see her face, and I can't focus on anything for more than a second before the truth serum threatens to pull me down again.

"Because." I bite my lip, as if trying to stop the words from rushing out. I don't know when I became so good at acting, but I guess it's not that different from lying, which I have always had a talent for. "Because I couldn't hold a gun, okay? Not after shooting . . . him. My friend Will. I couldn't hold a gun without panicking."

Evelyn's eyes pinch tighter. I suspect that even in the softest parts of her, there is no sympathy for me.

"So Marcus told you he was working under my orders," she says, "and even knowing what you do about his rather tense relationship with both the Dauntless and the factionless, you believed him?"

"Yes."

"I can see why you didn't choose Erudite." She laughs.

My cheeks tingle. I would like to slap her, as I'm sure many of the people in this room would, though they wouldn't dare to admit it. Evelyn has us all trapped in the city, controlled by armed factionless patrolling the streets. She knows that whoever holds the guns holds the power. And with Jeanine Matthews dead, there is no one left to challenge her for it.

From one tyrant to another. That is the world we know, now.

"Why didn't you tell anyone about this?" she says.

"I didn't want to have to admit to any weakness," I say. "And I didn't want Four to know I was working with his father. I knew he wouldn't like it." I feel new words rising in my throat, prompted by the truth serum. "I brought you the truth about our city and the reason we are in it. If you aren't thanking me for it, you should at least *do* something about it instead of sitting here on this mess you made, pretending it's a throne!"

Evelyn's mocking smile twists like she has just tasted something unpleasant. She leans in close to my face, and I see for the first time how old she is; I see the lines that frame her eyes and mouth, and the unhealthy pallor she wears from years of eating far too little. Still, she is handsome like her son. Near-starvation could not take that.

"I am doing something about it. I am making a new world," she says, and her voice gets even quieter, so that I can barely hear her. "I was Abnegation. I have known the truth far longer than you have, Beatrice Prior. I don't know how you're getting away with this, but I promise you, you will not have a place in my new world, especially not with my son."

I smile a little. I shouldn't, but it's harder to suppress gestures and expressions than words, with this weight in my veins. She believes that Tobias belongs to her now. She doesn't know the truth, that he belongs to himself.

Evelyn straightens, folding her arms.

"The truth serum has revealed that while you may be a fool, you are no traitor. This interrogation is over. You may leave."

"What about my friends?" I say sluggishly. "Christina, Cara. They didn't do anything wrong either."

"We will deal with them soon," Evelyn says.

I stand, though I'm weak and dizzy from the serum. The room is packed with people, shoulder to shoulder, and I can't find the exit for a few long seconds, until someone takes my arm, a boy with warm brown skin and a wide smile—Uriah. He guides me to the door. Everyone starts talking.

+++

Uriah leads me down the hallway to the elevator bank. The elevator doors spring open when he touches the button, and I follow him in, still not steady on my feet. When the doors close, I say, "You don't think the part about the mess and the throne was too much?"

"No. She expects you to be hotheaded. She might have been suspicious if you hadn't been."

I feel like everything inside me is vibrating with energy, in anticipation of what is to come. I am free. We're going to find a way out of the city. No more waiting, pacing a cell, demanding answers that I won't get from the guards.

The guards did tell me a few things about the new factionless order this morning. Former faction members are required to move closer to Erudite headquarters and mix, no more than four members of a particular faction in each dwelling. We have to mix our clothing, too. I was given a yellow Amity shirt and black Candor pants earlier as a result of that particular edict.

"All right, we're this way. . . ." Uriah leads me out of the elevator. This floor of Erudite headquarters is all glass, even the walls. Sunlight refracts through it and casts slivers of rainbows across the floor. I shield my eyes with one hand and follow Uriah to a long, narrow room with beds on either side. Next to each bed is a glass cabinet for clothes and books, and a small table.

"It used to be the Erudite initiate dormitory," Uriah says. "I reserved beds for Christina and Cara already."

Sitting on a bed near the door are three girls in red shirts—Amity girls, I would guess—and on the left side of the room, an older woman lies on one of the beds, her spectacles dangling from one ear—possibly one of the Erudite. I know I should try to stop putting people in factions when I see them, but it's an old habit, hard to break.

Uriah falls on one of the beds in the back corner. I sit on the one next to his, glad to be free and at rest, finally.

"Zeke says it sometimes takes a little while for the factionless to process exonerations, so they should be out later," Uriah says.

For a moment I feel relieved that everyone I care about will be out of prison by tonight. But then I remember that Caleb is still there, because he was a well-known lackey of Jeanine Matthews, and the factionless will never exonerate him. But just how far they will go to destroy the mark Jeanine Matthews left on this city, I don't know.

I don't care, I think. But even as I think it, I know it's a lie. He's still my brother.

"Good," I say. "Thanks, Uriah."

He nods, and leans his head against the wall to prop it up.

"How are you?" I say. "I mean . . . Lynn . . ."

Uriah had been friends with Lynn and Marlene as long as I'd known them, and now both of them are dead. I feel like I might be able to understand—after all, I've lost two friends too, Al to the pressures of initiation and Will to the attack simulation and my own hasty actions. But I don't want to pretend that our suffering is the same. For one thing, Uriah knew his friends better than I did.

"I don't want to talk about it." Uriah shakes his head. "Or think about it. I just want to keep moving."

"Okay. I understand. Just . . . let me know if you need . . ."

"Yeah." He smiles at me and gets up. "You're okay here, right? I told my mom I'd visit tonight, so I have to go soon. Oh—almost forgot to tell you—Four said he wants to meet you later."

I pull up straighter. "Really? When? Where?"

"A little after ten, at Millennium Park. On the lawn." He smirks. "Don't get too excited, your head will explode."

CHAPTER FOUR

TOBIAS

MY MOTHER ALWAYS sits on the edges of things—chairs, ledges, tables—as if she suspects she will have to flee in an instant. This time it's Jeanine's old desk in Erudite headquarters that she sits on the edge of, her toes balanced on the floor and the cloudy light of the city glowing behind her. She is a woman of muscle twisted around bone.

"I think we have to talk about your loyalty," she says, but she doesn't sound like she's accusing me of something, she just sounds tired. For a moment she seems so worn that I feel like I can see right through her, but then she straightens, and the feeling is gone.

"Ultimately, it was you who helped Tris and got that video released," she says. "No one else knows that, but *I* know it."

"Listen." I lean forward to prop my elbows on my knees. "I didn't know what was in that file. I trusted Tris's judgment more than my own. That's all that happened."

I thought telling Evelyn that I broke up with Tris would make it easier for my mother to trust me, and I was right—she has been warmer, more open, ever since I told that lie.

"And now that you've seen the footage?" Evelyn says. "What do you think now? Do you think we should leave the city?"

I know what she wants me to say—that I see no reason to join the outside world—but I'm not a good liar, so instead I select a part of the truth.

"I'm afraid of it," I say. "I'm not sure it's smart to leave the city knowing the dangers that might be out there."

She considers me for a moment, biting the inside of her cheek. I learned that habit from her—I used to chew my skin raw as I waited for my father to come home, unsure which version of him I would encounter, the one the Abnegation trusted and revered, or the one whose hands struck me.

I run my tongue along the bite scars and swallow the memory like it's bile.

She slides off the desk and moves to the window. "I've been receiving disturbing reports of a rebel organization among us." She looks up, raising an eyebrow. "People always organize into groups. That's a fact of our existence. I just didn't expect it to happen this quickly."

"What kind of organization?"

"The kind that wants to leave the city," she says. "They released some kind of manifesto this morning. They call themselves the Allegiant." When she sees my confused look, she adds, "Because they're *allied* with the original purpose of our city, see?"

"The original purpose—you mean, what was in the Edith Prior video? That we should send people outside when the city has a large Divergent population?"

"That, yes. But also living in factions. The Allegiant claim that we're meant to be in factions because we've been in them since the beginning." She shakes her head. "Some people will always fear change. But we can't indulge them."

With the factions dismantled, part of me has felt like a man released from a long imprisonment. I don't have to evaluate whether every thought I have or choice I make fits into a narrow ideology. I don't want the factions back.

But Evelyn hasn't liberated us like she thinks—she's just made us all factionless. She's afraid of what we would choose, if we were given actual freedom. And that means that no matter what I believe about the factions, I'm relieved that someone, somewhere, is defying her.

I arrange my face into an empty expression, but my heart is beating faster than before. I have had to be careful, to stay in Evelyn's good graces. It's easy for me to lie to everyone else, but it's more difficult to lie to her, the only person who knew all the secrets of our Abnegation house, the violence contained within its walls.

"What are you going to do about them?" I say.

"I am going to get them under control, what else?"

The word "control" makes me sit up straight, as rigid as the chair beneath me. In this city, "control" means needles and serums and seeing without seeing; it means simulations, like the one that almost made me kill Tris, or the one that made the Dauntless into an army.

"With simulations?" I say slowly.

She scowls. "Of course not! I am not Jeanine Matthews!"

Her flare of anger sets me off. I say, "Don't forget that I barely know you, Evelyn."

She winces at the reminder. "Then let me tell you that I will never resort to simulations to get my way. Death would be better."

It's possible that death is what she will use—killing people would certainly keep them quiet, stifle their revolution before it begins. Whoever the Allegiant are, they need to be warned, and quickly.

"I can find out who they are," I say.

"I'm sure that you can. Why else would I have told you about them?"

There are plenty of reasons she would tell me. To test me. To catch me. To feed me false information. I know what my mother is—she is someone for whom the end of a thing justifies the means of getting there, the same as my father, and the same, sometimes, as me.

"I'll do it, then. I'll find them."

I rise, and her fingers, brittle as branches, close around my arm. "Thank you."

I force myself to look at her. Her eyes are close above her nose, which is hooked at the end, like my own. Her skin is a middling color, darker than mine. For a moment I see her in Abnegation gray, her thick hair bound back with a dozen pins, sitting across the dinner table from me. I see her crouched in front of me, fixing my mismatched shirt buttons before I go to school, and standing at the window, watching the uniform street for my father's car, her hands clasped—no, clenched, her tan knuckles white with tension. We were united in fear then, and now that she isn't afraid anymore, part of me wants to see what it would be like to unite with her in strength.

I feel an ache, like I betrayed her, the woman who used to be my only ally, and I turn away before I can take it all back and apologize.

I leave Erudite headquarters amid a crowd of people, my eyes confused, hunting for faction colors automatically when there are none left. I am wearing a gray shirt, blue jeans, black shoes—new clothes, but beneath them, my Dauntless tattoos. It is impossible to erase my choices. Especially these.

CHAPTER FIVE

TRIS

I SET MY watch alarm for ten o'clock and fall asleep right away, without even shifting to a comfortable position. A few hours later the beeps don't wake me, but the frustrated shout of someone across the room does. I turn off the alarm, run my fingers through my hair, and half walk, half jog to one of the emergency staircases. The exit at the bottom will let me out in the alley, where I probably won't be stopped.

Once I'm outside, the cool air wakes me up. I pull my sleeves down over my fingers to keep them warm. Summer is finally ending. There are a few people milling around the entrance to Erudite headquarters, but none of them notices me creeping across Michigan Avenue. There are some advantages to being small.

I see Tobias standing in the middle of the lawn, wearing mixed faction colors—a gray T-shirt, blue jeans, and a black sweatshirt with a hood, representing all the factions my aptitude test told me I was qualified for. A backpack rests against his feet.

"How did I do?" I say when I'm close enough for him to hear me.

"Very well," he says. "Evelyn still hates you, but Christina and Cara have been released without questioning."

"Good." I smile.

He pinches the front of my shirt, right over my stomach, and tugs me toward him, kissing me softly.

"Come on," he says as he pulls away. "I have a plan for this evening."

"Oh, really?"

"Yes, well, I realized that we've never been on an actual date."

"Chaos and destruction do tend to take away a person's dating possibilities."

"I would like to experience this 'date' phenomenon." He walks backward, toward the mammoth metal structure at the other end of the lawn, and I follow him. "Before you, I only went on group dates, and they were usually a disaster. They always ended up with Zeke making out with whatever girl he intended to make out with, and me sitting in awkward silence with some girl that I had somehow offended in some way early on."

"You're not very nice," I say, grinning.

"You're one to talk."

"Hey, I could be nice if I tried."

"Hmm." He taps his chin. "Say something nice, then."

"You're very good-looking."

He smiles, his teeth a flash in the dark. "I like this 'nice' thing."

We reach the end of the lawn. The metal structure is larger and stranger up close than it was from far away. It's really a stage, and arcing above it are massive metal plates that curl in different directions, like an exploded aluminum can. We walk around one of the plates on the right side to the back of the stage, which rises at an angle from the ground. There, metal beams support the plates from behind. Tobias secures his backpack on his shoulders and grabs one of the beams. Climbing.

"This feels familiar," I say. One of the first things we did together was scale the Ferris wheel, but that time it was me, not him, who compelled us to climb higher.

I push up my sleeves and follow him. My shoulder is still sore from the bullet wound, but it is mostly healed. Still, I bear most of my weight with my left arm and try to push with my feet whenever possible. I look down at the tangle of bars beneath me and beyond them, the ground, and laugh.

Tobias climbs to a spot where two metal plates meet in a V, leaving enough room for two people to sit. He scoots back, wedging himself between the two plates, and reaches for my waist to help me when I get close enough. I don't really need the help, but I don't say so—I am too busy enjoying his hands on me.

He takes a blanket out of his backpack and covers us with it, then produces two plastic cups.

"Would you like a clear head or a fuzzy one?" he says, peering into the bag.

"Um . . ." I tilt my head. "Clear. I think we have some things to talk about, right?"

"Yes."

He takes out a small bottle with clear, bubbling liquid in it, and as he twists open the cap, says, "I stole it from the Erudite kitchens. Apparently it's delicious."

He pours some in each cup, and I take a sip. Whatever it is, it's sweet as syrup and lemon-flavored and makes me cringe a little. My second sip is better.

"Things to talk about," he says.

"Right."

"Well . . ." Tobias frowns into his cup. "Okay, so I understand why you worked with Marcus, and why you felt like you couldn't tell me. But . . ."

"But you're angry," I say. "Because I lied to you. On several occasions."

He nods, not looking at me. "It's not even the Marcus thing. It's further back than that. I don't know if you can understand what it was like to wake up alone, and know that you had gone"—*to your death*, is what I suspect he wants to say, but he can't even say the words—"to Erudite headquarters."

"No, I probably can't." I take another sip, turning the sugary drink over in my mouth before swallowing. "Listen, I . . . I used to think about giving my life for things, but I didn't understand what 'giving your life' really was until it was right there, about to be taken from me."

I look up at him, and finally, he looks back at me.

"I know now," I say. "I know I want to live. I know I want to be honest with you. But . . . but I can't do that, I won't do it, if you won't trust me, or if you talk to me in that condescending way you sometimes do—"

"Condescending?" he says. "You were doing ridiculous, risky things—"

"Yeah," I say. "And do you really think it helped to talk to me like I was a child who didn't know any better?"

"What else was I supposed to do?" he demands. "You wouldn't see reason!"

"Maybe reason wasn't what I needed!" I sit forward, not able to pretend I am relaxed anymore. "I felt like I was being eaten alive by guilt, and what I needed was your patience and your kindness, not for you to *yell* at me. Oh, and for you to constantly keep your plans from me like I couldn't possibly handle—"

"I didn't want to burden you more than you already were."

"So do you think I'm a strong person, or not?" I scowl at him. "Because you seem to think I can take it when you're scolding me, but you don't think I can handle anything else? What does that mean?"

"Of course I think you're a strong person." He shakes his head. "I just . . . I'm not used to telling people things. I'm used to handling things on my own."

"I'm reliable," I say. "You can trust me. And you can let me be the judge of what I can handle."

"Okay," he says, nodding. "But no more lies. Not ever."

"Okay."

I feel stiff and squeezed, like my body was just forced into something too small for it. But that's not how I want the conversation to end, so I reach for his hand.

"I'm sorry I lied to you," I say. "I really am."

"Well," he says. "I didn't mean to make you feel like I didn't respect you."

We stay there for a while, our hands clasped. I lean back against the metal plate. Above me, the sky is blank and dark, the moon shielded by clouds. I find a star ahead of us, as the clouds shift, but it seems to be the only one.

When I tilt my head back, though, I can see the line of buildings along Michigan Avenue, like a row of sentries keeping watch over us.

I am quiet until the stiff, squeezed feeling leaves me. In its place I now feel relief. It isn't usually that easy for me to let go of anger, but the past few weeks have been strange for both of us, and I am happy to release the feelings I have been holding on to, the anger and the fear that he hates me and the guilt from working with his father behind his back.

"This stuff is kind of gross," he says, draining his cup and setting it down.

"Yes, it is," I say, staring at what remains in mine. I drink it in one gulp, wincing as the bubbles burn my throat. "I don't know what the Erudite are always bragging about. Dauntless cake is much better."

"I wonder what the Abnegation treat would have been, if they had one."

"Stale bread."

He laughs. "Plain oatmeal."

"Milk."

"Sometimes I think I believe everything they taught us," he says. "But obviously not, since I'm sitting here holding your hand right now without having married you first."

"What do the Dauntless teach about . . . that?" I say, nodding to our hands.

"What do the Dauntless teach, hmm." He smirks. "Do whatever you want, but use protection, is what they teach."

I raise my eyebrows. Suddenly my face feels warm.

"I think I'd like to find a middle ground for myself," he says. "To find that place between what I want and what I think is wise."

"That sounds good." I pause. "But what do you want?"

I think I know the answer, but I want to hear him say it.

"Hmm." He grins, and leans forward onto his knees. He presses his hands to the metal plate, framing my head with his arms, and kisses me, slowly, on my mouth, under my jaw, right above my collarbone. I stay still, nervous about doing anything, in case it's stupid or he doesn't like it. But then I feel like a statue, like I am not really here at all, and so I touch his waist, hesitantly.

Then his lips are on mine again, and he pulls his shirt out from under my hands so that I am touching his bare skin. I come to life, pressing closer, my hands creeping up his back, sliding over his shoulders. His breaths come faster and so do mine, and I taste the lemon-syrup-fizz we just drank and I smell the wind on his skin and all I want is more, more.

I push his shirt up. A moment ago I was cold, but I don't think either of us is cold now. His arm wraps around my waist, strong and certain, and his free hand tangles in my hair and I slow down, drinking it in—the smoothness of his skin, marked up and down with black ink, and the insistence of the kiss, and the cool air wrapped around us both.

I relax, and I no longer feel like some kind of Divergent soldier, defying serums and government leaders alike. I feel softer, lighter, and like it is okay to laugh a little as his fingertips brush over my hips and the small of my back, or to sigh into his ear when he pulls me against him, burying his face in the side of my neck so that he can kiss me there. I feel like myself, strong and weak at once—allowed, at least for a little while, to be both.

I don't know how long it is before we get cold again, and huddle under the blanket together.

"It's getting more difficult to be wise," he says, laughing into my ear.

I smile at him. "I think that's how it's supposed to be."

CHAPTER SIX

TOBIAS

SOMETHING IS BREWING.

I can feel it as I walk the cafeteria line with my tray, and see it in the huddled heads of a group of factionless as they lean over their oatmeal. Whatever is about to happen will happen soon.

Yesterday when I left Evelyn's office I lingered in the hallway to eavesdrop on her next meeting. Before she closed the door, I heard her say something about a demonstration. The question that is itching at the back of my mind is: Why didn't she tell me?

She must not trust me. That means I'm not doing as good a job as her pretend right-hand man as I think I am.

I sit down with the same breakfast as everyone else: a

bowl of oatmeal with a sprinkle of brown sugar on it, and a mug of coffee. I watch the group of factionless as I spoon it into my mouth without tasting it. One of them—a girl, maybe fourteen—keeps flicking her eyes toward the clock.

I'm halfway done with breakfast when I hear the shouts. The nervy factionless girl jolts from her seat as if stuck with a live wire, and they all start toward the door. I am right behind them, elbowing my way past slow-movers through the lobby of Erudite headquarters, where the portrait of Jeanine Matthews still lies in shreds on the floor.

A group of factionless has already gathered outside, in the middle of Michigan Avenue. A layer of pale clouds covers the sun, making the daylight hazy and dull. I hear someone shout, "Death to the factions!" and others pick up the phrase, turning it into a chant, until it fills my ears, *Death to the factions, death to the factions*. I see their fists in the air, like excitable Dauntless, but without the Dauntless joy. Their faces are twisted with rage.

I push toward the middle of the group, and then I see what they're all gathered around: The huge, man-sized faction bowls from the Choosing Ceremony are turned on their sides, their contents spilling across the road, coals and glass and stone and earth and water all mingling together.

I remember slicing into my palm to add my blood to the

coals, my first act of defiance against my father. I remember the surge of power inside me, and the rush of relief. Escape. These bowls were my escape.

Edward stands among them, shards of glass ground to dust beneath his heel, a sledgehammer held above his head. He brings it down on one of the overturned bowls, forcing a dent into the metal. Coal dust rises into the air.

I have to stop myself from running at him. He can't destroy it, not that bowl, not the Choosing Ceremony, not the symbol of my triumph. Those things should not be destroyed.

The crowd is swelling, not just with factionless wearing black armbands with empty white circles on them, but with people from every former faction, their arms bare. An Erudite man—his faction still indicated by his neatly parted hair—bursts free of the crowd just as Edward is pulling back the sledgehammer for another swing. He wraps his soft, ink-smudged hands around the handle, just above Edward's, and they push into each other, teeth gritted.

I see a blond head across the crowd—Tris, wearing a loose blue shirt without sleeves, showing the edges of the faction tattoos on her shoulders. She tries to run to Edward and the Erudite man, but Christina stops her with both hands.

The Erudite man's face turns purple. Edward is taller

and stronger than he is. He has no chance; he's a fool for trying. Edward rips the sledgehammer handle from the Erudite man's hands and swings again. But he's off balance, dizzy with rage—the sledgehammer hits the Erudite man in the shoulder at full force, metal cracking bone.

For a moment all I hear is the Erudite man's screams. It's like everyone is taking a breath.

Then the crowd explodes into a frenzy, everyone running toward the bowls, toward Edward, toward the Erudite man. They collide with one another and then with me, shoulders and elbows and heads hitting me over and over again.

I don't know where to run: to the Erudite man, to Edward, to Tris? I can't think; I can't breathe. The crowd carries me toward Edward, and I grab his arm.

"Let go!" I shout over the noise. His single bright eye fixes on me, and he bares his teeth, trying to wrench himself away.

I bring my knee up, into his side. He stumbles back, losing his grip on the sledgehammer. I hold it close to my leg and start toward Tris.

She is somewhere in front of me, struggling toward the Erudite man. I watch as a woman's elbow hits her in the cheek, sending her reeling backward. Christina shoves the woman away.

Then a gun goes off. Once, twice. Three times.

The crowd scatters, everyone running in terror from the threat of bullets, and I try to see who, if anyone, was shot, but the rush of bodies is too intense. I can barely see anything.

Tris and Christina crouch next to the Erudite man with the shattered shoulder. His face is bloody and his clothes are dirty with footprints. His combed Erudite hair is tousled. He isn't moving.

A few feet away from him, Edward lies in a pool of his own blood. The bullet hit him in the gut. There are other people on the ground too, people I don't recognize, people who got trampled or shot. I suspect the bullets were meant for Edward and Edward alone—the others were just bystanders.

I look around wildly but I don't see the shooter. Whoever it was seems to have dissolved into the crowd.

I drop the sledgehammer next to the dented bowl and kneel beside Edward, Abnegation stones digging into my kneecaps. His remaining eye moves back and forth beneath his eyelid—he's alive, for now.

"We have to get him to the hospital," I say to whoever is listening. Almost everyone is gone.

I look over my shoulder at Tris and the Erudite man, who hasn't moved. "Is he . . . ?"

Her fingers are on his throat, taking his pulse, and her eyes are wide and empty. She shakes her head. No, he is not alive. I didn't think he was.

I close my eyes. The faction bowls are printed on my eyelids, tipped on their sides, their contents in a pile on the street. The symbols of our old way of life, destroyed—a man dead, others injured—and for what?

For nothing. For Evelyn's empty, narrow vision: a city where factions are wrenched away from people against their will.

She wanted us to have more than five choices. Now we have none.

I know for sure, then, that I can't be her ally, and I never could have.

"We have to go," Tris says, and I know she's not talking about leaving Michigan Avenue or taking Edward to the hospital; she's talking about the city.

"We have to go," I repeat.

+++

The makeshift hospital at Erudite headquarters smells like chemicals, almost gritty in my nose. I close my eyes as I wait for Evelyn.

I'm so angry I don't even want to sit here, I just want to pack up my things and leave. She must have planned that demonstration, or she wouldn't have known about it the day before, and she must have known that it would get out of control, with tensions running as high as they are. But she did it anyway. Making a big statement about the factions was more important to her than safety or the potential loss of lives. I don't know why that surprises me.

I hear the elevator doors slide open, and her voice: "Tobias!"

She rushes toward me and seizes my hands, which are sticky with blood. Her dark eyes are wide with fear as she says, "Are you hurt?"

She's worried about me. The thought is a little pinprick of heat inside me—she must love me, to worry about me. She must still be capable of love.

"The blood is Edward's. I helped carry him here."

"How is he?" she says.

I shake my head. "Dead."

I don't know how else to say it.

She shrinks back, releasing my hands, and sits on one of the waiting room chairs. My mother embraced Edward after he defected from Dauntless. She must have taught him to be a warrior again, after the loss of his eye and his faction and his footing. I never knew they were so close, but I can see it now, in the gleam of tears in her eyes and the trembling of her fingers. It's the most emotion I've seen her show since I was a child, since my father slammed her into our living room walls.

I press the memory away as if stuffing it into a drawer that is too small for it.

"I'm sorry," I say. I don't know if I really mean it or if I'm just saying it so she still thinks I'm on her side. Then I add tentatively, "Why didn't you tell me about the demonstration?"

She shakes her head. "I didn't know about it."

She's lying. I know. I decide to let her. In order to stay on her good side, I have to avoid conflict with her. Or maybe I just don't want to press the issue with Edward's death looming over both of us. Sometimes it's hard for me to tell where strategy ends and sympathy for her begins.

"Oh." I scratch behind my ear. "You can go in and see him, if you want."

"No." She seems far away. "I know what bodies look like." Drifting further.

"Maybe I should go."

"Stay," she says. She touches the empty chair between us. "Please."

I take the seat beside her, and though I tell myself that I am just an undercover agent obeying his supposed leader, I feel like I am a son comforting his grieving mother.

We sit with our shoulders touching, our breaths falling into the same rhythm, and we don't say a word.

CHAPTER SEVEN

TRIS

CHRISTINA TURNS A black stone over and over in her hand as we walk. It takes me a few seconds to realize that it's actually a piece of coal, from the Dauntless Choosing Ceremony bowl.

"I didn't really want to bring this up, but I can't stop thinking about it," she says. "That of the ten transfer initiates we started with, only six are still alive."

Ahead of us is the Hancock building, and beyond it, Lake Shore Drive, the lazy strip of pavement that I once flew over like a bird. We walk the cracked sidewalk side by side, our clothes smeared with Edward's blood, now dry.

It hasn't hit me yet: that Edward, by far the most talented transfer initiate we had, the boy whose blood I cleaned off the dormitory floor, is dead. He's dead now.

"And of the nice ones," I say, "it's just you, me, and . . . Myra, probably."

I haven't seen Myra since she left the Dauntless compound with Edward, right after his eye was claimed by a butter knife. I know they broke up not long after that, but I never found out where she went. I don't think I ever exchanged more than a few words with her anyway.

A set of doors to the Hancock building are already open, dangling from their hinges. Uriah said that he would come here early to turn on the generator, and sure enough, when I touch my finger to the elevator button, it glows through my fingernail.

"Have you been here before?" I say as we walk into the elevator.

"No," Christina says. "Not inside, I mean. I didn't get to go zip lining, remember?"

"Right." I lean against the wall. "You should try to go before we leave."

"Yeah." She's wearing red lipstick. It reminds me of the way candy stains children's skin if they eat it too sloppily. "Sometimes I get where Evelyn's coming from. So many awful things have happened, sometimes it feels like a good idea to stay here and just . . . try to clean up this mess before we get ourselves involved in another." She smiles a little. "But of course, I'm not going to do that," she adds. "I'm not even sure why. Curiosity, I guess."

"Have you talked to your parents about it?"

Sometimes I forget that Christina isn't like me, with no family loyalty to tie her to one place anymore. She has a mother and a little sister, both former Candor.

"They have to look after my sister," she says. "They don't know if it's safe out there; they don't want to risk her."

"But they would be okay with you leaving?"

"They were okay with me joining another faction. They'll be okay with this, too," she says. She looks down at her shoes. "They just want me to live an honest life, you know? And I can't do that here. I just know that I can't."

The elevator doors open, and the wind hits us immediately, still warm but woven with threads of winter cold. I hear voices coming from the roof, and I climb the ladder to get to them. It bounces with each of my footsteps, but Christina holds it steady for me until I reach the top.

Uriah and Zeke are there, throwing pebbles off the roof and listening for the clatter when they hit the windows. Uriah tries to bump Zeke's elbow before he throws, to mess him up, but Zeke is too quick for him.

"Hey," they say in unison when they spot Christina and me.

"Wait, are you guys related or something?" Christina

says, grinning. They both laugh, but Uriah looks a little dazed, like he's not quite connected to this moment or this place. I guess losing someone the way he lost Marlene can do that to a person, though that's not what it did to me.

There are no slings on the roof for the zip line, and that's not why we came. I don't know why the others did, but I wanted to be up high—I wanted to see as far as I could. But all the land west of where I am is black, like it's draped in a dark blanket. For a moment I think I can make out a glimmer of light on the horizon, but the next it's gone, just a trick of the eyes.

The others are quiet too. I wonder if we're all thinking the same thing.

"What do you think's out there?" Uriah finally says.

Zeke just shrugs, but Christina ventures a guess. "What if it's just more of the same? Just . . . more crumbling city, more factions, more of everything?"

"Can't be," Uriah says, shaking his head. "There has to be something *else*."

"Or there's nothing," Zeke suggests. "Those people who put us all in here, they could just be dead. Everything could be empty."

I shiver. I had never thought of that before, but he's right—we don't know what's happened out there since they put us in here, or how many generations have lived and died since they did. We could be the last people left.

"It doesn't matter," I say, more sternly than I mean to. "It doesn't matter what's out there, we have to see it for ourselves. And then we'll deal with it once we have."

We stand there for a long time. I follow the bumpy edges of buildings with my eyes until all the lit windows smear into a line. Then Uriah asks Christina about the riot, and our still, silent moment passes as if carried away by the wind.

+++

The next day, Evelyn stands among the pieces of Jeanine Matthews's portrait in the Erudite headquarters lobby and announces a new set of rules. Former faction members and factionless alike are gathered in the space and spilling out into the street to hear what our new leader has to say, and factionless soldiers line the walls, their fingers poised over the triggers of their guns. Keeping us under control.

"Yesterday's events made it clear that we are no longer able to trust each other," she says. She looks ashen and exhausted. "We will be introducing more structure into everyone's lives until our situation is more stable. The first of these measures is a curfew: Everyone is required to return to their assigned living spaces at nine o'clock at night. They will not leave those spaces until eight o'clock the next morning. Guards will be patrolling the streets at all hours to keep us safe."

I snort and try to cover it up with a cough. Christina elbows me in the side and touches her finger to her lips. I don't know why she cares—it's not like Evelyn can hear me from all the way at the front of the room.

Tori, former leader of Dauntless, ousted by Evelyn herself, stands a few feet away from me, her arms crossed. Her mouth twitches into a sneer.

"It's also time to prepare for our new, factionless way of life. Starting today, everyone will begin to learn the jobs the factionless have done for as long as we can remember. We will then *all* do those jobs on a rotation schedule, in addition to the other duties that have traditionally been performed by the factions." Evelyn smiles without really smiling. I don't know how she does it. "We will all contribute equally to our new city, as it should be. The factions have divided us, but now we will be united. Now, and forever."

All around me the factionless cheer. I just feel uneasy. I don't disagree with her, exactly, but the same faction members who rose up against Edward yesterday won't remain quiet after this, either. Evelyn's hold on this city is not as strong as she might like.

+ + +

I don't want to wrestle with the crowds after Evelyn's announcement, so I weave through the hallways until I find one of the staircases in the back, the one we climbed to reach Jeanine's laboratory not too long ago. The steps were crowded with bodies then. Now they are clean and cool, like nothing ever happened here.

As I walk past the fourth floor, I hear a yell, and some scuffling sounds. I open the door to a cluster of people—young, younger than I am, and all sporting factionless armbands—gathered around a young man on the ground.

Not just a young man—a Candor, dressed in black and white from head to toe.

I run toward them, and when I see a tall factionless girl draw back her foot to kick again, I shout, "Hey!"

No use—the kick hits the Candor boy in the side, and he groans, twisting away from it.

"Hey!" I yell again, and this time the girl turns. She's much taller than I am—a good six inches, in fact—but I'm only angry, not afraid.

"Back up," I say. "Back away from him."

"He's in violation of the dress code. I'm well within my rights, and I don't take orders from faction lovers," she says, her eyes on the ink creeping over my collarbone.

"Becks," the factionless boy beside her says. "That's the Prior video girl."

The others look impressed, but the girl just sneers. "So?"

"So," I say, "I had to hurt a lot of people to get through Dauntless initiation, and I'll do it to you, too, if I have to."

I unzip my blue sweatshirt and toss it at the Candor boy, who looks at me from the ground, blood streaming from his eyebrow. He pushes himself up, still holding his side with one hand, and pulls the sweatshirt around his shoulders like a blanket.

"There," I say. "Now he's not violating the dress code."

The girl tests the situation in her mind, evaluating whether she wants to fight me or not. I can practically hear what she's thinking—I'm small, so I'm an easy target, but I'm Dauntless, so I'm not that easy to beat. Maybe she knows that I've killed people, or maybe she just doesn't want to get into trouble, but she's losing her nerve; I can tell by the uncertain set of her mouth.

"You'd better watch your back," she says.

"I guarantee you that I don't need to," I say. "Now get out of here."

I stay just long enough to see them scatter, then keep walking. The Candor boy calls, "Wait! Your sweatshirt!"

"Keep it!" I call back.

I turn a corner that I think will take me to another staircase, but I end up in another blank hallway, just like the last one I was in. I think I hear footsteps behind me, and I spin around, ready to fight the factionless girl off, but there's no one there.

I must be getting paranoid.

I open one of the doors off the main corridor, hoping to find a window so I can reorient myself, but I find only a ransacked laboratory, beakers and test tubes scattered across each counter. Torn pieces of paper litter the floor, and I'm bending to pick one up when the lights shut off.

I lunge toward the door. A hand grabs my arm and drags me to the side. Someone shoves a sack over my head while someone else pushes me against the wall. I thrash against them, struggling with the fabric covering my face, and all I can think is, *Not again not again not again*. I twist one arm free and punch, hitting someone in a shoulder or a chin, I can't tell.

"Hey!" a voice says. "That *hurt*!"

"We're sorry for frightening you, Tris," another voice says, "but anonymity is integral to our operation. We mean you no harm."

"Let *go* of me, then!" I say, almost growling. All the hands holding me to the wall fall away.

"Who are you?" I demand.

"We are the Allegiant," the voice replies. "And we are many, yet we are no one. . . ."

I can't help it: I laugh. Maybe it's the shock—or the fear, my pounding heart slowing by the second, my hands shaking with relief.

The voice continues, "We have heard that you are not loyal to Evelyn Johnson and her factionless lackeys."

"This is ridiculous."

"Not as ridiculous as trusting someone with your identity when you don't have to."

I try to see through the fibers of whatever is over my head, but they are too dense and it is too dark. I try to relax against the wall, but it's difficult without my vision to orient me. I crush the side of a beaker under my shoe.

"No, I'm not loyal to her," I say. "Why does that matter?"

"Because it means you want to leave," the voice says. I feel a prickle of excitement. "We want to ask you for a favor, Tris Prior. We're going to have a meeting tomorrow night, at midnight. We want you to bring your Dauntless friends."

"Okay," I say. "Let me ask you this: If I'm going to see who you are tomorrow, why is it so important to keep this thing over my head today?"

This seems to temporarily stump whoever I'm talking to.

"A day contains many dangers," the voice says. "We'll see you tomorrow, at midnight, in the place where you made your confession."

All at once, the door swings open, blowing the sack against my cheeks, and I hear running footsteps down the hallway. By the time I'm able to pull the sack from my head, the corridor is silent. I look down at it—it's a dark-blue pillowcase with the words "Faction before blood" painted on it.

Whoever they are, they certainly have a flair for the dramatic.

The place where you made your confession.

There's only one place that could be: Candor headquarters, where I succumbed to the truth serum.

+++

When I finally make it back to the dormitory that evening, I find a note from Tobias tucked under the glass of water on my bedside table.

VI—

Your brother's trial will be tomorrow morning, and it will be private. I can't go or I'll raise suspicion, but I'll get you the verdict as soon as possible. Then we can make some kind of plan.

No matter what, this will be over soon.

—IV

CHAPTER EIGHT

TRIS

IT'S NINE O'CLOCK. They could be deciding Caleb's verdict right now, as I tie my shoes, as I straighten my sheets for the fourth time today. I put my hands through my hair. The factionless only make trials private when they feel the verdict is obvious, and Caleb was Jeanine's right-hand man before she was killed.

I shouldn't worry about his verdict. It's already decided. All of Jeanine's closest associates will be executed.

Why do you care? I ask myself. *He betrayed you. He didn't try to stop* your *execution.*

I don't care. I do care. I don't know.

"Hey, Tris," Christina says, rapping her knuckles against the door frame. Uriah lurks behind her. He still smiles all the time, but now his smiles look like they're made of water, about to drip down his face.

"You had some news?" she says.

I check the room again, though I already know it's empty. Everyone is at breakfast, as required by our schedules. I asked Uriah and Christina to skip a meal so that I could tell them something. My stomach is already rumbling.

"Yeah," I say.

They sit on the bed across from mine, and I tell them about getting cornered in one of the Erudite laboratories the night before, about the pillowcase and the Allegiant and the meeting.

"I'm surprised all you did was punch one of them," Uriah says.

"Well, I was outnumbered," I say, feeling defensive. It wasn't very Dauntless of me to just trust them immediately, but these are strange times. And I'm not sure how Dauntless I really am, anyway, now that the factions are gone.

I feel a strange little ache at the thought, right in the middle of my chest. Some things are hard to let go of.

"So what do you think they want?" Christina says. "Just to leave the city?"

"It sounds that way, but I don't know," I say.

"How do we know they're not Evelyn's people, trying to trick us into betraying her?"

"I don't know that, either," I say. "But it's going to be impossible to get out of the city without someone's help, and I'm not just going to stay here, learning how to drive buses and going to bed when I'm told to."

Christina gives Uriah a worried look.

"Hey," I say. "You don't have to come, but I need to get out of here. I need to know who Edith Prior was, and who's waiting for us outside the fence, if anyone. I don't know why, but I need to."

I take a deep breath. I'm not sure where that swell of desperation came from, but now that I've acknowledged it, it's impossible to ignore, like a living thing has awakened from a long sleep inside me. It writhes in my stomach and throat. I need to leave. I need the truth.

For once, the weak smile playing over Uriah's lips is gone. "So do I," he says.

"Okay," Christina says. Her dark eyes are still troubled, but she shrugs. "So we go to the meeting."

"Good. Can one of you tell Tobias? I'm supposed to be keeping my distance, since we're 'broken up,'" I say. "Let's meet in the alley at eleven thirty."

"I'll tell him. I think I'm in his group today," Uriah says. "Learning about the factories. I can't *wait*." He smirks.

"Can I tell Zeke, too? Or is he not trustworthy enough?"

"Go ahead. Just make sure he doesn't spread it around."

I check my watch again. Nine fifteen. Caleb's verdict has to be decided by now; it's almost time for everyone to go learn their factionless jobs. I feel like the slightest thing could make me jump right out of my skin. My knee bounces of its own volition.

Christina puts her hand on my shoulder, but she doesn't ask me about it, and I'm grateful. I don't know what I would say.

+++

Christina and I weave a complicated path through Erudite headquarters on our way to the back staircase, avoiding patrolling factionless. I pull my sleeve down over my wrist. I drew a map on my arm before I left—I know how to get to Candor headquarters from here, but I don't know the side streets that will keep us away from prying factionless eyes.

Uriah waits for us just outside the door. He wears all black, but I can see a hint of Abnegation gray peeking over the collar of his sweatshirt. It's strange to see my Dauntless friends in Abnegation colors, as if they've been with me my entire life. Sometimes it feels that way anyway.

"I told Four and Zeke, but they're going to meet us there," Uriah says. "Let's go."

We run in a pack down the alley toward Monroe Street. I resist the urge to wince at each of our loud footsteps. It's more important to be quick than silent at this point, anyway. We turn onto Monroe, and I check behind us for factionless patrols. I see dark shapes moving closer to Michigan Avenue, but they disappear behind the row of buildings without stopping.

"Where's Cara?" I whisper to Christina, when we're on State Street and far enough away from Erudite headquarters that it's safe to talk.

"I don't know, I don't think she got an invitation," Christina says. "Which is really bizarre. I know she wants to—"

"Shh!" Uriah says. "Next turn?"

I use my watch light to see the words written on my arm. "Randolph Street!"

We settle into a rhythm, our shoes slapping on the pavement, our breaths pulsing almost in unison. Despite the burn in my muscles, it feels good to run.

My legs ache by the time we reach the bridge, but then I see the Merciless Mart across the marshy river, abandoned and unlit, and I smile through the pain. My pace slows when I am across the bridge, and Uriah slings an arm across my shoulders.

"And now," he says, "we get to walk up a million flights of stairs."

"Maybe they turned the elevators on?"

"Not a chance." He shakes his head. "I bet Evelyn's monitoring all the electricity usage—it's the best way to figure out if people are meeting in secret."

I sigh. I may like to run, but I hate climbing stairs.

+++

When we finally reach the top of the stairs, our chests heaving, it is five minutes to midnight. The others go ahead while I catch my breath near the elevator bank. Uriah was right—there isn't a single light on that I can see, apart from the exit signs. It is in their blue glow that I see Tobias emerge from the interrogation room up ahead.

Since our date I have spoken to him only in covert messages. I have to resist the urge to throw myself at him and brush my fingers over the curl of his lip and the crease in his cheek when he smiles and the hard line of his eyebrow and jaw. But it's two minutes to midnight. We don't have any time.

He wraps his arms around me and holds me tight for a few seconds. His breaths tickle my ear, and I close my eyes, letting myself finally relax. He smells like wind and sweat and soap, like Tobias and like safety.

"Should we go in?" he says. "Whoever they are, they're probably prompt."

"Yes." My legs are trembling from overexertion—I can't imagine going down the stairs and running back to Erudite headquarters later. "Did you find out about Caleb?"

He winces. "Maybe we should talk about that later."

That's all the answer I need.

"They're going to execute him, aren't they," I say softly.

He nods, and takes my hand. I don't know how to feel. I try not to feel anything.

Together we walk into the room where Tobias and I were once interrogated under the influence of truth serum. *The place where you made your confession.*

A circle of lit candles is arranged on the floor over one of the Candor scales set into the tile. There is a mix of familiar and unfamiliar faces in the room: Susan and Robert stand together, talking; Peter is alone on the side of the room, his arms crossed; Uriah and Zeke are with Tori and a few other Dauntless; Christina is with her mother and sister; and in a corner are two nervous-looking Erudite. New outfits can't erase the divisions between us; they are ingrained.

Christina beckons to me. "This is my mom, Stephanie,"

she says, indicating a woman with gray streaks in her dark curly hair. "And my sister, Rose. Mom, Rose, this is my friend Tris, and my initiation instructor, Four."

"Obviously," Stephanie says. "We saw their interrogations several weeks ago, Christina."

"I know that, I was just being *polite*—"

"Politeness is deception in—"

"Yeah, yeah, I know." Christina rolls her eyes.

Her mother and sister, I notice, look at each other with something like wariness or anger or both. Then her sister turns to me and says, "So you killed Christina's boyfriend."

Her words create a cold feeling inside me, like a streak of ice divides one side of my body from the other. I want to answer, to defend myself, but I can't find the words.

"Rose!" Christina says, scowling at her. At my side, Tobias straightens, his muscles tensing. Ready for a fight, as always.

"I just thought we would air everything out," Rose says. "It wastes less time."

"And you wonder why I left our faction," Christina says. "Being honest doesn't mean you say whatever you want, whenever you want. It means that what you choose to say is true."

"A lie of omission is still a lie."

"You want the truth? I'm uncomfortable and don't want to be here right now. I'll see you guys later." She takes my arm and walks Tobias and me away from her family, shaking her head the whole time. "Sorry about that. They're not really the forgiving type."

"It's fine," I say, though it's not.

I thought that when I received Christina's forgiveness, the hard part of Will's death would be over. But when you kill someone you love, the hard part is never over. It just gets easier to distract yourself from what you've done.

My watch reads twelve o'clock. A door across the room opens, and in walk two lean silhouettes. The first is Johanna Reyes, former spokesperson of Amity, identifiable by the scar that crosses her face and the hint of yellow peeking out from under her black jacket. The second is another woman, but I can't see her face, just that she is wearing blue.

I feel a spike of terror. She looks almost like . . . Jeanine.

No, I saw her die. Jeanine is dead.

The woman comes closer. She is statuesque and blond, like Jeanine. A pair of glasses dangles from her front pocket, and her hair is in a braid. An Erudite from head to foot, but not Jeanine Matthews.

Cara.

Cara and Johanna are the leaders of the Allegiant?

"Hello," Cara says, and all conversation stops. She

smiles, but on her the expression looks compulsory, like she's just adhering to a social convention. "We aren't supposed to be here, so I'm going to keep this meeting short. Some of you—Zeke, Tori—have been helping us for the past few days."

I stare at Zeke. *Zeke* has been helping Cara? I guess I forgot that he was once a Dauntless spy. Which is probably when he proved his loyalty to Cara—he had some kind of friendship with her before she left Erudite headquarters not long ago.

He looks at me, wiggles his eyebrows, and grins.

Johanna continues, "Some of you are here because we want to ask for your help. All of you are here because you don't trust Evelyn Johnson to determine the fate of this city."

Cara touches her palms together in front of her. "We believe in following the guidance of the city's founders, which has been expressed in two ways: the formation of the factions, and the Divergent mission expressed by Edith Prior, to send people outside the fence to help whoever is out there once we have a large Divergent population. We believe that even if we have not reached that Divergent population size, the situation in our city has become dire enough to send people outside the fence anyway.

"In accordance with the intentions of our city's founders, we have two goals: to overthrow Evelyn and the factionless so that we can reestablish the factions, and to send some of our number outside the city to see what's out there. Johanna will be heading up the former effort, and I will be heading up the latter, which is what we will mostly be focusing on tonight." She presses a loose strand of hair back into her braid. "Not many of us will be able to go, because a crowd that large would draw too much attention. Evelyn won't let us leave without a fight, so I thought it would be best to recruit people who I know to be experienced with surviving danger."

I glance at Tobias. We certainly are experienced with danger.

"Christina, Tris, Tobias, Tori, Zeke, and Peter are my selections," Cara says. "You have all proven your skills to me in one way or another, and it's for that reason that I'd like to ask you to come with me outside the city. You are under no obligation to agree, of course."

"Peter?" I demand, without thinking. I can't imagine what Peter could have done to "prove his skills" to Cara.

"He kept the Erudite from killing you," Cara says mildly. "Who do you think provided him with the technology to fake your death?"

I raise my eyebrows. I had never thought about it before—too much happened after my failed execution for me to dwell on the details of my rescue. But of course, Cara was the only well-known defector from Erudite at that time, the only person Peter would have known to ask for help. Who else could have helped him? Who else would have known how?

I don't raise another objection. I don't want to leave this city with Peter, but I'm too desperate to leave to make a fuss about it.

"That's a lot of Dauntless," a girl at the side of the room says, looking skeptical. She has thick eyebrows that don't stop growing in the middle, and pale skin. When she turns her head, I see black ink right behind her ear. A Dauntless transfer to Erudite, no doubt.

"True," Cara says. "But what we need right now are people with the skills to get out of the city unscathed, and I think Dauntless training makes them highly qualified for that task."

"I'm sorry, but I don't think I can go," Zeke says. "I couldn't leave Shauna here. Not after her sister just . . . well, you know."

"I'll go," Uriah says, his hand popping up. "I'm Dauntless. I'm a good shot. And I provide much-needed eye candy."

I laugh. Cara does not seem to be amused, but she nods. "Thank you."

"Cara, you'll need to get out of the city fast," the Dauntless-turned-Erudite girl says. "Which means you should get someone to operate the trains."

"Good point," Cara says. "Does anyone here know how to drive a train?"

"Oh. I do," the girl says. "Was that not implied?"

The pieces of the plan come together. Johanna suggests we take Amity trucks from the end of the railroad tracks out of the city, and she volunteers to supply them to us. Robert offers to help her. Stephanie and Rose volunteer to monitor Evelyn's movements in the hours before the escape, and to report any unusual behavior to the Amity compound by two-way radio. The Dauntless who came with Tori offer to find weapons for us. The Erudite girl prods at any weaknesses she sees, and so does Cara, and soon they are all shored up, like we have just built a secure structure.

There is only one question left. Cara asks it:

"When should we go?"

And I volunteer an answer:

"Tomorrow night."

CHAPTER NINE

TOBIAS

THE NIGHT AIR slips into my lungs, and I feel like it is one of my last breaths. Tomorrow I will leave this place and seek another.

Uriah, Zeke, and Christina start toward Erudite headquarters, and I hold Tris's hand to keep her back.

"Wait," I say. "Let's go somewhere."

"Go somewhere? But . . ."

"Just for a little while." I tug her toward the corner of the building. At night I can almost see what the water looked like when it filled the empty canal, dark and patterned with moonlit ripples. "You're with me, remember? They're not going to arrest you."

A twitch at the corner of her mouth—almost a smile.

Around the corner, she leans against the wall and I stand in front of her, the river at my back. She's wearing something dark around her eyes to make their color stand out, bright and striking.

"I don't know what to do." She presses her hands to her face, curling her fingers into her hair. "About Caleb, I mean."

"You don't?"

She moves one hand aside to look at me.

"Tris." I set my hands on the wall on either side of her face and lean into them. "You don't want him to die. I know you don't."

"The thing is . . ." She closes her eyes. "I'm so . . . *angry*. I try not to think about him because when I do I just want to . . ."

"I know. God, I know." My entire life I've daydreamed about killing Marcus. Once I even decided how I would do it—with a knife, so I could feel the warmth leave him, so I could be close enough to watch the light leave his eyes. Making that decision frightened me as much as his violence ever did.

"My parents would want me to save him, though." Her eyes open and lift to the sky. "They would say it's selfish to let someone die just because they wronged you. Forgive, forgive, forgive."

"This isn't about what they want, Tris."

"Yes, it is!" She presses away from the wall. "It's always about what they want. Because he belongs to them more than he belongs to me. And I want to make them proud of me. It's all I want."

Her pale eyes are steady on mine, determined. I have never had parents who set good examples, parents whose expectations were worth living up to, but she did. I can see them within her, the courage and the beauty they pressed into her like a handprint.

I touch her cheek, sliding my fingers into her hair. "I'll get him out."

"What?"

"I'll get him out of his cell. Tomorrow, before we leave." I nod. "I'll do it."

"Really? Are you sure?"

"Of course I'm sure."

"I . . ." She frowns up at me. "Thank you. You're . . . amazing."

"Don't say that. You haven't found out about my ulterior motives yet." I grin. "You see, I didn't bring you here to talk to you about Caleb, actually."

"Oh?"

I set my hands on her hips and push her gently back against the wall. She looks up at me, her eyes clear and eager. I lean in close enough to taste her breaths, but pull back when she leans in, teasing.

She hooks her fingers in my belt loops and pulls me against her, so I have to catch myself on my forearms. She tries to kiss me but I tilt my head to dodge her, kissing just under her ear, then along her jaw to her throat. Her skin is soft and tastes like salt, like a night run.

"Do me a favor," she whispers into my ear, "and never have pure motives again."

She puts her hands on me, touching all the places I am marked, down my back and over my sides. Her fingertips slip under the waistband of my jeans and hold me against her. I breathe against the side of her neck, unable to move.

Finally we kiss, and it is a relief. She sighs, and I feel a wicked smile creep across my face.

I lift her up, letting the wall bear most of her weight, and her legs drape around my waist. She laughs into another kiss, and I feel strong, but so does she, her fingers stern around my arms. The night air slips into my lungs, and I feel like it is one of my first breaths.

CHAPTER TEN

TOBIAS

THE BROKEN BUILDINGS in the Dauntless sector look like doorways to other worlds. Ahead of me I see the Pire piercing the sky.

The pulse in my fingertips marks the passing seconds. The air still feels rich in my lungs, though summer is drawing to a close. I used to run all the time and fight all the time because I cared about muscles. Now my feet have saved me too often, and I can't separate running and fighting from what they are: a way to escape danger, a way to stay alive.

When I reach the building, I pace before the entrance to catch my breath. Above me, panes of glass reflect light in every direction. Somewhere up there is the chair I sat in while I was running the attack simulation, and a smear of Tris's father's blood on the wall. Somewhere up there, Tris's voice pierced the simulation I was under, and I felt her hand on my chest, drawing me back to reality.

I open the door to the fear landscape room and flip open the small black box that was in my back pocket to see the syringes inside. This is the box I have always used, padded around the needles; it is a sign of something sick inside me, or something brave.

I position the needle over my throat and close my eyes as I press down on the plunger. The black box clatters to the ground, but by the time I open my eyes, it has disappeared.

I stand on the roof of the Hancock building, near the zip line where the Dauntless flirt with death. The clouds are black with rain, and the wind fills my mouth when I open it to breathe. To my right, the zip line snaps, the wire cord whipping back and shattering the windows below me.

My vision tightens around the roof edge, trapping it in the center of a pinhole. I can hear my own exhales despite the whistling wind. I force myself to walk to the edge. The rain pounds against my shoulders and head, dragging me toward the ground. I tip my weight forward just a little and fall, my jaw clamped around my screams, muffled and suffocated by my own fear.

After I land, I don't have a second to rest before the walls close in around me, the wood slamming into my spine, and then my head, and then my legs. Claustrophobia. I pull my arms in to my chest, close my eyes, and try not to panic.

I think of Eric in his fear landscape, willing his terror into submission with deep breathing and logic. And Tris, conjuring weapons out of thin air to attack her worst nightmares. But I am not Eric, and I am not Tris. What am I? What do *I* need, to overcome my fears?

I know the answer, of course I do: I need to deny them the power to control me. I need to know that I am stronger than they are.

I breathe in and slam my palms against the walls to my left and right. The box creaks, and then breaks, the boards crashing to the concrete floor. I stand above them in the dark.

Amar, my initiation instructor, taught us that our fear landscapes were always in flux, shifting with our moods and changing with the little whispers of our nightmares. Mine was always the same, until a few weeks ago. Until I proved to myself that I could overpower my father. Until I discovered someone I was terrified to lose.

I don't know what I will see next.

I wait for a long time without anything changing. The room is still dark, the floor still cold and hard, my heart still beating faster than normal. I look down to check my watch and discover that it's on the wrong hand—I usually wear mine on my left, not my right, and my watchband isn't gray, it's black.

Then I notice bristly hairs on my fingers that weren't there before. The calluses on my knuckles are gone. I look down, and I am wearing gray slacks and a gray shirt; I am thicker around the middle and thinner through the shoulders.

I lift my eyes to a mirror that now stands in front of me. The face staring back at mine is Marcus's.

He winks at me, and I feel the muscles around my eye contracting as he does, though I didn't tell them to. Without warning, his—my—*our* arms jerk toward the glass and reach into it, closing around the neck of my reflection. But then the mirror disappears, and my—his—*our* hands are around our own throat, dark patches creeping into the edge of our vision. We sink to the ground, and the grip is as tight as iron.

I can't think. I can't think of a way out of this one.

By instinct, I scream. The sound vibrates against my hands. I picture those hands as mine really are, large with slender fingers and calloused knuckles from hours at the punching bag. I imagine my reflection as water running over Marcus's skin, replacing every piece of him with a piece of me. I remake myself in my own image.

I am kneeling on the concrete, gasping for air.

My hands tremble, and I run my fingers over my neck, my shoulders, my arms. Just to make sure.

I told Tris, on the train to meet Evelyn a few weeks ago, that Marcus was still in my fear landscape, but that he had changed. I spent a long time thinking about it; it crowded my thoughts every night before I slept and clamored for attention every time I woke. I was still afraid of him, I knew, but in a different way—I was no longer a child, afraid of the threat my terrifying father posed to my safety. I was a man, afraid of the threat he posed to my character, to my future, to my identity.

But even that fear, I know, does not compare to the one that comes next. Even though I know it's coming, I want to open a vein and drain the serum from my body rather than see it again.

A pool of light appears on the concrete in front of me. A hand, the fingers bent into a claw, reaches into the light, followed by another hand, and then a head, with stringy blond hair. The woman coughs and drags herself into the circle of light, inch by inch. I try to move toward her, to help her, but I am frozen.

The woman turns her face toward the light, and I see that she is Tris. Blood spills over her lips and curls around her chin. Her bloodshot eyes find mine, and she wheezes, "Help."

She coughs red onto the floor, and I throw myself toward her, somehow knowing that if I don't get to her soon, the light will leave her eyes. Hands wrap around my arms and shoulders and chest, forming a cage of flesh and bone, but I keep straining toward her. I claw at the hands holding me, but I only end up scratching myself.

I shout her name, and she coughs again, this time more blood. She screams for help, and I scream for her, and I don't hear anything, I don't feel anything, but my heartbeat, but my own terror.

She drops to the ground, tensionless, and her eyes roll back into her head. It's too late.

The darkness lifts. The lights return. Graffiti covers the walls of the fear landscape room, and across from me are the mirror-windows to the observation room, and in the corners are the cameras that record each session, all where they're supposed to be. My neck and back are covered in sweat. I wipe my face with the hem of my shirt and walk to the opposite door, leaving my black box with its syringe and needle behind.

I don't need to relive my fears anymore. All I need to do now is try to overcome them.

+ + +

I know from experience that confidence alone can get a person into a forbidden place. Like the cells on the third floor of Erudite headquarters.

Not here, though, apparently. A factionless man stops me with the end of his gun before I reach the door, and I am nervous, choking.

"Where you going?"

I put my hand on his gun and push it away from my arm. "Don't point that thing at me. I'm here on Evelyn's orders. I'm going to see a prisoner."

"I didn't hear about any after-hours visits today."

I drop my voice low, so he feels like he's hearing a secret. "That's because she didn't want it on the record."

"Chuck!" someone calls out from the stairs above us. It's Therese. She makes a waving motion as she walks down. "Let him through. He's fine."

I nod to Therese and keep moving. The debris in the hallway has been swept clean, but the broken lightbulbs haven't been replaced, so I walk through stretches of darkness, like patches of bruises, on my way to the right cell.

When I reach the north corridor, I don't go straight to the cell, but rather to the woman who stands at the end. She is middle-aged, with eyes that droop at the edges and a mouth held in a pucker. She looks like everything exhausts her, including me.

"Hi," I say. "My name is Tobias Eaton. I'm here to collect a prisoner, on orders from Evelyn Johnson."

Her expression doesn't change when she hears my name, so for a few seconds I'm sure I'll have to knock her unconscious to get what I want. She takes a piece of crumpled paper from her pocket and flattens it against her left palm. On it is a list of prisoners' names and their corresponding room numbers.

"Name?" she says.

"Caleb Prior. 308A."

"You're Evelyn's son, right?"

"Yeah. I mean . . . yes." She doesn't seem like the kind of person who likes the word "yeah."

She leads me to a blank metal door with 308A on it—I wonder what it was used for when our city didn't require so many cells. She types in the code, and the door springs open.

"I guess I'm supposed to pretend I don't see what you're about to do?" she says.

She must think I'm here to kill him. I decide to let her.

"Yes," I say.

"Do me a favor and put in a good word for me with Evelyn. I don't want so many night shifts. The name's Drea."

"You got it."

She gathers the paper into her fist and shoves it back into her pocket as she walks away. I keep my hand on the door handle until she reaches her post again and turns to the side so she isn't facing me. It seems like she's done this a few times before. I wonder how many people have disappeared from these cells at Evelyn's command.

I walk in. Caleb Prior sits at a metal desk, bent over a book, his hair piled on one side of his head.

"What do you want?" he says.

"I hate to break this to you—" I pause. I decided a few hours ago how I wanted to handle this—I want to teach Caleb a lesson. And it will involve a few lies. "You know, actually, I kind of don't hate it. Your execution's been moved up a few weeks. To tonight."

That gets his attention. He twists in his chair and stares at me, his eyes wild and wide, like prey faced with a predator.

"Is that a joke?"

"I'm really bad at telling jokes."

"No." He shakes his head. "No, I have a few weeks, it's not *tonight*, no—"

"If you shut up, I'll give you an hour to adjust to this new information. If you don't shut up, I'll knock you out and shoot you in the alley outside before you wake up. Make your choice now."

Seeing an Erudite process something is like watching the inside of a watch, the gears all turning, shifting, adjusting, working together to form a particular function, which in this case is to make sense of his imminent demise.

Caleb's eyes shift to the open door behind me, and he seizes the chair, turning and swinging it into my body. The legs hit me, hard, which slows me down just enough to let him slip by.

I follow him into the hallway, my arms burning from where the chair hit me. I am faster than he is—I slam into his back and he hits the floor face-first, without bracing himself. With my knee against his back, I pull his wrists together and squeeze them into a plastic loop. He groans, and when I pull him to his feet, his nose is bright with blood.

Drea's eyes touch mine for just a moment, then move away.

I drag him down the hallway, not the way I came, but another way, toward an emergency exit. We walk down a flight of narrow stairs where the echo of our footsteps layers over itself, dissonant and hollow. Once I'm at the bottom, I knock on the exit door.

Zeke opens it, a stupid grin on his face.

"No trouble with the guard?"

"No."

"I figured Drea would be easy to get by. She doesn't care about anything."

"It sounded like she had looked the other way before."

"That doesn't surprise me. Is this Prior?"

"In the flesh."

"Why's he bleeding?"

"Because he's an idiot."

Zeke offers me a black jacket with a factionless symbol stitched into the collar. "I didn't know that idiocy caused people to just start spontaneously bleeding from the nose."

I wrap the jacket around Caleb's shoulders and fasten one of the buttons over his chest. He avoids my eyes.

"I think it's a new phenomenon," I say. "The alley's clear?"

"Made sure of it." Zeke holds out his gun, handle first. "Careful, it's loaded. Now it would be great if you would hit me so I'm more convincing when I tell the factionless you stole it from me."

"You want me to hit you?"

"Oh, like you've never wanted to. Just do it, Four."

I do like to hit people—I like the explosion of power and energy, and the feeling that I am untouchable because I can hurt people. But I hate that part of myself, because it is the part of me that is the most broken.

Zeke braces himself and I curl my hand into a fist.

"Do it fast, you pansycake," he says.

I decide to aim for the jaw, which is too strong to break but will still show a good bruise. I swing, hitting him right where I mean to. Zeke groans, clutching his face with both hands. Pain shoots up my arm, and I shake my hand out.

"Great." Zeke spits at the side of the building. "Well, I guess that's it."

"Guess so."

"I probably won't be seeing you again, will I? I mean, I know the others might come back, but you . . ." He trails off, but picks up the thought again a moment later. "Just seems like you'll be happy to leave it behind, that's all."

"Yeah, you're probably right." I look at my shoes. "You sure you won't come?"

"Can't. Shauna can't wheel around where you guys are going, and it's not like I'm gonna leave her, you know?" He touches his jaw, lightly, testing the skin. "Make sure Uri doesn't drink too much, okay?"

"Yeah," I say.

"No, I mean it," he says, and his voice dips down the way it always does when he's being serious, for once. "Promise you'll look out for him?"

It's always been clear to me, since I met them, that Zeke

and Uriah were closer than most brothers. They lost their father when they were young, and I suspect Zeke began to walk the line between parent and sibling after that. I can't imagine what it feels like for Zeke to watch him leave the city now, especially as broken by grief as Uriah is by Marlene's death.

"I promise," I say.

I know I should leave, but I have to stay in this moment for a little while, feeling its significance. Zeke was one of the first friends I made in Dauntless, after I survived initiation. Then he worked in the control room with me, watching the cameras and writing stupid programs that spelled out words on the screen or played guessing games with numbers. He never asked me for my real name, or why a first-ranked initiate ended up in security and instruction instead of leadership. He demanded nothing from me.

"Let's just hug already," he says.

Keeping one hand firm on Caleb's arm, I wrap my free arm around Zeke, and he does the same.

When we break apart, I pull Caleb down the alley, and can't resist calling back, "I'll miss you."

"You too, sweetie!"

He grins, and his teeth are white in the twilight. They are the last thing I see of him before I have to turn and set out at a trot for the train.

"You're going somewhere," says Caleb, between breaths. "You and some others."

"Yeah."

"Is my sister going?"

The question awakes inside me an animal rage that won't be satisfied by sharp words or insults. It will only be satisfied by smacking his ear hard with the flat of my hand. He winces and hunches his shoulders, preparing for a second strike.

I wonder if that's what I looked like when my father did it to me.

"She is not your sister," I say. "You betrayed her. You tortured her. You took away the only family she had left. And because . . . what? Because you wanted to keep Jeanine's secrets, wanted to stay in the city, safe and sound? You are a coward."

"I am not a coward!" Caleb says. "I knew if—"

"Let's go back to the arrangement where you keep your mouth closed."

"Fine," he says. "Where are you taking me, anyway? You can kill me just as well here, can't you?"

I pause. A shape moves along the sidewalk behind us, slippery in my periphery. I twist and hold up my gun, but the shape disappears into the yawn of an alley.

I keep walking, pulling Caleb with me, listening for footsteps behind me. We scatter broken glass with our shoes. I watch the dark buildings and the street signs, dangling from their hinges like late-clinging leaves in autumn. Then I reach the station where we'll catch the train, and lead Caleb up a flight of metal steps to the platform.

I see the train coming from a long way off, making its last journey through the city. Once, the trains were a force of nature to me, something that continued along their path regardless of what we did inside the city limits, something pulsing and alive and powerful. Now I have met the men and women who operate them, and some of that mystery is gone, but what they mean to me will never be gone—my first act as a Dauntless was to jump on one, and every day afterward they were the source of my freedom, they gave me the power to move within this world when I had once felt so trapped in the Abnegation sector, in the house that was a prison to me.

When it comes closer, I cut the tie around Caleb's wrists with a pocketknife and keep a firm hold on his arm.

"You know how to do this, right?" I say. "Get in the last car."

He unbuttons the jacket and drops it on the ground. "Yeah."

Starting at one end of the platform, we run together along the worn boards, keeping pace with the open door. He doesn't reach for the handle, so I push him toward it. He stumbles, then grabs it and pulls himself into the last car. I am running out of space—the platform is ending—I seize the handle and swing myself in, my muscles absorbing the pull forward.

Tris stands inside the car, wearing a small, crooked smile. Her black jacket is zipped up to her throat, framing her face in darkness. She grabs my collar and pulls me in for a kiss. As she pulls away, she says, "I always loved watching you do that."

I grin.

"Is this what you had planned?" Caleb demands from behind me. "For her to be here when you kill me? That's—"

"*Kill* him?" Tris asks me, not looking at her brother.

"Yeah, I let him think he was being taken to his execution," I say, loud enough that he can hear. "You know, sort of like he did to you in Erudite headquarters."

"I . . . it isn't true?" His face, lit by the moon, is slack with shock. I notice that his shirt's buttons are in the wrong buttonholes.

"No," I say. "I just saved your life, actually."

He starts to say something, and I interrupt him. "Might not want to thank me just yet. We're taking you with us. Outside the fence."

Outside the fence—the place he once tried so hard to avoid that he turned on his own sister. It seems a more fitting punishment than death, anyway. Death is so quick, so certain. Where we're going now, nothing is certain.

He looks frightened, but not as frightened as I thought he would be. I feel like I understand, then, the way he ranks things in his mind: his life, first; his comfort in a world of his own making, second; and somewhere after that, the lives of the people he is supposed to love. He is the sort of despicable person who has no understanding of how despicable he is, and my badgering him with insults won't change that; nothing will. Rather than angry, I just feel heavy, useless.

I don't want to think about him anymore. I take Tris's hand and lead her to the other side of the car, so we can watch the city disappear behind us. We stand side by side in the open doorway, each of us holding one of the handles. The buildings create a dark, jagged pattern on the sky.

"We were followed," I say.

"We'll be careful," she answers.

"Where are the others?"

"In the first few cars," she says. "I thought we should be alone. Or as alone as we can get."

She smiles at me. These are our last moments in the city. Of course we should spend them alone.

"I'm really going to miss this place," she says.

"Really?" I say. "My thoughts are more like, 'Good riddance.'"

"There's *nothing* you'll miss? No good memories?" She elbows me.

"Fine." I smile. "There are a few."

"Any that don't involve me?" she says. "That sounds self-centered. You know what I mean."

"Sure, I guess," I say, shrugging. "I mean, I got to have a different life in Dauntless, a different name. I got to be Four, thanks to my initiation instructor. He gave me the name."

"Really?" She tilts her head. "Why haven't I met him?"

"Because he's dead. He was Divergent." I shrug again, but I don't feel casual about it. Amar was the first person who noticed that I was Divergent, and he helped me to hide it. But he couldn't hide his own Divergence, and that killed him.

She touches my arm, lightly, but doesn't say anything. I shift, uncomfortable.

"See?" I say. "Too many bad memories here. I'm ready to leave."

I feel empty, not because of sadness, but because of relief, all the tension flowing out of me. Evelyn is in that city, and Marcus, and all the grief and nightmares and bad memories, and the factions that kept me trapped inside one version of myself. I squeeze Tris's hand.

"Look," I say, pointing at a distant cluster of buildings. "There's the Abnegation sector."

She smiles, but her eyes are glassy, like a dormant part of her is fighting its way out and spilling over. The train hisses over the rails, a tear drops down Tris's cheek, and the city disappears into the darkness.

CHAPTER ELEVEN

TRIS

THE TRAIN SLOWS down when we get closer to the fence, a signal from the driver that we should get off soon. Tobias and I sit in the doorway of the car as it moves lazily over the tracks. He puts his arm around me and touches his nose to my hair, taking a breath. I look at him, at the collarbone peeking out from the neck of his T-shirt, at the faint curl of his lip, and I feel something heating up inside me.

"What are you thinking about?" he says into my ear, softly.

I jerk to attention. I look at him all the time, but not always like *that*—I feel like he just caught me doing something embarrassing. "Nothing! Why?"

"No reason." He pulls me closer to his side, and I rest my head on his shoulder, taking deep breaths of the cool air. It still smells like summer, like grass baking in the heat of the sun.

"It looks like we're getting close to the fence," I say.

I can tell because the buildings are disappearing, leaving just fields, dotted with the rhythmic glow of lightning bugs. Behind me, Caleb sits near the other door, hugging his knees. His eyes find mine at just the wrong moment, and I want to scream into the darkest parts of him so he can finally hear me, finally understand what he did to me, but instead I just hold his stare until he can't take it anymore and he looks away.

I stand, using the handle to steady me, and Tobias and Caleb do the same. At first Caleb tries to stand behind us, but Tobias pushes him forward, right up to the edge of the car.

"You first. On my mark!" he says. "And . . . go!"

He gives Caleb a push, just enough to get him off the car floor, and my brother disappears. Tobias goes next, leaving me alone in the train car.

It's stupid to miss a thing when there are so many people to miss instead, but I miss this train already, and all the others that carried me through the city, *my* city, after I was brave enough to ride them. I brush my fingers over the car wall, just once, and then jump. The train is moving so slowly that I overcompensate with my landing, too used to running off the momentum, and I fall. The dry grass scrapes my palms and I push myself to my feet, searching the darkness for Tobias and Caleb.

Before I find them, I hear Christina. "Tris!"

She and Uriah come toward me. He is holding a flashlight, and he looks far more alert than he did this afternoon, which is a good sign. Behind them are more lights, more voices.

"Did your brother make it?" Uriah says.

"Yeah." Finally I see Tobias, his hand gripping Caleb's arm, coming toward us.

"Not sure why an Erudite like you can't get it through his head," Tobias is saying, "but you aren't going to be able to outrun me."

"He's right," says Uriah. "Four's fast. Not as fast as me, but definitely faster than a Nose like you."

Christina laughs. "A what?"

"Nose." Uriah touches the side of his nose. "It's a play on words. 'Knows' with a 'K,' knowledge, Erudite . . . get it? It's like Stiff."

"The Dauntless have the weirdest slang. Pansycake, Nose . . . is there a term for the Candor?"

"Of course." Uriah grins. "Jerks."

Christina shoves Uriah, hard, making him drop the flashlight. Tobias, laughing, leads us to the rest of the group, standing a few feet away. Tori waves her flashlight in the air to get everyone's attention, then says, "All right, Johanna and the trucks will be about a ten-minute walk from here, so let's get going. And if I hear a word from anyone, I will beat you senseless. We're not out yet."

We move closer together like sections of a tightened shoelace. Tori walks a few feet in front of us, and from the back, in the dark, she reminds me of Evelyn, her limbs lean and wiry, her shoulders back, so sure of herself it's almost frightening. By the light of the flashlights I can just make out the tattoo of a hawk on the back of her neck, the first thing I spoke to her about when she administered my aptitude test. She told me it was a symbol of a fear she had overcome, a fear of the dark. I wonder if that fear still creeps up on her now, though she worked so hard to face it—I wonder if fears ever really go away, or if they just lose their power over us.

She moves farther away from us by the minute, her pace more like a jog than a walk. She is eager to leave, to escape this place where her brother was murdered and she rose to prominence only to be thwarted by a factionless woman who wasn't supposed to be alive.

She is so far ahead that when the shots go off, I only see

her flashlight fall, not her body.

"Split up!" Tobias's voice roars over the sound of our cries, our chaos. "Run!"

I search in the dark for his hand, but I don't find it. I grab the gun Uriah gave me before we left and hold it out from my body, ignoring the way my throat tightens at the feel of it. I can't run into the night. I need light. I sprint in the direction of Tori's body—of her fallen flashlight.

I hear but do not hear the gunshots, and the shouting, and the running footsteps. I hear but do not hear my heartbeat. I crouch next to the shaft of light she dropped and pick up the flashlight, intending to just grab it and keep running, but in its glow I see her face. It shines with sweat, and her eyes roll beneath her eyelids, like she is searching for something but is too tired to find it.

One of the bullets found her stomach, and the other found her chest. There is no way she will recover from this. I may be angry with her for fighting me in Jeanine's laboratory, but she's still Tori, the woman who guarded the secret of my Divergence. My throat tightens as I remember following her into the aptitude test room, my eyes on her hawk tattoo.

Her eyes shift in my direction and focus on me. Her eyebrows furrow, but she doesn't speak.

I shift the flashlight into the crook of my thumb and

reach for her hand to squeeze her sweaty fingers.

I hear someone approaching, and I aim flashlight and gun in the same direction. The beam hits a woman wearing a factionless armband, with a gun pointed at my head. I fire, clenching my teeth so hard they squeak.

The bullet hits the woman in the stomach and she screams, firing blindly into the night.

I look back down at Tori, and her eyes are closed, her body still. Pointing my flashlight at the ground, I sprint away from her and from the woman I just shot. My legs ache and my lungs burn. I don't know where I'm going, if I'm running into danger or away from it, but I keep running as long as I can.

Finally I see a light in the distance. At first I think it's another flashlight, but as I draw closer I realize it is larger and steadier than a flashlight—it's a headlight. I hear an engine, and crouch in the tall grass to hide, switching my flashlight off and keeping my gun ready. The truck slows, and I hear a voice:

"Tori?"

It sounds like Christina. The truck is red and rusted, an Amity vehicle. I straighten, pointing the light at myself so she'll see me. The truck stops a few feet ahead of me, and Christina leaps out of the passenger seat, throwing her arms around me. I replay it in my mind to make it real,

Tori's body falling, the factionless woman's hands covering her stomach. It doesn't work. It doesn't feel real.

"Thank God," Christina says. "Get in. We're going to find Tori."

"Tori's dead," I say plainly, and the word "dead" makes it real for me. I wipe tears from my cheeks with the heels of my hands and struggle to control my shuddering breaths. "I—I shot the woman who killed her."

"What?" Johanna sounds frantic. She leans over from the driver's seat. "What did you say?"

"Tori's gone," I say. "I saw it happen."

Johanna's expression is shrouded by her hair. She presses her next breath out.

"Well, let's find the others, then."

I get into the truck. The engine roars as Johanna presses the gas pedal, and we bump over the grass in search of the others.

"Did you see any of them?" I say.

"A few. Cara, Uriah." Johanna shakes her head. "No one else."

I wrap my hand around the door handle and squeeze. If I had tried harder to find Tobias . . . if I hadn't stopped for Tori . . .

What if Tobias didn't make it?

"I'm sure they're all right," Johanna says. "That boy of

yours knows how to take care of himself."

I nod, without conviction. Tobias can take care of himself, but in an attack, surviving is an accident. It doesn't take skill to stand in a place where no bullets find you, or to fire into the dark and hit a man you didn't see. It is all luck, or providence, depending on what you believe. And I don't know—have never known—exactly what I believe.

He's all right he's all right he's all right.

Tobias is all right.

My hands tremble, and Christina squeezes my knee. Johanna steers us toward the rendezvous point, where she saw Uriah and Cara. I watch the speedometer needle climb, then hold steady at seventy-five. We jostle one another in the cab, thrown this way and that way by the uneven ground.

"There!" Christina points. There is a cluster of lights ahead of us, some just pinpricks, like flashlights, and others round, like headlights.

We pull up close, and I see him. Tobias sits on the hood of the other truck, his arm soaked with blood. Cara stands in front of him with a first aid kit. Caleb and Peter sit on the grass a few feet away. Before Johanna has stopped the truck completely, I open the door and get out, running toward him. Tobias stands up, ignoring Cara's orders to stay put, and we collide, his uninjured arm wrapping around my back and lifting me off my feet. His back is wet with sweat, and when he kisses me, he tastes like salt.

All the knots of tension inside me come apart at once. I feel, just for a moment, like I am remade, like I am brand-new.

He's all right. We're out of the city. He's all right.

CHAPTER TWELVE

Tobias

My arm throbs like a second heartbeat from the bullet graze. Tris's knuckles brush mine as she lifts her hand to point at something on our right: a series of long, low buildings lit by blue emergency lamps.

"What are those?" Tris says.

"The other greenhouses," Johanna says. "They don't require much manpower, but we grow and raise things in large quantities there—animals, raw material for fabric, wheat, and so on."

Their panes glow in the starlight, obscuring the treasures I imagine to be inside them, small plants with berries dangling from their branches, rows of potato plants buried in the earth.

"You don't show them to visitors," I say. "We never saw them."

"Amity keeps a number of secrets," Johanna says, and she sounds proud.

The road ahead of us is long and straight, marked with cracks and swollen patches. Alongside it are gnarled trees, broken lampposts, old power lines. Every so often, there is an isolated square of sidewalk with weeds forcing their way through the concrete, or a pile of rotting wood, a collapsed dwelling.

The more time I spend thinking about this landscape that every Dauntless patrol was told was normal, the more I see an old city rising up around me, the buildings lower than the ones we left behind, but just as numerous. An old city that was transformed into empty land for the Amity to farm. In other words, an old city that was razed, burned to cinders, and crushed into the ground, even the roads disappearing, the earth left to run wild over the wreckage.

I put my hand out the window, and the wind wraps around my fingers like locks of hair. When I was very young, my mother pretended she could shape things from the wind, and she would give them to me to use, like hammers and nails, or swords, or roller skates. It was a game we played in the evenings, on the front lawn, before Marcus got home. It took away our dread.

In the bed of the truck, behind us, are Caleb, Christina,

and Uriah. Christina and Uriah sit close enough for their shoulders to touch, but they are looking in opposite directions, more like strangers than friends. Just behind us is another truck, driven by Robert, which carries Cara and Peter. Tori was supposed to be with them. The thought makes me feel hollow, empty. She administered my aptitude test. She made me think, for the first time, that I could leave Abnegation—that I had to. I feel like I owe her something, and she died before I could give it to her.

"This is it," Johanna says. "The outer limit of the Dauntless patrols."

No fence or wall marks the divide between the Amity compound and the outer world, but I remember monitoring the Dauntless patrols from the control room, making sure they didn't go farther than the limit, which is marked by a series of signs with Xs on them. The patrols were structured so that the trucks would run out of gas if they went too far, a delicate system of checks and balances that preserved our safety and theirs—and, I now realize, the secret the Abnegation kept.

"Have they ever gone past the limit?" says Tris.

"A few times," says Johanna. "It was our responsibility to deal with that situation when it came up."

Tris gives her a look, and she shrugs.

"Every faction has a serum," Johanna says. "The Dauntless serum gives hallucinated realities, Candor's gives the truth, Amity's gives peace, Erudite's gives death—" At this, Tris visibly shudders, but Johanna continues as if it didn't happen. "And Abnegation's resets memory."

"Resets *memory*?"

"Like Amanda Ritter's memory," I say. "She said, 'There are many things I am happy to forget,' remember?"

"Yes, exactly," says Johanna. "The Amity are charged with administering the Abnegation serum to anyone who goes out past the limit, just enough to make them forget the experience. I'm sure some of them have slipped past us, but not many."

We are silent then. I turn the information over and over in my mind. There is something deeply wrong with taking a person's memories—even though I know it was necessary to keep our city safe for as long as it needed to be, I feel it in the pit of my stomach. Take a person's memories, and you change who they are.

Swelling inside me is the feeling that I am about to jump out of my own skin, because the farther we get outside the outer limit of the Dauntless patrols, the closer we get to seeing what lies outside the only world I've ever known. I am terrified and thrilled and confused and a hundred different things at once.

I see something up ahead of us, in the light of early morning, and grab Tris's hand.

"Look," I say.

CHAPTER THIRTEEN

TRIS

THE WORLD BEYOND ours is full of roads and dark buildings and collapsing power lines.

There is no life in it, as far as I can see; no movement, no sound but the wind and my own footsteps.

It's like the landscape is an interrupted sentence, one side dangling in the air, unfinished, and the other, a completely different subject. On our side of that sentence is empty land, grass and stretches of road. On the other side are two concrete walls with half a dozen sets of train tracks between them. Up ahead, there is a concrete bridge built across the walls, and framing the tracks are buildings, wood and brick and glass, their windows dark, trees growing around them, so wild their branches have grown together.

A sign on the right says 90.

"What do we do now?" Uriah asks.

"We follow the tracks," I say, but quietly, so only I hear it.

+++

We get out of the trucks at the divide between our world and theirs—whoever "they" are. Robert and Johanna say a brief good-bye, turn the trucks around, and drive back into the city. I watch them go. I can't imagine coming this far and then turning back, but I guess there are things they have to do in the city. Johanna still has an Allegiant rebellion to organize.

The rest of us—me, Tobias, Caleb, Peter, Christina, Uriah, and Cara—set out with our meager possessions along the railroad tracks.

The tracks are not like the ones in the city. They are polished and sleek, and instead of boards running perpendicular to their path, there are sheets of textured metal. Up ahead I see one of the trains that runs along them, abandoned near the wall. It is metal-plated on the top and front, like a mirror, with tinted windows all along the side. When we draw closer, I see rows of benches inside it with maroon cushions on them. People must not jump on and off these trains.

Tobias walks behind me on one of the rails, his arms held out from his sides to maintain his balance. The others are spread out over the tracks, Peter and Caleb near one wall, Cara near the other. No one talks much, except to point out something new, a sign or a building or a hint of what this world was like, when there were people in it.

The concrete walls alone hold my attention—they are covered with strange pictures of people with skin so smooth they hardly look like people anymore, or colorful bottles with shampoo or conditioner or vitamins or unfamiliar substances inside them, words I don't understand, "vodka" and "Coca-Cola" and "energy drink." The colors and shapes and words and pictures are so garish, so abundant, that they are mesmerizing.

"Tris." Tobias puts his hand on my shoulder, and I stop.

He tilts his head and says, "Do you hear that?"

I hear footsteps and the quiet voices of our companions. I hear my own breaths, and his. But running beneath them is a quiet rumble, inconsistent in its intensity. It sounds like an engine.

"Everyone stop!" I shout.

To my surprise, everyone does, even Peter, and we gather together in the center of the tracks. I see Peter draw his gun and hold it up, and I do the same, both hands joined together to steady it, remembering the ease with which I used to lift it. That ease is gone now.

Something appears around the bend up ahead. A black truck, but larger than any truck I've ever seen, large enough to hold more than a dozen people in its covered bed.

I shudder.

The truck bumps over the tracks and comes to a stop twenty feet away from us. I can see the man driving it—he has dark skin and long hair that is in a knot at the back of his head.

"God," Tobias says, and his hands tighten around his own gun.

A woman gets out of the front seat. She looks to be around Johanna's age, her skin patterned with dense freckles and her hair so dark it's almost black. She hops to the ground and puts up both hands, so we can see that she isn't armed.

"Hello," she says, and smiles nervously. "My name is Zoe. This is Amar."

She jerks her head to the side to indicate the driver, who has gotten out of the truck too.

"Amar is dead," Tobias says.

"No, I'm not. Come on, Four," Amar says.

Tobias's face is tight with fear. I don't blame him. It's not every day you see someone you care about come back from the dead.

The faces of all the people I've lost flash into my mind. Lynn. Marlene. Will. Al.

My father. My mother.

What if they're still alive, like Amar? What if the curtain that separates us is not death but a chain-link fence and some land?

I can't stop myself from hoping, foolish as it is.

"We work for the same organization that founded your city," Zoe says as she glares at Amar. "The same organization Edith Prior came from. And . . ."

She reaches into her pocket and takes out a partially crumpled photograph. She holds it out, and then her eyes find mine in the crowd of people and guns.

"I think you should look at this, Tris," she says. "I'll step forward and leave it on the ground, then back up. All right?"

She knows my name. My throat tightens with fear. *How* does she know my name? And not just my name—my nickname, the name I chose when I joined Dauntless?

"All right," I say, but my voice is hoarse, so the words barely escape.

Zoe steps forward, sets the photograph down on the train tracks, then moves back to her original position. I leave the safety of our numbers and crouch near the photograph, watching her the whole time. Then I back up, photograph in hand.

It shows a row of people in front of a chain-link fence, their arms slung across one another's shoulders and backs. I see a child version of Zoe, recognizable by her freckles, and a few people I don't recognize. I am about to ask her what the point of me looking at this picture is when I recognize the young woman with dull blond hair, tied back, and a wide smile.

My mother. What is my mother doing next to these people?

Something—grief, pain, longing—squeezes my chest.

"There is a lot to explain," Zoe says. "But this isn't really the best place to do it. We'd like to take you to our headquarters. It's a short drive from here."

Still holding up his gun, Tobias touches my wrist with his free hand, guiding the photograph closer to his face. "That's your mother?" he asks me.

"It's *Mom?*" Caleb says. He pushes past Tobias to see the picture over my shoulder.

"Yes," I say to both of them.

"Think we should trust them?" Tobias says to me in a low voice.

Zoe doesn't look like a liar, and she doesn't sound like one either. And if she knows who I am, and knew how to find us here, it's probably because she has some form of access to the city, which means she is probably telling the truth about being with the group that Edith Prior came from. And then there's Amar, who is watching every movement Tobias makes.

"We came out here because we wanted to find these people," I say. "We have to trust someone, don't we? Or else we're just walking around in a wasteland, possibly starving to death."

Tobias releases my wrist and lowers his gun. I do the same. The others follow suit slowly, with Christina putting hers down last.

"Wherever we go, we have to be free to leave at any time," Christina says. "Okay?"

Zoe places her hand on her chest, right over her heart. "You have my word."

I hope, for all our sakes, that her word is worth having.

CHAPTER FOURTEEN

TOBIAS

I STAND ON the edge of the truck bed, holding the structure that supports the cloth cover. I want this new reality to be a simulation that I could manipulate if I could only make sense of it. But it's not, and I can't make sense of it.

Amar is alive.

"Adapt!" was one of his favorite commands during my initiation. Sometimes he yelled it so often that I would dream it; it woke me like an alarm clock, requiring more of me than I could provide. *Adapt.* Adapt faster, adapt better, adapt to things that no man should have to.

Like this: leaving a wholly formed world and discovering another one.

Or this: discovering that your dead friend is actually alive and driving the truck you're riding in.

Tris sits behind me, on the bench that wraps around the truck bed, the creased photo in her hands. Her fingers hover over her mother's face, almost touching it but not quite. Christina sits on one side of her, and Caleb is on the other. She must be letting him stay just to see the photograph; her entire body recoils from him, pressing into Christina's side.

"That's your mom?" Christina says.

Tris and Caleb both nod.

"She's so young there. Pretty, too," Christina adds.

"Yes she is. Was, I mean."

I expect Tris to sound sad as she replies, like she's aching at the memory of her mother's fading beauty. Instead her voice is nervous, her lips pursed in anticipation. I hope that she isn't brewing false hope.

"Let me see it," Caleb says, stretching his hand out to his sister.

Silently, and without really looking at him, she passes him the photograph.

I turn back to the world we are driving away from—the end of the train tracks. The huge expanses of field. And in the distance, the Hub, barely visible in the haze that covers the city's skyline. It's a strange feeling, seeing it from this place, like I can still touch it if I stretch my hand far enough, though I have traveled so far away from it.

Peter moves toward the edge of the truck bed next to

me, holding the canvas to steady himself. The train tracks curve away from us now, and I can't see the fields anymore. The walls on either side of us gradually disappear as the land flattens out, and I see buildings everywhere, some small, like the Abnegation houses, and some wide, like city buildings turned on their sides.

Trees, overgrown and huge, grow beyond the cement fixtures intended to keep them enclosed, their roots sprawling over the pavement. Perched on the edge of one rooftop is a row of black birds like the ones tattooed on Tris's collarbone. As the truck passes, they squawk and scatter into the air.

This is a wild world.

Just like that, it is too much for me to bear, and I have to back up and sit on one of the benches. I cradle my head in my hands, keeping my eyes shut so I can't take in any new information. I feel Tris's strong arm across my back, pulling me sideways into her narrow frame. My hands are numb.

"Just focus on what's right here, right now," Cara says from across the truck. "Like how the truck is moving. It'll help."

I try it. I think about how hard the bench is beneath me and how the truck always vibrates, even on flat ground, buzzing in my bones. I detect its tiny movements left and right, forward and back, and absorb each bounce as it rolls over the rails. I focus until everything goes dark around us, and I don't feel the passage of time or the panic of discovery, I feel only our movement over the earth.

"You should probably look around now," Tris says, and she sounds weak.

Christina and Uriah stand where I stood, peering around the edge of the canvas wall. I look over their shoulders to see what we're driving toward. There is a tall fence stretching wide across the landscape, which looks empty compared to the densely packed buildings I saw before I sat down. The fence has vertical black bars with pointed ends that bend outward, as if to skewer anyone who might try to climb over it.

A few feet past it is another fence, this one chain-link, like the one around the city, with barbed wire looped over the top. I hear a loud buzz coming from the second fence, an electric charge. People walk the space between them, carrying guns that look a little like our paintball guns, but far more lethal, powerful pieces of machinery.

A sign on the first fence reads BUREAU OF GENETIC WELFARE.

I hear Amar's voice, speaking to the armed guards, but I don't know what he's saying. A gate in the first fence opens to admit us, and then a gate in the second. Beyond the two fences is . . . order.

As far as I can see, there are low buildings separated by trimmed grass and fledgling trees. The roads that connect them are well maintained and well marked, with arrows pointing to various destinations: GREENHOUSES, straight ahead; SECURITY OUTPOST, left; OFFICERS' RESIDENCES, right; COMPOUND MAIN, straight ahead.

I get up and lean around the truck to see the compound, half my body hanging over the road. The Bureau of Genetic Welfare isn't tall, but it's still huge, wider than I can see, a mammoth of glass and steel and concrete. Behind the compound are a few tall towers with bulges at the top—I don't know why, but I think of the control room when I see them, and wonder if that's what they are.

Aside from the guards between the fences, there are few people outside. Those who are stop to watch us, but we drive away so quickly I don't see their expressions.

The truck stops before a set of double doors, and Peter is the first to jump down. The rest of us spill out on the pavement behind him, and we are shoulder to shoulder, standing so close I can hear how fast everyone is breathing. In the city we were divided by faction, by age, by history, but here all those divisions fall away. We are all we have.

"Here we go," mutters Tris, as Zoe and Amar approach.

Here we go, I say to myself.

+++

"Welcome to the compound," says Zoe. "This building used to be O'Hare Airport, one of the busiest airports in the country. Now it's the headquarters of the Bureau of Genetic Welfare—or just the Bureau, as we call it around here. It's an agency of the United States government."

I feel my face going slack. I know all the words she's saying—except I'm not sure what an "airport" or "united states" is—but they don't make sense to me all together. I'm not the only one who looks confused—Peter raises both eyebrows as if asking a question.

"Sorry," she says. "I keep forgetting how little you all know."

"I believe it's *your* fault if we don't know anything, not ours," Peter points out.

"I should rephrase." Zoe smiles gently. "I keep forgetting how little information we provided you with. An airport is a hub for air travel, and—"

"*Air* travel?" says Christina, incredulous.

"One of the technological developments that wasn't necessary for us to know about when we were inside the city was air travel," says Amar. "It's safe, fast, and amazing."

"Wow," says Tris.

She looks excited. I, however, think of speeding

through the air, high above the compound, and feel like I might throw up.

"Anyway. When the experiments were first developed, the airport was converted into this compound so that we could monitor the experiments from a distance," Zoe says. "I'm going to walk you to the control room to meet David, the leader of the Bureau. You will see a lot of things you don't understand, but it may be best to get some preliminary explanations before you start asking me about them. So take note of the things you want to learn more about, and feel free to ask me or Amar later."

She starts toward the entrance, and the doors part for her, pulled open by two armed guards who smile in greeting as she passes them. The contrast between the friendly greeting and the weapons propped against their shoulders is almost humorous. The guns are huge, and I wonder how they feel to shoot, if you can feel the deadly power in them just by curling your finger around the trigger.

Cool air rushes over my face as I walk into the compound. Windows arch high above my head, letting in pale light, but that is the most appealing part about the place—the tile floor is dull with dirt and age, and the walls are gray and blank. Ahead of us is a sea of people and machinery, with a sign over it that says SECURITY CHECKPOINT. I don't understand why they need so much security if they're already protected by two layers of fence, one of which is electrified, and a few layers of guards, but this is not my world to question.

No, this is not my world at all.

Tris touches my shoulder and points down the long entryway. "Look at that."

Standing at the far end of the room, outside the security checkpoint, is a huge block of stone with a glass apparatus suspended above it. It's a clear example of the things we will see here that we don't understand. I also don't understand the hunger in Tris's eyes, devouring everything around us as if it alone can sustain her. Sometimes I feel like we are the same, but sometimes, like right now, I feel the separation between our personalities like I've just run into a wall.

Christina says something to Tris, and they both grin. Everything I hear is muffled and distorted.

"Are you all right?" Cara asks me.

"Yeah," I say automatically.

"You know, it would be perfectly logical for you to be panicking right now," she says. "No need to continually insist upon your unshakable masculinity."

"My . . . what?"

She smiles, and I realize that she was joking.

All the people at the security checkpoint step aside,

forming a tunnel for us to walk through. Ahead of us, Zoe announces, "Weapons are not allowed inside this facility, but if you leave them at the security checkpoint you can pick them up as you exit, if you choose to do so. After you drop them off, we'll go through the scanners and be on our way."

"That woman is irritating," Cara says.

"What?" I say. "Why?"

"She can't separate herself from her own knowledge," she says as she draws her weapon. "She keeps saying things like they're obvious when they are not, in fact, obvious."

"You're right," I say without conviction. "That is irritating."

Ahead of me, I see Zoe putting her gun into a gray container and then walking into a scanner—it is a man-sized box with a tunnel through the middle, just wide enough for a body. I draw my own gun, which is heavy with unused bullets, and put it in the container the security guard holds out to me, where all the others' guns are.

I watch Zoe go through the scanner, then Amar, Peter, Caleb, Cara, and Christina. As I stand at the edge of it, at the walls that will squeeze my body between them, I feel the beginnings of panic again, the numb hands and the tight chest. The scanner reminds me of the wooden box that traps me in my fear landscape, squeezing my bones together.

I cannot, will not panic here.

I force my feet to move into the scanner, and stand in the middle, where all the others stood. I hear something moving in the walls on either side of me, and then there's a high-pitched beep. I shudder, and all I can see is the guard's hand, motioning me forward.

It is now okay to escape.

I stumble out of the scanner, and the air opens up around me. Cara gives me a pointed look, but doesn't say anything.

When Tris takes my hand after going through the scanner herself, I barely feel it. I remember going through my fear landscape with her, our bodies pressed together in the wooden box that enclosed us, my palm against her chest, feeling her heartbeat. It's enough to ground me in reality again.

Once Uriah is through, Zoe waves us forward again.

Beyond the security checkpoint, the facility is not as dingy as it was before. The floors are still tile, but they are polished to perfection, and there are windows everywhere. Down one long hallway I see rows of lab tables and computers, and it reminds me of Erudite headquarters, but it's brighter here, and nothing seems to be hidden.

Zoe leads us down a darker passageway on the right. As we walk past people, they stop to watch, and I feel their eyes on me like little beams of heat, making me warm from throat to cheeks.

We walk for a long time, deeper into the compound, and then Zoe stops, facing us.

Behind her is a large circle of blank screens, like moths circling a flame. People within the circle sit at low desks, typing furiously on still more screens, these ones facing out instead of in. It's a control room, but it's out in the open, and I'm not sure what they're observing here, since all the screens are dark. Clustered around the screens that face in are chairs and benches and tables, like people gather here to watch at their leisure.

A few feet in front of the control room is an older man wearing a smile and a dark blue uniform, just like all the others. When he sees us approaching, he spreads his hands as if to welcome us. David, I assume.

"This," the man says, "is what we've waited for since the very beginning."

CHAPTER FIFTEEN

TRIS

I TAKE THE photograph from my pocket. The man in front of me—David—is in it, next to my mother, his face a little smoother, his middle a little trimmer.

I cover my mother's face with my fingertip. All the hope growing inside me has withered. If my mother, or my father, or my friends were still alive, they would have been waiting by the doors for our arrival. I should have known better than to think what happened with Amar—whatever it was—could happen again.

"My name is David. As Zoe probably told you already, I am the leader of the Bureau of Genetic Welfare. I'm going to do my best to explain things," David says. "The first thing you should know is that the information Edith

Prior gave you is only partly true."

At the name "Prior" his eyes settle on me. My body shakes with anticipation—ever since I saw that video I've been desperate for answers, and I'm about to get them.

"She provided only as much information as you needed to meet the goals of our experiments," says David. "And in many cases, that meant oversimplifying, omitting, and even outright falsehood. Now that you are here, there is no need for any of those things."

"You all keep talking about 'experiments,'" Tobias says. "*What* experiments?"

"Yes, well, I was getting to that." David looks at Amar. "Where did they start when they explained it to you?"

"Doesn't matter where you start. You can't make it easier to take," Amar says, picking at his cuticles.

David considers this for a moment, then clears his throat.

"A long time ago, the United States government—"

"The united what?" Uriah asks.

"It's a country," says Amar. "A large one. It has specific borders and its own governing body, and we're in the middle of it right now. We can talk about it later. Go ahead, sir."

David presses his thumb into his palm and massages his hand, clearly disconcerted by all the interruptions.

He begins again:

"A few centuries ago, the government of this country became interested in enforcing certain desirable behaviors in its citizens. There had been studies that indicated that violent tendencies could be partially traced to a person's genes—a gene called 'the murder gene' was the first of these, but there were quite a few more, genetic predispositions toward cowardice, dishonesty, low intelligence—all the qualities, in other words, that ultimately contribute to a broken society."

We were taught that the factions were formed to solve a problem, the problem of our flawed natures. Apparently the people David is describing, whoever they were, believed in that problem too.

I know so little about genetics—just what I can see passed down from parent to child, in my face and in friends' faces. I can't imagine isolating a gene for murder, or cowardice, or dishonesty. Those things seem too nebulous to have a concrete location in a person's body. But I'm not a scientist.

"Obviously there are quite a few factors that determine personality, including a person's upbringing and experiences," David continues, "but despite the peace and prosperity that had reigned in this country for nearly a century, it seemed advantageous to our ancestors to reduce the risk of these undesirable qualities showing up in our population by correcting them. In other words, by editing humanity.

"That's how the genetic manipulation experiment was born. It takes several generations for any kind of genetic manipulation to manifest, but people were selected from the general population in large numbers, according to their backgrounds or behavior, and they were given the option to give a gift to our future generations, a genetic alteration that would make their descendants just a little bit better."

I look around at the others. Peter's mouth is puckered with disdain. Caleb is scowling. Cara's mouth has fallen open, like she is hungry for answers and intends to eat them from the air. Christina just looks skeptical, one eyebrow raised, and Tobias is staring at his shoes.

I feel like I am not hearing anything new—just the same philosophy that spawned the factions, driving people to manipulate their genes instead of separating into virtue-based groups. I understand it. On some level I even agree with it. But I don't know how it relates to us, here, now.

"But when the genetic manipulations began to take effect, the alterations had disastrous consequences. As it turns out, the attempt had resulted not in corrected genes, but in damaged ones," David says. "Take away someone's fear, or low intelligence, or dishonesty . . . and you take away their compassion. Take away someone's aggression and you take away their motivation, or their ability to assert themselves. Take away their selfishness and you take away their sense of self-preservation. If you think about it, I'm sure you know exactly what I mean."

I tick off each quality in my mind as he says it—fear, low intelligence, dishonesty, aggression, selfishness. He *is* talking about the factions. And he's right to say that every faction loses something when it gains a virtue: the Dauntless, brave but cruel; the Erudite, intelligent but vain; the Amity, peaceful but passive; the Candor, honest but inconsiderate; the Abnegation, selfless but stifling.

"Humanity has never been perfect, but the genetic alterations made it worse than it had ever been before. This manifested itself in what we call the Purity War. A civil war, waged by those with damaged genes, against the government and everyone with pure genes. The Purity War caused a level of destruction formerly unheard of on American soil, eliminating almost half of the country's population."

"The visual is up," says one of the people at a desk in the control room.

A map appears on the screen above David's head. It is an unfamiliar shape, so I'm not sure what it's supposed to represent, but it is covered with patches of pink, red, and dark-crimson lights.

"This is our country before the Purity War," David says. "And *this* is after—"

The lights start to recede, the patches shrinking like puddles of water drying in the sun. Then I realize that the red lights were people—people, disappearing, their lights going out. I stare at the screen, unable to wrap my mind around such a substantial loss.

David continues, "When the war was finally over, the people demanded a permanent solution to the genetic problem. And that is why the Bureau of Genetic Welfare was formed. Armed with all the scientific knowledge at our government's disposal, our predecessors designed experiments to restore humanity to its genetically pure state."

"They called for genetically damaged individuals to come forward so that the Bureau could alter their genes. The Bureau then placed them in secure environments to settle in for the long haul, equipped with basic versions of the serums to help them control their society. They would wait for the passage of time—for the generations to pass, for each one to produce more genetically healed humans. Or, as you currently know them . . . the Divergent."

Ever since Tori told me the word for what I am—Divergent—I have wanted to know what it means. And here is the simplest answer I have received: "Divergent" means that my genes are healed. Pure. Whole. I should feel relieved to know the real answer at last. But I just feel like something is off, itching in the back of my mind.

I thought that "Divergent" explained everything that I am and everything that I could be. Maybe I was wrong.

I am starting to feel short of breath as the revelations begin to work their way into my mind and heart, as David peels the layers of lies and secrets away. I touch my chest to feel my heartbeat, to try to steady myself.

"Your city is one of those experiments for genetic healing, and by far the most successful one, because of the behavioral modification portion. The factions, that is." David smiles at us, like it's something we should be proud of, but I am not proud. They created us, they shaped our world, they told us what to believe.

If they told us what to believe, and we didn't come to it on our own, is it still true? I press my hand harder against my chest. *Steady.*

"The factions were our predecessors' attempt to incorporate a 'nurture' element to the experiment—they discovered that mere genetic correction was not enough to change the way people behaved. A new social order, combined with the genetic modification, was determined to be the most complete solution to the behavioral problems that the genetic damage had created." David's smile fades as he looks around at all of us. I don't know what he expected—for us to smile back? He continues, "The factions were later introduced to most of our other experiments, three of which are currently active. We have gone to great lengths to protect you, observe you, and learn from you."

Cara runs her hands over her hair, as if checking for loose strands. Finding none, she says, "So when Edith Prior said we were supposed to determine the cause of Divergence and come out and help you, that was . . ."

"'Divergent' is the name we decided to give to those who have reached the desired level of genetic healing," says David. "We wanted to make sure that the leaders of your city valued them. We didn't expect the leader of Erudite to start hunting them down—or for the Abnegation to even tell her what they were—and contrary to what Edith Prior said, we never *really* intended for you to send a Divergent army out to us. We don't, after all, truly need your help. We just need your healed genes to remain intact and to be passed on to future generations."

"So what you're saying is that if we're not Divergent, we're *damaged*," Caleb says. His voice is shaking. I never thought I would see Caleb on the verge of tears because of something like this, but he is.

Steady, I tell myself again, and take another deep, slow breath.

"*Genetically* damaged, yes," says David. "However, we were surprised to discover that the behavioral modification component of our city's experiment was quite effective—up until recently, it actually helped quite a bit with the behavioral problems that made the genetic manipulation so problematic to begin with. So generally, you would not be able to tell whether a person's genes were damaged or healed from their behavior."

"I'm smart," Caleb says. "So you're saying that because my ancestors were *altered* to be smart, I, their descendant, can't be fully compassionate. I, and every other genetically damaged person, am limited by my damaged genes. And the Divergent are not."

"Well," says David, lifting a shoulder. "Think about it."

Caleb looks at me for the first time in days, and I stare back. Is that the explanation for Caleb's betrayal—his damaged genes? Like a disease that he can't heal, and can't control? It doesn't seem right.

"Genes aren't everything," Amar says. "People, even genetically damaged people, make choices. That's what matters."

I think of my father, a born Erudite, not Divergent; a man who could not help but be smart, choosing Abnegation, engaging in a lifelong struggle against his own nature, and ultimately fulfilling it. A man warring with himself, just as I war with myself.

That internal war doesn't seem like a product of genetic damage—it seems completely, purely *human*.

I look at Tobias. He is so washed out, so slouched, he looks like he might pass out. He's not alone in his reaction: Christina, Peter, Uriah, and Caleb all look stunned. Cara has the hem of her shirt pinched between her fingers, and she is moving her thumb over the fabric, frowning.

"This is a lot to process," says David.

That is an understatement.

Beside me, Christina snorts.

"And you've all been up all night," David finishes, like there was no interruption. "So I'll show you to a place where you can get some rest and food."

"Wait," I say. I think of the photograph in my pocket, and how Zoe knew my name when she gave it to me. I think of what David said, about observing us and learning from us. I think of the rows of screens, blank, right in front of me. "You said you've been observing us. How?"

Zoe purses her lips. David nods to one of the people at the desks behind him. All at once, all the screens turn on, each of them showing footage from different cameras. On the ones nearest to me, I see Dauntless headquarters. The Merciless Mart. Millennium Park. The Hancock building. The Hub.

"You've always known that the Dauntless observe the

city with security cameras," David says. "Well, we have access to those cameras too."

They've been watching us.

+ + +

I think about leaving.

We walk past the security checkpoint on our way to wherever David is taking us, and I think about walking through it again, picking up my gun, and running from this place where they've been watching me. Since I was small. My first steps, my first words, my first day of school, my first kiss.

Watching, when Peter attacked me. When my faction was put under a simulation and turned into an army. When my parents died.

What else have they seen?

The only thing that stops me from going is the photograph in my pocket. I can't leave these people before I find out how they knew my mother.

David takes us through the compound to a carpeted area with potted plants on either side. The wallpaper is old and yellowed, peeling from the corners of the walls. We follow him into a large room with high ceilings and wood floors and lights that glow orange-yellow. There are cots arranged in two straight rows, with trunks beside them for what we brought with us, and large windows with elegant curtains on the opposite end of the room. When I get closer to them, I see that they're worn and frayed at the edges.

David tells us that this part of the compound was a hotel, connected to the airport by a tunnel, and this room was once the ballroom. Again the words mean nothing to us, but he doesn't seem to notice.

"This is just a temporary dwelling, of course. Once you decide what to do, we will settle you somewhere else, whether it's in this compound or elsewhere. Zoe will ensure that you are well taken care of," he says. "I will be back tomorrow to see how you're all doing."

I look back at Tobias, who is pacing back and forth in front of the windows, gnawing on his fingernails. I never realized he had that habit. Maybe he was never distressed enough to do it before.

I could stay and try to comfort him, but I need answers about my mother, and I'm not going to wait any longer. I'm sure that Tobias, of all people, will understand. I follow David into the hallway. Just outside the room he leans against the wall and scratches the back of his neck.

"Hi," I say. "My name is Tris. I believe you knew my mother."

He jumps a little, but eventually smiles at me. I cross my arms. I feel the same way I did when Peter pulled my towel away during Dauntless initiation, to be cruel:

exposed, embarrassed, angry. Maybe it's not fair to direct all of that at David, but I can't help it. He's the leader of this compound—of the Bureau.

"Yes, of course," he says. "I recognize you."

From where? The creepy cameras that followed my every move? I pull my arms tighter across my chest.

"Right." I wait a beat, then say, "I need to know about my mother. Zoe gave me a picture of her, and you were standing right next to her in it, so I figured you could help."

"Ah," he says. "Can I see the picture?"

I take it out of my pocket and offer it to him. He smooths it down with his fingertips, and there is a strange smile on his face as he looks at it, like he's caressing it with his eyes. I shift my weight from one foot to the other—I feel like I'm intruding on a private moment.

"She took a trip back to us once," he says. "Before she settled into motherhood. That's when we took this."

"*Back* to you?" I say. "Was she one of you?"

"Yes," David says simply, like it's not a word that changes my entire world. "She came from this place. We sent her into the city when she was young to resolve a problem in the experiment."

"So she knew," I say, and my voice shakes, but I don't know why. "She *knew* about this place, and what was outside the fence."

David looks puzzled, his bushy eyebrows furrowed. "Well, of course."

The shaking moves down my arms and into my hands, and soon my entire body is shuddering, as if rejecting some kind of poison that I've swallowed, and the poison is knowledge, the knowledge of this place and its screens and all the lies I built my life on. "She knew you were *watching* us at every moment . . . watching as she *died* and my father died and everyone started killing each other! And did you send in someone to help her, to help me? No! No, all you did was take notes."

"Tris . . ."

He tries to reach for me, and I push his hand away. "Don't call me that. You shouldn't know that name. You shouldn't know anything about us."

Shivering, I walk back into the room.

+++

Back inside, the others have picked their beds and put their things down. It's just us in here, no intruders. I lean against the wall by the door and push my palms down the front of my pants to get the sweat off.

No one seems to be adjusting well. Peter lies facing the wall. Uriah and Christina sit side by side, having a conversation in low voices. Caleb is massaging his temples with his fingertips. Tobias is still pacing and gnawing on his fingernails. And Cara is on her own, dragging her hand over her face. For the first time since I met her, she looks upset, the Erudite armor gone.

I sit down across from her. "You don't look so good."

Her hair, usually smooth and perfect in its knot, is disheveled. She glowers at me. "That's kind of you to say."

"Sorry," I say. "I didn't mean it that way."

"I know." She sighs. "I'm . . . I'm an Erudite, you know."

I smile a little. "Yeah, I know."

"No." Cara shakes her head. "It's the only thing I am. Erudite. And now they've told me that's the result of some kind of flaw in my genetics . . . and that the factions themselves are just a mental prison to keep us under control. Just like Evelyn Johnson and the factionless said." She pauses. "So why form the Allegiant? Why bother to come out here?"

I didn't realize how much Cara had already cleaved to the idea of being an Allegiant, loyal to the faction system, loyal to our founders. For me it was just a temporary identity, powerful because it could get me out of the city. For her the attachment must have been much deeper.

"It's still good that we came out here," I say. "We found out the truth. That's not valuable to you?"

"Of course it is," Cara says softly. "But it means I need

other words for what I am."

Just after my mother died, I grabbed hold of my Divergence like it was a hand outstretched to save me. I needed that word to tell me who I was when everything else was coming apart around me. But now I'm wondering if I need it anymore, if we ever really *need* these words, "Dauntless," "Erudite," "Divergent," "Allegiant," or if we can just be friends or lovers or siblings, defined instead by the choices we make and the love and loyalty that binds us.

"Better check on him," Cara says, nodding to Tobias.

"Yeah," I say.

I cross the room and stand in front of the windows, staring at what we can see of the compound, which is just more of the same glass and steel, pavement and grass and fences. When he sees me, he stops pacing and stands next to me instead.

"You all right?" I say to him.

"Yeah." He sits on the windowsill, facing me, so we're at eye level. "I mean, no, not really. Right now I'm just thinking about how meaningless it all was. The faction system, I mean."

He rubs the back of his neck, and I wonder if he's thinking about the tattoos on his back.

"We put everything we had into it," he says. "All of us. Even if we didn't realize we were doing it."

"That's what you're thinking about?" I raise my eyebrows. "Tobias, they were *watching* us. Everything that happened, everything we did. They didn't intervene, they just invaded our privacy. Constantly."

He rubs his temple with his fingertips. "I guess. That's not what's bothering me, though."

I must give him an incredulous look without meaning to, because he shakes his head. "Tris, I worked in the Dauntless control room. There were cameras everywhere, all the time. I tried to warn you that people were watching you during your initiation, remember?"

I remember his eyes shifting to the ceiling, to the corner. His cryptic warnings, hissed between his teeth. I never realized he was warning me about cameras—it just never occurred to me before.

"It used to bother me," he says. "But I got over it a long time ago. We always thought we were on our own, and now it turns out we were right—they left us on our own. That's just the way it is."

"I guess I don't accept that," I say. "If you see someone in trouble, you should help them. Experiment or not. And . . . God." I cringe. "All the things they saw."

He smiles at me, a little.

"What?" I demand.

"I was just thinking of some of the things they saw,"

he says, putting his hand on my waist. I glare at him for a moment, but I can't sustain it, not with him grinning at me like that. Not knowing that he's trying to make me feel better. I smile a little.

I sit next to him on the windowsill, my hands wedged between my legs and the wood. "You know, the Bureau setting up the factions is not much different than what we thought happened: A long time ago, a group of people decided that the faction system would be the best way to live—or the way to get people to live the best lives they could."

He doesn't respond at first, just chews on the inside of his lip and looks at our feet, side by side on the floor. My toes brush the ground, not quite reaching it.

"That helps, actually," he says. "But there's so much that was a lie, it's hard to figure out what was true, what was real, what matters."

I take his hand, slipping my fingers between his. He touches his forehead to mine.

I catch myself thinking, *Thank God for this*, out of habit, and then I understand what he's so concerned about. What if my parents' God, their whole belief system, is just something concocted by a bunch of scientists to keep us under control? And not just their beliefs about God and whatever else is out there, but about right and wrong, about selflessness? Do all those things have to change because we know how our world was made?

I don't know.

The thought rattles me. So I kiss him—slowly, so I can feel the warmth of his mouth and the gentle pressure and his breaths as we pull away.

"Why is it," I say, "that we always find ourselves surrounded by people?"

"I don't know," he says. "Maybe because we're stupid."

I laugh, and it's laughter, not light, that casts out the darkness building within me, that reminds me I am still alive, even in this strange place where everything I've ever known is coming apart. I know some things—I know that I'm not alone, that I have friends, that I'm in love. I know where I came from. I know that I don't want to die, and for me, that's something—more than I could have said a few weeks ago.

+++

That night we push our cots just a little closer together, and look into each other's eyes in the moments before we fall asleep. When he finally drifts off, our fingers are twisted together in the space between the beds.

I smile a little, and let myself go too.

CHAPTER SIXTEEN

TOBIAS

THE SUN STILL hasn't completely set when we fall asleep, but I wake a few hours later, at midnight, my mind too busy for rest, swarming with thoughts and questions and doubts. Tris released me earlier, and her fingers now brush the floor. She is sprawled over the mattress, her hair covering her eyes.

I shove my feet into my shoes and walk the hallways, shoelaces slapping the carpets. I am so accustomed to the Dauntless compound that I am not used to the creak of wooden floors beneath me—I am used to the scrape and echo of stone, and the roar and pulse of water in the chasm.

A week into my initiation, Amar—worried that I was becoming increasingly isolated and obsessive—invited me to join some of the older Dauntless for a game of Dare.

For my dare, we went back to the Pit for me to get my first tattoo, the patch of Dauntless flames covering my rib cage. It was agonizing. I relished every second of it.

I reach the end of one hallway and find myself in an atrium, surrounded by the smell of wet earth. Everywhere plants and trees are suspended in water, the same way they were in the Amity greenhouses. In the center of the room is a tree in a giant water tank, lifted high above the floor so I can see the tangle of roots beneath it, strangely human, like nerves.

"You're not nearly as vigilant as you used to be," Amar says from behind me. "Followed you all the way here from the hotel lobby."

"What do you want?" I tap the tank with my knuckles, sending ripples through the water.

"I thought you might like an explanation for why I'm not dead," he says.

"I thought about it," I say. "They never let us see your body. It wouldn't be that hard to fake a death if you never show the body."

"Sounds like you've got it all figured out." Amar claps his hands together. "Well, I'll just go, then, if you're not curious. . . ."

I cross my arms.

Amar runs a hand over his black hair, tying it back with a rubber band. "They faked my death because I was

Divergent, and Jeanine had started killing the Divergent. They tried to save as many as they could before she got to them, but it was tricky, you know, because she was always a step ahead."

"Are there others?" I say.

"A few," he says.

"Any named Prior?"

Amar shakes his head. "No, Natalie Prior is actually dead, unfortunately. She was the one who helped me get out. She also helped this other guy too . . . George Wu. Know him? He's on a patrol right now, or he would have come with me to get you. His sister is still inside the city."

The name clutches at my stomach.

"Oh God," I say, and I lean into the tank wall.

"What? You know him?"

I shake my head.

I can't imagine it. There were just a few hours between Tori's death and our arrival. On a normal day, a few hours can contain long stretches of watch-checking, of empty time. But yesterday, just a few hours placed an impenetrable barrier between Tori and her brother.

"Tori is his sister," I say. "She tried to leave the city with us."

"*Tried* to," repeats Amar. "Ah. Wow. That's . . ."

Both of us are quiet for a while. George will never get to reunite with his sister, and she died thinking he had been murdered by Jeanine. There isn't anything to say—at least, not anything that's worth saying.

Now that my eyes have adjusted to the light, I can see that the plants in this room were selected for beauty, not practicality—flowers and ivy and clusters of purple or red leaves. The only flowers I've ever seen are wildflowers, or apple blossoms in the Amity orchards. These are more extravagant than those, vibrant and complex, petals folded into petals. Whatever this place is, it has not needed to be as pragmatic as our city.

"That woman who found your body," I say. "Was she just . . . lying about it?"

"People can't really be trusted to lie consistently." He quirks his eyebrows. "Never thought I would say that phrase—it's true, anyway. She was reset—her memory was altered to include me jumping off the Pire, and the body that was planted wasn't actually me. But it was too messed up for anyone to notice."

"She was reset. You mean, with the Abnegation serum."

"We call it 'memory serum,' since it doesn't technically just belong to the Abnegation, but yeah. That's the one."

I was angry with him before. I'm not really sure why. Maybe I was just angry that the world had become such a complicated place, that I have never known even a fraction of the truth about it. Or that I allowed myself to grieve for someone who was never really gone, the same way

I grieved for my mother all the years I thought she was dead. Tricking someone into grief is one of the cruelest tricks a person can play, and it's been played on me twice.

But as I look at him, my anger ebbs away, like the changing of the tide. And standing in the place of my anger is my initiation instructor and friend, alive again.

I grin.

"So you're alive," I say.

"More importantly," he says, pointing at me, "you are no longer upset about it."

He grabs my arm and pulls me into an embrace, slapping my back with one hand. I try to return his enthusiasm, but it doesn't come naturally—when we break apart, my face is hot. And judging by how he bursts into laughter, it's also bright red.

"Once a Stiff, always a Stiff," he says.

"Whatever," I say. "So do you like it here, then?"

Amar shrugs. "I don't really have a choice, but yeah, I like it fine. I work in security, obviously, since that's all I was trained to do. We'd love to have you, but you're probably too good for it."

"I haven't quite resigned myself to staying here just yet," I say. "But thanks, I guess."

"There's nowhere better out there," he says. "All the other cities—that's where most of the country lives, in these big metropolitan areas, like our city—are dirty and dangerous, unless you know the right people. Here at least there's clean water and food and safety."

I shift my weight, uncomfortable. I don't want to think about staying here, making this my home. I already feel trapped by my own disappointment. This is not what I imagined when I thought of escaping my parents and the bad memories they gave me. But I don't want to disturb the peace with Amar now that I finally feel like I have my friend back, so I just say, "I'll take that under advisement."

"Listen, there's something else you should know."

"What? More resurrections?"

"It's not exactly a resurrection if I was never dead, is it?" Amar shakes his head. "No, it's about the city. Someone heard it in the control room today—Marcus's trial is scheduled for tomorrow morning."

I knew it was coming—I knew Evelyn would save him for last, would savor every moment she spent watching him squirm under truth serum like he was her last meal. I just didn't realize that I would be able to see it, if I wanted to. I thought I was finally free of them, all of them, forever.

"Oh," is all I can say.

I still feel numb and confused when I walk back to the dormitory later and crawl back into bed. I don't know what I'll do.

CHAPTER SEVENTEEN

TRIS

I WAKE JUST before the sun. No one else stirs in their cot—Tobias's arm is draped over his eyes, but his shoes are now on, like he got up and walked around in the middle of the night. Christina's head is buried beneath her pillow. I lay for a few minutes, finding patterns in the ceiling, then put on my shoes and run my fingers through my hair to flatten it.

The hallways in the compound are empty except for a few stragglers. I assume they are just finishing the night shift, because they are hunched over screens, their chins propped on their hands, or slumped against broomsticks, barely remembering to sweep. I put my hands in my pockets and follow the signs to the entrance. I want to get a better look at the sculpture I saw yesterday.

Whoever built this place must have loved light. There is glass in the curve of each hallway's ceiling and along each lower wall. Even now, when it is barely morning, there is plenty of light to see by.

I check my back pocket for the badge Zoe handed to me at dinner last night, and pass the security checkpoint with it in hand. Then I see the sculpture, a few hundred yards away from the doors we entered through yesterday, gloomy and massive and mysterious, like a living entity.

It is a huge slab of dark stone, square and rough, like the rocks at the bottom of the chasm. A large crack runs through the middle of it, and there are streaks of lighter rock near the edges. Suspended above the slab is a glass tank of the same dimensions, full of water. A light placed above the center of the tank shines through the water, refracting as it ripples. I hear a faint noise, a drop of water hitting the stone. It comes from a small tube running through the center of the tank. At first I think the tank is just leaking, but another drop falls, then a third, and a fourth, at the same interval. A few drops collect, and then disappear down a narrow channel in the stone. They must be intentional.

"Hello." Zoe stands on the other side of the sculpture. "I'm sorry, I was about to go to the dormitory for you, then saw you heading this way and wondered if you were lost."

"No, I'm not lost," I say. "This is where I meant to go."

"Ah." She stands beside me and crosses her arms. She is about as tall as I am, but she stands straighter, so she seems taller. "Yeah, it's pretty weird, right?"

As she talks I watch the freckles on her cheeks, dappled like sunlight through dense leaves.

"Does it mean something?"

"It's the symbol of the Bureau of Genetic Welfare," she says. "The slab of stone is the problem we're facing. The tank of water is our potential for changing that problem. And the drop of water is what we're actually able to do, at any given time."

I can't help it—I laugh. "Not very encouraging, is it?"

She smiles. "That's one way of looking at it. I prefer to look at it another way—which is that if they are persistent enough, even tiny drops of water, over time, can change the rock forever. And it will never change back."

She points to the center of the slab, where there is a small impression, like a shallow bowl carved into the stone.

"That, for example, wasn't there when they installed this thing."

I nod, and watch the next drop fall. Even though I'm wary of the Bureau and everyone in it, I can feel the quiet hope of the sculpture working its way through me. It's a practical symbol, communicating the patient attitude that has allowed the people here to stay for so long, watching and waiting. But I have to ask.

"Wouldn't it be more effective to unleash the whole tank at once?" I imagine the wave of water colliding with the rock and spilling over the tile floor, collecting around my shoes. Doing a little at once can fix something, eventually, but I feel like when you believe that something is truly a problem, you throw everything you have at it, because you just can't help yourself.

"Momentarily," she says. "But then we wouldn't have any water left to do anything else, and genetic damage isn't the kind of problem that can be solved with one big charge."

"I understand that," I say. "I'm just wondering if it's a good thing to resign yourself quite this much to small steps when you could take some big ones."

"Like what?"

I shrug. "I guess I don't really know. But it's worth thinking about."

"Fair enough."

"So . . . you said you were looking for me?" I say. "Why?"

"Oh!" Zoe touches her forehead. "It slipped my mind. David asked me to find you and take you to the labs.

There's something there that belonged to your mother."

"My mother?" My voice comes out sounding strangled and too high. She leads me away from the sculpture and toward the security checkpoint again.

"Fair warning: You might get stared at," Zoe says as we walk through the security scanner. There are more people in the hallways up ahead now than there were earlier—it must be time for them to start work. "Your face is a familiar one here. People in the Bureau watch the screens often, and for the past few months, you've been involved in a lot of interesting things. A lot of the younger people think you're downright heroic."

"Oh, good," I say, a sour taste in my mouth. "Heroism is what I was focused on. Not, you know, trying not to die."

Zoe stops. "I'm sorry. I didn't mean to make light of what you've been through."

I still feel uncomfortable with the idea that everyone has been watching us, like I need to cover myself or hide where they can't look at me anymore. But there's not much Zoe can do about it, so I don't say anything.

Most of the people walking the halls wear variations of the same uniform—it comes in dark blue or dull green, and some of them wear the jackets or jumpsuits or sweatshirts open, revealing T-shirts of a wide variety of colors, some with pictures drawn on them.

"Do the colors of the uniforms mean anything?" I ask Zoe.

"Yes, actually. Dark blue means scientist or researcher, and green means support staff—they do maintenance, upkeep, things like that."

"So they're like the factionless."

"No," she says. "No, the dynamic is different here—everyone does what they can to support the mission. Everyone is valued and important."

She was right: People do stare at me. Most of them just look at me for a little too long, but some point, and some even say my name, like it belongs to them. It makes me feel cramped, like I can't move the way I want to.

"A lot of the support staff used to be in the experiment in Indianapolis—another city, not far from here," Zoe says. "But for them, this transition has been a little bit easier than it will be for you—Indianapolis didn't have the behavioral components of your city." She pauses. "The factions, I mean. After a few generations, when your city didn't tear itself apart and the others did, the Bureau implemented the faction components in the newer cities—Saint Louis, Detroit, and Minneapolis—using the relatively new Indianapolis experiment as a control group. The Bureau always placed experiments in the Midwest, because there's more space between urban areas here. Out east everything is closer together."

"So in Indianapolis you just . . . corrected their genes and shoved them in a city somewhere? Without factions?"

"They had a complex system of rules, but . . . yes, that's essentially what happened."

"And it didn't work very well?"

"No." She purses her lips. "Genetically damaged people who have been conditioned by suffering and are not taught to live differently, as the factions would have taught them to, are very destructive. That experiment failed quickly—within three generations. Chicago—your city—and the other cities that have factions have made it through much more than that."

Chicago. It's so strange to have a name for the place that was always just home to me. It makes the city smaller in my mind.

"So you guys have been doing this for a long time," I say.

"Quite some time, yes. The Bureau is different from most government agencies, because of the focused nature of our work and our contained, relatively remote location. We pass on knowledge and purpose to our children, instead of relying on appointments or hiring. I've been training for what I'm doing now for my entire life."

Through the abundant windows I see a strange vehicle—it's shaped like a bird, with two wing structures and a pointed nose, but it has wheels, like a car.

"Is that for air travel?" I say, pointing at it.

"Yes." She smiles. "It's an airplane. We might be able to take you up in one sometime, if it doesn't seem too *daunting* for you."

I don't react to the play on words. I can't quite forget how she recognized me on sight.

David is standing near one of the doors up ahead. He raises his hand in a wave when he sees us.

"Hello, Tris," he says. "Thank you for bringing her, Zoe."

"You're welcome, sir," Zoe says. "I'll leave you to it, then. Lots of work to do."

She smiles at me, then walks away. I don't want her to leave—now that she's gone, I'm left with David and the memory of how I yelled at him yesterday. He doesn't say anything about it, just scans his badge in the door sensor to open it.

The room beyond it is an office with no windows. A young man, maybe Tobias's age, sits at one desk, and another one, across the room, is empty. The young man looks up when we come in, taps something on his computer screen, and stands.

"Hello, sir," he says. "Can I help you?"

"Matthew. Where's your supervisor?" David says.

“He’s foraging for food in the cafeteria,” Matthew says.

“Well, maybe you can help me, then. I’ll need Natalie Wright’s file loaded on a portable screen. Can you do that?”

Wright? I think. Was that my mother’s real last name?

“Of course,” Matthew says, and he sits again. He types something on his computer and pulls up a series of documents that I’m not close enough to see clearly. “Okay, it just has to transfer.

“You must be Natalie’s daughter, Beatrice.” He props his chin on his hand and looks at me critically. His eyes are so dark they look black, and they slant a little at the edges. He does not look impressed or surprised to see me. “You don’t look much like her.”

“Tris,” I say automatically. But I find it comforting that he doesn’t know my nickname—that must mean he doesn’t spend all his time staring at the screens like our lives in the city are entertainment. “And yeah, I know.”

David pulls a chair over, letting it screech on the tile, and pats it.

“Sit. I’ll give you a screen with all Natalie’s files on it so that you and your brother can read them yourselves, but while they’re loading I might as well tell you the story.”

I sit on the edge of the chair, and he sits behind the desk of Matthew’s supervisor, turning a half-empty coffee cup in circles on the metal.

"Let me start by saying that your mother was a fantastic discovery. We located her almost by accident inside the damaged world, and her genes were nearly perfect." David beams. "We took her out of a bad situation and brought her here. She spent several years here, but then we encountered a crisis within your city's walls, and she volunteered to be placed inside to resolve it. I'm sure you know all about that, though."

For a few seconds all I can do is blink at him. My mother came from outside this place? Where?

It hits me, again, that she walked these halls, watched the city on the screens in the control room. Had she sat in this chair? Had her feet touched these tiles? Suddenly I feel like there are invisible marks of my mother everywhere, on every wall and doorknob and pillar.

I grip the edge of the seat and try to organize my thoughts enough to ask a question.

"No, I don't know," I say. "What crisis?"

"The Erudite representative had just begun to kill the Divergent, of course," he says. "His name was Nor—Norman?"

"Norton," says Matthew. "Jeanine's predecessor. Seems he passed on the idea of killing off the Divergent to her, right before his heart attack."

"Thank you. Anyway, we sent Natalie in to investigate

the situation and to stop the deaths. We never dreamed she would be in there for so long, of course, but she was useful—we had never thought about having an insider before, and she was able to do many things that were invaluable to us. As well as building a life for herself, which obviously includes you."

I frown. "But the Divergent were still being killed when I was an initiate."

"You only know about the ones who died," David says. "Not about the ones who didn't die. Some of them are here, in this compound. I believe you met Amar earlier? He's one of them. Some of the rescued Divergent needed some distance from your experiment—it was too hard for them to watch the people they had once known and loved going about their lives, so they were trained to integrate into life outside the Bureau. But yes, she did important work, your mother."

She also told quite a few lies, and very few truths. I wonder if my father knew who she was, where she was really from. He was an Abnegation leader, after all, and as such, one of the keepers of the truth. I have a sudden, horrifying thought: What if she only married him because she was supposed to, as part of her mission in the city? What if their entire relationship was a sham?

"So she wasn't really born Dauntless," I say as I sort

through the lies that must have been.

"When she first entered the city, it was as a Dauntless, because she already had tattoos and that would have been hard to explain to the natives. She was sixteen, but we said she was fifteen so she would have some time to adjust. Our intention was for her to . . ." He lifts a shoulder. "Well, you should read her file. I can't do a sixteen-year-old perspective justice."

As if on cue, Matthew opens a desk drawer and takes out a small, flat piece of glass. He taps it with one fingertip, and an image appears on it. It's one of the documents he just had open on his computer. He offers the tablet to me. It's sturdier than I expected it to be, hard and strong.

"Don't worry, it's practically indestructible," David says. "I'm sure you want to return to your friends. Matthew, would you please walk Miss Prior back to the hotel? I have some things to take care of."

"And I don't?" Matthew says. Then he winks. "Kidding, sir. I'll take her."

"Thank you," I say to David, before he walks out.

"Of course," he says. "Let me know if you have any questions."

"Ready?" Matthew says.

He's tall, maybe the same height as Caleb, and his black hair is artfully tousled in the front, like he spent a lot of time making it look like he'd just rolled out of bed that way. Under his dark blue uniform he wears a plain black T-shirt and a black string around his throat. It shifts over his Adam's apple when he swallows.

I walk with him out of the small office and down the hallway again. The crowd that was here before has thinned. They must have settled in to work, or breakfast. There are whole lives being lived in this place, sleeping and eating and working, bearing children and raising families and dying. This is a place my mother called home, once.

"I wonder when you're going to freak out," he says. "After finding out all this stuff at once."

"I'm not going to freak out," I say, feeling defensive. *I already did,* I think, but I'm not going to admit to that.

Matthew shrugs. "I would. But fair enough."

I see a sign that says HOTEL ENTRANCE up ahead. I clutch the screen to my chest, eager to get back to the dormitory and tell Tobias about my mother.

"Listen, one of the things my supervisor and I do is genetic testing," Matthew says. "I was wondering if you and that other guy—Marcus Eaton's son?—would mind coming in so that I can test your genes."

"Why?"

"Curiosity." He shrugs. "We haven't gotten to test the genes of someone in such a late generation of the experiment before, and you and Tobias seem to be somewhat . . . odd, in your manifestations of certain things."

I raise my eyebrows.

"You, for example, have displayed extraordinary serum resistance—most of the Divergent aren't as capable of resisting serums as you are," Matthew says. "And Tobias can resist simulations, but he doesn't display some of the characteristics we've come to expect of the Divergent. I can explain in more detail later."

I hesitate, not sure if I want to see my genes, or Tobias's genes, or to compare them, like it matters. But Matthew's expression seems eager, almost childlike, and I understand curiosity.

"I'll ask him if he's up for it," I say. "But I would be willing. When?"

"This morning okay?" he says. "I can come get you in an hour or so. You can't get into the labs without me anyway."

I nod. I feel excited, suddenly, to learn more about my genes, which feels like the same thing as reading my mother's journal: I will get pieces of her back.

CHAPTER EIGHTEEN

TOBIAS

IT'S STRANGE TO see people you don't know well in the morning, with sleepy eyes and pillow creases in their cheeks; to know that Christina is cheerful in the morning, and Peter wakes up with his hair perfectly flat, but Cara communicates only through a series of grunts, inching her way, limb by limb, toward coffee.

The first thing I do is shower and change into the clothes they provided for us, which aren't much different from the clothes I am accustomed to, but all the colors are mixed together like they don't mean anything to the people here, and they probably don't. I wear a black shirt and blue jeans and try to convince myself that it feels normal, that I feel normal, that I am adapting.

My father's trial is today. I haven't decided if I'm going to watch it or not.

When I return, Tris is already fully dressed, perched on the edge of one of the cots, like she's ready to leap to her feet at any moment. Just like Evelyn.

I grab a muffin from the tray of breakfast food that someone brought us, and sit across from her. "Good morning. You were up early."

"Yeah," she says, scooting her foot forward so it's wedged between mine. "Zoe found me at that big sculpture thing this morning—David had something to show me." She picks up the glass screen resting on the cot beside her. It glows when she touches it, showing a document. "It's my mother's file. She wrote a journal—a small one, from the look of it, but still." She shifts like she's uncomfortable. "I haven't looked at it much yet."

"So," I say, "why aren't you reading it?"

"I don't know." She puts it down, and the screen turns off automatically. "I think I'm afraid of it."

Abnegation children rarely know their parents in any significant way, because Abnegation parents never reveal themselves the way other parents do when their children grow to a particular age. They keep themselves wrapped in gray cloth armor and selfless acts, convinced that to share is to be self-indulgent. This is not just a piece of

Tris's mother, recovered; it's one of the first and last honest glimpses Tris will ever get of who Natalie Prior was.

I understand, then, why she holds it like it's a magical object, something that could disappear in a moment. And why she wants to leave it undiscovered for a while, which is the same way I feel about my father's trial. It could tell her something she doesn't want to know.

I follow her eyes across the room to where Caleb sits, chewing on a bite of cereal—morosely, like a pouting child.

"Are you going to show it to him?" I say.

She doesn't respond.

"Usually I don't advocate giving him anything," I say. "But in this case . . . this doesn't really just belong to you."

"I know that," she says, a little tersely. "Of course I'll show it to him. But I think I want to be alone with it first."

I can't argue with that. Most of my life has been spent keeping information close, turning it over and over in my mind. The impulse to share anything is a new one, the impulse to hide as natural as breathing.

She sighs, then breaks a piece off the muffin in my hand. I flick her fingers as she pulls away. "Hey. There are plenty more just five feet to your right."

"Then you shouldn't be so worried about losing some of yours," she says, grinning.

"Fair enough."

She pulls me toward her by the front of my shirt and

kisses me. I slip my hand under her chin and hold her still as I kiss her back.

Then I notice that she's stealing another pinch of muffin, and I pull away, glaring at her.

"Seriously," I say. "I'll get you one from that table. It'll only take me a second."

She grins. "So, there's something I wanted to ask you. Would you be up for undergoing a little genetic test this morning?"

The phrase "a little genetic test" strikes me as an oxymoron.

"Why?" I say. Asking to see my genes feels a little like asking me to strip down.

"Well, this guy I met—Matthew is his name—works in one of the labs here, and he says they would be interested in looking at our genetic material for research," she says. "And he asked about you, specifically, because you're sort of an anomaly."

"Anomaly?"

"Apparently you display some Divergent characteristics and you don't display others," she says. "I don't know. He's just curious about it. You don't have to do it."

The air around my head feels warmer and heavier. To alleviate the discomfort I touch the back of my neck, scratching at my hairline.

Sometime in the next hour or so, Marcus and Evelyn

will be on the screens. Suddenly I know that I can't watch.

So even though I don't *really* want to let a stranger examine the puzzle pieces that make up my existence, I say, "Sure. I'll do it."

"Great," she says, and she eats another pinch of my muffin. A piece of hair falls into her eyes, and I am brushing it back before she even notices it. She covers my hand with her own, which is warm and strong, and the corners of her mouth curl into a smile.

The door opens, admitting a young man with slanted, angular eyes and black hair. I recognize him immediately as George Wu, Tori's younger brother. "Georgie" was the name she called him.

He smiles a giddy smile, and I feel the urge to back away, to put more space between me and his impending grief.

"I just got back," he says, breathless. "They told me my sister set out with you guys, and—"

Tris and I exchange a troubled look. All around us, the others are noticing George by the door and going quiet, the same kind of quiet you hear at an Abnegation funeral. Even Peter, who I would expect to crave other people's pain, looks bewildered, shifting his hands from his waist to his pockets and back again.

"And . . ." George begins again. "Why are you all looking at me like that?"

Cara steps forward, about to bear the bad news, but I can't imagine Cara sharing it well, so I get up, talking over her.

"Your sister did leave with us," I say. "But we were attacked by the factionless, and she . . . didn't make it."

There is so much that phrase doesn't say—how quick it was, and the sound of her body hitting the earth, and the chaos of everyone running into the night, stumbling over the grass. I didn't go back for her. I should have—of all the people in our party, I knew Tori best, knew how tightly her hands squeezed the tattoo needle and how her laugh sounded rough, like it had been scraped with sandpaper.

George touches the wall behind him for stability. "What?"

"She gave her life defending us," Tris says with surprising gentleness. "Without her, none of us would have made it out."

"She's . . . dead?" George says weakly. He leans his entire body into the wall, and his shoulders sag.

I see Amar in the hallway, a piece of toast in his hand and a smile quickly fading from his face. He sets the toast down on a table by the door.

"I tried to find you earlier to tell you," Amar says.

Last night Amar said George's name so casually, I didn't think they really knew each other. Apparently they do.

George's eyes turn glassy, and Amar pulls him into an embrace with one arm. George's fingers are bent at harsh angles into Amar's shirt, the knuckles white with tension. I don't hear him cry, and maybe he doesn't, maybe all he needs to do is hold on to something. I have only hazy memories of my own grief over my mother, when I thought she was dead—just the feeling that I was separate from everything around me, and this constant sensation of needing to swallow something. I don't know what it's like for other people.

Eventually, Amar leads George out of the room, and I watch them walk down the hallway side by side, talking in low voices.

+++

I barely remember that I agreed to participate in a genetic test until someone else appears at the door to the dormitory—a boy, or not really a boy, since he looks about as old as I am. He waves to Tris.

"Oh, that's Matthew," she says. "I guess we should get going."

She takes my hand and leads me toward the doorway. Somehow I missed her mentioning that "Matthew" wasn't a crusty old scientist. Or maybe she didn't mention it at all.

Don't be stupid, I think.

Matthew sticks out his hand. "Hi. It's nice to meet you. I'm Matthew."

"Tobias," I say, because "Four" sounds strange here, where people would never identify themselves by how many fears they have. "You too."

"So let's go to the labs, I guess," he says. "They're this way."

The compound is thick with people this morning, all dressed in green or dark blue uniforms that pool around the ankles or stop several inches above the shoe, depending on the height of the person. The compound is full of open areas that branch off the major hallways, like chambers of a heart, each marked with a letter and a number, and the people seem to be moving between them, some carrying glass devices like the one Tris brought back this morning, some empty-handed.

"What's with the numbers?" says Tris. "Just a way of labeling each area?"

"They used to be gates," says Matthew. "Meaning that each one has a door and a walkway that led to a particular airplane going to a particular destination. When they converted the airport into the compound, they ripped out all the chairs people used to wait for their flights in and replaced them with lab equipment, mostly taken from schools in the city. This area of the compound is basically a giant laboratory."

"What are they working on? I thought you were just observing the experiments," I say, watching a woman rush from one side of the hallway to the other with a screen balanced on both palms like an offering. Beams of light stretch across the polished tile, slanting through the ceiling windows. Through the windows everything looks peaceful, every blade of grass trimmed and the wild trees swaying in the distance, and it's hard to imagine that people are destroying one another out there because of "damaged genes" or living under Evelyn's strict rules in the city we left.

"Some of them are doing that. Everything that they notice in all the remaining experiments has to be recorded and analyzed, so that requires a lot of manpower. But some of them are also working on better ways to treat the genetic damage, or developing the serums for our own use instead of the experiments' use—dozens of projects. All you have to do is come up with an idea, gather a team together, and propose it to the council that runs the compound under David. They usually approve anything that isn't too risky."

"Yeah," says Tris. "Wouldn't want to take any risks."

She rolls her eyes a little.

"They have a good reason for their endeavors," Matthew says. "Before the factions were introduced, and the serums with them, the experiments all used to be under near-constant assault from within. The serums help the people in the experiment to keep things under control, especially the memory serum. Well, I guess no one's working on that right now—it's in the Weapons Lab."

"Weapons Lab." He says the words like they're fragile in his mouth. Sacred words.

"So the Bureau gave us the serums, in the beginning," Tris says.

"Yes," he says. "And then the Erudite continued to work on them, to perfect them. Including your brother. To be honest, we got some of our serum developments from them, by observing them in the control room. Only they didn't do much with the memory serum—the Abnegation serum. We did a lot more with that, since it's our greatest weapon."

"A weapon," Tris repeats.

"Well, it arms the cities against their own rebellions, for one thing—erase people's memories and there's no need to kill them; they just forget what they were fighting about. And we can also use it against rebels from the fringe, which is about an hour from here. Sometimes fringe dwellers try to raid, and the memory serum stops them without killing them."

"That's . . ." I start.

"Still kind of awful?" Matthew supplies. "Yes, it is. But the higher-ups here think of it as our life support, our breathing machine. Here we are."

I raise my eyebrows. He just spoke out against his own leaders so casually I almost missed it. I wonder if that's the kind of place this is—where dissent can be expressed in public, in the middle of a normal conversation, instead of in secret spaces, with hushed voices.

He scans his card at a heavy door on our left, and we walk down another hallway, this one narrow and lit with pale, fluorescent light. He stops at a door marked GENE THERAPY ROOM 1. Inside, a girl with light brown skin and a green jumpsuit is replacing the paper that covers the exam table.

"This is Juanita, the lab technician. Juanita, this is—"

"Yeah, I know who they are," she says, smiling. Out of the corner of my eye I see Tris stiffen, chafing against the reminder that our lives have been on camera. But she doesn't say anything about it.

The girl offers me her hand. "Matthew's supervisor is the only person who calls me Juanita. Except Matthew, apparently. I'm Nita. You'll need two tests prepared?"

Matthew nods.

"I'll get them." She opens a set of cabinets across the room and starts pulling things out. All of them are encased in plastic and paper and have white labels. The room is full of the sound of crinkling and ripping.

"How do you guys like it here so far?" she asks us.

"It's been an adjustment," I say.

"Yeah, I know what you mean." Nita smiles at me. "I came from one of the other experiments—the one in Indianapolis, the one that failed. Oh, you don't know where Indianapolis is, do you? It's not far from here. Less than an hour by plane." She pauses. "That won't mean anything to you either. You know what? It's not important."

She takes a syringe and needle from its plastic-paper wrapping, and Tris tenses.

"What's that for?" Tris says.

"It's what will enable us to read your genes," Matthew says. "Are you okay?"

"Yeah," Tris says, but she's still tense. "I just . . . don't like to be injected with strange substances."

Matthew nods. "I swear it's just going to read your genes. That's all it does. Nita can vouch for it."

Nita nods.

"Okay," Tris says. "But . . . can I do it to myself?"

"Sure," Nita says. She prepares the syringe, filling it with whatever they intend to inject us with, and offers it to Tris.

"I'll give you the simplified explanation of how this

works," Matthew says as Nita brushes Tris's arm with antiseptic. The smell is sour, and it nips at the inside of my nose.

"The fluid is packed with microcomputers. They are designed to detect specific genetic markers and transmit the data to a computer. It will take them about an hour to give me as much information as I need, though it would take them much longer to read all your genetic material, obviously."

Tris sticks the needle into her arm and presses the plunger.

Nita beckons my arm forward and drags the orange-stained gauze over my skin. The fluid in the syringe is silver-gray, like fish scales, and as it flows into me through the needle, I imagine the microscopic technology chewing through my body, reading me and analyzing me. Beside me, Tris holds a cotton ball to her pricked skin and offers me a small smile.

"What are the . . . microcomputers?" Matthew nods, and I continue. "What are they looking for, exactly?"

"Well, when our predecessors at the Bureau inserted 'corrected' genes into your ancestors, they also included a genetic tracker, which is basically something that shows us that a person has achieved genetic healing. In this case, the genetic tracker is awareness during simulations—it's something we can easily test for, which shows us if your genes are healed or not. That's one of the reasons why everyone in the city has to take the aptitude test at sixteen—if they're aware during the test, that shows us that they might have healed genes."

I add the aptitude test to a mental list of things that were once so important to me, cast aside because it was just a ruse to get these people the information or result they wanted.

I can't believe that awareness during simulations, something that made me feel powerful and unique, something Jeanine and the Erudite *killed* people for, is actually just a sign of genetic healing to these people. Like a special code word, telling them I'm in their genetically healed society.

Matthew continues, "The only problem with the genetic tracker is that being aware during simulations and resisting serums doesn't necessarily mean that a person is Divergent, it's just a strong correlation. Sometimes people will be aware during simulations or be able to resist serums even if they still have damaged genes." He shrugs. "That's why I'm interested in your genes, Tobias. I'm curious to see if you're actually Divergent, or if your simulation awareness just makes it look like you are."

Nita, who is clearing the counter, presses her lips together like she is holding words inside her mouth. I feel suddenly uneasy. There's a chance I'm not actually Divergent?

"All that's left is to sit and wait," Matthew says. "I'm going to go get breakfast. Do either of you want something to eat?"

Tris and I both shake our heads.

"I'll be back soon. Nita, keep them company, would you?"

Matthew leaves without waiting for Nita's response, and Tris sits on the examination table, the paper crinkling beneath her and tearing where her leg hangs over the edge. Nita puts her hands in her jumpsuit pockets and looks at us. Her eyes are dark, with the same sheen as a puddle of oil beneath a leaking engine. She hands me a cotton ball, and I press it to the bubble of blood inside my elbow.

"So you came from a city experiment," says Tris. "How long have you been here?"

"Since the Indianapolis experiment was disbanded, which was about eight years ago. I could have integrated into the greater population, outside the experiments, but that felt too overwhelming." Nita leans against the counter. "So I volunteered to come here. I used to be a janitor. I'm moving through the ranks, I guess."

She says it with a certain amount of bitterness. I suspect that here, as in Dauntless, there is a limit to her climb through the ranks, and she is reaching it earlier than she would like to. The same way I did, when I chose my job in the control room.

"And your city, it didn't have factions?" Tris says.

"No, it was the control group—it helped them to figure out that the factions were actually effective by comparison. It had a lot of rules, though—curfew, wake-up times, safety regulations. No weapons allowed. Stuff like that."

"What happened?" I say, and a moment later I wish I hadn't asked, because the corners of Nita's mouth turn down, like the memory hangs heavy from each side.

"Well, a few of the people inside still knew how to make weapons. They made a bomb—you know, an explosive—and set it off in the government building," she says. "Lots of people died. And after that, the Bureau decided our experiment was a failure. They erased the memories of the bombers and relocated the rest of us. I'm one of the only ones who wanted to come here."

"I'm sorry," Tris says softly. Sometimes I still forget to look for the gentler parts of her. For so long all I saw was the strength, standing out like the wiry muscles in her arms or the black ink marking her collarbone with flight.

"It's all right. It's not like you guys don't know about stuff like this," says Nita. "With what Jeanine Matthews did, and all."

"Why haven't they shut our city down?" Tris says. "The

same way they did to yours?"

"They might still shut it down," says Nita. "But I think the Chicago experiment, in particular, has been a success for so long that they'll be a little reluctant to just ditch it now. It was the first one with factions."

I take the cotton ball away from my arm. There is a tiny red dot where the needle went in, but it isn't bleeding anymore.

"I like to think I would have chosen Dauntless," says Nita. "But I don't think I would have had the stomach for it."

"You'd be surprised what you have the stomach for, when you have to," Tris says.

I feel a pang in the middle of my chest. She's right. Desperation can make a person do surprising things. We would both know.

+++

Matthew returns right at the hour mark, and he sits at the computer for a long time after that, his eyes flicking back and forth as he reads the screen. A few times he makes a revelatory noise, a "hmm!" or an "ah!" The longer he waits to tell us something, anything, the more tense my muscles become, until my shoulders feel like they are made of stone instead of flesh. Finally he looks up and turns the screen around so we can see what's on it.

"This program helps us to interpret the data in an understandable way. What you see here is a simplified depiction of a particular DNA sequence in Tris's genetic material," he says.

The picture on the screen is a complicated mass of lines and numbers, with certain parts selected in yellow and red. I can't make any sense of the picture beyond that—it is above my level of comprehension.

"These selections here suggest healed genes. We wouldn't see them if the genes were damaged." He taps certain parts of the screen. I don't understand what he's pointing at, but he doesn't seem to notice, caught up in his own explanation. "These selections over here indicate that the program also found the genetic tracker, the simulation awareness. The combination of healed genes and simulation awareness genes is just what I expected to see from a Divergent. Now, this is the strange part."

He touches the screen again, and the screen changes, but it remains just as confusing, a web of lines, tangled threads of numbers.

"This is the map of Tobias's genes," Matthew says. "As you can see, he has the right genetic components for simulation awareness, but he doesn't have the same 'healed' genes that Tris does."

My throat is dry, and I feel like I've been given bad news, but I still haven't entirely grasped what that bad news is.

"What does that mean?" I ask.

"It means," Matthew says, "that you are not Divergent. Your genes are still damaged, but you have a genetic anomaly that allows you to be aware during simulations anyway. You have, in other words, the appearance of a Divergent without actually being one."

I process the information slowly, piece by piece. I'm not Divergent. I'm not like Tris. I'm genetically damaged.

The word "damaged" sinks inside me like it's made of lead. I guess I always knew there was something wrong with me, but I thought it was because of my father, or my mother, and the pain they bequeathed to me like a family heirloom, handed down from generation to generation. And this means that the one good thing my father had—his Divergence—didn't reach me.

I don't look at Tris—I can't bear it. Instead I look at Nita. Her expression is hard, almost angry.

"Matthew," she says. "Don't you want to take this data to your lab to analyze?"

"Well, I was planning on discussing it with our subjects here," Matthew says.

"I don't think that's a good idea," Tris says, sharp as a blade.

Matthew says something I don't really hear; I'm listening to the thump of my heart. He taps the screen again, and the picture of my DNA disappears, so the screen is blank, just glass. He leaves, instructing us to visit his lab if we want more information, and Tris, Nita, and I stand in the room in silence.

"It's not that big a deal," Tris says firmly. "Okay?"

"You don't get to tell me it's not a big deal!" I say, louder than I mean to be.

Nita busies herself at the counter, making sure the containers there are lined up, though they haven't moved since we first came in.

"Yeah, I do!" Tris exclaims. "You're the same person you were five minutes ago and four months ago and eighteen years ago! This doesn't change anything about you."

I hear something in her words that's right, but it's hard to believe her right now.

"So you're telling me this affects nothing," I say. "The truth affects nothing."

"What truth?" she says. "These people tell you there's something wrong with your genes, and you just believe it?"

"It was right there." I gesture to the screen. "You saw it."

"I also see you," she says fiercely, her hand closing around my arm. "And I know who you are."

I shake my head. I still can't look at her, can't look at anything in particular. "I . . . need to take a walk. I'll see you later."

"Tobias, wait—"

I walk out, and some of the pressure inside me releases as soon as I'm not in that room anymore. I walk down the cramped hallway that presses against me like an exhale, and into the sunlit halls beyond it. The sky is bright blue now. I hear footsteps behind me, but they're too heavy to belong to Tris.

"Hey." Nita twists her foot, making it squeak against the tile. "No pressure, but I'd like to talk to you about all this . . . genetic-damage stuff. If you're interested, meet me here tonight at nine. And . . . no offense to your girl or anything, but you might not want to bring her."

"Why?" I say.

"She's a GP—genetically pure. So she can't understand that—well, it's hard to explain. Just trust me, okay? She's better off staying away for a little while."

"Okay."

"Okay." Nita nods. "Gotta go."

I watch her run back toward the gene therapy room, and then I keep walking. I don't know where I'm going, exactly, just that when I walk, the frenzy of information I've learned in the past day stops moving quite so fast, stops shouting quite so loud inside my head.

CHAPTER NINETEEN

TRIS

I DON'T GO after him, because I don't know what to say.

When I found out I was Divergent, I thought of it as a secret power that no one else possessed, something that made me different, better, stronger. Now, after comparing my DNA to Tobias's on a computer screen, I realize that "Divergent" doesn't mean as much as I thought it did. It's just a word for a particular sequence in my DNA, like a word for all people with brown eyes or blond hair.

I lean my head into my hands. But these people still think it means something—they still think it means I'm healed in a way that Tobias is not. And they want me to just trust that, believe it.

Well, I don't. And I'm not sure why Tobias does—why

he's so eager to believe that he is damaged.

I don't want to think about it anymore. I leave the gene therapy room just as Nita is walking back to it.

"What did you say to him?" I say.

She's pretty. Tall but not too tall, thin but not too thin, her skin rich with color.

"I just made sure he knew where he was going," she says. "It's a confusing place."

"It certainly is." I start toward—well, I don't know where I'm going, but it's away from Nita, the pretty girl who talks to my boyfriend when I'm not there. Then again, it's not like it was a long conversation.

I spot Zoe at the end of the hallway, and she waves me toward her. She looks more relaxed now than she did earlier this morning, her forehead smooth instead of creased, her hair loose over her shoulders. She shoves her hands into the pockets of her jumpsuit.

"I just told the others," she says. "We've scheduled a plane ride in two hours for those who want to go. Are you up for it?"

Fear and excitement squirm together in my stomach, just like they did before I was strapped in on the zip line atop the Hancock building. I imagine hurtling into the air in a car with wings, the energy of the engine and the rush of wind through all the spaces in the walls and the possibility, however slight, that something will fail and I will plummet to my death.

"Yes," I say.

"We're meeting at gate B14. Follow the signs!" She flashes a smile as she leaves.

I look through the windows above me. The sky is clear and pale, the same color as my own eyes. There is a kind of inevitability in it, like it has always been waiting for me, maybe because I relish height while others fear it, or maybe because once you have seen the things that I have seen, there is only one frontier left to explore, and it is above.

+++

The metal stairs leading down to the pavement screech with each of my footsteps. I have to tilt my head back to look at the airplane, which is bigger than I expected it to be, and silver-white. Just below the wing is a huge cylinder with spinning blades inside it. I imagine the blades sucking me in and spitting me out the other side, and shudder a little.

"How can something that big stay in the sky?" Uriah says from behind me.

I shake my head. I don't know, and I don't want to think about it. I follow Zoe up another set of stairs, this one connected to a hole in the side of the plane. My hand shakes when I grab the railing, and I look over my shoulder one last time, to check if Tobias caught up to us. He isn't there. I haven't seen him since the genetic test.

I duck when I go through the hole, though it's taller than my head. Inside the airplane are rows and rows of seats covered in ripped, fraying blue fabric. I choose one near the front, next to a window. A metal bar pushes against my spine. It feels like a chair skeleton with barely any flesh to support it.

Cara sits behind me, and Peter and Caleb move toward the back of the plane and sit near each other, next to the window. I didn't know they were friends. It seems fitting, given how despicable they both are.

"How old is this thing?" I ask Zoe, who stands near the front.

"Pretty old," she says. "But we've completely redone the important stuff. It's a nice size for what we need."

"What do you use it for?"

"Surveillance missions, mostly. We like to keep an eye on what's happening in the fringe, in case it threatens what's happening in here." Zoe pauses. "The fringe is a large, sort of chaotic place between Chicago and the nearest government-regulated metropolitan area, Milwaukee, which is about a three-hour drive from here."

I would like to ask what exactly *is* happening in the

fringe, but Uriah and Christina sit in the seats next to me, and the moment is lost. Uriah puts an armrest down between us and leans over me to look out the window.

"If the Dauntless knew about this, everyone would be getting in line to learn how to drive it," he says. "Including me."

"No, they would be strapping themselves to the wings." Christina pokes his arm. "Don't you know your own faction?"

Uriah pokes her cheek in response, then turns back to the window again.

"Have either of you seen Tobias lately?" I say.

"No, haven't seen him," Christina says. "Everything okay?"

Before I can answer, an older woman with lines around her mouth stands in the aisle between the rows of seats and claps her hands.

"My name is Karen, and I'll be flying this plane today!" she announces. "It may seem frightening, but remember: The odds of us crashing are actually much lower than the odds of a car crash."

"So are the odds of survival if we *do* crash," Uriah mutters, but he's grinning. His dark eyes are alert, and he looks giddy, like a child. I haven't seen him this way since Marlene died. He's handsome again.

Karen disappears into the front of the plane, and Zoe

sits across the aisle from Christina, twisting around to call out instructions like "Buckle your seat belts!" and "Don't stand up until we've reached our cruising altitude!" I'm not sure what cruising altitude is, and she doesn't explain it, in true Zoe fashion. It was almost a miracle that she remembered to explain the fringe earlier.

The plane starts to move backward, and I'm surprised by how smooth it feels, like we're already floating over the ground. Then it turns and glides over the pavement, which is painted with dozens of lines and symbols. My heart beats faster the farther we go away from the compound, and then Karen's voice speaks through an intercom: "Prepare for takeoff."

I clench the armrests as the plane lurches into motion. The momentum presses me back against the skeleton chair, and the view out the window turns into a smear of color. Then I feel it—the lift, the rising of the plane, and I see the ground stretching wide beneath us, everything getting smaller by the second. My mouth hangs open and I forget to breathe.

I see the compound, shaped like the picture of a neuron I once saw in my science textbook, and the fence that surrounds it. Around it is a web of concrete roads with buildings sandwiched between them.

And then suddenly, I can't even see the roads or the buildings anymore, because there is just a sheet of gray and green and brown beneath us, and farther than I can see in any direction is land, land, land.

I don't know what I expected. To see the place where the world ends, like a giant cliff hanging in the sky?

What I didn't expect is to know that I have been a person standing in a house that I can't even see from here. That I have walked a street among hundreds—thousands—of other streets.

What I didn't expect is to feel so, so small.

"We can't fly too high or too close to the city because we don't want to draw attention, so we'll observe from a great distance. Coming up on the left side of the plane is some of the destruction caused by the Purity War, before the rebels resorted to biological warfare instead of explosives," Zoe says.

I have to blink tears from my eyes before I can see it, what looks at first to be a group of dark buildings. Upon further examination, I realize that the buildings aren't supposed to be dark—they're charred beyond recognition. Some of them are flattened. The pavement between them is broken in pieces like a cracked eggshell.

It resembles certain parts of the city, but at the same time, it doesn't. The city's destruction could have been caused by people. This had to have been caused by something else, something bigger.

"And now you'll get a brief look at Chicago!" Zoe says.

"You'll see that some of the lake was drained so that we could build the fence, but we left as much of it intact as possible."

At her words I see the two-pronged Hub as small as a toy in the distance, the jagged line of our city interrupting the sea of concrete. And beyond it, a brown expanse—the marsh—and just past that . . . blue.

Once I slid down a zip line from the Hancock building and imagined what the marsh looked like full of water, blue-gray and gleaming under the sun. And now that I can see farther than I have ever seen, I know that far beyond our city's limits, it is just like what I imagined, the lake in the distance glinting with streaks of light, marked with the texture of waves.

The plane is silent around me except for the steady roar of the engine.

"Whoa," says Uriah.

"Shh," Christina replies.

"How big is it compared to the rest of the world?" Peter says from across the plane. He sounds like he's choking on each word. "Our city, I mean. In terms of land area. What percentage?"

"Chicago takes up about two hundred twenty-seven square miles," says Zoe. "The land area of the planet is a little less than two hundred million square miles. The percentage is . . . so small as to be negligible."

She delivers the facts calmly, as if they mean nothing to her. But they hit me square in the stomach, and I feel squeezed, like something is crushing me into myself. So much space. I wonder what it's like in the places beyond ours; I wonder how people live there.

I look out the window again, taking slow, deep breaths into a body too tense to move. And as I stare out at the land, I think that this, if nothing else, is compelling evidence for my parents' God, that our world is so massive that it is completely out of our control, that we cannot possibly be as large as we feel.

So small as to be negligible.

It's strange, but there's something in that thought that makes me feel almost . . . free.

+ + +

That evening, when everyone else is at dinner, I sit on the window ledge in the dormitory and turn on the screen David gave me. My hands tremble as I open the file labeled "Journal."

The first entry reads:

> David keeps asking me to write down what I experienced. I think he expects it to be horrifying, maybe even wants it to be. I guess parts of it were, but they were bad for everyone, so it's not like I'm special.

I grew up in a single-family home in Milwaukee, Wisconsin. I never knew much about who was inside the territory outside the city (which everyone around here calls "the fringe"), just that I wasn't supposed to go there. My mom was in law enforcement; she was explosive and impossible to please. My dad was a teacher; he was pliable and supportive and useless. One day they got into it in the living room and things got out of hand, and he grabbed her and she shot him. That night she was burying his body in the backyard while I assembled a good portion of my possessions and left through the front door. I never saw her again.

Where I grew up, tragedy is all over the place. Most of my friends' parents drank themselves stupid or yelled too much or had stopped loving each other a long time ago, and that was just the way of things, no big deal. So when I left I'm sure I was just another item on a long list of awful things that had happened in our neighborhood in the past year.

I knew that if I went anyplace official, like to another city, the government types would just make me go home to my mom, and I didn't think I would ever be able to look at her without seeing the streak of blood my dad's head left on the living room carpet, so I didn't go anyplace official. I went to the fringe, where a whole bunch of people are living in a little colony made of tarp and aluminum in some of the postwar wreckage, living on scraps and burning old papers for warmth because the government can't provide, since they're spending all their resources trying to put us back together again, and have been for over a century after the war ripped us apart. Or they won't provide. I don't know.

One day I saw a grown man beating up one of the kids in the fringe, and I hit him over the head with a plank to get him to stop and he died, right there in the street. I was only thirteen. I ran. I got snatched by some guy in a van, some guy who looked like police. But he didn't take me to the side of the road to shoot me and he didn't take me to jail; he just took me to this secure area and tested my genes and told me all about the city experiments and how my genes were cleaner than other people's. He even showed me a map of my genes on a screen to prove it.

But I killed a man just like my mother did. David says it's okay because I didn't mean to, and because he was about to kill that little kid. But I'm pretty sure my mom didn't mean to kill my dad, either, so what difference does that make, meaning or not meaning to do something? Accident or on purpose, the result is the same, and that's one fewer life than there should be in the world.

That's what I experienced, I guess. And to hear David talk about it, it's like it all happened because a long, long time ago people tried to mess with human nature and ended up making it worse.

I guess that makes sense. Or I'd like it to.

My teeth dig into my lower lip. Here in the Bureau compound, people are sitting in the cafeteria right now, eating and drinking and laughing. In the city, they're probably doing the same thing. Ordinary life surrounds me, and I am alone with these revelations.

I clutch the screen to my chest. My mother was from here. This place is both my ancient and my recent history. I can feel her in the walls, in the air. I can feel her settled inside me, never to leave again. Death could not erase her; she is permanent.

The cold from the glass seeps through my shirt, and I shiver. Uriah and Christina walk through the door to the dormitory, laughing about something. Uriah's clear eyes and steady footsteps fill me with a sense of relief, and my eyes well up with tears all of a sudden. He and Christina both look alarmed, and they lean against the windows on either side of me.

"You okay?" she says.

I nod and blink the tears away. "Where have you guys been today?"

"After the plane ride we went and watched the screens in the control room for a while," Uriah says. "It's really weird to see what they're up to now that we're gone. Just more of the same—Evelyn's a jerk, so are all her lackeys, and so on—but it was like getting a news report."

"I don't think I'd like to look at those," I say. "Too . . . creepy and invasive."

Uriah shrugs. "I don't know, if they want to watch me scratch my butt or eat dinner, I feel like that says more about them than about me."

I laugh. "How often *are* you scratching your butt, exactly?"

He jostles me with his elbow.

"Not to derail the conversation from *butts*, which we can all agree is incredibly important—" Christina smiles a little. "But I'm with you, Tris. Just watching those screens made me feel awful, like I was doing something sneaky. I think I'll be staying away from now on."

She points to the screen in my lap, where the light still glows around my mother's words. "What's that?"

"As it turns out," I say, "my mother was from here. Well, she was from the world outside, but then she came here, and when she was fifteen, she was placed in Chicago as a Dauntless."

Christina says, "Your mother was from here?"

I nod. "Yeah. Insane. Even weirder, she wrote this journal and left it with them. That's what I was reading before you came in."

"Wow," Christina says softly. "That's good, right? I mean, that you get to learn more about her."

"Yeah, it's good. And no, I'm not still upset, you can stop looking at me like that." The look of concern that had been building on Uriah's face disappears.

I sigh. "I just keep thinking . . . that in some way I belong here. Like maybe this place can be home."

Christina pinches her eyebrows together.

"Maybe," she says, and I feel like she doesn't believe it, but it's nice of her to say it anyway.

"I don't know," Uriah says, and he sounds serious now. "I'm not sure anywhere will feel like home again. Not even if we went back."

Maybe that's true. Maybe we're strangers no matter where we go, whether it's to the world outside the Bureau, or here in the Bureau, or back in the experiment. Everything has changed, and it won't stop changing anytime soon.

Or maybe we'll make a home somewhere inside ourselves, to carry with us wherever we go—which is the way I carry my mother now.

Caleb walks into the dormitory. There's a stain on his shirt that looks like sauce, but he doesn't seem to notice it—he has the look in his eye that I now recognize as intellectual fascination, and for a moment I wonder what he's been reading, or watching, to make him look that way.

"Hi," he says, and he almost makes a move toward me,

but he must see my revulsion, because he stops in the middle of a step.

I cover the screen with my palm, though he can't see it from across the room, and stare at him, unable—or unwilling—to say anything in reply.

"You think you'll ever speak to me again?" he says sadly, his mouth turning down at the corners.

"If she does, I'll die of shock," Christina says coldly.

I look away. The truth is, sometimes I want to just forget about everything that's happened and return to the way we were before either of us chose a faction. Even if he was always correcting me, reminding me to be selfless, it was better than this—this feeling that I need to protect even my mother's journal from him, so that he can't poison it like he's done to everything else. I get up and slip it under my pillow.

"Come on," Uriah says to me. "Want to go with us to get some dessert?"

"You didn't already have some?"

"So what if I did?" Uriah rolls his eyes and puts his arm across my shoulders, steering me toward the door.

Together the three of us walk toward the cafeteria, leaving my brother behind.

CHAPTER TWENTY

TOBIAS

"WASN'T SURE IF you would come," Nita says to me.

When she turns to lead me wherever we're going, I see that her loose shirt is low in the back, and there's a tattoo on her spine, but I can't make out what it is.

"You get tattoos too, here?" I say.

"Some people do," she says. "The one on my back is of broken glass." She pauses, the kind of pause you take when you're deciding whether or not to share something personal. "I got it because it suggests damage. It's . . . sort of a joke."

There's that word again, "damage," the one that's been sinking and surfacing, sinking and surfacing in my mind since the genetic test. If it's a joke, it's not a funny one even for Nita—she spits out the explanation like it tastes bitter to her.

We walk down one of the tiled corridors, nearly empty now at the end of a workday, and down a flight of stairs. As we descend, blue and green and purple and red lights dance over the walls, shifting between colors with each second. The tunnel at the bottom of the stairs is wide and dark, with only the strange light to guide us. The floor here is old tile, and even through my shoe soles, it feels grainy with dirt and dust.

"This part of the airport was completely redone and expanded when they first moved in here," Nita says. "For a while, after the Purity War, all the laboratories were underground, to keep them safer if they were attacked. Now it's just the support staff who goes down here."

"Is that who you want me to meet?"

She nods. "Support staff is more than just a job. Almost all of us are GDs—genetically damaged, leftovers from the failed city experiments or the descendants of other leftovers or people pulled in from the outside, like Tris's mother, except without her genetic advantage. And all of the scientists and leaders are GPs—genetically pure, descendants of people who resisted the genetic engineering movement in the first place. There are some exceptions, of course, but so few I could list them all for you if I wanted to."

I am about to ask why the division is so strict, but I can figure it out for myself. The so-called "GPs" grew up in this community, their worlds saturated by experiments and observation and learning. The "GDs" grew up in the experiments, where they only had to learn enough to survive until the next generation. The division is based on knowledge, based on qualifications—but as I learned from the factionless, a system that relies on a group of uneducated people to do its dirty work without giving them a way to rise is hardly fair.

"I think your girl's right, you know," Nita says. "Nothing has changed; now you just have a better idea of your own limitations. Every human being has limitations, even GPs."

"So there's an upward limit to . . . what? My compassion? My conscience?" I say. "That's the reassurance you have for me?"

Nita's eyes study me, carefully, and she doesn't respond.

"This is ridiculous," I say. "Why do you, or they, or anyone get to determine my limits?"

"It's just the way things are, Tobias," Nita says. "It's just genetic, nothing more."

"That's a lie," I say. "It's about more than genes, here, and you know it."

I feel like I need to leave, to turn and run back to the dormitory. The anger is boiling and churning inside me, filling me with heat, and I'm not even sure who it's for. For Nita, who has just accepted that she is somehow limited, or for whoever told her that? Maybe it's for everyone.

We reach the end of the tunnel, and she nudges a heavy wooden door open with her shoulder. Beyond it is a bustling, glowing world. The room is lit by small, bright bulbs on strings, but the strings are so densely packed that a web of yellow and white covers the ceiling. On one end of the room is a wooden counter with glowing bottles behind it, and a sea of glasses on top of it. There are tables and chairs on the left side of the room, and a group of people with musical instruments on the right side. Music fills the air, and the only sounds I recognize—from my limited experience with the Amity—are plucked guitar strings and drums.

I feel like I am standing beneath a spotlight and everyone is watching me, waiting for me to move, speak, something. For a moment it's hard to hear anything over the music and the chatter, but after a few seconds I get used to it, and I hear Nita when she says, "This way! Want a drink?"

I'm about to answer when someone runs into the room. He's short, and the T-shirt he wears hangs from his body, two sizes too large for him. He gestures for the musicians to stop playing, and they do, just long enough for him to shout, "It's verdict time!"

Half the room gets up and rushes toward the door. I give Nita a questioning look, and she frowns, creating a crease in her forehead.

"Whose verdict?" I say.

"Marcus's, no doubt," she replies.

And I'm running.

+++

I sprint back down the tunnel, finding the open spaces between people and pushing my way through if there are none. Nita runs at my heels, shouting for me to stop, but I can't stop. I am separate from this place and these people and my own body, and besides, I have always been a good runner.

I take the stairs three at a time, clutching the railing for balance. I don't know what I am so eager for—Marcus's conviction? His exoneration? Do I hope that Evelyn finds him guilty and executes him, or do I hope that she spares him? I can't tell. To me each outcome feels like it is made of the same substance. Everything is either Marcus's evil or Marcus's mask, Evelyn's evil or Evelyn's mask.

I don't have to remember where the control room is,

because the people in the hallway lead me to it. When I reach it, I push my way to the front of the crowd and there they are, my parents, shown on half the screens. Everyone moves away from me, whispering, except Nita, who stands beside me, catching her breath.

Someone turns up the volume, so we can all hear their voices. They crackle, distorted by the microphones, but I know my father's voice; I can hear it shift at all the right times, lift in all the right places. I can almost predict his words before he says them.

"You took your time," he says, sneering. "Savoring the moment?"

I stiffen. This is not Marcus's mask. This is not the person who the city knows as my father—the patient, calm leader of Abnegation who would never hurt anyone, least of all his own son or wife. This is the man who slid his belt out loop by loop and wrapped it around his knuckles. This is the Marcus I know best, and the sight of him, like the sight of him in my fear landscape, turns me into a child.

"Of course not, Marcus," my mother says. "You have served this city well for many years. This is not a decision I or any of my advisers have taken lightly."

Marcus is not wearing his mask, but Evelyn is wearing hers. She sounds so genuine she almost convinces me.

"I and the former representatives of the factions have

had a lot to consider. Your years of service, the loyalty you have inspired among your faction members, my lingering feelings for you as my former husband . . ."

I snort.

"I am still your husband," Marcus says. "The Abnegation do not allow divorce."

"They do in cases of spousal abuse," Evelyn replies, and I feel that same old feeling again, the hollowness and the weight. I can't believe she just admitted that in public.

But then, she now wants the people in the city to see her a certain way—not as the heartless woman who took control of their lives, but as the woman Marcus attacked with his might, the secret he hid behind a clean house and pressed gray clothing.

I know, then, what the outcome of this will be.

"She's going to kill him," I say.

"The fact remains," says Evelyn, almost sweetly, "that you have committed egregious crimes against this city. You deceived innocent children into risking their lives for your purposes. Your refusal to follow the orders of myself and Tori Wu, the former leader of Dauntless, resulted in countless deaths in the Erudite attack. You betrayed your peers by failing to do as we agreed and by failing to fight against Jeanine Matthews. You betrayed your own faction by revealing what was supposed to be a guarded secret."

"I did not—"

"I am not finished," Evelyn says. "Given your record of service to this city, we have decided on an alternate solution. You will not, unlike the other former faction representatives, be forgiven and allowed to consult on issues regarding this city. Nor will you be executed as a traitor. Instead, you will be sent outside the fence, beyond the Amity compound, and you will not be allowed to return."

Marcus looks surprised. I don't blame him.

"Congratulations," says Evelyn. "You have the privilege of beginning again."

Should I feel relieved, that my father isn't going to be executed? Angry, that I came so close to finally escaping him, but instead he'll still be in this world, still hanging over my head?

I don't know. I don't feel anything. My hands go numb, so I know I'm panicking, but I don't really feel it, not the way I normally do. I am overwhelmed with the need to be somewhere else, so I turn and leave my parents and Nita and the city where I once lived behind me.

CHAPTER TWENTY-ONE

TRIS

THEY ANNOUNCE THE attack drill in the morning, over the intercom, as we eat breakfast. The crisp, female voice instructs us to lock the door to whatever room we are in from the inside, cover the windows, and sit quietly until the alarms no longer sound. "It will take place at the top of the hour," she says.

Tobias looks worn and pale, with dark circles under his eyes. He picks at a muffin, pinching small pieces off and sometimes eating them, sometimes forgetting to.

Most of us woke up late, at ten, I suspect because there was no reason not to. When we left the city, we lost our factions, our sense of purpose. Here there is nothing to do but wait for something to happen, and far from making me feel relaxed, it makes me feel jittery and tense. I am used to having something to do, something to fight, all the time. I try to remind myself to relax.

"They took us up in a plane yesterday," I say to Tobias. "Where were you?"

"I just had to walk around. Process things." He sounds terse, irritated. "How was it?"

"Amazing, actually." I sit across from him so that our knees touch in the space between our beds. "The world is . . . a lot bigger than I thought it was."

He nods. "I probably wouldn't have enjoyed it. Heights, and all."

I don't know why, but his reaction disappoints me. I want him to say that he wishes he had been there with me, to experience it with me. Or at least to ask me what I mean when I say that it was amazing. But all he can say is that he wouldn't have liked it?

"Are you all right?" I say. "You look like you barely slept."

"Well, yesterday carried quite the revelation," he says, putting his forehead into his hand. "You can't really blame me for being upset about it."

"I mean, you can be upset about whatever you want," I say, frowning. "But from my perspective, it doesn't seem like there's much to be upset about. I know it's a shock, but as I said, you're still the same person you were yesterday and the day before, no matter what these people say about it."

He shakes his head. "I'm not talking about my genes. I'm talking about Marcus. You really have no idea, do you?" The question is accusatory, but his tone isn't. He gets up to toss his muffin in the trash.

I feel raw and frustrated. Of course I knew about Marcus. It was buzzing around the room when I woke up. But for some reason I didn't think it would upset him to know his father wasn't going to be executed. Apparently I was wrong.

It doesn't help that the alarms sound at that exact moment, preventing me from saying anything else to him. They are loud, screeching, so painful to listen to that I can barely think, let alone move. I keep one hand clamped over my ear and slide my other hand under my pillow to pick up the screen with my mother's journal on it.

Tobias locks the door and draws the curtains closed, and everyone sits on their cots. Cara wraps a pillow around her head. Peter just sits with his back against the wall, his eyes closed. I don't know where Caleb is—researching whatever made him so distant yesterday, probably—or where Christina and Uriah are—exploring the compound, maybe. Yesterday after dessert they seemed determined to discover every corner of the place. I decided to discover my mother's thoughts about it instead—she wrote several entries about her first impressions of the compound, the strange cleanliness of the place, how everyone smiled all the time, how she fell in love with the city by watching it in the control room.

I turn on the screen, hoping to distract myself from the noise.

Today I volunteered to go inside the city. David said the Divergent are dying and someone has to stop it, because that's a waste of our best genetic material. I think that's a pretty sick way to put it, but David doesn't mean it that way—he just means that if it wasn't the Divergent dying, we wouldn't intervene until a certain level of destruction, but since it's them it has to be taken care of now.

Just a few years, he said. All I have here are a few friends, no family, and I'm young enough that it will be easy to insert me—just wipe and resupply a few people's memories, and I'm in. They'll put me in Dauntless, at first, because I already have tattoos, and that would be hard to explain to the people inside the experiment. The only problem is that at my Choosing Ceremony next year I'll have to join Erudite, because that's where the killer is, and I'm not sure I'm smart enough to make it through initiation. David says it doesn't matter, he can alter my results, but that feels wrong. Even if the Bureau thinks the factions don't mean anything, that they're just a kind of behavioral modification that will help with the damage, those people believe they do, and it feels wrong to play with their system.

I've been watching them for a couple years now, so there's not much I need to know about fitting in. I bet I know the city better than they do, at this point. It's going to be difficult to send my updates—someone might notice that I'm connecting to a distant server instead of an intra-city server, so my entries will probably come less often, if at all. It will be hard to separate myself from everything I know, but maybe it will be good. Maybe it will be a fresh start.

I could really use one of those.

It's a lot to take in, but I find myself rereading the sentence: *The only problem is that at my Choosing Ceremony next year I'll have to join Erudite, because that's where the killer is*. I don't know what killer she's referring to—Jeanine Matthews's predecessor, maybe?—but more confusing even than that is that she *didn't* join Erudite.

What happened to make her join Abnegation instead?

The alarms stop, and my ears feel muffled in their absence. The others trickle out slowly, but Tobias lingers for a moment, tapping his fingers against his leg. I don't speak to him—I'm not sure I want to hear what he has to say right now, when we're both on edge.

But all he says is, "Can I kiss you?"

"Yes," I say, relieved.

He bends down and touches my cheek, then kisses me softly.

Well, he knows how to improve my mood, at least.

"I didn't think about Marcus. I should have," I say.

He shrugs. "It's over now."

I know it's not over. It's never over with Marcus; the wrongs he committed are too great. But I don't press the issue.

"More journal entries?" he says.

"Yes," I say. "Just some memories of the compound so far. But it's getting interesting."

"Good," he says. "I'll leave you with it."

He smiles a little, but I can tell he's still tired, still upset. I don't try to stop him from going. In a way, it feels like we are leaving each other to our grief, his over the loss of his Divergence and whatever hopes he had for Marcus's trial, and mine, finally, over the loss of my parents.

I tap the screen to read the next entry.

Dear David,

I raise my eyebrows. Now she's writing to David?

Dear David,

I'm sorry, but it's not going to happen the way we

planned it. I can't do it. I know you're just going to think I'm being a stupid teenager, but this is my life and if I'm going to be here for years, I have to do this my way. I'll still be able to do my job from outside of Erudite. So tomorrow, at the Choosing Ceremony, Andrew and I are going to choose Abnegation together.

I hope you're not angry. I guess even if you are, I won't hear about it.

—Natalie

I read the entry again, and again, letting the words sink in. *Andrew and I are going to choose Abnegation together.*

I smile into my hand, lean my head against the window, and let the tears fall in silence.

My parents did love each other. Enough to forsake plans and factions. Enough to defy "faction before blood." Blood before faction—no, *love* before faction, always.

I turn off the screen. I don't want to read anything that will spoil this feeling: that I am adrift in calm waters.

It's strange how, even though I should be grieving, I feel like I am actually getting back pieces of her, word by word, line by line.

CHAPTER TWENTY-TWO

TRIS

THERE ARE ONLY a dozen more entries in the file, and they don't tell me everything I want to know, though they do give me more questions. And instead of just containing her thoughts and impressions, they are all written *to* someone.

Dear David,

I thought you were more my friend than my supervisor, but I guess I was wrong.

What did you think would happen when I came in here, that I would live single and alone forever? That I wouldn't get attached to anyone? That I wouldn't make any of my own choices?

I left *everything* behind to come in here when no one else wanted to. You should be thanking me instead of accusing me of losing sight of my mission. Let's get this straight: I'm not going to forget why I'm here just because I chose Abnegation and I'm going to get married. I deserve to have a life of my own. One that *I* choose, not one that you and the Bureau choose for me. You should know all about that—you should understand why this life would appeal to me after all I've seen and been through.

Honestly, I don't really think you care that I didn't choose Erudite like I was supposed to. It sounds like you're actually just jealous. And if you want me to keep updating you, you'll apologize for doubting me. But if you don't, I won't send you any more updates, and I certainly won't leave the city to visit anymore. It's up to you.

—Natalie

I wonder if she was right about David. The thought itches at my mind. Was he really jealous of my father? Did his jealousy fade over time? I can only see their relationship from her eyes, and I'm not sure she's the most accurate source of information about it.

I can tell she's getting older in the entries, her language becoming more refined as time separates her from the fringe where she once lived, her reactions becoming more moderate. She's growing up.

I check the date on the next entry. It's a few months later, but it's not addressed to David the way some of the others have been. The tone is different too—not as familiar, more straightforward.

I tap the screen, flipping through the entries. It takes me ten taps to reach an entry that is addressed to David again. The date on the entry suggests that it came a full two years later.

Dear David,

I got your letter. I understand why you can't be on the receiving end of these updates anymore, and I'll respect your decision, but I'll miss you.

I wish you every happiness.

—Natalie

I try to flip forward, but the journal entries are over. The last document in the file is a certificate of death. The cause of death says *multiple gunshot wounds to the torso.* I rock back and forth a little, to dispel the image of her collapsing in the street from my mind. I don't want to think about her death. I want to know more about her and my father, and her and David. Anything to distract me from the way her life ended.

+++

It's a sign of how desperate I am for information—and action—that I go to the control room with Zoe later that morning. She talks to the manager of the control room about a meeting with David as I stare, determined, at my feet, not wanting to see what's on the screens. I feel like if I allow myself to look at them, even for a moment, I will become addicted to them, lost in the old world because I don't know how to navigate this new one.

As Zoe finishes her conversation, though, I can't keep my curiosity in check. I look at the large screen hanging over the desks. Evelyn is sitting on her bed, running her hands over something on her bedside table. I move closer to see what it is, and the woman at the desk in front of me says, "This is the Evelyn cam. We track her 24-7."

"Can you hear her?"

"Only if we turn the volume up," the woman replies. "We mostly keep the sound off, though. Hard to listen to that much chatter all day."

I nod. "What is that she's touching?"

"Some kind of sculpture, I don't know." The woman shrugs. "She stares at it a lot, though."

I recognize it from somewhere—from Tobias's room, where I slept after my almost-execution in Erudite headquarters. It's made of blue glass, an abstract shape that looks like falling water frozen in time.

I touch my fingertips to my chin as I search my memory. He told me that Evelyn gave it to him when he was young, and instructed him to hide it from his father, who wouldn't approve of a useless-but-beautiful object, Abnegation that he was. I didn't think much of it at the time, but it must mean something to her, if she carried it all the way from the Abnegation sector to Erudite headquarters to keep on her bedside table. Maybe it was her way of rebelling against the faction system.

On the screen, Evelyn balances her chin on her hand and stares at the sculpture for a moment. Then she gets up and shakes out her hands and leaves the room.

No, I don't think the sculpture is a sign of rebellion. I think it's just a reminder of Tobias. Somehow I never realized that when Tobias charged out of the city with me, he wasn't just a rebel defying his leader—he was a son abandoning his mother. And she is grieving over it.

Is he?

Fraught with difficulty as their relationship has been, those ties never really break. They can't possibly.

Zoe touches my shoulder. "You wanted to ask me something?"

I nod and turn away from the screens. Zoe was young in the photograph where she stood next to my mother, but she was still there, so I figure she must know something. I would have asked David, but as the leader of the Bureau, he is difficult to find.

"I wanted to know about my parents," I say. "I'm reading her journal, and I guess I'm having a hard time figuring out how they even met, or why they joined Abnegation together."

Zoe nods slowly. "I'll tell you what I know. Mind walking with me to the labs? I need to leave a message with Matthew."

She holds her hands behind her back, resting them at the bottom of her spine. I am still holding the screen David gave me. It's marked all over with my fingerprints, and warm from my constant touch. I understand why Evelyn keeps touching that sculpture—it's the last piece of her son she has, just like this is the last piece of my mother that I have. I feel closer to her when it's with me.

I think that's why I can't give it to Caleb, even though he has a right to see it. I'm not sure I can let go of it yet.

"They met in a class," Zoe says. "Your father, though a very smart man, never quite got the knack of psychology, and the teacher—an Erudite, unsurprisingly—was very hard on him for it. So your mother offered to help him after school, and he told his parents he was doing some kind of school project. They did this for several weeks, and then started to meet in secret—I think one of their favorite places was the fountain south of Millennium Park. Buckingham Fountain? Right by the marsh?"

I imagine my mother and father sitting beside a fountain, under the spray of water, their feet skimming the concrete bottom. I know the fountain Zoe is referring to hasn't been operational for a long time, so the spraying water was never there, but the picture is prettier that way.

"The Choosing Ceremony was approaching, and your father was eager to leave Erudite because he saw something terrible—"

"What? What did he see?"

"Well, your father was a good friend of Jeanine Matthews," says Zoe. "He saw her performing an experiment on a factionless man in exchange for something—food, or clothing, something like that. Anyway, she was testing the fear-inducing serum that was later incorporated into Dauntless initiation—long ago, the fear simulations weren't generated by a person's individual fears, you see, just general fears like heights or spiders or something—and Norton, then the representative of Erudite, was there, letting it go on for far longer than it should have. The factionless man was never quite right again. And that was the last straw for your father."

She pauses in front of the door to the labs to open it with her ID badge. We walk into the dingy office where David gave me my mother's journal. Matthew is sitting with his nose three inches from his computer screen, his eyes narrow. He barely registers our presence when we walk in.

I feel overwhelmed by the desire to smile and cry at the same time. I sit down in a chair next to the empty desk, my hands clasped between my knees. My father was a difficult man. But he was also a good one.

"Your father wanted out of Erudite, and your mother didn't want in, no matter what her mission was—but she still wanted to be near Andrew, so they chose Abnegation together." She pauses. "This caused a rift between your mother and David, as I'm sure you saw. He eventually apologized, but said he couldn't receive updates from her anymore—I don't know why, he wouldn't say—and after that her reports were very short, very informational. Which is why they're not in that journal."

"But she was still able to carry out her mission in Abnegation."

"Yes. And she was much happier there, I think, than she would have been among the Erudite," Zoe says. "Of course, Abnegation turned out to be no better, in some ways. It seems there's no escaping the reach of genetic damage. Even the Abnegation leadership was poisoned by it."

I frown. "Are you talking about Marcus? Because he's Divergent. Genetic damage had nothing to do with it."

"A man surrounded by genetic damage cannot help but mimic it with his own behavior," Zoe says. "Matthew, David wants to set up a meeting with your supervisor to discuss one of the serum developments. Last time Alan completely forgot about it, so I was wondering if you could escort him."

"Sure," Matthew says without looking away from his computer. "I'll get him to give me a time."

"Lovely. Well, I have to go—I hope that answered your question, Tris." She smiles at me and slips out the door.

I sit hunched, with my elbows on my knees. Marcus was Divergent—genetically pure, just like me. But I don't accept that he was a bad person because he was surrounded by genetically damaged people. So was I. So was Uriah. So was my mother. But none of us lashed out at our loved ones.

"Her argument has a few holes in it, doesn't it," says Matthew. He's watching me from behind his desk, tapping his fingers on the arm of his chair.

"Yeah," I say.

"Some of the people here want to blame genetic damage for everything," he says. "It's easier for them to accept than the truth, which is that they can't know everything about people and why they act the way they do."

"Everyone has to blame something for the way the world is," I say. "For my father it was the Erudite."

"I probably shouldn't tell you that the Erudite were always my favorite, then," Matthew says, smiling a little.

"Really?" I straighten. "Why?"

"I don't know, I guess I agree with them. That if everyone would just keep learning about the world around them, they would have far fewer problems."

"I've been wary of them my whole life," I say, resting my chin on my hand. "My father hated the Erudite, so I learned to hate them too, and everything they did with their time. Only now I'm thinking he was wrong. Or just . . . biased."

"About the Erudite or about learning?"

I shrug. "Both. So many of the Erudite helped me when I didn't ask them to." Will, Fernando, Cara—all Erudite, all some of the best people I've known, however briefly. "They were so focused on making the world a better place." I shake my head. "What Jeanine did has nothing to do with a thirst for knowledge leading to a thirst for power, like my father told me, and everything to do with her being terrified of how big the world is and how powerless that made her. Maybe it was the Dauntless who had it right."

"There's an old phrase," Matthew says. "Knowledge is power. Power to do evil, like Jeanine . . . or power to do good, like what we're doing. Power itself is not evil. So knowledge itself is not evil."

"I guess I grew up suspicious of both. Power and knowledge," I say. "To the Abnegation, power should only be given to people who don't want it."

"There's something to that," Matthew says. "But maybe it's time to grow out of that suspicion."

He reaches under the desk and takes out a book. It is thick, with a worn cover and frayed edges. On it is printed HUMAN BIOLOGY.

"It's a little rudimentary, but this book helped to teach me what it is to be human," he says. "To be such a complicated, mysterious piece of biological machinery, and more amazing still, to have the capacity to analyze that machinery! That is a special thing, unprecedented in all of evolutionary history. Our ability to know about ourselves and the world is what makes us human."

He hands me the book and turns back to the computer. I look down at the worn cover and run my fingers along the edge of the pages. He makes the acquisition of knowledge feel like a secret, beautiful thing, and an ancient thing. I feel like, if I read this book, I can reach backward through all the generations of humanity to the very first one, whenever it was—that I can participate in something many times larger and older than myself.

"Thank you," I say, and it's not for the book. It's for giving something back to me, something I lost before I was able to really have it.

+++

The lobby of the hotel smells like candied lemon and bleach, an acrid combination that burns my nostrils when I breathe it in. I walk past a potted plant with a garish flower blossoming among its branches, and toward the dormitory that has become our temporary home here. As I walk I wipe the screen with the hem of my shirt, trying to get rid of some of my fingerprints.

Caleb is alone in the dormitory, his hair tousled and his eyes red from sleep. He blinks at me when I walk in and toss the biology book onto my bed. I feel a sickening ache in my stomach and press the screen with our mother's file against my side. *He's her son. He has a right to read her journal, just like you.*

"If you have something to say," he says, "just say it."

"Mom lived here." I blurt it out like a long-held secret, too loud and too fast. "She came from the fringe, and they brought her here, and she lived here for a couple years, then went into the city to stop the Erudite from killing the Divergent."

Caleb blinks at me. Before I lose my nerve, I hold out the screen for him to take. "Her file is here. It's not very long, but you should read it."

He gets up and closes his hand around the glass. He's so much taller than he used to be, so much taller than I am. For a few years when we were children, I was the taller one, even though I was almost a year younger. Those were some of our best years, the ones where I didn't feel like he was bigger or better or smarter or more selfless than I was.

"How long have you known this?" he says, narrowing his eyes.

"It doesn't matter." I step back. "I'm telling you now. You can keep that, by the way. I'm done with it."

He wipes the screen with his sleeve and navigates with deft fingers to our mother's first journal entry. I expect him to sit down and read it, thus ending the conversation, but instead he sighs.

"I have something to show you, too," he says. "About Edith Prior. Come on."

It's her name, not my lingering attachment to him, that draws me after him when he starts to walk away.

He leads me out of the dormitory and down the hallway and around corners to a room far away from any that I have seen in the Bureau compound. It is long and narrow, the walls covered with shelves that bear identical blue-gray books, thick and heavy as dictionaries. Between the first two rows is a long wooden table with chairs tucked beneath it. Caleb flips the light switch, and pale light fills the room, reminding me of Erudite headquarters.

"I've been spending a lot of time here," he says. "It's the

record room. They keep some of the Chicago experiment data in here."

He walks along the shelves on the right side of the room, running his fingers over the book spines. He pulls out one of the volumes and lays it flat on the table, so it spills open, its pages covered in text and pictures.

"Why don't they keep all this on computers?"

"I assume they kept these records before they developed a sophisticated security system on their network," he says without looking up. "Data never fully disappears, but paper can be destroyed forever, so you can actually get rid of it if you don't want the wrong people to get their hands on it. It's safer, sometimes, to have everything printed out."

His green eyes shift back and forth as he searches for the right place, his fingers nimble, built for turning pages. I think of how he disguised that part of himself, wedging books between his headboard and the wall in our Abnegation house, until he dropped his blood in the Erudite water on the day of our Choosing Ceremony. I should have known, then, that he was a liar, with loyalty only to himself.

I feel that sickening ache again. I can hardly stand to be in here with him, the door closing us in, nothing but the table between us.

"Ah, here." He touches his finger to a page, then spins

the book around to show me.

It looks like a copy of a contract, but it's handwritten in ink:

I, Amanda Marie Ritter, of Peoria, Illinois, give my consent to the following procedures:

- The "genetic healing" procedure, as defined by the Bureau of Genetic Welfare: "a genetic engineering procedure designed to correct the genes specified as 'damaged' on page three of this form."
- The "reset procedure," as defined by the Bureau of Genetic Welfare: "a memory-erasing procedure designed to make an experiment participant more fit for the experiment."

I declare that I have been thoroughly instructed as to the risks and benefits of these procedures by a member of the Bureau of Genetic Welfare. I understand that this means I will be given a new background and a new identity by the Bureau and inserted into the experiment in Chicago, Illinois, where I will live out the remainder of my days.

I agree to reproduce at least twice to give my corrected genes the best possible chance of survival. I understand that I will be encouraged to do this when I am reeducated after the reset procedure.

I also give my consent for my children and my children's children, etc., to continue in this experiment until such time as the Bureau of Genetic Welfare deems it to be complete. They will be instructed in the false history that I myself will be given after the reset procedure.

Signed,

Amanda Marie Ritter

Amanda Marie Ritter. She was the woman in the video, Edith Prior, my ancestor.

I look up at Caleb, whose eyes are alight with knowledge, like there's a live wire running through each of them.

Our ancestor.

I pull out one of the chairs and sit. "She was Dad's ancestor?"

He nods and sits down across from me. "Seven generations back, yes. An aunt. Her brother is the one who carried on the Prior name."

"And this is . . ."

"It's a consent form," he says. "Her consent form for joining the experiment. The endnotes say that this was just a first draft—she was one of the original experiment designers. A member of the Bureau. There were only a few Bureau members in the original experiment; most of the people in the experiment weren't working for the government."

I read the words again, trying to make sense of them. When I saw her in the video, it seemed so logical that she would become a resident of our city, that she would immerse herself in our factions, that she would volunteer to leave behind everything she left behind. But that was before I knew what life was like outside the city, and it doesn't seem as horrific as what Edith described in her message to us.

She delivered a skillful manipulation in that video, which was intended to keep us contained and dedicated to the vision of the Bureau—*the world outside the city is badly broken, and the Divergent need to come out here and heal it*. It's not quite a lie, because the people in the Bureau do believe that healed genes will fix certain things, that if we integrate into the general population and pass our genes on, the world will be a better place. But they didn't need the Divergent to march out of our city like an army to fight injustice and save everyone, as Edith suggested. I wonder if Edith Prior believed her own words, or if she just said them because she had to.

There's a photograph of her on the next page, her mouth in a firm line, wisps of brown hair hanging around her face. She must have seen something terrible, to volunteer for her memory to be erased and her entire life remade.

"Do you know why she joined?" I say.

Caleb shakes his head. "The records suggest—though they're fairly vague on this front—that people joined the experiment so their families could escape extreme poverty—the families of the subjects were offered a monthly stipend for the subject's participation, for upward of ten years. But obviously that wasn't Edith's motivation, since she worked for the Bureau. I suspect something traumatic must have happened to her, something she was determined to forget."

I frown at her photograph. I can't imagine what kind of poverty would motivate a person to forget themselves and everyone they loved so their families could get a monthly stipend. I may have lived on Abnegation bread and vegetables for most of my life, with nothing to spare, but I was never that desperate. Their situation must have been much worse than anything I saw in the city.

I can't imagine why Edith was that desperate either. Or maybe it's just that she didn't have anyone to keep her memory for.

"I was interested in the legal precedent for giving consent on behalf of one's descendants," Caleb says. "I think it's an extrapolation of giving consent for one's children under eighteen, but it seems a little odd."

"I guess we all decide our children's fates just by making our own life decisions," I say vaguely. "Would we have chosen the same factions we did if Mom and Dad hadn't chosen Abnegation?" I shrug. "I don't know. Maybe we wouldn't have felt as stifled. Maybe we would have become different people."

The thought creeps into my mind like a slithering creature—*Maybe we would have become better people. People who don't betray their own sisters.*

I stare at the table in front of me. For the past few minutes it was easy to pretend that Caleb and I were just brother and sister again. But a person can only keep reality—and anger—at bay for so long before the truth comes back again. As I raise my eyes to his, I think of looking at him in just this way, when I was still a prisoner in Erudite headquarters. I think of being too tired to fight with him anymore, or to hear his excuses; too tired to care that my brother had abandoned me.

I ask tersely, "Edith joined Erudite, didn't she? Even though she took an Abnegation name?"

"Yes!" He doesn't seem to notice my tone. "In fact, most of our ancestors were in Erudite. There were a few Abnegation outliers, and one or two Candor, but the through line is fairly consistent."

I feel cold, like I might shiver and then shatter.

"So I suppose you've used this as an excuse in your twisted mind for what you did," I say steadily. "For joining

Erudite, for being loyal to them. I mean, if you were supposed to be one of them all along, then 'faction before blood' is an acceptable thing to believe, right?"

"Tris . . ." he says, and his eyes plead with me for understanding, but I do not understand. I won't.

I stand up. "So now I know about Edith and you know about our mother. Good. Let's just leave it at that, then."

Sometimes when I look at him I feel the ache of sympathy toward him, and sometimes I feel like I want to wrap my hands around his throat. But right now I just want to escape, and pretend this never happened. I walk out of the records room, and my shoes squeak on the tile floor as I run back to the hotel. I run until I smell sweet citrus, and then I stop.

Tobias is standing in the hallway outside the dormitory. I am breathless, and I can feel my heartbeat even in my fingertips; I am overwhelmed, teeming with loss and wonder and anger and longing.

"Tris," Tobias says, his brow furrowed with concern. "Are you all right?"

I shake my head, still struggling for air, and crush him against the wall with my body, my lips finding his. For a moment he tries to push me away, but then he must decide that he doesn't care if I'm all right, doesn't care if he's all right, doesn't care. We haven't been alone together in days. Weeks. Months.

His fingers slide into my hair, and I hold on to his arms to stay steady as we press together like two blades at a stalemate. He is stronger than anyone I know, and warmer than anyone else realizes; he is a secret that I have kept, and will keep, for the rest of my life.

He leans down and kisses my throat, hard, and his hands smooth over me, securing themselves at my waist. I hook my fingers in his belt loops, my eyes closing. In that moment I know exactly what I want; I want to peel away all the layers of clothing between us, strip away everything that separates us, the past and the present and the future.

I hear footsteps and laughter at the end of the hallway, and we break apart. Someone—probably Uriah—whistles, but I barely hear it over the pulsing in my ears.

Tobias's eyes meet mine, and it's like the first time I really looked at him during my initiation, after my fear simulation; we stare too long, too intently. "Shut up," I call out to Uriah, without looking away.

Uriah and Christina walk into the dormitory, and Tobias and I follow them, like nothing happened.

CHAPTER TWENTY-THREE

TOBIAS

THAT NIGHT WHEN my head hits the pillow, heavy with thoughts, I hear something crinkle beneath my cheek. A note under my pillowcase.

T—

Meet me outside the hotel entrance at eleven. I need to talk to you.

—Nita

I look at Tris's cot. She's sprawled on her back, and there is a piece of hair covering her nose and mouth that shifts with each exhale. I don't want to wake her, but I feel strange, going to meet a girl in the middle of the night without telling her about it. Especially now that we're trying so hard to be honest with each other.

I check my watch. It's ten to eleven.

Nita's just a friend. You can tell Tris tomorrow. It might be urgent.

I push the blankets back and shove my feet into my shoes—I sleep in my clothes these days. I pass Peter's cot, then Uriah's. The top of a flask peeks out from beneath Uriah's pillow. I pinch it between my fingers and carry it toward the door, where I slide it under the pillow on one of the empty cots. I haven't been looking after him as well as I promised Zeke I would.

Once I'm in the hallway, I tie my shoes and smooth my hair down. I stopped cutting it like the Abnegation when I wanted the Dauntless to see me as a potential leader, but I miss the ritual of the old way, the buzz of the clippers and the careful movements of my hands, knowing more by touch than by sight. When I was young, my father used to do it, in the hallway on the top floor of our Abnegation house. He was always too careless with the blade, and scraped the back of my neck, or nicked my ear. But he never complained about having to cut my hair for me. That's something, I guess.

Nita is tapping her foot. This time she wears a white short-sleeved shirt, her hair pulled back. She smiles, but it doesn't quite reach her eyes.

"You look worried," I say.

"That's because I am," she answers. "Come on, there's a place I've been wanting to show you."

She leads me down dim hallways, empty except for the occasional janitor. They all seem to know Nita—they wave at her, or smile. She puts her hands in her pockets, guiding her eyes carefully away from mine every time we happen to look at each other.

We go through a door without a security sensor to keep it locked. The room beyond it is a wide circle with a chandelier marking its center with dangling glass. The floors are polished wood, dark, and the walls, covered in sheets of bronze, gleam where the light touches them. There are names inscribed on the bronze panels, dozens of names.

Nita stands beneath the glass chandelier and holds her arms out, wide, to encompass the room in her gesture.

"These are the Chicago family trees," she says. "Your family trees."

I move closer to one of the walls and read through the names, searching for one that looks familiar. At the end, I find one: Uriah Pedrad and Ezekiel Pedrad. Next to each name is a small "DD," and there is a dot next to Uriah's name, and it looks freshly carved. Marking him as Divergent, probably.

"Do you know where mine is?" I say.

She crosses the room and touches one of the panels.

"The generations are matrilineal. That's why Jeanine's records said Tris was 'second generation'—because her mother came from outside the city. I'm not sure how Jeanine knew that, but I guess we'll never find out."

I approach the panel that bears my name with trepidation, though I'm not sure what I have to fear from seeing my name and my parents' names carved into bronze. I see a vertical line connecting Kristin Johnson to Evelyn Johnson, and a horizontal one connecting Evelyn Johnson to Marcus Eaton. Below the two names is just one: Tobias Eaton. The small letters beside my name are "AD," and there's a dot there too, though I now know I'm not actually Divergent.

"The first letter is your faction of origin," she says, "and the second is your faction of choice. They thought that keeping track of the factions would help them trace the path of the genes."

My mother's letters: "EAF." The "F" is for "factionless," I assume.

My father's letters: "AA," with a dot.

I touch the line connecting me to them, and the line connecting Evelyn to her parents, and the line connecting them to their parents, all the way back through eight generations, counting my own. This is a map of what I've always known, that I am tied to them, bound forever to this empty inheritance no matter how far I run.

"While I appreciate you showing me this," I say, and I feel sad, and tired, "I'm not sure why it had to happen in the middle of the night."

"I thought you might want to see it. And I had something I wanted to talk to you about."

"More reassurance that my limitations don't define me?" I shake my head. "No thanks, I've had enough of that."

"No," she says. "But I'm glad you said that."

She leans against the panel, covering Evelyn's name with her shoulder. I step back, not wanting to be so close to her that I can see the ring of lighter brown around her pupils.

"That conversation I had with you last night, about genetic damage . . . it was actually a test. I wanted to see how you would react to what I said about damaged genes, so I would know whether I could trust you or not," she says. "If you accepted what I said about your limitations, the answer would have been no." She slides a little closer to me, so her shoulder covers Marcus's name too. "See, I'm not really on board with being classified as 'damaged.'"

I think of the way she spat out the explanation of the tattoo of broken glass on her back like it was poison.

My heart starts to beat harder, so I can feel my pulse in

my throat. Bitterness has replaced the good humor in her voice, and her eyes have lost their warmth. I am afraid of her, afraid of what she says—and thrilled by it too, because it means I don't have to accept that I am smaller than I once believed.

"I take it you aren't on board with it either," she says.

"No. I'm not."

"There are a lot of secrets in this place," she says. "One of them is that, to them, a GD is expendable. Another is that some of us are not just going to sit back and take it."

"What do you mean, expendable?" I say.

"The crimes they have committed against people like us are serious," Nita says. "And hidden. I can show you evidence, but that will have to come later. For now, what I can tell you is that we're working against the Bureau, for good reasons, and we want you with us."

I narrow my eyes. "Why? What is it you want from me, exactly?"

"Right now I want to offer you an opportunity to see what the world is like outside the compound."

"And what you get in return is . . . ?"

"Your protection," she says. "I'm going to a dangerous place, and I can't tell anyone else from the Bureau about it. You're an outsider, which means it's safer for me to trust you, and I know you know how to defend yourself. And if you come with me, I'll show you that evidence you want to see."

She touches her heart, lightly, as if swearing on it. My skepticism is strong, but my curiosity is stronger. It's not hard for me to believe that the Bureau would do bad things, because every government I've ever known has done bad things, even the Abnegation oligarchy, of which my father was the head. And even beyond that reasonable suspicion, I have brewing inside me the desperate hope that I am not damaged, that I am worth more than the corrected genes I pass on to any children I might have.

So I decide to go along with this. For now.

"Fine," I say.

"First," she says, "before I show you anything, you have to accept that you won't be able to tell anyone—even Tris—about what you see. Are you all right with that?"

"She's trustworthy, you know." I promised Tris I wouldn't keep secrets from her anymore. I shouldn't get into situations where I'll have to do it again. "Why can't I tell her?"

"I'm not saying she isn't trustworthy. It's just that she doesn't have the skill set we need, and we don't want to put anyone at risk that we don't have to. See, the Bureau doesn't want us to organize. If we believe we're not 'damaged,' then we're saying that everything they're doing—the experiments, the genetic alterations, all of it—is a waste of time. And no one wants to hear that their life's work is a sham."

I know all about that—it's like finding out that the factions are an artificial system, designed by scientists to keep us under control for as long as possible.

She pulls away from the wall, and then she says the only thing she could possibly say to make me agree:

"If you tell her, you would be depriving her of the choice I'm giving you now. You would force her to become a coconspirator. By keeping this from her, you would be protecting her."

I run my fingers over my name, carved into the metal panel, Tobias Eaton. These are my genes, this is my mess. I don't want to pull Tris into it.

"All right," I say. "Show me."

+++

I watch her flashlight beam bob up and down with her footsteps. We just retrieved a bag from a mop closet down the hall—she was ready for this. She leads me deep into the underground hallways of the compound, past the place where the GDs gather, to a corridor where the electricity no longer flows. At a certain place she crouches and slides her hand along the ground until her fingers reach a latch. She hands me the flashlight and pulls back the latch, lifting a door from the tile.

"It's an escape tunnel," she says. "They dug it when they first came here, so there would always be a way to escape during an emergency."

From her bag she takes a black tube and twists off the top. It sprays sparks of light that glow red against her skin. She releases it over the doorway and it falls several feet, leaving a streak of light on my eyelids. She sits on the edge of the hole, her backpack secure around her shoulders, and drops.

I know it's just a short way down, but it feels like more with the space open beneath me. I sit, the silhouette of my shoes dark against the red sparks, and push myself forward.

"Interesting," Nita says when I land. I lift up the flashlight, and she holds the flare out in front of her as we walk down the tunnel, which is just wide enough for the two of us to walk side by side, and just tall enough for me to straighten up. It smells rich and rotten, like mold and dead air. "I forgot you were afraid of heights."

"Well, I'm not afraid of much else," I say.

"No need to get defensive!" She smiles. "I actually have always wanted to ask you about that."

I step over a puddle, the soles of my shoes gripping the gritty tunnel floor.

"Your third fear," she says. "Shooting that woman. Who was she?"

The flare goes out, so the flashlight I'm holding is our only guide through the tunnel. I shift my arm to create more space between us, not wanting to skim her arm in the dark.

"She wasn't anyone in particular," I say. "The fear was shooting her."

"You were afraid of shooting people?"

"No," I say. "I was afraid of my considerable capacity to kill."

She is silent, and so am I. That's the first time I've ever said those words out loud, and now I hear how strange they are. How many young men fear that there is a monster inside them? People are supposed to fear others, not themselves. People are supposed to aspire to become their fathers, not shudder at the thought.

"I've always wondered what would be in my fear landscape." She says it in a hushed tone, like a prayer. "Sometimes I feel like there is so much to be afraid of, and sometimes I feel like there is nothing left to fear."

I nod, though she can't see me, and we keep moving, the flashlight beam bouncing, our shoes scraping, the moldy air rushing toward us from whatever is on the other end.

+++

After twenty minutes of walking, we turn a corner and I smell fresh wind, cold enough to make me shudder. I turn off the flashlight, and the moonlight at the end of the tunnel guides us to our exit.

The tunnel let us out somewhere in the wasteland we drove through to get to the compound, among the crumbling buildings and overgrown trees breaking through the pavement. Parked a few feet away is an old truck, the back covered in shredded, threadbare canvas. Nita kicks one of the tires to test it, then climbs into the driver's seat. The keys already dangle from the ignition.

"Whose truck?" I say when I get into the passenger's seat.

"It belongs to the people we're going to meet. I asked them to park it here," she says.

"And who are they?"

"Friends of mine."

I don't know how she finds her way through the maze of streets before us, but she does, steering the truck around tree roots and fallen streetlights, flashing the headlights at animals that scamper at the edge of my vision.

A long-legged creature with a brown, spare body picks

its way across the street ahead of us, almost as tall as the headlights. Nita eases on the brakes so she doesn't hit it. Its ears twitch, and its dark, round eyes watch us with careful curiosity, like a child.

"Sort of beautiful, aren't they?" she says. "Before I came here I'd never seen a deer."

I nod. It is elegant, but hesitant, halting.

Nita presses the horn with her fingertips, and the deer moves out of the way. We accelerate again, then reach a wide, open road suspended across the railroad tracks I once walked down to reach the compound. I see its lights up ahead, the one bright spot in this dark wasteland.

And we are traveling northeast, away from it.

+++

It is a long time before I see electric light again. When I do, it is along a narrow, patchy street. The bulbs dangle from a cord strung along the old streetlights.

"We stop here." Nita jerks the wheel, pulling the truck into an alley between two brick buildings. She takes the keys from the ignition and looks at me. "Check in the glove box. I asked them to give us weapons."

I open the compartment in front of me. Sitting on top of some old wrappers are two knives.

"How are you with a knife?" she says.

The Dauntless taught initiates how to throw knives even before the changes to initiation that Max made before I joined them. I never liked it, because it seemed like a way to encourage the Dauntless flair for theatrics, rather than a useful skill.

"I'm all right," I say with a smirk. "I never thought that skill would actually be worth anything, though."

"I guess the Dauntless are good for something after all . . . *Four*," she says, smiling a little. She takes the larger of the two knives, and I take the smaller one.

I am tense, turning the handle in my fingers as we walk down the alley. Above me the windows flicker with a different kind of light—flames, from candles or lanterns. At one point, when I glance up, I see a curtain of hair and dark eye sockets staring back at me.

"People live here," I say.

"This is the very edge of the fringe," Nita says. "It's about a two-hour drive from Milwaukee, which is a metropolitan area north of here. Yeah, people live here. These days people don't venture too far away from cities, even if they want to live outside the government's influence, like the people here."

"Why do they want to live outside the government's influence?" I know what living outside the government is like, by watching the factionless. They were always hungry, always cold in the winter and hot in the summer, always struggling to survive. It's not an easy life to choose—you have to have a good reason for it.

"Because they're genetically damaged," Nita says, glancing at me. "Genetically damaged people are technically—legally—equal to genetically pure people, but only on paper, so to speak. In reality they're poorer, more likely to be convicted of crimes, less likely to be hired for good jobs . . . you name it, it's a problem, and has been since the Purity War, over a century ago. For the people who live in the fringe, it seemed more appealing to opt out of society completely rather than to try to correct the problem from within, like I intend to do."

I think of the fragment of glass tattooed on her skin. I wonder when she got it—I wonder what put that dangerous look in her eyes, what put such drama in her speech, what made her become a revolutionary.

"How do you plan on doing that?"

She sets her jaw and says, "By taking away some of the Bureau's power."

The alley opens up to a wide street. Some people prowl along the edges, but others walk right in the middle, in lurching groups, bottles swinging from their hands. Everyone I see is young—not many adults in the fringe, I guess.

I hear shouting up ahead, and glass shattering on the pavement. A crowd there stands in a circle around two punching, kicking figures.

I start toward them, but Nita grabs my arm and drags me toward one of the buildings.

"Not the time to be a hero," she says.

We approach the door to the building on the corner. A large man stands beside it, spinning a knife in his palm. When we walk up the steps, he stops the knife and tosses it into his other hand, which is gnarled with scars.

His size, his deftness with the weapon, his scarred and dusty appearance—they are all supposed to intimidate me. But his eyes are like that deer's eyes, large and wary and curious.

"We're here to see Rafi," she says. "We're from the compound."

"You can go in, but your knives stay here," the man says. His voice is higher, lighter than I expected. He could be a gentle man, maybe, if this were a different kind of place. As it is, I see that he isn't gentle, doesn't even know what that means.

Even though I myself have discarded any kind of softness as useless, I find myself thinking that something important is lost if this man has been forced to deny his own nature.

"Not a chance," Nita says.

"Nita, is that you?" says a voice from inside. It is expressive, musical. The man to whom it belongs is short, with a wide smile. He comes to the doorway. "Didn't I tell you to just let them in? Come in, come in."

"Hi, Rafi," she says, her relief obvious. "Four, this is Rafi. He's an important man in the fringe."

"Nice to meet you," Rafi says, and he beckons for us to follow him.

Inside is a large, open room lit by rows of candles and lanterns. There is wooden furniture strewn everywhere, all the tables empty but one.

A woman sits in the back of the room, and Rafi slides into the chair beside her. Though they don't look the same—she has red hair and a generous frame; his features are dark and his body, spare as wire—they have the same sort of look, like two stones hewn by the same chisel.

"Weapons on the table," Rafi says.

This time, Nita obeys, putting her knife on the edge of the table right in front of her. She sits. I do the same. Across from us, the woman surrenders a gun.

"Who's this?" the woman says, jerking her head toward me.

"This is my associate," Nita says. "Four."

"What kind of a name is 'Four'?" She doesn't ask with a

sneer, the way people have often asked me that question.

"The kind you get inside the city experiment," Nita says. "For having only four fears."

It occurs to me that she might have introduced me by that name just to have an opportunity to share where I'm from. Does it give her some kind of leverage? Does it make me more trustworthy to these people?

"Interesting." The woman taps the table with her index finger. "Well, *Four*, my name is Mary."

"Mary and Rafi lead the Midwest branch of a GD rebel group," Nita says.

"Calling it a 'group' makes us sound like old ladies playing cards," Rafi says smoothly. "We're more of an uprising. Our reach stretches across the country—there's a group for every metropolitan area that exists, and regional overseers for the Midwest, South, and East."

"Is there a West?" I say.

"Not anymore," Nita says quietly. "The terrain was too difficult to navigate and the cities too spread out for it to be sensible to live there after the war. Now it's wild country."

"So it's true what they say," Mary says, her eyes catching the light like slivers of glass as she looks at me. "The people in the city experiments really don't know what's outside."

"Of course it's true, why would they?" Nita says.

Fatigue, a weight behind my eyes, creeps up on me suddenly. I have been a part of too many uprisings in my short life. The factionless, and now this GD one, apparently.

"Not to cut the pleasantries short," Mary says, "but we shouldn't spend much time here. We can't keep people out for long before they come sniffing around."

"Right," Nita says. She looks at me. "Four, can you make sure nothing's happening outside? I need to talk to Mary and Rafi privately for a little while."

If we were alone, I would ask why I can't be here when she talks to them, or why she bothered to bring me in when I could have stood guard outside the whole time. I guess I haven't actually agreed to help her yet, and she must have wanted them to meet me for some reason. So I just get up, taking my knife with me, and walk to the door where Rafi's guard watches the street.

The fight across the street has died down. A lone figure lies on the pavement. For a moment I think it's still moving, but then I realize that's because someone is rifling through its pockets. It's not a figure—it's a body.

"Dead?" I say, and the word is just an exhale.

"Yep. If you can't defend yourself here, you won't last a night."

"Why do people come here, then?" I frown. "Why don't

they just go back to the cities?"

He's quiet for so long that I think he must not have heard my question. I watch the thief turn the dead person's pockets inside out and abandon the body, slipping into one of the nearby buildings. Finally, Rafi's guard speaks:

"Here, there's a chance that if you die, someone will care. Like Rafi, or one of the other leaders," the guard says. "In the cities, if you get killed, definitely no one will give a damn, not if you're a GD. The worst crime I've ever seen a GP get charged with for killing a GD was 'manslaughter.' Bullshit."

"Manslaughter?"

"It means the crime is deemed an accident," Rafi's smooth, lilting voice says behind me. "Or at least not as severe as, say, first-degree murder. *Officially*, of course, we're all to be treated the same, yes? But that is rarely put into practice."

He stands beside me, his arms folded. I see, when I look at him, a king surveying his own kingdom, which he believes is beautiful. I look out at the street, at the broken pavement and the limp body with its turned-out pockets and the windows flickering with firelight, and I know the beauty he sees is just freedom—freedom to be seen as a whole man instead of a damaged one.

I saw that freedom, once, when Evelyn beckoned to me from among the factionless, called me out of my faction to become a more complete person. But it was a lie.

"You're from Chicago?" Rafi says to me.

I nod, still looking at the dark street.

"And now that you are out? How does the world seem to you?" he says.

"Mostly the same," I say. "People are just divided by different things, fighting different wars."

Nita's footsteps creak on the floorboards inside, and when I turn she is standing right behind me, her hands buried in her pockets.

"Thanks for arranging this," Nita says, nodding to Rafi. "It's time for us to go."

We make our way down the street again, and when I turn to look at Rafi, he has his hand up, waving good-bye.

+++

As we walk back to the truck, I hear screams again, but this time they are the screams of a child. I walk past snuffling, whimpering sounds and think of when I was younger, crouched in my bedroom, wiping my nose on one of my sleeves. My mother used to scrub the cuffs with a sponge before throwing them in the wash. She never said anything about it.

When I get into the truck, I already feel numb to this place and its pain, and I am ready to get back to the dream of the compound, the warmth and the light and the feeling of safety.

"I'm having trouble understanding why this place is preferable to city life," I say.

"I've only been to a city that wasn't an experiment once," Nita says. "There's electricity, but it's on a ration system—each family only gets so many hours a day. Same with water. And there's a lot of crime, which is blamed on genetic damage. There are police, too, but they can only do so much."

"So the Bureau compound," I say. "It's easily the best place to live, then."

"In terms of resources, yes," Nita says. "But the same social system that exists in the cities also exists in the compound; it's just a little harder to see."

I watch the fringe disappear in the rearview mirror, distinct from the abandoned buildings around it only by that string of electric lights draped over the narrow street.

We drive past dark houses with boarded-up windows, and I try to imagine them clean and polished, as they must have been at some point in the past. They have fenced-in yards that must have once been trim and green, windows that must once have glowed in the evenings. I imagine that the lives lived here were peaceful ones, quiet ones.

"What did you come out here to talk to them about, exactly?" I say.

"I came out here to solidify our plans," Nita says. I notice, in the glow of the dashboard light, that there are a few cuts on her lower lip, like she has spent too much time biting it. "And I wanted them to meet you, to put a face on the people inside the faction experiments. Mary used to be suspicious that people like you were actually colluding with the government, which of course isn't true. Rafi, though . . . he was the first person to give me proof that the Bureau, the government, was lying to us about our history."

She pauses after she says it, like that will help me to feel the weight of it, but I don't need time or silence or space to believe her. I have been lied to by my government for my entire life.

"The Bureau talks about this golden age of humanity before the genetic manipulations in which everyone was genetically pure and everything was peaceful," Nita says. "But Rafi showed me old photographs of *war*."

I wait a beat. "So?"

"So?" Nita demands, incredulous. "If genetically pure people caused war and total devastation in the past at the same magnitude that genetically damaged people supposedly do now, then what's the basis for thinking that we need to spend so many resources and so much time working to correct genetic damage? What's the use of the experiments at all, except to convince the right people that the government is doing something to make all our lives better, even though it's not?"

The truth changes everything—isn't that why Tris was so desperate to get the Edith Prior video shown that she allied herself with my father to do it? She knew that the truth, whatever it was, would change our struggle, would shift our priorities forever. And here, now, a lie has changed the struggle, a lie has shifted priorities forever. Instead of working against the poverty or crime that have run rampant over this country, these people have chosen to work against genetic damage.

"Why? Why spend so much time and energy fighting something that isn't really a problem?" I demand, suddenly frustrated.

"Well, the people fighting it now probably fight it because they have been taught that it *is* a problem. That's another thing that Rafi showed me—examples of the propaganda the government released about genetic damage," Nita says. "But initially? I don't know. It's probably a dozen things. Prejudice against GDs? Control, maybe? Control the genetically damaged population by teaching them that there's something wrong with them, and control the genetically pure population by teaching them that they're healed and whole? These things don't happen overnight, and they don't happen for just one reason."

I lean the side of my head against the cold window and close my eyes. There is too much information buzzing in my brain to focus on any single part of it, so I give up trying and let myself drift off.

By the time we make it back through the tunnel and I find my bed, the sun is about to rise, and Tris's arm is hanging over the edge of her bed again, her fingertips brushing the floor.

I sit down across from her, for a moment watching her sleeping face and thinking of what we agreed, that night in Millennium Park: no more lies. She promised me, and I promised her. And if I don't tell her about what I heard and saw tonight, I will be going back on that promise. And for what? To protect her? For Nita, a girl I barely know?

I brush her hair away from her face, gently, so I don't wake her.

She doesn't need my protection. She's strong enough on her own.

CHAPTER TWENTY-FOUR

TRIS

PETER IS ACROSS the room, gathering a stack of books into a pile and shoving them into a bag. He bites down on a red pen and carries the bag out of the room; I hear the books inside it smacking against his leg as he walks down the hallway. I wait until I can't hear them anymore before I turn to Christina.

"I've been trying not to ask you, but I'm giving up," I say. "What's going on with you and Uriah?"

Christina, sprawled across her cot with one long leg dangling over the edge, gives me a look.

"What? You've been spending a lot of time together," I say. "Like a lot."

It's sunny today, the light glowing through the white

curtains. I don't know how, but the dormitory smells like sleep—like laundry and shoes and night sweats and morning coffee. Some of the beds are made, and some still have rumpled sheets bunched up at the bottom or the side. Most of us came from Dauntless, but I'm struck by how different we are anyway. Different habits, different temperaments, different ways of seeing the world.

"You may not believe me, but it's not like that." Christina props herself up on her elbows. "He's grieving. We're both bored. Also, he's *Uriah*."

"So? He's good-looking."

"Good-looking, but he can't have a serious conversation to save his life." Christina shakes her head. "Don't get me wrong, I like to laugh, but I also want a relationship to mean something, you know?"

I nod. I do know—better than most people, maybe, because Tobias and I aren't really the joking type.

"Besides," she says, "not every friendship turns into a romance. I haven't tried to kiss you yet."

I laugh. "True."

"Where have *you* been lately?" Christina says. She wiggles her eyebrows. "With Four? Doing a little . . . addition? Multiplication?"

I cover my face with my hands. "That was the worst joke I've ever heard."

"Don't dodge the question."

"No 'addition' for us," I say. "Not yet, anyway. He's been a little preoccupied with the whole 'genetic damage' thing."

"Ah. *That* thing." She sits up.

"What do you think about it?" I say.

"I don't know. I guess it makes me angry." She frowns. "No one likes to be told there's something wrong with them, especially something like their genes, which they can't change."

"You think there's really something wrong with you?"

"I guess so. It's like a disease, right? They can see it in our genes. That's not really up for debate, is it?"

"I'm not saying your genes aren't different," I say. "I'm just saying that doesn't mean one set is damaged and one set isn't. The genes for blue eyes and brown eyes are different too, but are blue eyes 'damaged'? It's like they just arbitrarily decided that one kind of DNA was bad and the other was good."

"Based on the evidence that GD behavior was worse," Christina points out.

"Which could be caused by a lot of things," I retort.

"I don't know why I'm arguing with you when I'd really like for you to be right," Christina says, laughing. "But don't you think a bunch of smart people like these Bureau scientists could figure out the cause of bad behavior?"

"Sure," I say. "But I think that no matter how smart,

people usually see what they're already looking for, that's all."

"Maybe you're biased too," she says. "Because you have friends—and a boyfriend—with this genetic issue."

"Maybe." I know I'm fumbling for an explanation, one I may not really believe, but I say it anyway: "I guess I don't see a reason to believe in genetic damage. Will it make me treat other people better? No. The opposite, maybe."

And besides, I see what it's doing to Tobias, how it's making him doubt himself, and I don't understand how anything good can possibly come from it.

"You don't believe things because they make your life better, you believe them because they're true," she points out.

"But"—I speak slowly as I mull that over—"isn't looking at the result of a belief a good way of evaluating if it's true?"

"Sounds like a Stiff way of thinking." She pauses. "I guess my way is very Candor, though. God, we really can't escape factions no matter where we go, can we?"

I shrug. "Maybe it's not so important to escape them."

Tobias walks into the dormitory, looking pale and exhausted, like he always does these days. His hair is pushed up on one side from lying on his pillow, and he's still wearing what he wore yesterday. He's been sleeping in his clothes since we came to the Bureau.

Christina gets up. "Okay, I'm going to go. And leave you two . . . to *all this space*. Alone." She gestures at all the empty beds, and then winks conspicuously at me as she walks out of the dormitory.

Tobias smiles a little, but not enough to make me think he's actually happy. And instead of sitting next to me, he lingers at the foot of my bed, his fingers fumbling over the hem of his shirt.

"There's something I want to talk to you about," he says.

"Okay," I say, and I feel a spike of fear in my chest, like a jump on a heart monitor.

"I want to ask you to promise not to get mad," he says, "but . . ."

"But you know I don't make stupid promises," I say, my throat tight.

"Right." He does sit, then, in the curve of blankets left unmade on his bed. He avoids my eyes. "Nita left a note under my pillow, telling me to meet her last night. And I did."

I straighten, and I can feel an angry heat spreading through me as I picture Nita's pretty face, Nita's graceful feet, walking toward my boyfriend.

"A pretty girl asks you to meet her late at night, and you *go*?" I demand. "And then you want me not to get *mad* about it?"

“It’s not about that with Nita and me. At all,” he says hastily, finally looking at me. “She just wanted to show me something. She doesn’t believe in genetic damage, like she led me to believe. She has a plan to take away some of the Bureau’s power, to make GDs more equal. We went to the fringe.”

He tells me about the underground tunnel that leads outside, and the ramshackle town in the fringe, and the conversation with Rafi and Mary. He explains the war that the government kept hidden so that no one would know that “genetically pure” people are capable of incredible violence, and the way GDs live in the metropolitan areas where the government still has real power.

As he speaks, I feel suspicion toward Nita building inside me, but I don’t know where it comes from—the gut instinct I usually trust, or my jealousy. When he finishes, he looks at me expectantly, and I purse my lips, trying to decide.

“How do you know she’s telling you the truth?” I say.

“I don’t,” he says. “She promised to show me evidence. Tonight.” He takes my hand. “I’d like you to come.”

“And Nita will be okay with that?”

“I don’t really care.” His fingers slide between mine. “If she really needs my help, she’ll have to figure out how to be okay with it.”

I look at our joined fingers, at the fraying cuff of his gray shirt and the worn knee of his jeans. I don't want to spend time with Nita and Tobias together, knowing that her supposed genetic damage gives her something in common with him that I will never have. But this is important to him, and I want to know if there's evidence of the Bureau's wrongdoing as much as he does.

"Okay," I say. "I'll go. But don't for a second think that I actually believe she's not interested in you for more than your genetic code."

"Well," he says. "Don't for a second think I'm interested in anyone but you."

He puts his hand on the back of my neck and draws my mouth toward his.

The kiss and his words both comfort me, but my unease doesn't completely disappear.

CHAPTER TWENTY-FIVE

TOBIAS

TRIS AND I meet Nita in the hotel lobby after midnight, among the potted plants with their unfurling flowers, a tame wilderness. When Nita sees Tris at my side, her face tightens like she just tasted something bitter.

"You promised you wouldn't tell her," she says, pointing at me. "What happened to protecting her?"

"I changed my mind," I say.

Tris laughs, harshly. "That's what you told him, that he would be protecting me? That's a pretty skillful manipulation. Well done."

I raise my eyebrows at her. I never thought of it as a manipulation, and that scares me a little. I can usually rely on myself to see a person's ulterior motives, or to invent them in my mind, but I was so used to my desire to protect Tris, especially after almost losing her, that I didn't even think twice.

Or I was so used to lying instead of telling difficult truths that I welcomed the chance to deceive her.

"It wasn't a manipulation, it was the truth." Nita doesn't look angry anymore, just tired, her hand sliding over her face and then smoothing back her hair. She isn't defensive, which means she might be telling the truth. "You could be arrested just for knowing what you know and not reporting it. I thought it would be better to avoid that."

"Well, too late," I say. "Tris is coming. Is that a problem?"

"I would rather have both of you than neither of you, and I'm sure that's the implied ultimatum," Nita says, rolling her eyes. "Let's go."

+++

Tris, Nita, and I walk back through the silent, still compound to the laboratories where Nita works. None of us speaks, and I am conscious of every squeak of my shoes, every voice in the distance, every snap of every closing door. I feel like we're doing something forbidden, though technically we aren't. Not yet, anyway.

Nita stops by the door to the laboratories and scans her card. We follow her past the gene therapy room where I saw a map of my genetic code, farther into the heart of the compound than I have been yet. It's dark and grim back here, and clumps of dust dance over the floor when we walk past.

Nita pushes another door open with her shoulder, and we walk into a storage room. Dull metal drawers cover the walls, labeled with paper numbers, the ink worn off with time. In the center of the room is a lab table with a computer and a microscope, and a young man with slicked-back blond hair.

"Tobias, Tris, this is my friend Reggie," Nita says. "He's also a GD."

"Nice to meet you," Reggie says with a smile. He shakes Tris's hand, then mine, his grip firm.

"Let's show them the slides first," Nita says.

Reggie taps the computer screen and beckons us closer. "Not gonna bite."

Tris and I exchange a glance, then stand behind Reggie at the table to see the screen. Pictures start flashing on it, one after another. They're in grayscale and look grainy and distorted—they must be very old. It takes me only a few seconds to realize that they are photographs of suffering: narrow, pinched children with huge eyes, ditches full of bodies, huge mounds of burning papers.

The photographs move so fast, like book pages

fluttering in the breeze, that I get only impressions of horrors. Then I turn my face away, unable to look any longer. I feel a deep silence grow inside me.

At first, when I look at Tris, her expression is like still water—like the images we just saw caused no ripples. But then her mouth quivers, and she presses her lips together to disguise it.

"Look at these weapons." Reggie brings up a photograph with a man in uniform holding a gun and points. "That kind of gun is incredibly old. The guns used in the Purity War were *much* more advanced. Even the Bureau would agree with that. It's gotta be from a really old conflict. Which must have been waged by genetically *pure* people, since genetic manipulation didn't exist back then."

"How do you hide a *war*?" I say.

"People are isolated, starving," Nita says quietly. "They know only what they're taught, they see only the information that's made available to them. And who controls all that? The government."

"Okay." Tris's head bobs, and she's talking too fast, nervous. "So they're lying about your—*our* history. That doesn't mean they're the enemy, it just means they're a group of grossly misinformed people trying to . . . better the world. In an ill-advised way."

Nita and Reggie glance at each other.

"That's the thing," Nita says. "They're hurting people."

She puts her hand on the counter and leans into it, leans toward us, and again I see the revolutionary building strength inside her, taking over the parts of her that are young woman and GD and laboratory worker.

"When the Abnegation wanted to reveal the great truth of their world sooner than they were supposed to," she says slowly, "and Jeanine wanted to stifle them . . . the Bureau was all too happy to provide her with an incredibly advanced simulation serum—the attack simulation that enslaved the minds of the Dauntless, that resulted in the destruction of Abnegation."

I take a moment to let that sink in.

"That can't be true," I say. "Jeanine told me that the highest proportion of Divergent—the genetically *pure*—in any faction was in Abnegation. You just said the Bureau values the genetically pure enough to send someone in to save them; why would they help Jeanine kill them?"

"Jeanine was wrong," Tris says distantly. "Evelyn said so. The highest proportion of Divergent was among the factionless, not Abnegation."

I turn to Nita.

"I still don't see why they would risk that many Divergent," I say. "I need evidence."

"Why do you think we came here?" Nita switches on

another set of lights that illuminate the drawers, and paces along the left wall. "It took me a long time to get clearance to go in here," she says. "Even longer to acquire the knowledge to understand what I saw. I had help from one of the GPs, actually. A sympathizer."

Her hand hovers over one of the low drawers. From it she takes a vial of orange liquid.

"Look familiar?" she asks me.

I try to remember the shot they gave me before the attack simulation began, right before the final round of Tris's initiation. Max did it, inserted the needle into the side of my neck as I had done myself dozens of times. Right before he did the glass vial caught the light, and it was orange, just like whatever Nita is holding.

"The colors match," I say. "So?"

Nita carries the vial to the microscope. Reggie takes a slide from a tray near the computer and, using a dropper, puts two drops of the orange liquid in its center, then seals the liquid in place with a second slide. As he places it on the microscope, his fingers are careful but certain; they are the movements of someone who has performed the same action hundreds of times.

Reggie taps the computer screen a few times, opening a program called "MicroScan."

"This information is free and available to anyone

who knows how to use this equipment and has the system password, which the GP sympathizer graciously gave me," Nita says. "So in other words, it's not all that hard to access, but no one would think to examine it very closely. And GDs don't have system passwords, so it's not like we would have known about it. This storage room is for obsolete experiments—failures, or outdated developments, or useless things."

She looks through the microscope, using a knob on the side to focus the lens.

"Go ahead," she says.

Reggie presses a button on the computer, and paragraphs of text appear under the "MicroScan" bar at the top of the screen. He points to a paragraph in the middle of the page, and I read it.

"'Simulation Serum v4.2. Coordinates a large number of targets. Transmits signals over long distances. Hallucinogen from original formula not included—simulated reality is predetermined by program master.'"

That's it.

That's the attack simulation serum.

"Now why would the Bureau have this unless they had developed it?" Nita says. "They were the ones who put the serums into the experiments, but they usually left the serums alone, let the city residents develop them further. If Jeanine was the one who developed it, they wouldn't have stolen it from her. If it's here, it's because *they* made it."

I stare at the illuminated slide in the microscope, at the orange droplet swimming in the eyepiece, and release a shaky breath.

Tris says, breathless, "Why?"

"Abnegation was about to reveal the truth to everyone inside the city. And you've seen what's happened now that the city knows the truth: Evelyn is effectively a dictator, the factionless are squashing the faction members, and I'm sure the factions will rise up against them sooner or later. Many people will die. Telling the truth risks the safety of the experiment, no question," Nita says. "So a few months ago, when the Abnegation were on the verge of causing that destruction and instability by revealing Edith Prior's video to your city, the Bureau probably thought, better that the Abnegation should suffer a great loss—even at the expense of several Divergent—than the whole city suffer a great loss. Better to end the lives of the Abnegation than to risk the experiment. So they reached out to someone who they knew would agree with them. Jeanine Matthews."

Her words surround me and bury themselves inside me.

I set my hands on the lab table, letting it cool my palms, and look at my distorted reflection in the brushed metal.

I may have hated my father for most of my life, but I never hated his faction. Abnegation's quiet, their community, their routine, always seemed good to me. And now most of those kind, giving people are dead. Murdered, at the hands of the Dauntless, at the urging of Jeanine, with the power of the Bureau to back her.

Tris's mother and father were among them.

Tris stands so still, her hands dangling limply, turning red with the flush of her blood.

"This is the problem with their blind commitment to these experiments," Nita says next to us, as if sliding the words into the empty spaces of our minds. "The Bureau values the experiments above GD lives. It's obvious. And now, things could get even worse."

"Worse?" I say. "*Worse* than killing most of the Abnegation? How?"

"The government has been threatening to shut down the experiments for almost a year now," Nita says. "The experiments keep falling apart because the communities can't live in peace, and David keeps finding ways to restore peace just in the nick of time. And if anything else goes wrong in Chicago, he can do it again. He can reset all the experiments at any time."

"*Reset* them," I say.

"With the Abnegation memory serum," Reggie says. "Well, really, it's the Bureau's memory serum. Every man, woman, and child will have to begin again."

Nita says tersely, "Their entire lives *erased*, against their will, for the sake of solving a genetic damage 'problem' that doesn't actually exist. These people have the power to do that. And no one should have that power."

I remember the thought I had, after Johanna told me about the Amity administering the memory serum to Dauntless patrols—that when you take a person's memories, you change who they are.

Suddenly I don't care what Nita's plan is, as long as it means striking the Bureau as hard as we can. What I have learned in the past few days has made me feel like there is nothing about this place worth salvaging.

"What's the plan?" says Tris, her voice flat, almost mechanical.

"I'll let my friends from the fringe in through the underground tunnel," Nita says. "Tobias, you will shut off the security system as I do, so that we aren't caught—it's nearly the same technology you worked with in the Dauntless control room; it should be easy for you. Then Rafi, Mary, and I will break into the Weapons Lab and steal the memory serum so the Bureau can't use it. Reggie's been helping behind the scenes, but he'll be opening the tunnel for us on the day of the attack."

"What will you do with a bunch of memory serum?" I say.

"Destroy it," Nita says, even-keeled.

I feel strange, empty like a deflated balloon. I don't know what I had in mind when Nita talked about her plan, but it wasn't this—this feels so small, so passive as an act of retaliation against the people responsible for the attack simulation, the people who told me that there was something wrong with me at my very core, in my genetic code.

"That's *all* you intend to do," Tris says, finally looking away from the microscope. She narrows her eyes at Nita. "You know that the Bureau is responsible for the murders of hundreds of people, and your plan is to . . . take away their memory serum?"

"I don't remember inviting your critique of my plan."

"I'm not critiquing your plan," Tris says. "I'm telling you I don't believe you. You hate these people. I can tell by the way you talk about them. Whatever you intend to do, I think it's far worse than stealing some serum."

"The memory serum is what they use to keep the experiments running. It's their greatest source of power over your city, and I want to take it away. I'd say that's a hard enough blow for now." Nita sounds gentle, like she's explaining something to a child. "I never said this was all I was ever going to do. It's not always wise to strike as hard as you can at the first opportunity. This is a long race, not a sprint."

Tris just shakes her head.

"Tobias, are you in?" Nita says.

I look from Tris, with her tense, stiff posture, to Nita, who is relaxed, ready. I don't see whatever Tris sees, or hear it. And when I think about saying no, I feel like my body will collapse in on itself. I have to do something. Even if it feels small, I have to do something, and I don't understand why Tris doesn't feel the same desperation inside her.

"Yes," I say. Tris turns to me, her eyes wide, incredulous. I ignore her. "I can disable the security system. I'll need some Amity peace serum, do you have access to that?"

"I do." Nita smiles a little. "I'll send you a message with the timing. Come on, Reggie. Let's leave these two to . . . talk."

Reggie nods to me, and then to Tris, and then he and Nita both leave the room, easing the door closed behind them so it doesn't make a sound.

Tris turns to me, her arms folded like two bars across her body, keeping me out.

"I can't believe you," she said. "She's *lying*. Why can't you see that?"

"Because it's not *there*," I say. "I can tell when someone's lying just as well as you can. And in this situation, I think your judgment might be clouded by something else. Something like jealousy."

"I am not *jealous*!" she says, scowling at me. "I am being smart. She has something bigger planned, and if I were you, I would run far away from anyone who lies to me about what they want me to participate in."

"Well, you're not me." I shake my head. "God, Tris. These people murdered your parents, and you're not going to do something about it?"

"I never said I wasn't going to do anything," she says tersely. "But I don't have to buy into the first plan I hear, either."

"You know, I brought you here because I wanted to be honest with you, not so that you could make snap judgments about people and tell me what to do!"

"Remember what happened last time you didn't trust my 'snap judgments'?" Tris says coldly. "You found out that I was right. I was right about Edith Prior's video changing everything, and I was right about Evelyn, and I'm right about this."

"Yeah. You're always right," I say. "Were you right about running into dangerous situations without weapons? Were you right about lying to me and going on a death march to Erudite headquarters in the middle of the night? Or about Peter, were you right about him?"

"Don't throw those things in my face." She points at

me, and I feel like I'm a child getting lectured by a parent. "I never said I was perfect, but you—you can't even see past your own desperation. You went along with Evelyn because you were desperate for a parent, and now you're going along with this because you're desperate not to be *damaged*—"

The word shivers through me.

"I am not damaged," I say quietly. "I can't believe you have so little faith in me that you would tell me not to trust myself." I shake my head. "And I don't need your *permission*."

I start toward the door, and as my hand closes around the handle, she says, "Just leaving so that you can have the last word, that's really mature!"

"So is being suspicious of someone's motives just because she's pretty," I say. "I guess we're even."

I leave the room.

I am not a desperate, unsteady child who throws his trust around. I am not damaged.

CHAPTER TWENTY-SIX

TRIS

I TOUCH MY forehead to the eyepiece of the microscope. The serum swims before me, orange-brown.

I was so busy looking for Nita's lies that I barely registered the truth: In order to get their hands on this serum, the Bureau must have developed it, and somehow delivered it to Jeanine to use. I pull away. Why would Jeanine work with the Bureau when she so badly wanted to stay in the city, away from them?

But I guess the Bureau and Jeanine shared a common goal. Both wanted the experiment to continue. Both were terrified of what would happen if it didn't. Both were willing to sacrifice innocent lives to do it.

I thought this place could be home. But the Bureau is

full of killers. I rock back on my heels as if pushed back by some invisible force, then walk out of the room, my heart beating fast.

I ignore the few people dawdling in the corridor in front of me. I just push farther into the Bureau compound, farther and farther into the belly of the beast.

Maybe this place could be home, I hear myself saying to Christina.

These people murdered your parents, Tobias's words echo in my head.

I don't know where I'm going except that I need space, and air. I clutch my ID in my hand and half walk, half run past the security barrier to the sculpture. There is no light shining into the tank now, though the water still falls from it, one drop for every second that passes. I stand for a little while, watching it. And then, across the slab of stone, I see my brother.

"Are you all right?" he says tentatively.

I am not all right. I was beginning to feel that I had finally found a place to stay, a place that was not so unstable or corrupt or controlling that I could actually belong there. You would think that I would have learned by now—such a place does not exist.

"No," I say.

He starts to move around the stone block, toward me. "What is it?"

"What is it." I laugh. "Let me put it this way: I just found out you're not the worst person I know."

I drop into a crouch and push my fingers through my hair. I feel numb and terrified of my own numbness. The Bureau is responsible for my parents' deaths. Why do I have to keep repeating it to myself to believe it? What's wrong with me?

"Oh," he says. "I'm . . . sorry?"

All I can manage is a small grunt.

"You know what Mom told me once?" he says, and the way he says *Mom*, like he didn't *betray* her, sets my teeth on edge. "She said that everyone has some evil inside them, and the first step to loving anyone is to recognize the same evil in ourselves, so we're able to forgive them."

"Is that what you want me to do?" I say dully as I stand. "I may have done bad things, Caleb, but I would *never* deliver you to your own execution."

"You can't say that," he says, and it sounds like he's pleading with me, begging me to say that I am just like him, no better. "You didn't know how persuasive Jeanine was—"

Something inside me snaps like a brittle rubber band.

I punch him in the face.

All I can think about is how the Erudite stripped me of my watch and my shoes and led me to the bare table where they would take my life. A table that Caleb may as well have set up himself.

I thought I was beyond this kind of anger, but as he stumbles back with his hands on his face, I pursue him, grabbing the front of his shirt and slamming him against the stone sculpture and screaming that he is a coward and a traitor and that I will kill him, I will kill him.

One of the guards comes toward me, and all she has to do is put her hand on my arm and the spell is broken. I release Caleb's shirt. I shake out my stinging hand. I turn and walk away.

+++

There's a beige sweater draped over the empty chair in Matthew's lab, the sleeve brushing the floor. I've never met his supervisor. I'm beginning to suspect that Matthew does all the real work.

I sit on top of the sweater and examine my knuckles. A few of them are split from punching Caleb, and dotted with faint bruises. It seems fitting that the blow would leave a mark on both of us. That's how the world works.

Last night, when I went back to the dormitory, Tobias wasn't there, and I was too angry to sleep. In the hours that I lay awake, staring at the ceiling, I decided that while I wasn't going to participate in Nita's plan, I also wasn't going to stop it. The truth about the attack simulation brewed hate for the Bureau inside me, and I want to watch it break apart from within.

Matthew is talking science. I'm having trouble paying attention.

"—doing some genetic analysis, which is fine, but before, we were developing a way to make the memory compound behave as a virus," he says. "With the same rapid replication, the same ability to spread through the air. And then we developed a vaccination for it. Just a temporary one, only lasts for forty-eight hours, but still."

I nod. "So . . . you were making it so you could set up other city experiments more efficiently, right?" I say. "No need to inject everyone with the memory serum when you can just release it and let it spread."

"Exactly!" He seems excited that I'm actually interested in what he's saying. "And it's a better model for having the option to select particular members of a population to opt out—you inoculate them, the virus spreads within twenty-four hours, and it has no effect on them."

I nod again.

"You okay?" Matthew says, his coffee mug poised near his mouth. He puts it down. "I heard the security guards had to pull you off someone last night."

"It was my brother. Caleb."

"Ah." Matthew raises an eyebrow. "What did he do this time?"

"Nothing, really." I pinch the sweater sleeve between my fingers. Its edges are all fraying, wearing with time. "I was wired to explode anyway; he just got in the way."

I already know, by looking at him, the question he's asking, and I want to explain it all to him, everything that Nita showed me and told me. I wonder if I can trust him.

"I heard something yesterday," I say, testing the waters. "About the Bureau. About my city, and the simulations."

He straightens up and gives me a strange look.

"What?" I say.

"Did you hear that something from Nita?" he says.

"Yes. How did you know that?"

"I've helped her a couple times," he says. "I let her into that storage room. Did she tell you anything else?"

Matthew is Nita's informant? I stare at him. I never thought that Matthew, who went out of his way to show me the difference between my "pure" genes and Tobias's "damaged" genes, might be helping Nita.

"Something about a plan," I say slowly.

He gets up and walks toward me, oddly tense. I lean away from him by instinct.

"Is it happening?" he says. "Do you know when?"

"What's going on?" I say. "Why would you help Nita?"

"Because all this 'genetic damage' nonsense is ridiculous," he says. "It's very important that you answer my questions."

"It is happening. And I don't know when, but I think it will be soon."

"Shit." Matthew puts his hands on his face. "Nothing good can come of this."

"If you don't stop saying cryptic things, I'm going to slap you," I say, getting to my feet.

"I was helping Nita until she told me what she and those fringe people wanted to do," Matthew says. "They want to get to the Weapons Lab and—"

"—steal the memory serum, yeah, I heard."

"No." He shakes his head. "No, they don't want the memory serum, they want the death serum. Similar to the one the Erudite have—the one you were supposed to be injected with when you were almost executed. They're going to use it for assassinations, a lot of them. Set off an aerosol can and it's easy, see? Give it to the right people and you have an explosion of anarchy and violence, which is exactly what those fringe people want."

I do see. I see the tilt of a vial, the quick press of a button on an aerosol can. I see Abnegation bodies and Erudite bodies sprawled over streets and staircases. I see the little pieces of this world that we've managed to cling to bursting into flames.

"I thought I was helping her with something smarter," Matthew says. "If I had known I was helping her start another war, I wouldn't have done it. We have to do something about this."

"I told him," I say softly, but not to Matthew, to myself. "I told him she was lying."

"We may have a problem with the way we treat GDs in this country, but it's not going to be solved by killing a bunch of people," he says. "Now come on, we're going to David's office."

I don't know what's right or wrong. I don't know anything about this country or the way it works or what it needs to change. But I do know that a bunch of death serum in the hands of Nita and some people from the fringe is no better than a bunch of death serum in the Weapons Lab of the Bureau. So I chase Matthew down the hallway outside. We walk quickly in the direction of the front entrance, where I first entered this compound.

When we walk past the security checkpoint, I spot Uriah near the sculpture. He lifts a hand to wave to me, his mouth pressed into a line that could be a smile if he was trying harder. Above his head, light refracts through the water tank, the symbol of the compound's slow, pointless struggle.

I'm just passing the security checkpoint when I see the

wall next to Uriah explode.

It is like fire blossoming from a bud. Shards of glass and metal spray from the center of the bloom, and Uriah's body is among them, a limp projectile. A deep rumble moves through me like a shudder. My mouth is open; I am screaming his name, but I can't hear myself over the ringing in my ears.

Around me, everyone is crouched, their arms curled around their heads. But I am on my feet, watching the hole in the compound wall. No one comes through it.

Seconds later, everyone around me starts running away from the blast, and I hurl myself against them, shoulder first, toward Uriah. An elbow hits me in the side and I fall down, my face scraping something hard and metal—the side of a table. I struggle to my feet, wiping blood from my eyebrow with a sleeve. Fabric slides over my arms, and limbs, hair, and wide eyes are all I can see, except the sign over their heads that says COMPOUND EXIT.

"Signal the alarms!" one of the guards at the security checkpoint screams. I duck under an arm and trip to the side.

"I did!" another guard shouts. "They aren't working!"

Matthew grabs my shoulder and yells into my ear. "What are you doing? Don't go *toward*—"

I move faster, finding an empty channel where there

are no people to obstruct my path. Matthew runs after me.

"We shouldn't be going to the explosion site—whoever set it off is already in the building," he says. "Weapons Lab, now! Come on!"

The Weapons Lab. Holy words.

I think of Uriah lying on the tile surrounded by glass and metal. My body is straining toward him, every muscle, but I know there's nothing I can do for him right now. The more important thing for me to do is to use my knowledge of chaos, of attacks, to keep Nita and her friends from stealing the death serum.

Matthew was right. Nothing good can come of this.

Matthew takes the lead, plunging into the crowd like it is a pool of water. I try to look only at the back of his head, to keep track of him, but the oncoming faces distract me, the mouths and eyes rigid with terror. I lose him for a few seconds and then find him again, several yards ahead, turning right at the next hallway.

"Matthew!" I shout, and I push my way through another group of people. Finally I catch up, grabbing the back of his shirt. He turns and grabs my hand.

"Are you okay?" he says, staring just above my eyebrow. In the rush I almost forgot about my cut. I press my sleeve to it, and it comes away red, but I nod.

"I'm fine! Let's go!"

We sprint side by side down the hallway—this one is not as crowded as the others, but I can see that whoever infiltrated the building has been here already. There are guards lying on the floor, some alive and some not. I see a gun on the tile near a drinking fountain and lurch toward it, breaking my grip on Matthew's hand.

I grab the gun and offer it to Matthew. He shakes his head. "I've never fired one."

"Oh, for God's sake." My finger curls around the trigger. It's different from the guns we had in the city—it doesn't have a barrel that shifts to the side, or the same tension in the trigger, or even the same distribution of weight. It's easier to hold, as a result, because it doesn't spark the same memories.

Matthew is gasping for air. So am I, only I don't notice it the same way, because I've done this sprint through chaos so many times. The next hallway he guides us to is empty except for one fallen soldier. She's not moving.

"It's not far," he says, and I touch my finger to my lips to tell him to be quiet.

We slow to a walk, and I squeeze the gun, my sweat making it slip. I don't know how many bullets are in it, or how to check. When we pass the soldier, I pause to search her for a weapon. I find a gun tucked under her hip, where she fell on her own wrist. Matthew stares at her, unblinking, as I take her weapon.

"Hey," I say quietly. "Just keep moving. Move now, process later."

I elbow him and lead the way down the hallway. Here the hallways are dim, the ceilings crossed with bars and pipes. I can hear people ahead and don't need Matthew's whispered directions to find them.

When we reach the place where we're supposed to turn, I press against the wall and look around the corner, careful to keep myself as hidden as possible.

There's a set of double-walled glass doors that look as heavy as metal doors would be, but they're open. Beyond them is a cramped hallway, empty except for three people in black. They wear heavy clothing and carry guns so big I'm not sure I would be able to lift one. Their faces are covered with dark fabric, disguising all but their eyes.

On his knees before the double doors is David, a gun barrel pressed to his temple, blood trailing down his chin. And standing among the invaders, wearing the same mask as the others, is a girl with a dark ponytail.

Nita.

CHAPTER TWENTY-SEVEN

TRIS

"GET US IN, David," Nita says, her voice garbled by the mask.

David's eyes slide lazily to the side, to the man pointing the gun at him.

"I don't believe you'll shoot me," he says. "Because I'm the only one in this building who knows this information, and you want that serum."

"Won't shoot you in the head, maybe," the man says, "but there are other places."

The man and Nita exchange a look. Then the man shifts the gun down, to David's feet, and fires. I squeeze my eyes shut as David's screams fill the hallway. He might be one of the people who offered Jeanine Matthews the attack simulation, but I still don't relish his screams of pain.

I stare at the guns I carry, one in each hand, my fingers pale against the black triggers. I imagine myself trimming back all the stray branches of my thoughts, focusing on just this place, just this time.

I put my mouth right next to Matthew's ear and mutter, "Go for help. Now."

Matthew nods and starts down the hallway. To his credit, he moves quietly, his footsteps silent on the tile. At the end of the hallway he looks back at me, and then disappears around the bend.

"I'm sick of this shit," the red-haired woman says. "Just blow up the doors."

"An explosion would activate one of the backup security measures," says Nita. "We need the pass code."

I look around the corner again, and this time, David's eyes shift to mine. His face is pale and shiny with sweat, and there is a wide pool of blood around his ankles. The others are looking at Nita, who takes a black box from her pocket and opens it to reveal a syringe and needle.

"Thought you said that stuff doesn't work on him," the man with the gun says.

"I said he could *resist* it, not that it didn't work at all," she says. "David, this is a very potent blend of truth serum and fear serum. I'm going to stick you with it if you don't tell us the pass code."

"I know this is just the fault of your genes, Nita," David

says weakly. "If you stop now, I can help you, I can—"

Nita smiles a twisted smile. With relish, she sticks the needle in his neck and presses the plunger. David slumps over, and then his body shudders, and shudders again.

He opens his eyes wide and screams, staring at the empty air, and I know what he's seeing, because I've seen it myself, in Erudite headquarters, under the influence of the terror serum. I watched my worst fears come to life.

Nita kneels in front of him and grabs his face.

"David!" she says urgently. "I can make it stop if you tell us how to get into this room. Hear me?"

He pants, and his eyes aren't focused on her, but rather on something over her shoulder. "Don't do it!" he shouts, and he lunges forward, toward whatever phantom the serum is showing him. Nita puts an arm across his chest to keep him steady, and he screams, "Don't—!"

Nita shakes him. "I'll stop them from doing it if you tell me how to get in!"

"Her!" David says, and tears gleam in his eyes. "The—the name—"

"Whose name?"

"We're running out of time!" the man with the gun trained on David says. "Either we get the serum or we kill him—"

"Her," David says, pointing at the space in front of him.

Pointing at me.

I stretch my arms around the corner of the wall and fire twice. The first bullet hits the wall. The second hits the man in the arm, so the huge weapon topples to the floor. The red-haired woman points her weapon at me—or the part of me that she can see, half hidden by the wall—and Nita screams, "Hold your fire!"

"Tris," Nita says, "you don't know what you're doing—"

"You're probably right," I say, and I fire again. This time my hand is steadier, my aim is better; I hit Nita's side, right above her hip. She screams into her mask and clutches the hole in her skin, sinking to her knees, her hands covered in blood.

David surges toward me with a grimace of pain as he puts weight on his injured leg. I wrap my arm around his waist and swing his body around so he's between me and the remaining soldiers. Then I press one of my guns to the back of his head.

They all freeze. I can feel my heartbeat in my throat, in my hands, behind my eyes.

"Fire, and I'll shoot him in the head," I say.

"You wouldn't kill your own leader," the red-haired woman says.

"He's not my leader. I don't care if he lives or dies," I say. "But if you think I'm going to let you gain control of that death serum, you're insane."

I start to shuffle backward, with David whimpering in

front of me, still under the influence of the serum cocktail. I duck my head and turn my body sideways so it's safely behind his. I keep one of the guns against his head.

We reach the end of the hallway, and the woman calls my bluff. She fires, and hits David just above the knee, in his other leg. He collapses with a scream, and I am exposed. I dive to the ground, slamming my elbows into the floor, as a bullet goes past me, the sound vibrating inside my head.

Then I feel something hot spreading through my left arm, and I see blood and my feet scramble on the floor, searching for traction. I find it and fire blindly down the hallway. I grab David by the collar and drag him around the corner, pain searing through my left arm.

I hear running footsteps and groan. But they aren't coming from behind me; they're coming from in front. People surround me, Matthew among them, and some of them pick David up and run with him down the hallway. Matthew offers me his hand.

My ears are ringing. I can't believe I did it.

CHAPTER TWENTY-EIGHT

TRIS

THE HOSPITAL IS packed with people, all of them yelling or racing back and forth or yanking curtains shut. Before I sat down I checked all the beds for Tobias. He wasn't in any of them. I am still shaking with relief.

Uriah is not here either. He is in one of the other rooms, and the door is closed—not a good sign.

The nurse who dabs my arm with antiseptic is breathless and looks around at all the activity instead of at my wound. I'm told it's a minor graze, nothing to worry about.

"I can wait, if you need to do something else," I say. "I have to find someone anyway."

She purses her lips, then says, "You need stitches."

"It's just a graze!"

"Not your arm, your head," she says, pointing to a spot above my eye. I had almost forgotten about the cut in all the chaos, but it still hasn't stopped bleeding.

"Fine."

"I'm going to have to give you a shot of this numbing agent," she says, holding up a syringe.

I am so used to needles that I don't even react. She dabs my forehead with antiseptic—they are so careful about germs here—and I feel the sting and prickle of the needle, diminishing by the second as the numbing agent does its work.

I watch the people rush past as she stitches my skin—a doctor pulls off a pair of bloodstained rubber gloves; a nurse carries a tray of gauze, his shoes nearly slipping on the tile; a family member of someone injured wrings her hands. The air smells like chemicals and old paper and warm bodies.

"Any updates on David?" I say.

"He'll live, but it will take him a long time to walk again," she says. Her lips stop puckering, just for a few seconds. "Could have been a lot worse, if you hadn't been there. You're all set."

I nod. I wish I could tell her that I'm not a hero, that I was using him as a shield, like a wall of meat. I wish I could confess to being a person full of hate for the Bureau and for David, a person who would let someone else get riddled with bullets to save herself. My parents would be ashamed.

She places a bandage over the stitches to protect the wound, and gathers all the wrappers and soaked cotton balls into her fists to throw them away.

Before I can thank her, she is gone, off to the next bed, the next patient, the next injury.

Injured people line the hallway outside the emergency ward. I have gathered from the evidence that there was another explosion set off at the same time as the one near the entrance. Both were diversions. Our attackers got in through the underground tunnel, as Nita said they would. She never mentioned blowing holes in walls.

The doors at the end of the hallway open, and a few people rush in, carrying a young woman—Nita—between them. They put her on a cot near one of the walls. She groans, clutching at a roll of gauze that is pressed to the wound in her side. I feel strangely separate from her pain. I shot her. I had to. That's the end of it.

As I walk down the aisle between the wounded, I notice the uniforms. Everyone sitting here wears green. With few exceptions, they are all support staff. They are clutching bleeding arms or legs or heads, their injuries no better than my own, some much worse.

I catch my reflection in the windows just beyond the main corridor—my hair is stringy and limp, and the bandage dominates my forehead. David's blood and my blood smear my clothes in places. I need to shower and change, but first I have to find Tobias and Christina. I haven't seen either of them since before the invasion.

It doesn't take me long to find Christina—she is sitting in the waiting room when I walk out of the emergency ward, her knee jiggling so much that the person next to her is giving her dirty looks. She lifts a hand to greet me, but her eyes shift away from mine and toward the doors right afterward.

"You all right?" she asks me.

"Yeah," I say. "There's still no update on Uriah. I couldn't get into the room."

"These people make me crazy, you know that?" she says. "They won't tell anyone anything. They won't let us see him. It's like they think they own him and everything that happens to him!"

"They work differently here. I'm sure they'll tell you when they know something concrete."

"Well, they would tell *you*," she says, scowling. "But I'm not convinced they would give *me* a second look."

A few days ago I might have disagreed with her, unsure how influential their belief in genetic damage was on their behavior. I'm not sure what to do—not sure how to talk to her now that I have these advantages and she does not and there's nothing either of us can do about it. All I can think to do is be near her.

"I have to find Tobias, but I'll come back after I do and sit with you, okay?"

She finally looks at me, and her knee goes still. "They didn't tell you?"

My stomach clenches with fear. "Tell me what."

"Tobias was arrested," she says quietly. "I saw him sitting with the invaders right before I came in here. Some people saw him at the control room before the attack—they say he was disabling the alarm system."

There is a sad look in her eyes, like she pities me. But I already knew what Tobias did.

"Where are they?" I say.

I need to talk to him. And I know what I need to say.

CHAPTER TWENTY-NINE

TOBIAS

MY WRISTS STING from the plastic tie the guard squeezed around them. I probe my jaw with just my fingertips, testing the skin for blood.

"All right?" Reggie says.

I nod. I have dealt with worse injuries than this—I have been hit harder than I was by the soldier who slammed the butt of his gun into my jaw while he was arresting me. His eyes were wild with anger when he did it.

Mary and Rafi sit a few feet away, Rafi clutching a handful of gauze to his bleeding arm. A guard stands between us and them, keeping us separate. As I look at them, Rafi meets my eyes and nods. As if to say, *Well done.*

If I did well, why do I feel sick to my stomach?

"Listen," Reggie says, shifting so he's closer to me. "Nita and the fringe people are taking the fall. It'll be all right."

I nod again, without conviction. We had a backup plan for our probable arrest, and I'm not worried about its success. What I am worried about is how long it's taking them to deal with us, and how casual it has been—we have been sitting against a wall in an empty corridor since they caught the invaders more than an hour ago, and no one has come to tell us what will happen to us, or to ask us any questions. I haven't even seen Nita yet.

It puts a sour taste in my mouth. Whatever we did, it seems to have shaken them up, and I know of nothing that shakes people up as much as lost lives.

How many of those am I responsible for, because I participated in this?

"Nita told me they were going to steal memory serum," I say to Reggie, and I'm afraid to look at him. "Was that true?"

Reggie eyes the guard who stands a few feet away. We have already been yelled at once for talking.

But I know the answer.

"It wasn't, was it," I say. Tris was right. Nita was lying.

"Hey!" The guard marches toward us and sticks the barrel of her gun between us. "Move aside. No conversation allowed."

Reggie shifts to the right, and I make eye contact with the guard.

"What's going on?" I say. "What happened?"

"Oh, like you don't know," she answers. "Now keep your mouth shut."

I watch her walk away, and then I see a small blond girl appear at the end of the hallway. Tris. A bandage stretches across her forehead, and blood smears her clothes in the shape of fingers. She clutches a piece of paper in her fist.

"Hey!" the guard says. "What are you doing here?"

"Shelly," the other guard says, jogging over. "Calm down. That's the girl who saved David."

The girl who saved David—from what, exactly?

"Oh." Shelly puts her gun down. "Well, it's still a valid question."

"They asked me to bring you guys an update," Tris says, and she offers Shelly the piece of paper. "David is in recovery. He'll live, but they're not sure when he'll walk again. Most of the other injured have been cared for."

The sour taste in my mouth grows stronger. David can't walk. And what they've been doing all this time is caring for the injured. All this destruction, and for what? I don't even know. I don't know the truth.

What did I do?

"Do they have a casualty count?" Shelly asks.

"Not yet," Tris replies.

"Thanks for letting us know."

"Listen." She shifts her weight to one foot. "I need to talk to him."

She jerks her head toward me.

"We can't really—" Shelly starts.

"Just for a second, I promise," Tris says. "Please."

"Let her," the other guard says. "What could it hurt?"

"Fine," Shelly says. "I'll give you two minutes."

She nods to me, and I use the wall to push myself to my feet, my hands still bound in front of me. Tris comes closer, but not that close—the space, and her folded arms, form a barrier between us that may as well be a wall. She looks somewhere south of my eyes.

"Tris, I—"

"Want to know what your friends did?" she says. Her voice shakes, and I do not make the mistake of thinking it's from tears. It's from anger. "They weren't after the memory serum. They were after poison—death serum. So that they could kill a bunch of important government people and start a war."

I look down, at my hands, at the tile, at the toes of her shoes. A war. "I didn't know—"

"I was right. I was right, and you didn't listen. Again," she says, quiet. Her eyes lock on mine, and I find that I do not want the eye contact I craved, because it takes me apart, piece by piece. "Uriah was standing right in front of one of the explosives they set off as diversions. He's unconscious and they're not sure he'll wake up."

It's strange how a word, a phrase, a sentence, can feel like a blow to the head.

"What?"

All I can see is Uriah's face when he hit the net after the Choosing Ceremony, the giddy smile he wore as Zeke and I pulled him onto the platform next to the net. Or him sitting in the tattoo parlor, his ear taped forward so it wouldn't get in Tori's way as she drew a snake on his skin. Uriah might not wake up? Uriah, gone forever?

And I promised. I promised Zeke I would look after him, I *promised* . . .

"He's one of the last friends I have," she says, her voice breaking. "I don't know if I'll ever be able to look at you the same way again."

She walks away. I hear Shelly's muffled voice telling me to sit down, and I sink to my knees, letting my wrists rest on my legs. I struggle to find a way to escape this, the horror of what I've done, but there is no sophisticated logic that can liberate me; there is no way out.

I put my face in my hands and try not to think, try not to imagine anything at all.

+++

The overhead light in the interrogation room reflects a muddled circle in the center of the table. That is where I keep my eyes as I recite the story Nita gave me, the one that is so close to true I have no trouble telling it. When I'm finished, the man recording it taps out my last sentences on his screen, the glass lighting up with letters where his fingers touch it. Then the woman acting as David's proxy—Angela—says, "So you didn't know the reason Juanita asked you to disable the security system?"

"No," I say, which is true. I didn't know the real reason; I only knew a lie.

They put all the others under truth serum, but not me. The genetic anomaly that makes me aware during simulations also suggests I could be resistant to serums, so my truth serum testimony might not be reliable. As long as my story fits with the others, they will assume it's true. They don't know that, a few hours ago, all of us were inoculated against truth serum. Nita's informant among the GPs provided her with the inoculation serum months ago.

"How, then, did she compel you to do it?"

"We're friends," I say. "She is—was—one of the only friends I had here. She asked me to trust her, told me it was for a good reason, so I did it."

"And what do you think about the situation now?"

I finally look at her. "I've never regretted something so much in my life."

Angela's hard, bright eyes soften a little. She nods. "Well, your story fits with what the others told us. Given your newness to this community, your ignorance of the master plan, and your genetic deficiency, we are inclined to be lenient. Your sentence is parole—you must work for the good of this community, and stay on your best behavior, for one year. You will not be allowed to enter any private laboratories or rooms. You will not leave the confines of this compound without permission. You will check in every month with a parole officer who will be assigned to you at the conclusion of our proceedings. Do you understand these terms?"

With the words "genetic deficiency" lingering in my mind, I nod and say, "I do."

"Then we're finished here. You're free to go." She stands, pushing her chair back. The recorder also stands, and slips his screen into his bag. Angela touches the table so that I look up at her again.

"Don't be so hard on yourself," she says. "You're very young, you know."

I don't think my youth excuses it, but I accept her attempt at kindness without objection.

"Can I ask what's going to happen to Nita?" I say.

Angela presses her lips together. "Once she recovers from her substantial injuries, she will be transferred to our prison and will spend the duration of her life there," she says.

"She won't be executed?"

"No, we don't believe in capital punishment for the genetically damaged." Angela moves toward the door. "We can't have the same behavioral expectations for those with damaged genes as we do for those with pure genes, after all."

With a sad smile, she leaves the room, and doesn't close the door behind her. I stay in my seat for a few seconds, absorbing the sting of her words. I wanted to believe they were all wrong about me, that I was not limited by my genes, that I was no more damaged than any other person. But how can that be true, when my actions landed Uriah in the hospital, when Tris can't even look me in the eye, when so many people died?

I cover my face and grit my teeth as the tears fall, bearing the wave of despair like it is a fist, striking me. By the time I get up to leave, the cuffs of my sleeves, used to wipe my cheeks, are damp, and my jaw aches.

CHAPTER THIRTY

TRIS

"HAVE YOU BEEN in yet?"

Cara stands beside me, her arms folded. Yesterday Uriah was transferred from his secure room to a room with a viewing window, I suspect to keep us from asking to see him all the time. Christina sits by his bed now, grasping his limp hand.

I thought he would have come apart like a rag doll with a pulled thread, but he doesn't look that different, except for some bandages and scrapes. I feel like he could wake up at any moment, smiling and wondering why we're all staring at him.

"I was in there last night," I say. "It just didn't seem right to leave him alone."

"There is some evidence to suggest that, depending on the extent of his brain damage, he can on some level hear and feel us," says Cara. "Though I was told his prognosis is not good."

Sometimes I still want to smack her. As if I need to be reminded that Uriah is unlikely to recover. "Yeah."

After I left Uriah's side last night, I wandered the compound without any sense of direction. I should have been thinking of my friend, teetering between this world and whatever comes next, but instead I thought of what I said to Tobias. And how I felt when I looked at him, like something was breaking.

I didn't tell him it was the end of our relationship. I meant to, but when I was looking at him, the words were impossible to say. I feel tears welling up again, as they have every hour or so since yesterday, and I push them away, swallow them down.

"So you saved the Bureau," Cara says, turning to me. "You seem to get involved in a lot of conflict. I suppose we should all be grateful that you are steady in a crisis."

"I didn't save the Bureau. I have no interest in saving the Bureau," I retort. "I kept a weapon out of some dangerous hands, that's all." I wait a beat. "Did you just compliment me?"

"I am capable of recognizing another person's

strengths," Cara replies, and she smiles. "Additionally, I think *our* issues are now resolved, both on a logical and an emotional level." She clears her throat a little, and I wonder if it's finally acknowledging that she has emotions that makes her uncomfortable, or something else. "It sounds like you know something about the Bureau that has made you angry. I wonder if you could tell me what it is."

Christina rests her head on the edge of Uriah's mattress, her slender body collapsing sideways. I say wryly, "I wonder. We may never know."

"Hmm." The crease between Cara's eyebrows appears when she frowns, making her look so much like Will that I have to look away. "Maybe I should say please."

"Fine. You know Jeanine's simulation serum? Well, it wasn't hers." I sigh. "Come on. I'll show you. It'll be easier that way."

It would be just as easy to tell her what I saw in that old storage room, nestled deep in the Bureau laboratories. But the truth is, I just want to keep myself busy, so I don't think about Uriah. Or Tobias.

"It seems like we'll never reach the end of all these deceptions," Cara says as we walk toward the storage room. "The factions, the video Edith Prior left us . . . all lies, designed to make us behave a particular way."

"Is that what you really think about the factions?" I say. "I thought you loved being an Erudite."

"I did." She scratches the back of her neck, leaving little red lines on her skin from her fingernails. "But the Bureau made me feel like a fool for fighting for any of it, and for what the Allegiant stood for. And I don't like to feel foolish."

"So you don't think any of it was worthwhile," I say. "Any of the Allegiant stuff."

"You do?"

"It got us out," I say, "and it got us to the truth, and it was better than the factionless commune Evelyn had in mind, where no one gets to choose anything at all."

"I suppose," she says. "I just pride myself on being someone who can see through things, the faction system included."

"You know what the Abnegation used to say about pride?"

"Something unfavorable, I assume."

I laugh. "Obviously. They said it blinds people to the truth of what they are."

We reach the door to the labs, and I knock a few times so Matthew will hear me and let us in. As I wait for him to open the door, Cara gives me a strange look.

"The old Erudite writings said the same thing, more or less," she says.

I never thought the Erudite would say anything about pride—that they would even concern themselves with morality. It sounds like I was wrong. I want to ask her more, but then the door opens, and Matthew stands in the hallway, chewing on an apple core.

"Can you let me into the storage room?" I say. "I need to show Cara something."

He bites off the end of the apple core and nods. "Of course."

I cringe, imagining the bitter taste of apple seeds, and follow him.

CHAPTER THIRTY-ONE

TOBIAS

I CAN'T GO back to the staring eyes and unspoken questions of the dormitory. I know I shouldn't return to the scene of my great crime, even though it's not one of the secure areas I'm barred from entering, but I feel like I need to see what's happening inside the city. Like I need to remember that there is a world outside this one, where I am not hated.

I walk to the control room and sit in one of the chairs. Each screen in the grid above me shows a different part of the city: the Merciless Mart, the lobby of Erudite headquarters, Millennium Park, the pavilion outside the Hancock building.

For a long time I watch the people milling around inside

Erudite headquarters, their arms covered in factionless armbands, weapons at their hips, exchanging quick conversation or handing off cans of food for dinner, an old factionless habit.

Then I hear someone at the control room desks say, "There he is," to one of her coworkers, and I scan the screens to see what she's talking about. Then I see him, standing in front of the Hancock building: Marcus, near the front doors, checking his watch.

I get up and tap the screen with my index finger to turn on the sound. For a moment only the rush of air comes through the speakers just below the screen, but then, footsteps. Johanna Reyes approaches my father. He stretches his hand out for her to shake, but she doesn't, and my father is left with his hand dangling in the air, a piece of bait she did not take.

"I *knew* you stayed in the city," she says. "They're looking all over for you."

A few of the people milling around the control room gather behind me to watch. I hardly notice them. I am watching my father's arm return to his side in a fist.

"Have I done something to offend you?" Marcus says. "I contacted you because I thought you were a friend."

"I thought you contacted me because you know I'm still the leader of the Allegiant, and you want an ally," Johanna says, bending her neck so a lock of hair falls over her scarred eye. "And depending on what your aim is, I am still that, Marcus, but I think our friendship is over."

Marcus's eyebrows pinch together. My father has the look of a man who used to be handsome, but as he has aged, his cheeks have become hollow, his features harsh and strict. His hair, cropped close to his skull in the Abnegation style, does not help this impression.

"I don't understand," Marcus says.

"I spoke to some of my Candor friends," Johanna says. "They told me what your boy said when he was under truth serum. That nasty rumor Jeanine Matthews spread about you and your son . . . it was true, wasn't it?"

My face feels hot, and I shrink into myself, my shoulders curving in.

Marcus is shaking his head. "No, Tobias is—"

Johanna holds up a hand. She speaks with her eyes closed, like she can't stand to look at him. "Please. I have watched how your son behaves, how your wife behaves. I know what people who are stained with violence look like." She pushes her hair behind her ear. "We recognize our own."

"You can't possibly believe—" Marcus starts. He shakes his head. "I'm a disciplinarian, yes, but I only wanted what was best—"

"A husband should not *discipline* his wife," Johanna says. "Not even in Abnegation. And as for your son . . . well, let us say that I *do* believe it of you."

Johanna's fingers skip over the scar on her cheek. My heart overwhelms me with its rhythm. She knows. She knows, not because she heard me confess to my shame in the Candor interrogation room, but because she *knows*, she has experienced it herself, I'm sure of it. I wonder who it was for her—mother? Father? Someone else?

Part of me always wondered what my father would do if directly confronted with the truth. I thought he might shift from the self-effacing Abnegation leader to the nightmare I knew at home, that he might lash out and reveal himself for who he is. It would be a satisfying reaction for me to see, but it is not his real reaction.

He just stands there looking confused, and for a moment I wonder if he *is* confused, if in his sick heart he believes his own lies about disciplining me. The thought creates a storm inside me, a rumbling of thunder and a rush of wind.

"Now that I've been honest," Johanna says, a little more calm now, "you can tell me why you asked me to come here."

Marcus shifts to a new subject like the old one was never discussed. I see in him a man who divides himself into compartments and can switch between them on command. One of those compartments was reserved only for my mother and me.

The Bureau employees move the camera in closer, so that the Hancock building is just a black backdrop behind Marcus's and Johanna's torsos. I follow a girder diagonally across the screen so I don't have to look at him.

"Evelyn and the factionless are tyrants," Marcus says. "The peace we experienced among the factions, before Jeanine's first attack, *can* be restored, I'm sure of it. And I want to try to restore it. I think this is something you want too."

"It is," Johanna says. "How do you think we should go about it?"

"This is the part you might not like, but I hope you will keep an open mind," Marcus says. "Evelyn controls the city because she controls the weapons. If we take those weapons away, she won't have nearly as much power, and she can be challenged."

Johanna nods, and scrapes her shoe against the pavement. I can only see the smooth side of her face from this angle, the limp but curled hair, the full mouth.

"What would you like me to do?" she says.

"Let me join you in leading the Allegiant," he says. "I was an Abnegation leader. I was practically the leader of this entire city. People will rally behind me."

"People have rallied already," Johanna points out. "And not behind a person, but behind the desire to reinstate the factions. Who says I need you?"

"Not to diminish your accomplishments, but the Allegiant are still too insignificant to be any more than a small uprising," Marcus says. "There are more factionless than any of us knew. You do need me. You know it."

My father has a way of persuading people without charm that has always confused me. He states his opinions as if they're facts, and somehow his complete lack of doubt makes you believe him. That quality frightens me now, because I know what he told me: that I was broken, that I was worthless, that I was nothing. How many of those things did he make me believe?

I can see Johanna beginning to believe him, thinking of the small cluster of people she has gathered to the Allegiant cause. Thinking of the group she sent outside the fence, with Cara, and never heard from again. Thinking of how alone she is, and how rich his history of leadership is. I want to scream at her through the screens not to trust him, to tell her that he only wants the factions back because he knows he can then take up his place as their leader again. But my voice can't reach her, wouldn't be able to even if I was standing right next to her.

Carefully, Johanna says to him, "Can you promise me that you will, wherever possible, try to limit the destruction we will cause?"

Marcus says, "Of course."

She nods again, but this time it looks like she's nodding to herself.

"Sometimes we need to fight for peace," she says, more to the pavement than to Marcus. "I think this is one of those times. And I do think you would be useful for people to rally behind."

It's the beginning of the Allegiant rebellion I've been expecting since I first heard the group had formed. Even though it has seemed inevitable to me since I saw how Evelyn chose to rule, I feel sick. It seems like the rebellions never stop, in the city, in the compound, anywhere. There are just breaths between them, and foolishly, we call those breaths "peace."

I move away from the screen, intending to leave the control room behind me, to get some fresh air wherever I can.

But as I walk away, I catch sight of another screen, showing a dark-haired woman pacing back and forth in an office in Erudite headquarters. Evelyn—of course they keep footage of Evelyn on the most prominent screens in the control room, it only makes sense.

Evelyn pushes her hands into her hair, clenching her fingers around the thick locks. She drops to a crouch, papers littering the floor all around her, and I think, *She's crying*, but I'm not sure why, since I don't see her shoulders shake.

I hear, through the screen speakers, a knock on the office door. Evelyn straightens, pats her hair, wipes her face, and says, "Come in!"

Therese comes in, her factionless armband askew. "Just got an update from the patrols. They say they haven't seen any sign of him."

"Great." Evelyn shakes her head. "I exile him, and he stays inside the city. He must be doing this just to spite me."

"Or he's joined the Allegiant, and they're harboring him," Therese says, slinging her body across one of the office chairs. She twists paper into the floor with her boot soles.

"Well, obviously." Evelyn puts her arm against the window and leans into it, looking out over the city and beyond it, the marsh. "Thank you for the update."

"We'll find him," Therese says. "He can't have gone far. I swear we'll find him."

"I just want him to be gone," Evelyn says, her voice tight and small, like a child's. I wonder if she's still afraid of him, in the way that I'm still afraid of him, like a nightmare that keeps resurfacing during the day. I wonder how similar my mother and I are, deep down where it counts.

"I know," Therese says, and she leaves.

I stand for a long time, watching Evelyn stare out the window, her fingers twitching at her side.

I feel like what I have become is halfway between my mother and my father, violent and impulsive and desperate and afraid. I feel like I have lost control of what I have become.

CHAPTER THIRTY-TWO

TRIS

DAVID SUMMONS ME to his office the next day, and I am afraid that he remembers how I used him as a shield when I was backing away from the Weapons Lab, how I pointed a gun at his head and said I didn't care if he lived or died.

Zoe meets me in the hotel lobby and leads me through the main hallway and down another one, long and narrow, with windows on my right that show the small fleet of airplanes perched in rows on the concrete. Light snow touches the glass, an early taste of winter, and melts within seconds.

I sneak looks at her as we walk, hoping to see what she is like when she doesn't think anyone is watching, but she seems just the same as always—chipper, but businesslike. Like the attack never happened.

"He'll be in a wheelchair," she says when we reach the end of the narrow hallway. "It's best not to make a big deal of it. He doesn't like to be pitied."

"I don't pity him." I struggle to keep the anger out of my voice. It would make her suspicious. "He's not the first person to ever be hit with a bullet."

"I always forget that you have seen far more violence than we have," Zoe says, and she scans her card at the next security barrier we reach. I stare through the glass at the guards on the other side—they stand erect, their guns at their shoulders, facing forward. I get the sense they have to stand that way all day.

I feel heavy and achy, like my muscles are communicating a deeper, emotional pain. Uriah is still in a coma. I still can't look at Tobias when I see him in the dormitory, in the cafeteria, in the hallway, without seeing the exploded wall next to Uriah's head. I'm not sure when, or if, anything will ever get better, not sure if these wounds are the kind that can heal.

We walk past the guards, and the tile turns to wood beneath my feet. Small paintings with gilded frames line the walls, and just outside David's office is a pedestal with a bouquet of flowers on it. They are small touches, but the effect is that I feel like my clothes are smudged with dirt.

Zoe knocks, and a voice within calls out, "Come in!"

She opens the door for me but doesn't follow me in. David's office is spacious and warm, the walls lined with books where they are not lined with windows. On the left side is a desk with glass screens suspended above it, and on the right side is a small laboratory with wood furnishings instead of metal ones.

David sits in a wheelchair, his legs covered in a stiff material—to keep the bones in place so they can heal, I assume. He looks pale and wan, but healthy enough. Though I know that he had something to do with the attack simulation, and with all those deaths, I find it difficult to pair those actions with the man I see in front of me. I wonder if this is how it is with all evil men, that to someone, they look just like good men, talk like good men, are just as likable as good men.

"Tris." He pushes himself toward me and presses one of my hands between his. I keep my hand firmly in his, though his skin feels dry as paper and I am repulsed by him.

"You are so very brave," he says, and then he releases my hand. "How are your injuries?"

I shrug. "I've had worse. How are yours?"

"It will take me some time to walk again, but they're confident that I will. Some of our people are developing sophisticated leg braces anyway, so I can be their first test case if I have to," he says, the corners of his eyes crinkling. "Could you push me behind the desk again? I am still having trouble steering."

I do, guiding his stiff legs under the tabletop and letting the rest of him follow. When I'm sure he's positioned correctly, I sit in the chair across from him and try to smile. In order to find some way to avenge my parents, I need to keep his trust and his fondness for me intact. And I won't do that with a scowl.

"I asked you to come here mostly so that I could thank you," he says. "I can't think of many young people who would have come after me instead of running for cover, or who would have been able to save this compound the way you did."

I think of pressing a gun to his head and threatening his life, and swallow hard.

"You and the people you came with have been in a regrettable state of flux since your arrival," he says. "We aren't quite sure what to do with all of you, to be honest, and I'm sure you don't know what to do with yourselves, but I have thought of something I would like *you* to do. I am the official leader of this compound, but apart from that, we have a similar system of governance to the Abnegation, so I am advised by a small group of councilors. I would like you to begin training for that position."

My hands tighten around the armrests.

"You see, we are going to need to make some changes around here now that we have been attacked," he says. "We are going to have to take a stronger stand for our cause. And I think you know how to do that."

I can't argue with that.

"What . . ." I clear my throat. "What would training for that entail?"

"Attending our meetings, for one thing," he says, "and learning the ins and outs of our compound—how we function, from top to bottom, our history, our values, and so on. I can't allow you to be a part of the council in any official capacity at such a young age, and there is a track you must follow—assisting one of the current council members—but I am inviting you to travel down the road, if you would like to."

His eyes, not his voice, ask me the question.

The councilors are probably the same people who authorized the attack simulation and ensured that it was passed on to Jeanine at the right time. And he wants me to sit among them, learn to become them. Even though I can taste bile in the back of my mouth, I have no trouble answering.

"Of course," I say, and smile. "I would be honored."

If someone offers you an opportunity to get closer to your enemy, you always take it. I know that without having learned it from anyone.

He must believe my smile, because he grins.

"I thought you would say yes," he says. "It's something I wanted your mother to do with me, before she volunteered to enter the city. But I think she had fallen in love with the place from afar and couldn't resist it."

"Fallen in love . . . with the city?" I say. "No accounting for taste, I suppose."

It's just a joke, but my heart isn't in it. Still, David laughs, and I know I've said the right thing.

"You were . . . close with my mother, while she was here?" I say. "I've been reading her journal, but she's not very wordy."

"No, she wouldn't be, would she? Natalie was always very straightforward. Yes, we were close, your mother and I." His voice softens when he talks about her—he is no longer the toughened leader of this compound, but an old man, reflecting on some fonder past.

The past that happened before he got her killed.

"We had a similar history. I was also plucked right out of the damaged world as a child . . . my parents were severely dysfunctional people who were both taken to prison when I was young. Rather than succumbing to an adoption system overburdened with orphans, my siblings and I ran to the fringe—the same place where your mother also took refuge, years later—and only I came out of there alive."

I don't know what to say to that—I don't know what to do with the sympathy growing within me, for a man I know has done terrible things. I just stare at my hands, and I imagine that my insides are liquid metal hardening in the air, taking a shape they will never leave again.

"You'll have to go out there with our patrols tomorrow. You can see the fringe for yourself," he says. "It's something that's important for a future council member to see."

"I'd be very interested," I say.

"Lovely. Well, I hate to end our time together, but I have quite a bit of work to catch up on," he says. "I'll have someone notify you about the patrols, and our first council meeting is on Friday at ten in the morning, so I'll be seeing you soon."

I feel frantic—I didn't ask him what I wanted to ask him. I don't think there was ever an opportunity. It's too late now, anyway. I get up and move toward the doorway, but then he speaks again.

"Tris, I feel like I should be open with you, if we are to trust each other," he says.

For the first time since I've met him, David looks almost . . . afraid. His eyes are wide open, like a child's. But a moment later, the expression is gone.

"I may have been under the influence of a serum cocktail at the time," he says, "but I know what you said to them to keep them from shooting at us. I know you told them you would kill me to protect what was in the Weapons Lab."

My throat feels so tight I can hardly breathe.

"Don't be alarmed," he says. "It's one of the reasons why I offered you this opportunity."

"W-why?"

"You demonstrated the quality I most need in my advisers," he says. "Which is the ability to make sacrifices for the greater good. If we are going to win this fight against genetic damage, if we are going to save the experiments from being shut down, we will need to make sacrifices. You understand that, don't you?"

I feel a flash of anger and force myself to nod. Nita already told us that the experiments were in danger of being disbanded, so I am not surprised to hear it's true. But David's desperation to save his life's work doesn't excuse killing off a faction, *my* faction.

For a moment I stand with my hand on the doorknob, trying to gather myself together, and then I decide to take a risk.

"What would have happened, if they had set off another explosion to get into the Weapons Lab?" I say. "Nita said it would trigger a backup security measure if they did, but it seemed like the most obvious solution to their problem, to me."

"A serum would have been released into the air . . . one that masks could not have protected against, because it is absorbed into the skin," says David. "One that even the genetically pure cannot fight off. I don't know how Nita knows about it, since it's not supposed to be public knowledge, but I suppose we'll find out some other time."

"What does the serum do?"

His smile turns into a grimace. "Let's just say it's bad enough that Nita would rather be in prison for the rest of her life than come into contact with it."

He's right. He doesn't have to say anything more.

CHAPTER THIRTY-THREE

TOBIAS

"LOOK WHO IT is," Peter says as I walk into the dormitory. "The traitor."

There are maps spread across his cot and the one next to his. They are white and pale blue and dull green, and they draw me to them by some strange magnetism. On each one Peter has drawn a wobbly circle—around our city, around Chicago. He's marking the limits of where he's been.

I watch that circle shrink into each map, until it's just a bright red dot, like a drop of blood.

And then I back away, afraid of what it means that I am so small.

"If you think you're standing on some kind of moral

high ground, you're wrong," I say to Peter. "Why all the maps?"

"I'm having trouble wrapping my head around it, the size of the world," he says. "Some of the Bureau people have been helping me learn more about it. Planets and stars and bodies of water, things like that."

He says it casually, but I know from the frantic scribbling on maps that his interest isn't casual—it's obsessive. I was obsessive about my fears, once, in the same way, always trying to make sense of them, over and over again.

"Is it helping?" I say. I realize that I've never had a conversation with Peter that didn't involve yelling at him. Not that he didn't deserve it, but I don't know anything about him. I barely remember his last name from the initiate roster. Hayes. Peter Hayes.

"Sort of." He picks up one of the bigger maps. It shows the entire globe, pressed flat like kneaded dough. I stare at it long enough to make sense of the shapes on it, the blue stretches of water and the multicolored pieces of land. On one of the pieces is a red dot. He points at it. "That dot covers all the places we've ever been. You could cut that piece of land out of the ground and sink it into this ocean and no one would even notice."

I feel that fear again, the fear of my own size. "Right. So?"

"So? So everything I've ever worried about or said or

done, how can it possibly matter?" He shakes his head. "It doesn't."

"Of course it does," I say. "All that land is filled with people, every one of them different, and the things they do to each other matter."

He shakes his head again, and I wonder, suddenly, if this is how he comforts himself: by convincing himself that the bad things he's done don't matter. I see how the mammoth planet that terrifies me seems like a haven to him, a place where he can disappear into its great space, never distinguishing himself, and never being held responsible for his actions.

He bends over to untie his shoes. "So, have you been ostracized from your little crowd of devotees?"

"No," I say automatically. Then I add, "Maybe. But they aren't my devotees."

"Please. They're like the Cult of Four."

I can't help but laugh. "Jealous? Wish you had a Cult of Psychopaths to call your very own?"

One of his eyebrows twitches up. "If I was a psychopath, I would have killed you in your sleep by now."

"And added my eyeballs to your eyeball collection, no doubt."

Peter laughs too, and I realize that I am exchanging jokes and conversation with the initiate who stabbed

Edward in the eye and tried to kill my girlfriend—if she's still that. But then, he's also the Dauntless who helped us end the attack simulation and saved Tris from a horrible death. I am not sure which actions should weigh more heavily on my mind. Maybe I should forget them all, let him begin again.

"Maybe you should join my little group of hated people," says Peter. "So far Caleb and I are the only members, but given how easy it is to get on that girl's bad side, I'm sure our numbers will grow."

I stiffen. "You're right, it is easy to get on her bad side. All you have to do is try to get her killed."

My stomach clenches. *I* almost got her killed. If she had been standing closer to the explosion, she might be like Uriah, hooked up to tubes in the hospital, her mind quiet.

No wonder she doesn't know if she wants to stay with me or not.

The ease of a moment ago is gone. I cannot forget what Peter did, because he has not changed. He is still the same person who was willing to kill and maim and destroy to climb to the top of his initiate class. And I can't forget what I did either. I stand.

Peter leans against the wall and laces his fingers over his stomach. "I'm just saying, if she decides someone is worthless, everyone follows suit. That's a strange talent, for someone who used to be just another boring Stiff, isn't it? And maybe too much power for one person to have, right?"

"Her talent isn't for controlling other people's opinions," I say, "it's for usually being right about people."

He closes his eyes. "Whatever you say, Four."

All my limbs feel brittle with tension. I leave the dormitory and the maps with their red circles, though I'm not sure where else to go.

To me, Tris has always seemed magnetic in a way I could not describe, and that she was not aware of. I have never feared or hated her for it, the way Peter does, but then, I have always been in a position of strength myself, not threatened by her. Now that I have lost that position, I can feel the tug toward resentment, as strong and sure as a hand around my arm.

I find myself in the atrium garden again, and this time, light glows behind the windows. The flowers look beautiful and savage in the daylight, like vicious creatures suspended in time, motionless.

Cara jogs into the atrium, her hair askew and floating over her forehead. "There you are. It is frighteningly easy to lose people in this place."

"What is it?"

"Well—are you all right, Four?"

I bite down on my lip so hard I feel a pinch. "I'm fine. What is it?"

"We're having a meeting, and your presence is required."

"Who is 'we,' exactly?"

"GDs and GD sympathizers who don't want to let the Bureau get away with certain things," she says, and then she cocks her head to the side. "But better planners than the last ones you fell in with."

I wonder who told her. "You know about the attack simulation?"

"Better still, I recognized the simulation serum in the microscope when Tris showed it to me," Cara says. "Yes, I know."

I shake my head. "Well, I'm not getting involved in this again."

"Don't be a fool," she says. "The truth you heard is still true. These people are still responsible for the deaths of most of the Abnegation and the mental enslavement of the Dauntless and the utter destruction of our way of life, and something has to be done about them."

I'm not sure I want to be in the same room with Tris, knowing that we might be on the verge of ending, like standing on the edge of a cliff. It's easier to pretend it's not happening when I'm not around her. But Cara says it so simply I have to agree with her: yes, something has to be done.

She takes my hand and leads me down the hotel hallway. I know she's right, but I'm uncertain, uneasy about participating in another attempt at resistance. Still, I am already moving toward it, part of me eager for a chance to move again, instead of standing frozen before the surveillance footage of our city, as I have been.

When she's sure I'm following her, she releases my hand and tucks her stray hair behind her ears.

"It's still strange not to see you in blue," I say.

"It's time to let all that go, I think," she answers. "Even if I could go back, I wouldn't want to, at this point."

"You don't miss the factions?"

"I do, actually." She glances at me. Enough time has passed between Will's death and now that I no longer see him when I look at her, I just see Cara. I have known her far longer than I knew him. She has just a touch of his good-naturedness, enough to make me feel like I can tease her without offending her. "I thrived in Erudite. So many people devoted to discovery and innovation—it was lovely. But now that I know how large the world is . . . well. I suppose I have grown too large for my faction, as a consequence." She frowns. "I'm sorry, was that arrogant?"

"Who cares?"

"Some people do. It's nice to know you aren't one of them."

I notice, because I can't help it, that some of the people we pass on the way to the meeting give me nasty looks, or a wide berth. I have been hated and avoided before, as the son of Evelyn Johnson, factionless tyrant, but it bothers me more now. Now I know that I have done something to make myself worthy of that hatred; I have betrayed them all.

Cara says, "Ignore them. They don't know what it is to make a difficult decision."

"You wouldn't have done it, I bet."

"That is only because I have been taught to be cautious when I don't know all the information, and you have been taught that risks can produce great rewards." She looks at me sideways. "Or, in this case, no rewards."

She pauses at the door to the labs Matthew and his supervisor use, and knocks. Matthew tugs it open and takes a bite out of the apple he's holding. We follow him into the room where I found out I was not Divergent.

Tris is there, standing beside Christina, who looks at me like I am something rotten that needs to be discarded. And in the corner by the door is Caleb, his face stained with bruises. I am about to ask what happened to him when I realize that Tris's knuckles are also discolored, and that she very intentionally isn't looking at him.

Or at me.

"I think that's everyone," Matthew says. "Okay . . . so . . . um. Tris, I suck at this."

"You do, actually," she says with a grin. I feel a flare of jealousy. She clears her throat. "So, we know that these people are responsible for the attack on Abnegation, and that they can't be trusted to safeguard our city any longer. We know that we want to do something about it, and that the previous attempt to do something was . . ." Her eyes drift to mine, and her stare carves me into a smaller man. "Ill-advised," she finishes. "We can do better."

"What do you propose?" Cara says.

"All I know right now is that I want to expose them for what they are," Tris says. "The entire compound can't possibly know what their leaders have done, and I think we should show them. Maybe then they'll elect new leaders, ones who won't treat the people inside the experiments as expendable. I thought, maybe a widespread truth serum 'infection,' so to speak—"

I remember the weight of the truth serum, filling me in all my empty places, lungs and belly and face. I remember how impossible it seemed to me that Tris had lifted that weight enough to lie.

"Won't work," I say. "They're GPs, remember? GPs can resist truth serum."

"That's not necessarily true," Matthew says, pinching the string around his neck and then twisting it. "We don't see that many Divergent resisting truth serum. Just Tris, in recent memory. The capacity for serum resistance seems to be higher in some people than others—take yourself, for example, Tobias." Matthew shrugs. "Still, this is why I invited *you*, Caleb. You've worked on the serums before. You might know them as well as I do. Maybe we can develop a truth serum that is more difficult to resist."

"I don't want to do that kind of work anymore," Caleb says.

"Oh, shut—" starts Tris, but Matthew interrupts her.

"Please, Caleb," he says.

Caleb and Tris exchange a look. The skin on his face and on her knuckles is nearly the same color, purple-blue-green, as if drawn with ink. This is what happens when siblings collide—they injure each other the same way. Caleb sinks back against the countertop edge, touching the back of his head to the metal cabinets.

"Fine," Caleb says. "As long as you promise not to use this against me, Beatrice."

"Why would I?" Tris says.

"I can help," Cara says, lifting a hand. "I've worked on serums too, as an Erudite."

"Great." Matthew claps his hands together. "Meanwhile, Tris will be playing the spy."

"What about me?" Christina says.

"I was hoping you and Tobias could get in with Reggie," Tris says. "David wouldn't tell me about the backup security measures in the Weapons Lab, but Nita can't have been the only one who knew about them."

"You want me to get *in* with the guy who set off the explosives that put Uriah in a coma?" Christina says.

"You don't have to be friends," Tris says, "you just need to talk to him about what he knows. Tobias can help you."

"I don't need Four; I can do it myself," Christina says.

She shifts on the exam table, tearing the paper beneath her with her thigh, and gives me another sour look. I know it must be Uriah's blank face she sees when she looks at me. I feel like there is something stuck in my throat.

"You do need me, actually, because he already trusts me," I say. "And those people are very secretive, which means this will require subtlety."

"I can be subtle," Christina says.

"No, you can't."

"He's got a *point* . . ." Tris sings with a smile.

Christina smacks her arm, and Tris smacks her back.

"It's all settled, then," Matthew says. "I think we should meet again after Tris has been to the council meeting, which is on Friday. Come here at five."

He approaches Cara and Caleb and says something

about chemical compounds I don't quite understand. Christina walks out, bumping me with her shoulder as she leaves. Tris lifts her eyes to mine.

"We should talk," I say.

"Fine," she says, and I follow her into the hallway.

We stand next to the door until everyone else leaves. Her shoulders are drawn in like she's trying to make herself even smaller, trying to evaporate on the spot, and we stand too far apart, the entire width of the hallway between us. I try to remember the last time I kissed her and I can't.

Finally we're alone, and the hallway is quiet. My hands start to tingle and go numb, the way they always do when I panic.

"Do you think you'll ever forgive me?" I say.

She shakes her head, but says, "I don't know. I think that's what I need to figure out."

"You know . . . you *know* I never wanted Uriah to get hurt, right?" I look at the stitches crossing her forehead and I add, "Or you. I never wanted you to get hurt either."

She's tapping her foot, her body shifting with the movement. She nods. "I know that."

"I had to do something," I say. "I *had* to."

"A lot of people got hurt," she says. "All because you dismissed what I said, because—and this is the worst part, Tobias—because you thought I was being petty and *jealous*. Just some silly sixteen-year-old girl, right?" She shakes her head.

"I would never call you silly or petty," I say sternly. "I thought your judgment was clouded, yes. But that's all."

"That's enough." Her fingers slide through her hair and wrap around it. "It's just the same thing all over again, isn't it? You don't respect me as much as you say you do. When it comes down to it, you still believe I can't think rationally—"

"That is *not* what's happening!" I say hotly. "I respect you more than anyone. But right now I'm wondering what bothers you more, that I made a stupid decision or that I didn't make *your* decision."

"What's that supposed to mean?"

"It means," I say, "that you may have said you just wanted us to be honest with each other, but I think you really wanted me to always agree with you."

"I can't believe you would say that! You were *wrong*—"

"Yeah, I was wrong!" I'm shouting now, and I don't know where the anger came from, except that I can feel it swirling around inside me, violent and vicious and the strongest I have felt in days. "I was wrong, I made a huge mistake! My best friend's brother is as good as dead! And now you're acting like a parent, punishing me for it because I didn't do as I was told. Well, you are not my parent, Tris, and you don't get to tell me what to do, what to choose—!"

"Stop yelling at me," she says quietly, and she finally looks at me. I used to see all kinds of things in her eyes, love and longing and curiosity, but now all I see is anger. "Just stop."

Her quiet voice stalls the anger inside me, and I relax into the wall behind me, shoving my hands into my pockets. I didn't mean to yell at her. I didn't mean to get angry at all.

I stare, shocked, as tears touch her cheeks. I haven't seen her cry in a long time. She sniffs, and gulps, and tries to sound normal, but she doesn't.

"I just need some time," she says, choking on each word. "Okay?"

"Okay," I say.

She wipes her cheeks with her palms and walks down the hallway. I watch her blond head until it disappears around the bend, and I feel bare, like there's nothing left to protect me against pain. Her absence stings worst of all.

CHAPTER THIRTY-FOUR

TRIS

"THERE SHE IS," Amar says as I approach the group. "Here, I'll get you your vest, Tris."

"My . . . vest?" As promised by David yesterday, I'm going to the fringe this afternoon. I don't know what to expect, which usually makes me nervous, but I'm too worn-out from the past few days to feel much of anything.

"Bulletproof vest. The fringe is not all that safe," he says, and he reaches into a crate near the doors, sorting through a stack of thick black vests to find the right size. He emerges with one that still looks far too big for me. "Sorry, not much variety here. This will work just fine. Arms up."

He guides me into the vest and tightens the straps at my sides.

"I didn't know you would be here," I say.

"Well, what did you think I did at the Bureau? Just wandered around cracking jokes?" He smiles. "They found a good use for my Dauntless expertise. I'm part of the security team. So is George. We usually just handle compound security, but any time anyone wants to go to the fringe, I volunteer."

"Talking about me?" George, who was standing in the group by the doors. "Hi, Tris. I hope he's not saying anything bad."

George puts his arm across Amar's shoulders, and they grin at each other. George looks better than the last time I saw him, but grief leaves its mark on his expression, taking the crinkles out of the corners of his eyes when he smiles, taking the dimple from his cheek.

"I was thinking we should give her a gun," Amar says. He glances at me. "We don't normally give potential future council members weapons, because they have no clue how to use them, but it's pretty clear that you do."

"It's really all right," I say. "I don't need—"

"No, you're probably a better shot than most of them," George says. "We could use another Dauntless on board with us. Let me go get one."

A few minutes later I am armed and walking with Amar to the truck. He and I get in the far back, George and a woman named Ann get in the middle, and two older security officers named Jack and Violet get in the front. The back of the truck is covered with a hard black material. The back doors look opaque and black from the outside, but from the inside they're transparent, so we can see where we're going. I am nestled between Amar and stacks of equipment that block our view of the front of the truck. George peers over the equipment and grins when the truck starts, but other than that, it's just Amar and me.

I watch the compound disappear behind us. We drive through the gardens and outbuildings that surround it, and peeking out from behind the edge of the compound are the airplanes, white and stationary. We reach the fence, and the gates open for us. I hear Jack speaking to the soldier at the outer fence, telling him our plans and the contents of the vehicle—a series of words I don't understand—before we can be released into the wild.

I ask, "What's the purpose of this patrol? Beyond showing me how things work, I mean."

"We've always kept an eye on the fringe, which is the nearest genetically damaged area outside the compound. Mostly just research, studying how the genetically damaged behave," Amar says. "But after the attack, David and the council decided we needed more extensive surveillance set up there so we can prevent an attack from happening again."

We drive past the same kind of ruins I saw when we left the city—the buildings collapsing under their own weight, and the plants roaming wild over the land, breaking through concrete.

I don't know Amar, and I don't exactly trust him, but I have to ask:

"So you believe it all? All the stuff about genetic damage being the cause of . . . *this*?"

All his old friends in the experiment were GDs. Can he possibly believe that they're damaged, that there's something wrong with them?

"You don't?" Amar says. "The way I see it, the earth has been around for a long, long time. Longer than we can imagine. And before the Purity War, no one had ever done *this*, right?" He waves his hand to indicate the world outside.

"I don't know," I say. "I find it hard to believe that they didn't."

"Such a grim view of human nature you have," he says.

I don't respond.

He continues, "Anyway, if something like that had happened in our history, the Bureau would know about it."

That strikes me as naive, for someone who once lived in my city and saw, at least on the screens, how many secrets we kept from one another. Evelyn tried to control people by controlling weapons, but Jeanine was more ambitious—she knew that when you control information, or manipulate it, you don't need force to keep people under your thumb. They stay there willingly.

That is what the Bureau—and the entire government, probably—is doing: conditioning people to be happy under its thumb.

We ride in silence for a while, with just the sound of jiggling equipment and the engine to accompany us. At first I look at every building we pass, wondering what it once housed, and then they start to blend together for me. How many different kinds of ruin do you have to see before you resign yourself to calling it all "ruin"?

"We're almost at the fringe," George calls from the middle of the truck. "We're going to stop here and advance on foot. Everyone take some equipment and set it up—except Amar, who should just look after Tris. Tris, you're welcome to get out and have a look, but stay with Amar."

I feel like all my nerves are too close to the surface, and the slightest touch will make them fire. The fringe is where my mother retreated after witnessing a murder—it is where the Bureau found her and rescued her because they suspected her genetic code was sound. Now I will walk there, to the place where, in some ways, it all began.

The truck stops, and Amar shoves the doors open. He

holds his gun in one hand and beckons to me with the other. I jump out behind him.

There are buildings here, but they are not nearly as prominent as the makeshift homes, made of scrap metal and plastic tarps, piled up right next to one another like they are holding one another upright. In the narrow aisles between them are people, mostly children, selling things from trays, or carrying buckets of water, or cooking over open fires.

When the ones nearest to us see us, a young boy takes off running and screams, "Raid! Raid!"

"Don't worry about that," Amar says to me. "They think we're soldiers. Sometimes they raid to transport the kids to orphanages."

I barely acknowledge the comment. Instead I start walking down one of the aisles, as most people take off or shut themselves inside their lean-tos with cardboard or more tarp. I see them through the cracks between the walls, their houses not much more than a pile of food and supplies on one side and sleeping mats on the other. I wonder what they do in the winter. Or what they do for a toilet.

I think of the flowers inside the compound, and the wood floors, and all the beds in the hotel that are unoccupied, and say, "Do you ever help them?"

"We believe that the best way to help our world is to fix its genetic deficiencies," Amar says, like he's reciting it from memory. "Feeding people is just putting a tiny bandage on a gaping wound. It might stop the bleeding for a while, but ultimately the wound will still be there."

I can't respond. All I do is shake my head a little and keep walking. I am beginning to understand why my mother joined Abnegation when she was supposed to join Erudite. If she had really craved safety from Erudite's growing corruption, she could have gone to Amity or Candor. But she chose the faction where she could help the helpless, and dedicated most of her life to making sure the factionless were provided for.

They must have reminded her of this place, of the fringe.

I turn my head away from Amar so he won't see the tears in my eyes. "Let's go back to the truck."

"You all right?"

"Yeah."

We both turn around to head back to the truck, but then we hear gunshots.

And right after them, a shout. "Help!"

Everyone around us scatters.

"That's George," Amar says, and he takes off running down one of the aisles on our right. I chase him into the scrap-metal structures, but he's too quick for me, and this place is a maze—I lose him in seconds, and then I am alone.

As much automatic, Abnegation-bred sympathy as I have for the people living in this place, I am also afraid of them. If they are like the factionless, then they are surely desperate like the factionless, and I am wary of desperate people.

A hand closes around my arm and drags me backward, into one of the aluminum lean-tos. Inside everything is tinted blue from the tarp that covers the walls, insulating the structure against the cold. The floor is covered with plywood, and standing in front of me is a small, thin woman with a grubby face.

"You don't want to be out there," she says. "They'll lash out at anyone, no matter how young she is."

"They?" I say.

"Lots of angry people here in the fringe," the woman says. "Some people's anger makes them want to kill everyone they perceive as an enemy. Some people's makes them more constructive."

"Well, thank you for the help," I say. "My name is Tris."

"Amy. Sit."

"I can't," I say. "My friends are out there."

"Then you should wait until the hordes of people run

to wherever your friends are, and then sneak up on them from behind."

That sounds smart.

I sink to the floor, my gun digging into my leg. The bulletproof vest is so stiff it's hard to get comfortable, but I do the best I can to seem relaxed. I hear people running outside and shouting. Amy flicks the corner of the tarp back to see outside.

"So you and your friends aren't soldiers," Amy says, still looking outside. "Which means you must be Genetic Welfare types, right?"

"No," I say. "I mean, they are, but I'm from the city. I mean, Chicago."

Amy's eyebrows pop up high. "Damn. Has it been disbanded?"

"Not yet."

"That's unfortunate."

"Unfortunate?" I frown at her. "That's my home you're talking about, you know."

"Well your home is perpetuating the belief that genetically damaged people need to be fixed—that they're *damaged*, period, which they—we—are not. So yes, it's unfortunate that the experiments still exist. I won't apologize for saying so."

I hadn't thought about it that way. To me Chicago has

to keep existing because the people I have lost lived there, because the way of life I once loved continues there, though in a broken form. But I didn't realize that Chicago's very existence could be harmful to people outside who just want to be thought of as whole.

"It's time for you to go," Amy says, dropping the corner of the tarp. "They're probably in one of the meeting areas, northwest of here."

"Thank you again," I say.

She nods to me, and I duck out of her makeshift home, the boards creaking beneath my feet.

I move through the aisles, fast, glad that all the people scattered when we arrived so there is no one to block my way. I jump over a puddle of—well, I don't want to know what it is—and emerge into a kind of courtyard, where a tall, gangly boy has a gun pointed at George.

A small crowd of people surrounds the boy with the gun. They have distributed among them the surveillance equipment George was carrying, and they're destroying it, hitting it with shoes or rocks or hammers.

George's eyes shift to me, but I touch a finger to my lips, hastily. I am behind the crowd now; the one with the gun doesn't know I'm there.

"Put the gun down," George says.

"No!" the boy answers. His pale eyes keep shifting

from George to the people around him and back. "Went to a lot of trouble to get this, not gonna give it to you now."

"Then just . . . let me go. You can keep it."

"Not until you tell us where you've been taking our people!" the boy says.

"We haven't taken any of your people," George says. "We're not soldiers. We're just scientists."

"Yeah, right," the boy says. "A bulletproof vest? If that's not soldier shit, then I'm the richest kid in the States. Now tell me what I need to know!"

I move back so I'm standing behind one of the lean-tos, then put my gun around the edge of the structure and say, "Hey!"

Everyone in the crowd turns at once, but the boy with the gun doesn't stop aiming at George, like I'd hoped.

"I've got you in my sights," I say. "Leave now and I'll let you go."

"I'll shoot him!" the boy says.

"I'll shoot *you*," I say. "We're with the government, but we aren't soldiers. We don't know where your people are. If you let him go, we'll all leave quietly. If you kill him, I guarantee there *will* be soldiers here soon to arrest you, and they won't be as forgiving as we are."

At that moment Amar emerges into the courtyard behind George, and someone in the crowd screeches,

"There are more of them!" And everyone scatters. The boy with the gun dives into the nearest aisle, leaving George, Amar, and me alone. Still, I keep my gun up by my face, in case they decide to come back.

Amar wraps his arms around George, and George thumps his back with a fist. Amar looks at me, his face over George's shoulder. "Still don't think genetic damage is to blame for any of these troubles?"

I walk past one of the lean-tos and see a little girl crouching just inside the door, her arms wrapped around her knees. She sees me through the crack in the layered tarps and whimpers a little. I wonder who taught these people to be so terrified of soldiers. I wonder what made a young boy desperate enough to aim a gun at one of them.

"No," I say. "I don't."

I have better people to blame.

+++

By the time we get back to the truck, Jack and Violet are setting up a surveillance camera that wasn't stolen by people in the fringe. Violet has a screen in her hands with a long list of numbers on it, and she reads them to Jack, who programs them into his screen.

"Where have you guys been?" he says.

"We were attacked," George says. "We have to leave, now."

"Luckily, that's the last set of coordinates," Violet says. "Let's get going."

We pile into the truck again. Amar draws the doors shut behind us, and I set my gun on the floor with the safety on, glad to be rid of it. I didn't think I would be aiming a dangerous weapon at someone today when I woke up. I didn't think I would witness those kinds of living conditions, either.

"It's the Abnegation in you," Amar says. "That makes you hate that place. I can tell."

"It's a lot of things in me."

"It's just something I noticed in Four, too. Abnegation produces deeply serious people. People who automatically see things like need," he says. "I've noticed that when people switch to Dauntless, it creates some of the same types. Erudite who switch to Dauntless tend to turn cruel and brutal. Candor who switch to Dauntless tend to become boisterous, fight-picking adrenaline junkies. And Abnegation who switch to Dauntless become . . . I don't know, soldiers, I guess. Revolutionaries.

"That's what he could be, if he trusted himself more," he adds. "If Four wasn't so plagued with self-doubt, he would be one hell of a leader, I think. I've always thought that."

"I think you're right," I say. "It's when he's a follower

that he gets himself into trouble. Like with Nita. Or Evelyn."

What about you? I ask myself. *You wanted to make him a follower too.*

No, I didn't, I tell myself, but I'm not sure if I believe it.

Amar nods.

Images from the fringe keep rising up inside me like hiccups. I imagine the child my mother was, crouched in one of those lean-tos, scrambling for weapons because they meant an ounce of safety, choking on smoke to keep warm in the winter. I don't know why she was so willing to abandon that place after she was rescued. She became absorbed into the compound, and then worked on its behalf for the rest of her life. Did she forget about where she came from?

She couldn't have. She spent her entire life trying to help the factionless. Maybe it wasn't a fulfillment of her duty as an Abnegation—maybe it came from a desire to help people like the ones she had left.

Suddenly I can't stand to think of her, or that place, or the things I saw there. I grab on to the first thought that comes to my mind, to distract myself.

"So you and Tobias were good friends?"

"Is anyone good friends with him?" Amar shakes his head. "I gave him his nickname, though. I watched him face his fears and I saw how troubled he was, and I figured he could use a new life, so I started calling him 'Four.' But no, I wouldn't say we were good friends. Not as good as I wanted to be."

Amar leans his head back against the wall and closes his eyes. A small smile curls his lips.

"Oh," I say. "Did you . . . *like* him?"

"Now why would you ask that?"

I shrug. "Just the way you talk about him."

"I don't *like* him anymore, if that's what you're really asking. But yes, at one time I did, and it was clear that he did not return that particular sentiment, so I backed off," Amar says. "I'd prefer it if you didn't say anything."

"To Tobias? Of course I won't."

"No, I mean, don't say anything to anyone. And I'm not talking about just the thing with Tobias."

He looks at the back of George's head, now visible above the considerably diminished pile of equipment.

I raise an eyebrow at him. I'm not surprised he and George were drawn to each other. They're both Divergent who had to fake their own deaths to survive. Both outsiders in an unfamiliar world.

"You have to understand," Amar says. "The Bureau is obsessed with procreation—with passing on genes. And George and I are both GPs, so any entanglement that can't produce a stronger genetic code . . . It's not encouraged, that's all."

"Ah." I nod. "You don't have to worry about me. I'm not obsessed with producing strong genes." I smile wryly.

"Thank you," he says.

For a few seconds we sit quietly, watching the ruins turn to a blur as the truck picks up speed.

"I think you're good for Four, you know," he says.

I stare at my hands, curled in my lap. I don't feel like explaining to him that we're on the verge of breaking up—I don't know him, and even if I did, I wouldn't want to talk about it. All I can manage to say is, "Oh?"

"Yeah. I can see what you bring out in him. You don't know this because you've never experienced it, but Four without you is a much different person. He's . . . obsessive, explosive, insecure . . ."

"Obsessive?"

"What else do you call someone who repeatedly goes through his own fear landscape?"

"I don't know . . . determined." I pause. "Brave."

"Yeah, sure. But also a little bit crazy, right? I mean, most Dauntless would rather leap into the chasm than keep going through their fear landscapes. There's bravery and then there's masochism, and the line got a little hazy with him."

"I'm familiar with the line," I say.

"I know." Amar grins. "Anyway, all I'm saying is, any time you mash two different people against each other, you'll get problems, but I can see that what you guys have is worthwhile, that's all."

I wrinkle my nose. "*Mash* people against each other, really?"

Amar presses his palms together and twists them back and forth, to illustrate. I laugh, but I can't ignore the achy feeling in my chest.

CHAPTER THIRTY-FIVE

Tobias

I WALK TO the cluster of chairs closest to the windows in the control room and bring up the footage from different cameras throughout the city, one by one, searching for my parents. I find Evelyn first—she is in the lobby of Erudite headquarters, talking in a close huddle with Therese and a factionless man, her second and third in command now that I am gone. I turn up the volume on the microphone, but I still can't hear anything but muttering.

Through the windows along the back of the control room, I see the same empty night sky as the one above the city, interrupted only by small blue and red lights marking the runways for airplanes. It's strange to think we have that in common when everything else is so different here.

By now the people in the control room know that I was the one who disabled the security system the night before the attack, though I wasn't the one who slipped one of their night shift workers peace serum so that I could do it—that was Nita. But for the most part, they ignore me, as long as I stay away from their desks.

On another screen, I scroll through the footage again, looking for Marcus or Johanna, anything that can show me what's happening with the Allegiant. Every part of the city shows up on the screen, the bridge near the Merciless Mart and the Pire and the main thoroughfare of the Abnegation sector, the Hub and the Ferris wheel and the Amity fields, now worked by all the factions. But none of the cameras shows me anything.

"You've been coming here a lot," Cara says as she approaches. "Are you afraid of the rest of the compound? Or of something else?"

She's right, I have been coming to the control room a lot. It's just something to pass the time as I wait for my sentence from Tris, as I wait for our plan to strike the Bureau to come together, as I wait for something, *anything.*

"No," I say. "I'm just keeping an eye on my parents."

"The parents you hate?" She stands next to me, her arms folded. "Yes, I can see why you would want to spend every waking hour staring at people you want nothing to do with. It makes perfect sense."

"They're dangerous," I say. "More dangerous because no one else knows how dangerous they are but me."

"And what are you going to do from here, if they do something terrible? Send a smoke signal?"

I glare at her.

"Fine, fine." She puts up her hands in surrender. "I'm just trying to remind you that you aren't in their world anymore, you're in this one. That's all."

"Point taken."

I never thought of the Erudite as being particularly perceptive about relationships, or emotions, but Cara's discerning eyes see all kinds of things. My fear. My search for a distraction in my past. It's almost alarming.

I scroll past one of the camera angles and then pause, and scroll back. The scene is dark, because of the hour, but I see people alighting like a flock of birds around a building I don't recognize, their movements synchronized.

"They're doing it," Cara says, excited. "The Allegiant are actually attacking."

"Hey!" I shout to one of the women at the control room desks. The older one, who always gives me a nasty look when I show up, lifts her head. "Camera twenty-four! Hurry!"

She taps her screen, and everyone milling around the

surveillance area gathers around her. People passing by in the hallway stop to see what's happening, and I turn to Cara.

"Can you go get the others?" I say. "I think they should see this."

She nods, her eyes wild, and rushes away from the control room.

The people around the unfamiliar building wear no uniform to distinguish them, but they don't wear factionless armbands either, and they carry guns. I try to pick out a face, anything I recognize, but the footage is too blurry. I watch them arrange themselves, motioning to one another to communicate, dark arms waving in the darker night.

I wedge my thumbnail between my teeth, impatient for something, anything to happen. A few minutes later Cara arrives with the others at her back. When they reach the crowd of people around the primary screens, Peter says, "Excuse me!" loud enough to make people turn around. When they see who he is, they part for him.

"What's up?" Peter says to me when he's closer. "What's going on?"

"The Allegiant have formed an army," I say, pointing at the screen on the left. "There are people from every faction in it, even Amity and Erudite. I've been watching a lot lately."

"Erudite?" Caleb says.

"The Allegiant are the enemies of the new enemies, the factionless," Cara replies. "Which gives the Erudite and the Allegiant a common goal: to usurp Evelyn."

"Did you say there were Amity in an *army*?" Christina asks me.

"They're not really participating in the violence," I say. "But they are participating in the effort."

"The Allegiant raided their first weapons storehouse a few days ago," the young woman sitting at the control room desk nearest to us says over her shoulder. "This is their second. That's where they got those weapons. After the first raid, Evelyn had most of the weapons relocated, but this storehouse didn't make it in time."

My father knows what Evelyn knew: that the power to make people fear you is the only power you need. Weapons will do that for him.

"What's their goal?" Caleb says.

"The Allegiant are motivated by the desire to return to our original purpose in the city," Cara says. "Whether that means sending a group of people outside of it, as instructed by Edith Prior—which we thought was important at the time, though I've since learned that her instructions didn't really matter—or reinstating the factions by force. They're building up to an attack on the factionless stronghold. That's what Johanna and I discussed before I left. We did *not* discuss allying with your father, Tobias, but I suppose she's capable of making her own decisions."

I almost forgot that Cara was the leader of the Allegiant, before we left. Now I'm not sure she cares whether the factions survive or not, but she still cares about the people. I can tell by the way she watches the screens, eager but afraid.

Even over the chatter of the people around us, I hear the gunfire when it starts, just snaps and claps in the microphones. I tap the glass in front of me a few times, and the camera angle switches to one inside the building the invaders have just forced their way into. On a table within is a pile of small boxes—ammunition—and a few pistols. It's nothing compared to the guns the people here have, in all their abundance, but in the city, I know it's valuable.

Several men and women with factionless armbands guard the table, but they are falling fast, outnumbered by the Allegiant. I recognize a familiar face among them—Zeke, slamming the butt of his gun into a factionless man's jaw. The factionless are overcome within two minutes, falling to bullets I see only when they're already buried in flesh. The Allegiant spread through the room, stepping over bodies like they are just more debris, and gather everything they can. Zeke piles stray guns on the table, a hard look on his face that I've only seen a few times.

He doesn't even know what happened to Uriah.

The woman at the desk taps the screen in a few places. On one of the smaller screens above her is an image—a piece of the surveillance footage we just watched, frozen at a particular moment in time. She taps again, and the image moves closer to its targets, a man with close-cropped hair and a woman with long, dark hair covering one side of her face.

Marcus, of course. And Johanna—carrying a gun.

"Between them, they have managed to rally most of the loyal faction members to their cause. Surprisingly, though, the Allegiant still don't outnumber the factionless." The woman leans back in her chair and shakes her head. "There were far more factionless than we ever anticipated. It's difficult to get an accurate population count on a scattered population, after all."

"Johanna? Leading a rebellion? With a weapon? That makes no sense," Caleb says.

Johanna told me once that if the decisions had been up to her, she would have supported action against Erudite instead of the passivity the rest of her faction advocated. But she was at the mercy of her faction and their fear. Now, with the factions disbanded, it seems she has become something other than the mouthpiece of Amity or even the leader of the Allegiant. She has become a soldier.

"Makes more sense than you'd think," I say, and Cara nods along with my words.

I watch them empty the room of weapons and ammunition and move on, fast, scattering like seeds on the wind. I feel heavier, like I am bearing a new burden. I wonder if the people around me—Cara, Christina, Peter, even Caleb—feel the same way. The city, our city, is even closer to total destruction than it was before.

We can pretend that we don't belong there anymore, while we're living in relative safety in this place, but we do. We always will.

CHAPTER THIRTY-SIX

Tris

It's dark and snowing when we drive up to the entrance of the compound. The flakes blow across the road, as light as powdered sugar. It's just an early autumn snow; it will be gone in the morning. I take off my bulletproof vest as soon as I get out, and offer it to Amar along with my gun. I'm uncomfortable holding it now, and I used to think that my discomfort would go away with time, but now I'm not so sure. Maybe it never will, and maybe that's all right.

Warm air surrounds me as I pass through the doors. The compound looks cleaner than ever before, now that I've seen the fringe. The comparison is unsettling. How can I walk these squeaky floors and wear these starchy clothes when I know that those people are out there, wrapping their houses in tarp to stay warm?

But by the time I reach the hotel dormitory, the unsettled feeling is gone.

I scan the room for Christina, or for Tobias, but neither of them is there. Only Peter and Caleb are, Peter with a large book on his lap, scribbling notes on a nearby notepad, and Caleb reading our mother's journal on the screen, his eyes glassy. I try to ignore that.

"Have either of you seen . . ." But who do I want to talk to, Christina or Tobias?

"Four?" Caleb says, deciding for me. "I saw him in the genealogy room earlier."

"The . . . what room?"

"They have our ancestors' names on display in a room. Can I get a piece of paper?" he asks Peter.

Peter tears a sheet from the back of his notepad and hands it to Caleb, who scribbles something on it—directions. Caleb says, "I found our parents' names there earlier. On the right side of the room, second panel from the door."

He hands me the directions without looking at me. I look at his neat, even letters. Before I punched him, Caleb would have insisted on walking me himself, desperate for time to explain himself to me. But recently he has kept his distance, either because he's afraid of me or because he has finally given up.

Neither option makes me feel good.

"Thank you," I say. "Um . . . how's your nose?"

"It's fine," he says. "I think the bruise really brings out my eyes, don't you?"

He smiles a little, and so do I. But it's clear that neither of us knows what to do from here, because we've both run out of words.

"Wait, you were gone today, right?" he says after a second. "Something's happening in the city. The Allegiant rose up against Evelyn, attacked one of her weapons storehouses."

I stare at him. I haven't wondered about what was happening in the city for a few days now; I've been too wrapped up in what's happening here.

"The Allegiant?" I say. "The people currently led by *Johanna Reyes* . . . attacked a storehouse?"

Before we left, I was sure the city was about to explode into another conflict. I guess now it has. But I feel detached from it—almost everyone I care about is here.

"Led by Johanna Reyes and Marcus Eaton," Caleb says. "But Johanna was there, holding a gun. It was ludicrous. The Bureau people seemed really disturbed by it."

"Wow." I shake my head. "I guess it was just a matter of time."

We lapse into silence again, then walk away from each other at the same time, Caleb returning to his cot and me walking down the hallway, following Caleb's directions.

I see the genealogy room from a distance. The bronze walls seem to glow with warm light. Standing in the doorway, I feel like I am inside a sunset, the radiance surrounding me. Tobias's finger runs along the lines of his family tree—I assume—but idly, like he's not really paying attention to it.

I feel like I can see that obsessive streak Amar was referring to. I know that Tobias has been watching his parents on the screens, and now he is staring at their names, though there's nothing in this room he didn't already know. I was right to say that he was desperate, desperate for a connection to Evelyn, desperate not to be damaged, but I never thought about how those things were connected. I don't know how it would feel, to hate your own history and to crave love from the people who gave that history to you at the same time. How have I never seen the schism inside his heart? How have I never realized before that for all the strong, kind parts of him, there are also hurting, broken parts?

Caleb told me that our mother said there was evil in everyone, and the first step to loving someone else is to recognize that evil in ourselves, so we can forgive them.

So how can I hold Tobias's desperation against him, like I'm better than him, like I've never let my own brokenness blind me?

"Hey," I say, crushing Caleb's directions into my back pocket.

He turns, and his expression is stern, familiar. It looks the way it did the first few weeks I knew him, like a sentry guarding his innermost thoughts.

"Listen," I say. "I thought I was supposed to figure out if I could forgive you or not, but now I'm thinking you didn't do anything to me that I need to forgive, except maybe accusing me of being jealous of Nita. . . ."

He opens his mouth to interject, but I hold up a hand to stop him.

"If we stay together, I'll have to forgive you over and over again, and if you're still in this, you'll have to forgive me over and over again too," I say. "So forgiveness isn't the point. What I really should have been trying to figure out is whether we were still good for each other or not."

All the way home I thought about what Amar said, about every relationship having its problems. I thought about my parents, who argued more often than any other Abnegation parents I knew, who nonetheless went through each day together until they died.

Then I thought of how strong I have become, how

secure I feel with the person I now am, and how all along the way he has told me that I am brave, I am respected, I am loved and worth loving.

"And?" he says, his voice and his eyes and his hands a little unsteady.

"And," I say, "I think you're still the only person sharp enough to sharpen someone like me."

"I am," he says roughly.

And I kiss him.

His arms slip around me and hold me tight, lifting me onto the tips of my toes. I bury my face in his shoulder and close my eyes, just breathing in the clean smell of him, the smell of wind.

I used to think that when people fell in love, they just landed where they landed, and they had no choice in the matter afterward. And maybe that's true of beginnings, but it's not true of this, now.

I fell in love with him. But I don't just stay with him by default as if there's no one else available to me. I stay with him because I choose to, every day that I wake up, every day that we fight or lie to each other or disappoint each other. I choose him over and over again, and he chooses me.

CHAPTER THIRTY-SEVEN

Tris

I ARRIVE AT David's office for my first council meeting just as my watch shifts to ten, and he pushes himself into the hallway soon afterward. He looks even paler than he did the last time I saw him, and the dark circles under his eyes are pronounced, like bruises.

"Hello, Tris," he says. "Eager, are you? You're right on time."

I still feel a little weight in my limbs from the truth serum Cara, Caleb, and Matthew tested on me earlier, as part of our plan. They're trying to develop a powerful truth serum, one that even GPs as serum-resistant as I am are not immune to. I ignore the heavy feeling and say, "Of course I'm eager. It's my first meeting. Want help? You look tired."

"Fine, fine."

I move behind him and press into the handles of the wheelchair to get it moving.

He sighs. "I suppose I am tired. I was up all night dealing with our most recent crisis. Take a left here."

"What crisis is that?"

"Oh, you'll find out soon enough, let's not rush it."

We maneuver through the dim hallways of Terminal 5, as it is labeled—"an old name," David says—which have no windows, no hint of the world outside. I can almost feel the paranoia emanating from the walls, like the terminal itself is terrified of unfamiliar eyes. If only they knew what *my* eyes were searching for.

As I walk, I get a glimpse of David's hands, pressed to the armrests. The skin around his fingernails is raw and red, like he chewed it away overnight. The fingernails themselves are jagged. I remember when my own hands looked that way, when the memories of fear simulations crept into every dream and every idle thought. Maybe it's David's memories of the attack that are doing this to him.

I don't care, I think. *Remember what he did. What he would do again.*

"Here we are," David says. I push him through a set of double doors, propped open with doorstops. Most of the council members seem to be there, stirring tiny sticks in tiny cups of coffee, the majority of them men and women David's age. There are some younger members—Zoe is there, and she gives me a strained, but polite, smile when I walk in.

"Let's come to order!" David says as he wheels himself to the head of the conference table. I sit in one of the chairs along the edge of the room, next to Zoe. It's clear we're not supposed to be at the table with all the important people, and I'm okay with that—it'll be easier to doze off if things get boring, though if this new crisis is serious enough to keep David awake at night, I doubt it will.

"Last night I received a frantic call from the people in our control room," David says. "Evidently Chicago is about to erupt into violence again. Faction loyalists calling themselves the Allegiant have rebelled against factionless control, attacking weapons safe houses. What they don't know is that Evelyn Johnson has discovered a new weapon—stores of death serum kept hidden in Erudite headquarters. As we know, no one is capable of resisting death serum, not even the Divergent. If the Allegiant attack the factionless government, and Evelyn Johnson retaliates, the casualties will obviously be catastrophic."

I stare at the floor in front of my feet as the room bursts into conversation.

"Quiet," says David. "The experiments are already in

danger of being shut down if we cannot prove to our superiors that we are capable of controlling them. Another revolution in Chicago would only cement their belief that this endeavor has outlived its usefulness—something we cannot allow to happen if we want to continue to fight genetic damage."

Somewhere behind David's exhausted, haggard expression is something harder, stronger. I believe him. I believe that he will not allow it to happen.

"It's time to use the memory serum virus for a mass reset," he says. "And I think we should use it against all four experiments."

"*Reset* them?" I say, because I can't help myself. Everyone in the room looks at me at once. They seem to have forgotten that I, a former member of the experiments they're referring to, am in the room.

"'Resetting' is our word for widespread memory erasure," David says. "It is what we do when the experiments that incorporate behavioral modification are in danger of falling apart. We did it when we first created each experiment that had a behavioral modification component, and the last one in Chicago was done a few generations before yours." He gives me an odd smile. "Why did you think there was so much physical devastation in the factionless sector? There was an uprising, and we had to quell it as cleanly as possible."

I sit stunned in my chair, picturing the broken roads and shattered windows and toppled streetlights in the factionless sector of the city, the destruction that is evident nowhere else—not even north of the bridge, where the buildings are empty but seem to have been vacated peacefully. I always just took the broken-down sectors of Chicago in stride, as evidence of what happens when people are without community. I never dreamed that they were the result of an uprising—and a subsequent *resetting*.

I feel sick with anger. That they want to stop a revolution, not to save lives, but to save their precious experiment, would be enough. But why do they believe they have the right to rip people's memories, their identities, out of their heads, just because it's convenient for them?

But of course, I know the answer to that question. To them, the people in our city are just containers of genetic material—just GDs, valuable for the corrected genes they pass on, and not for the brains in their heads or the hearts in their chests.

"When?" one of the council members says.

"Within the next forty-eight hours," David says.

Everyone nods as if this is sensible.

I remember what he said to me in his office. *If we are*

going to win this fight against genetic damage, we will need to make sacrifices. You understand that, don't you? I should have known, then, that he would gladly trade thousands of GD memories—lives—for control of the experiments. That he would trade them without even thinking of alternatives—without feeling like he needed to bother to save them.

They're *damaged*, after all.

CHAPTER THIRTY-EIGHT

TOBIAS

I PROP UP my shoe on the edge of Tris's bed and tighten the laces. Through the large windows I see afternoon light winking in the side panels of the parked airplanes on the landing strip. GDs in green suits walk across the wings and crawl under the noses, checking the planes before takeoff.

"How's your project with Matthew going?" I say to Cara, who is two beds away. Tris let Cara, Caleb, and Matthew test their new truth serum on her this morning, but I haven't seen her since then.

Cara is pushing a brush through her hair. She glances around the room to make sure it's empty before she answers. "Not well. So far Tris was immune to the new version of the serum we created—it had no effect whatsoever. It's very strange that a person's genes would make them so resistant to mind manipulation of any kind."

"Maybe it's not her genes," I say, shrugging. I switch feet. "Maybe it's some kind of superhuman stubbornness."

"Oh, are we at the insult part of the breakup?" she says. "Because I got in a lot of practice after what happened with Will. I have several choice things to say about her nose."

"We didn't break up." I grin. "But it's nice to know you have such warm feelings for my girlfriend."

"I apologize, I don't know why I jumped to that conclusion." Cara's cheeks flush. "My feelings toward your girlfriend are mixed, yes, but for the most part I have a lot of respect for her."

"I know. I was just kidding. It's nice to see you get flustered every once in a while."

Cara glares at me.

"Besides," I say, "what's wrong with her nose?"

The door to the dormitory opens, and Tris walks in, hair unkempt and eyes wild. It unsettles me to see her so agitated, like the ground I'm standing on is no longer solid. I get up and smooth my hand over her hair to put it back into place. "What happened?" I say, my hand coming to rest on her shoulder.

"Council meeting," Tris says. She covers my hand with hers, briefly, then sits on one of the beds, her hands dangling between her knees.

"I hate to be repetitive," Cara says, "but . . . what happened?"

Tris shakes her head like she's trying to shake the dust out of it. "The council has made plans. Big ones."

She tells us, in fits and starts, about the council's plan to reset the experiments. As she speaks she wedges her hands under her legs and presses forward into them until her wrists turn red.

When she finishes I move to sit beside her, putting my arm across her shoulders. I look out the window, at the planes perched on the runway, gleaming and poised for flight. In less than two days those planes will probably drop the memory serum virus over the experiments.

Cara says to Tris, "What do you intend to do about it?"

"I don't know," Tris says. "I feel like I don't know what's right anymore."

They're similar, Cara and Tris, two women sharpened by loss. The difference is that Cara's pain has made her certain of everything, and Tris has guarded her uncertainty, protected it, despite all she's been through. She still approaches everything with a question instead of an answer. It is something I admire about her—something I should probably admire more.

For a few seconds we stew in silence, and I follow the path of my thoughts as they turn over and over one another.

"They can't do this," I say. "They can't erase everyone. They shouldn't have the power to do that." I pause. "All I can think is that this would be so much easier if we were dealing with a completely different set of people who could actually see *reason*. Then we might be able to find a balance between protecting the experiments and opening themselves up to other possibilities."

"Maybe we should import a new group of scientists," Cara says, sighing. "And discard the old ones."

Tris's face twists, and she touches a hand to her forehead, as if rubbing out some brief and inconvenient pain. "No," she says. "We don't even need to do that."

She looks up at me, her bright eyes holding me still.

"Memory serum," she says. "Alan and Matthew came up with a way to make the serums behave like viruses, so they could spread through an entire population without injecting everyone. That's how they're planning to reset the experiments. But we could reset *them*." She speaks faster as the idea takes shape in her mind, and her excitement is contagious; it bubbles inside me like the idea is mine and not hers. But to me it doesn't feel like she's suggesting a solution to our problem. It feels like she's suggesting that we cause yet another problem. "Reset the Bureau, and reprogram them without the propaganda, without the disdain for GDs. Then they'll never risk the memories of the people in the experiments again. The danger will be gone forever."

Cara raises her eyebrows. "Wouldn't erasing their memories also erase all of their knowledge? Thus rendering them useless?"

"I don't know. I think there's a way to target memories, depending on where the knowledge is stored in the brain, otherwise the first faction members wouldn't have known how to speak or tie their shoes or anything." Tris comes to her feet. "We should ask Matthew. He knows how it works better than I do."

I get up too, putting myself in her path. The streaks of sun caught on the airplane wings blind me so I can't see her face.

"Tris," I say. "Wait. You really want to erase the memories of a whole population against their will? That's the same thing *they're* planning to do to our friends and family."

I shield my eyes from the sun to see her cold look—the expression I saw in my mind even before I looked at her. She looks older to me than she ever has, stern and tough and worn by time. I feel that way, too.

"These people have no regard for human life," she says. "They're about to wipe the memories of all our friends and neighbors. They're responsible for the deaths of a large majority of our old faction." She sidesteps me and marches toward the door. "I think they're lucky I'm not going to kill them."

CHAPTER THIRTY-NINE

TRIS

MATTHEW CLASPS HIS hands behind his back.

"No, no, the serum doesn't erase all of a person's knowledge," he says. "Do you think we would design a serum that makes people forget how to speak or walk?" He shakes his head. "It targets explicit memories, like your name, where you grew up, your first teacher's name, and leaves implicit memories—like how to speak or tie your shoes or ride a bicycle—untouched."

"Interesting," Cara says. "That actually works?"

Tobias and I exchange a look. There's nothing like a conversation between an Erudite and someone who may as well be an Erudite. Cara and Matthew are standing too close together, and the longer they talk, the more hand gestures they make.

"Inevitably, some important memories will be lost," Matthew says. "But if we have a record of people's scientific discoveries or histories, they can relearn them in the hazy period after their memories are erased. People are very pliable then."

I lean against the wall.

"Wait," I say. "If the Bureau is going to load all of those planes with the memory serum virus to reset the experiments, will there be any serum left to use against the compound?"

"We'll have to get it first," Matthew says. "In less than forty-eight hours."

Cara doesn't appear to hear what I said. "After you erase their memories, won't you have to program them with new memories? How does that work?"

"We just have to reteach them. As I said, people tend to be disoriented for a few days after being reset, which means they'll be easier to control." Matthew sits, and spins in his chair once. "We can just give them a new history class. One that teaches facts rather than propaganda."

"We could use the fringe's slide show to supplement a basic history lesson," I say. "They have photographs of a war caused by GPs."

"Great." Matthew nods. "Big problem, though. The memory serum virus is in the Weapons Lab. The one Nita just tried—and *failed*—to break into."

"Christina and I were supposed to talk to Reggie," Tobias says, "but I think, given this new plan, we should talk to Nita instead."

"I think you're right," I say. "Let's go find out where she went wrong."

+++

When I first arrived here, I felt like the compound was huge and unknowable. Now I don't even have to consult the signs to remember how to get to the hospital, and neither does Tobias, who keeps stride with me on the way. It's strange how time can make a place shrink, make its strangeness ordinary.

We don't say anything to each other, though I can feel a conversation brewing between us. Finally I decide to ask.

"What's wrong?" I say. "You hardly said anything during the meeting."

"I just . . ." He shakes his head. "I'm not sure this is the right thing to do. They want to erase our friends' memories, so we decide to erase theirs?"

I turn to him and touch his shoulders lightly. "Tobias, we have forty-eight hours to stop them. If you can think of any other idea, anything else that could save our city, I'm open to it."

"I can't." His dark blue eyes look defeated, sad. "But we're acting out of desperation to save something that's important to us—just like the Bureau is. What's the difference?"

"The difference is what's right," I say firmly. "The people in the city, as a whole, are innocent. The people in the Bureau, who supplied Jeanine with the attack simulation, are not innocent."

His mouth puckers, and I can tell he doesn't completely buy it.

I sigh. "It's not a perfect situation. But when you have to choose between two bad options, you pick the one that saves the people you love and believe in most. You just do. Okay?"

He reaches for my hand, his hand warm and strong. "Okay."

"Tris!" Christina pushes through the swinging doors to the hospital and jogs toward us. Peter is on her heels, his dark hair combed smoothly to the side.

At first I think she's excited, and I feel a swell of hope—what if Uriah is awake?

But the closer she gets, the more obvious it is that she isn't excited. She's frantic. Peter lingers behind her, his arms crossed.

"I just spoke to one of the doctors," she says, breathless. "The doctor says Uriah's not going to wake up.

Something about . . . no brain waves."

A weight settles on my shoulders. I knew, of course, that Uriah might never wake up. But the hope that kept the grief at bay is dwindling, slipping away with each word she speaks.

"They were going to take him off life support right away, but I pleaded with them." She wipes one of her eyes fiercely with the heel of her hand, catching a tear before it falls. "Finally the doctor said he would give me four days. So I can tell his family."

His family. Zeke is still in the city, and so is their Dauntless mother. It never occurred to me before that they don't know what happened to him, and we never bothered to tell them, because we were all so focused on—

"They're going to reset the city in forty-eight hours," I say suddenly, and I grab Tobias's arm. He looks stunned. "If we can't stop them, that means Zeke and his mother will *forget him*."

They'll forget him before they have a chance to say good-bye to him. It will be like he never existed.

"What?" Christina demands, her eyes wide. "My *family* is in there. They can't reset everyone! How could they do that?"

"Pretty easily, actually," Peter says. I had forgotten that he was there.

"What are you even doing here?" I demand.

"I went to see Uriah," he says. "Is there a law against it?"

"You didn't even care about him," I spit. "What right do you have—"

"Tris." Christina shakes her head. "Not now, okay?"

Tobias hesitates, his mouth open like there are words waiting on his tongue.

"We have to go in," he says. "Matthew said we could inoculate people against the memory serum, right? So we'll go in, inoculate Uriah's family just in case, and take them back to the compound to say good-bye to him. We have to do it tomorrow, though, or we'll be too late." He pauses. "And you can inoculate your family too, Christina. I should be the one who tells Zeke and Hana, anyway."

Christina nods. I squeeze her arm, in an attempt at reassurance.

"I'm going too," Peter says. "Unless you want me to tell David what you're planning."

We all pause to look at him. I don't know what Peter wants with a journey into the city, but it can't be good. At the same time, we can't afford for David to find out what we're doing, not now, when there's no time.

"Fine," Tobias says. "But if you cause any trouble, I reserve the right to knock you unconscious and lock you in an abandoned building somewhere."

Peter rolls his eyes.

"How do we get there?" Christina says. "It's not like they just let people borrow cars."

"I bet we could get Amar to take you," I say. "He told me today that he always volunteers for patrols. So he knows all the right people. And I'm sure he would agree to help Uriah and his family."

"I should go ask him now. And someone should probably sit with Uriah . . . make sure that doctor doesn't go back on his word. Christina, not Peter." Tobias rubs the back of his neck, pawing at the Dauntless tattoo like he wants to tear it from his body. "And then I should figure out how to tell Uriah's family that he got killed when I was supposed to be looking out for him."

"Tobias—" I say, but he holds up a hand to stop me.

He starts to move away. "They probably won't let me visit Nita anyway."

Sometimes it's hard to know how to take care of people. As I watch Peter and Tobias walk away—keeping their distance from each other—I think it's possible that Tobias needs someone to run after him, because people have been letting him walk away, letting him withdraw, his entire life. But he's right: He needs to do this for Zeke, and I need to talk to Nita.

"Come on," Christina says. "Visiting hours are almost over. I'm going back to sit with Uriah."

+++

Before I go to Nita's room—identifiable by the security guard sitting by the door—I stop by Uriah's room with Christina. She sits in the chair next to him, which is creased with the contours of her legs.

It's been a long time since I've spoken to her like a friend, a long time since we laughed together. I was lost in the fog of the Bureau, in the promise of belonging.

I stand next to her and look at him. He doesn't really look injured anymore—there are some bruises, some cuts, but nothing serious enough to kill him. I tilt my head to see the snake tattoo wrapped around his ear. I know it's him, but he doesn't look much like Uriah without a wide smile on his face and his dark eyes bright, alert.

"He and I weren't really even that close," she says. "Just at the . . . the very end. Because he had lost someone who died, and so had I . . ."

"I know," I say. "You really helped him."

I drag a chair over to sit next to her. She clutches Uriah's hand, which stays limp on the sheets.

"Sometimes I just feel like I've lost all my friends," she says.

"You haven't lost Cara," I say. "Or Tobias. And Christina, you haven't lost me. You'll never lose me."

She turns to me, and somewhere in the haze of grief

we wrap our arms around each other, in the same desperate way we did when she told me she had forgiven me for killing Will. Our friendship has held up under an incredible weight, the weight of me shooting someone she loved, the weight of so many losses. Other bonds would have broken. For some reason, this one hasn't.

We stay clutched together for a long time, until the desperation fades.

"Thanks," she says. "You won't lose me, either."

"I'm pretty sure if I was going to, I would have already." I smile. "Listen, I have some things to catch you up on."

I tell her about our plan to stop the Bureau from resetting the experiments. As I speak, I think of the people she stands to lose—her father and mother, her sister—all those connections, forever altered or discarded, in the name of genetic purity.

"I'm sorry," I say when I finish. "I know you probably want to help us, but . . ."

"Don't be sorry." She stares at Uriah. "I'm still glad I'm going into the city." She nods a few times. "You'll stop them from resetting the experiment. I know you will."

I hope she's right.

+++

I only have ten minutes until visiting hours are over when I arrive at Nita's room. The guard looks up from his book and raises his eyebrow at me.

"Can I go in?" I say.

"Not really supposed to let people in there," he says.

"I'm the one who shot her," I say. "Does that count for anything?"

"Well." He shrugs. "As long as you promise not to shoot her again. And get out within ten minutes."

"It's a deal."

He has me take off my jacket to show that I'm not carrying any weapons, and then he lets me into the room. Nita jerks to attention—as much as she can, anyway. Half her body is encased in plaster, and one of her hands is cuffed to the bed, as if she could escape even if she wanted to. Her hair is messy, knotted, but of course, she's still pretty.

"What are you doing here?" she says.

I don't answer—I check the corners of the room for cameras, and there's one across from me, pointed at Nita's hospital bed.

"There aren't microphones," she says. "They don't really do that here."

"Good." I pull up a chair and sit beside her. "I'm here because I need important information from you."

"I already told them everything I felt like telling them." She glares at me. "I've got nothing more to say. Especially not to the person who shot me."

"If I hadn't shot you, I wouldn't be David's favorite person, and I wouldn't know all the things I know." I glance at the door, more from paranoia than an actual concern that someone is listening in. "We've got a new plan. Matthew and I. And Tobias. And it will require getting into the Weapons Lab."

"And you thought I could help you with that?" She shakes her head. "I couldn't get in the first time, remember?"

"I need to know what the security is like. Is David the only person who knows the pass code?"

"Not like . . . the only person ever," she says. "That would be stupid. His superiors know it, but he's the only person in the compound, yes."

"Okay, then what's the backup security measure? The one that is activated if you explode the doors?"

She presses her lips together so they almost disappear, and stares at the half-body cast covering her. "It's the death serum," she says. "In aerosol form, it's practically unstoppable. Even if you wear a clean suit or something, it works its way in eventually. It just takes a little more time that way. That's what the lab reports said."

"So they just automatically *kill* anyone who makes their way into that room without the pass code?" I say.

"It surprises you?"

"I guess not." I balance my elbows on my knees. "And there's no other way in except with David's code."

"Which, as you found out, he is completely unwilling to share," she says.

"There's no chance a GP could resist the death serum?" I say.

"No. Definitely not."

"Most GPs can't resist the truth serum, either," I say. "But I can."

"If you want to go flirt with death, be my guest." She leans back into the pillows. "I'm done with that now."

"One more question," I say. "Say I do want to flirt with death. Where do I get explosives to break through the doors?"

"Like I'm going to tell you that."

"I don't think you get it," I say. "If this plan succeeds, you won't be imprisoned for life anymore. You'll recover and you'll go free. So it's in your best interest to help me."

She stares at me like she is weighing and measuring me. Her wrist tugs against the handcuff, just enough that the metal carves a line into her skin.

"Reggie has the explosives," she says. "He can teach you how to use them, but he's no good in action, so for God's sake, don't bring him along unless you feel like babysitting."

"Noted," I say.

"Tell him it will require twice as much firepower to get through those doors than any others. They're extremely sturdy."

I nod. My watch beeps on the hour, signaling that my time is up. I stand and push my chair back to the corner where I found it.

"Thank you for the help," I say.

"What is the plan?" she says. "If you don't mind telling me."

I pause, hesitating over the words.

"Well," I say eventually. "Let's just say it will erase the phrase 'genetically damaged' from everyone's vocabulary."

The guard opens the door, probably to yell at me for overstaying my welcome, but I'm already making my way out. I look over my shoulder just once before going, and I see that Nita is wearing a small smile.

CHAPTER FORTY

TOBIAS

AMAR AGREES TO help us get into the city without requiring much persuasion, eager for an adventure, as I knew he would be. We agree to meet that evening for dinner to talk through the plan with Christina, Peter, and George, who will help us get a vehicle.

After I talk to Amar, I walk to the dormitory and lay with a pillow over my head for a long time, cycling through a script of what I will say to Zeke when I see him. *I'm sorry, I was doing what I thought I had to do, and everyone else was looking after Uriah, and I didn't think . . .*

People come into the room and leave it, the heat switches on and pushes through the vents and then turns off again, and all the while I am thinking through that script, concocting excuses and then discarding them, choosing the right tone, the right gestures. Finally I grow frustrated and take the pillow from my face and fling it against the opposite wall. Cara, who is just smoothing a clean shirt down over her hips, jumps back.

"I thought you were asleep," she says.

"Sorry."

She touches her hair, ensuring that each strand is secure. She is so careful in her movements, so precise—it reminds me of the Amity musicians plucking at banjo strings.

"I have a question." I sit up. "It's kind of personal."

"Okay." She sits across from me, on Tris's bed. "Ask it."

"How were you able to forgive Tris, after what she did to your brother?" I say. "Assuming you have, that is."

"Hmm." Cara hugs her arms close to her body. "Sometimes I think I have forgiven her. Sometimes I'm not certain I have. I don't know how—that's like asking how you continue on with your life after someone dies. You just do it, and the next day you do it again."

"Is there . . . any way she could have made it easier for you? Or any way she did?"

"Why are you asking this?" She sets her hand on my knee. "Is it because of Uriah?"

"Yes," I say firmly, and I shift my leg a little so her hand falls away. I don't need to be patted or consoled, like a child. I don't need her raised eyebrows, her soft voice, to coax an emotion from me that I would prefer to contain.

"Okay." She straightens, and when she speaks again, she sounds casual, the way she usually does. "I think the most crucial thing she did—admittedly without meaning to—was confess. There is a difference between admitting and confessing. Admitting involves softening, making excuses for things that cannot be excused; confessing just names the crime at its full severity. That was something I needed."

I nod.

"And after you've confessed to Zeke," she says, "I think it would help if you leave him alone for as long as he wants to be left alone. That's all you can do."

I nod again.

"But, Four," she adds, "you didn't kill Uriah. You didn't set off the bomb that injured him. You didn't make the plan that led to that explosion."

"But I did participate in the plan."

"Oh, shut up, would you?" She says it gently, smiling at me. "It happened. It was awful. You aren't perfect. That's all there is. Don't confuse your grief with guilt."

We stay in the silence and the loneliness of the otherwise empty dormitory for a few more minutes, and I try to let her words work themselves into me.

+++

I eat dinner with Amar, George, Christina, and Peter in the cafeteria, between the beverage counter and a row of trash cans. The bowl of soup before me went cold before I could eat all of it, and there are still crackers swimming in the broth.

Amar tells us where and when to meet, then we go to the hallway near the kitchens so we won't be seen, and he takes out a small black box with syringes inside it. He gives one to Christina, Peter, and me, along with an individually packaged antibacterial wipe, something I suspect only Amar will bother with.

"What's this?" Christina says. "I'm not going to inject it into my body unless I know what it is."

"Fine." Amar folds his hands. "There's a chance that we will still be in the city when a memory serum virus is deployed. You'll need to inoculate yourself against it unless you want to forget everything you now remember. It's the same thing you'll be injecting into your family's arms, so don't worry about it."

Christina turns her arm over and slaps the inside of her elbow until a vein stands at attention. Out of habit, I stick the needle into the side of my neck, the same way I did every time I went through my fear landscape—which was several times a week, at one point. Amar does the same thing.

I notice, however, that Peter only pretends to inject himself—when he presses the plunger down, the fluid runs down his throat, and he wipes it casually with a sleeve.

I wonder what it feels like to volunteer to forget everything.

+++

After dinner Christina walks up to me and says, "We need to talk."

We walk down the long flight of stairs that leads to the underground GD space, our knees bouncing in unison with each step, and down the multicolored hallway. At the end, Christina crosses her arms, purple light playing over her nose and mouth.

"Amar doesn't know we're going to try to stop the reset?" she says.

"No," I say. "He's loyal to the Bureau. I don't want to involve him."

"You know, the city is still on the verge of revolution," she says, and the light turns blue. "The Bureau's whole reason for resetting our friends and families is to stop them from killing each other. If we stop the reset, the Allegiant will attack Evelyn, Evelyn will turn the death serum loose, and a lot of people will die. I may still be mad at you, but I don't think you want that many people in the city to die. Your parents in particular."

I sigh. "Honestly? I don't really care about them."

"You can't be serious," she says, scowling. "They're your *parents*."

"I can be, actually," I say. "I want to tell Zeke and his mother what I did to Uriah. Apart from that, I really don't care what happens to Evelyn and Marcus."

"You may not care about your permanently messed-up family, but you should care about everyone else!" she says. She takes my arm in one strong hand and jerks me so that I look at her. "Four, my little sister is in there. If Evelyn and the Allegiant smack into each other, she could get hurt, and I won't be there to protect her."

I saw Christina with her family on Visiting Day, when she was still just a loudmouthed Candor transfer to me. I watched her mother fix the collar of Christina's shirt with a proud smile. If the memory serum virus is deployed, that memory will be erased from her mother's mind. If it's not, her family will be caught in the middle of another citywide battle for control.

I say, "So what are you suggesting we do?"

She releases me. "There has to be a way to prevent a huge blowup that doesn't involve forcibly erasing everyone's memories."

"Maybe," I concede. I hadn't thought about it because it didn't seem necessary. But it is necessary, of course it's necessary. "Did you have an idea for how to stop it?"

"It's basically one of your parents against the other one," Christina says. "Isn't there something you can say to them that will stop them from trying to kill each other?"

"Something I can *say* to them?" I say. "Are you kidding? They don't listen to anyone. They don't do anything that doesn't directly benefit them."

"So there's nothing you can do. You're just going to let the city rip itself to shreds."

I stare at my shoes, bathed in green light, mulling it over. If I had different parents—if I had reasonable parents, less driven by pain and anger and the desire for revenge—it might work. They might be compelled to listen to their son. Unfortunately, I do not have different parents.

But I could. I could if I wanted them. Just a slip of the memory serum in their morning coffee or their evening water, and they would be new people, clean slates, unblemished by history. They would have to be taught that they even had a son to begin with; they would need to learn my name again.

It's the same technique we're using to heal the compound. I could use it to heal them.

I look up at Christina.

"Get me some memory serum," I say. "While you, Amar, and Peter are looking for your family and Uriah's family, I'll take care of it. I probably won't have enough time to get to both of my parents, but one of them will do."

"How will you get away from the rest of us?"

"I need . . . I don't know, we need to add a complication. Something that requires one of us leaving the pack."

"What about flat tires?" Christina says. "We're going at night, right? So I can tell Amar to stop so I can go to the bathroom or something, slash the tires, and then we'll have to split up, so you can find another truck."

I consider this for a moment. I could tell Amar what's really going on, but that would require undoing the dense knot of propaganda and lies the Bureau has tied in his mind. Assuming I could even do it, we don't have time for that.

But we do have time for a well-told lie. Amar knows that my father taught me how to start a car with just the wires when I was younger. He wouldn't question me volunteering to find us another vehicle.

"That will work," I say.

"Good." She tilts her head. "So you're really going to erase one of your parents' memories?"

"What do you do when your parents are evil?" I say.

"Get a new parent. If one of them doesn't have all the baggage they currently have, maybe the two of them can negotiate a peace agreement or something."

She frowns at me for a few seconds like she wants to say something, but eventually, she just nods.

CHAPTER FORTY-ONE

TRIS

THE SMELL OF bleach tingles in my nose. I stand next to a mop in a storage room in the basement; I stand in the wake of what I just told everyone, which is that whoever breaks into the Weapons Lab will be going on a suicide mission. The death serum is unstoppable.

"The question is," Matthew says, "is this something we're willing to sacrifice a life for."

This is the room where Matthew, Caleb, and Cara were developing the new serum, before the plan changed. Vials and beakers and scribbled-on notebooks are scattered across the lab table in front of Matthew. The string he wears tied around his neck is in his mouth now, and he chews it absentmindedly.

Tobias leans against the door, his arms crossed. I

remember him standing that way during initiation, as he watched us fight each other, so tall and so strong I never dreamed he would give me more than a cursory glance.

"It's not just about revenge," I say. "It's not about what they did to the Abnegation. It's about stopping them before they do something equally bad to the people in all the experiments—about taking away their power to control thousands of lives."

"It is worth it," Cara says. "One death, to save thousands of people from a terrible fate? And cut the compound's power off at the knees, so to speak? Is it even a question?"

I know what she is doing—weighing a single life against so many lifetimes and memories, drawing an obvious conclusion from the scales. That is the way an Erudite mind works, and the way an Abnegation mind works, but I am not sure if they are the minds we need right now. One life against thousands of memories, of course the answer is easy, but does it have to be one of our lives? Do we have to be the ones who act?

But because I know what my answer will be to that question, my thoughts turn to another question. If it has to be one of us, who should it be?

My eyes shift from Matthew and Cara, standing behind the table, to Tobias, to Christina, her arm slung over a broom handle, and land on Caleb.

Him.

A second later I feel sick with myself.

"Oh, just come out with it," Caleb says, lifting his eyes to mine. "You want me to do it. You all do."

"No one said that," Matthew says, spitting out the string necklace.

"Everyone's staring at me," Caleb says. "Don't think I don't know it. I'm the one who chose the wrong side, who worked with Jeanine Matthews; I'm the one none of you care about, so I should be the one to die."

"Why do you think Tobias offered to get you out of the city before they executed you?" My voice comes out cold, quiet. The odor of bleach plays over my nose. "Because I don't care whether you live or die? Because I don't care about you at all?"

He should be the one to die, part of me thinks.

I don't want to lose him, another part argues.

I don't know which part to trust, which part to believe.

"You think I don't know hatred when I see it?" Caleb shakes his head. "I see it every time you look at me. On the rare occasions when you do look at me."

His eyes are glossy with tears. It's the first time since my near execution that I've seen him remorseful instead of defensive or full of excuses. It might also be the first time since then that I've seen him as my brother instead of the coward who sold me out to Jeanine Matthews. Suddenly I have trouble swallowing.

"If I do this . . ." he says.

I shake my head no, but he holds up a hand.

"Stop," he says. "Beatrice, if I do this . . . will you be able to forgive me?"

To me, when someone wrongs you, you both share the burden of that wrongdoing—the pain of it weighs on both of you. Forgiveness, then, means choosing to bear the full weight all by yourself. Caleb's betrayal is something we both carry, and since he did it, all I've wanted is for him to take its weight away from me. I am not sure that I'm capable of shouldering it all myself—not sure that I am strong enough, or good enough.

But I see him steeling himself against this fate, and I know that I *have* to be strong enough, and good enough, if he is going to sacrifice himself for us all.

I nod. "Yes," I choke out. "But that's not a good reason to do this."

"I have plenty of reasons," Caleb says. "I'll do it. Of course I will."

+++

I am not sure what just happened.

Matthew and Caleb stay behind to fit Caleb for the clean suit—the suit that will keep him alive in the Weapons Lab long enough to set off the memory serum virus. I wait until the others leave before leaving myself. I want to walk back to the dormitory with only my thoughts as company.

A few weeks ago, I would have volunteered to go on the suicide mission myself—and I did. I volunteered to go to Erudite headquarters, knowing that death waited for me there. But it wasn't because I was selfless, or because I was brave. It was because I was guilty and a part of me wanted to lose everything; a grieving, ailing part of me wanted to die. Is that what's motivating Caleb now? Should I really allow him to die so that he feels like his debt to me is repaid?

I walk the hallway with its rainbow of lights and go up the stairs. I can't even think of an alternative—would I be any more willing to lose Christina, or Cara, or Matthew? No. The truth is that I would be less willing to lose them, because they have been good friends to me and Caleb has not, not for a long time. Even before he betrayed me, he left me for the Erudite and didn't look back. I was the one who went to visit *him* during my initiation, and he spent the whole time wondering why I was there.

And I don't want to die anymore. I am up to the challenge of bearing the guilt and the grief, up to facing the difficulties that life has put in my path. Some days are harder than others, but I am ready to live each one of them. I can't sacrifice myself, this time.

In the most honest parts of me, I am able to admit that it was a relief to hear Caleb volunteer.

Suddenly I can't think about it anymore. I reach the hotel entrance and walk to the dormitory, hoping that I can just collapse into my bed and sleep, but Tobias is waiting in the hallway for me.

"You okay?" he says.

"Yes," I say. "But I shouldn't be." I touch a hand, briefly, to my forehead. "I feel like I've already been mourning him. Like he died the second I saw him in Erudite headquarters while I was there. You know?"

I confessed to Tobias, soon after that, that I had lost my entire family. And he assured me that he was my family now.

That is how it feels. Like everything between us is twisted together, friendship and love and family, so I can't tell the difference between any of them.

"The Abnegation have teachings about this, you know," he says. "About when to let others sacrifice themselves for you, even if it's selfish. They say that if the sacrifice is the ultimate way for that person to show you that they love you, you should let them do it." He leans one shoulder into the wall. "That, in that situation, it's the greatest gift you can give them. Just as it was when both of your parents died for you."

"I'm not sure it's love that's motivating him, though." I close my eyes. "It seems more like guilt."

"Maybe," Tobias admits. "But why would he feel guilty for betraying you if he didn't love you?"

I nod. I know that Caleb loves me, and always has, even when he was hurting me. I know that I love him, too. But this feels wrong anyway.

Still, I am able to be momentarily placated, knowing that this is something my parents might have understood, if they were here right now.

"This may be a bad time," he says, "but there's something I want to say to you."

I tense immediately, afraid that he's going to name some crime of mine that went unacknowledged, or a confession that's eating away at him, or something equally difficult. His expression is unreadable.

"I just want to thank you," he says, his voice low. "A group of scientists told you that my genes were damaged, that there was something wrong with me—they showed you test results that proved it. And even I started to believe it."

He touches my face, his thumb skimming my cheekbone, and his eyes are on mine, intense and insistent.

"You never believed it," he says. "Not for a second. You always insisted that I was . . . I don't know, whole."

I cover his hand with my own. "Well, you are."

"No one has ever told me that before," he says softly.

"It's what you deserve to hear," I say firmly, my eyes going cloudy with tears. "That you're whole, that you're worth loving, that you're the best person I've ever known."

Just as the last word leaves my mouth, he kisses me.

I kiss him back so hard it hurts, and twist my fingers into his shirt. I push him down the hallway and through one of the doors to a sparsely furnished room near the dormitory. I kick the door shut with my heel.

Just as I have insisted on his worth, he has always insisted on my strength, insisted that my capacity is greater than I believe. And I know, without being told, that's what love does, when it's right—it makes you more than you were, more than you thought you could be.

This is right.

His fingers slide over my hair and curl into it. My hands shake, but I don't care if he notices, I don't care if he knows that I'm afraid of how intense this feels. I draw his shirt into my fists, tugging him closer, and sigh his name against his mouth.

I forget that he is another person; instead it feels like he is another part of me, just as essential as a heart or an eye or an arm. I pull his shirt up and over his head. I run my hands over the skin I expose like it is my own.

His hands clutch at my shirt and I am removing it and then I remember, I remember that I am small and flat-chested and sickly pale, and I pull back.

He looks at me, not like he's waiting for an explanation, but like I am the only thing in the room worth looking at.

I look at him, too, but everything I see makes me feel worse—he is so handsome, and even the black ink curling over his skin makes him into a piece of art. A moment ago I was convinced that we were perfectly matched, and maybe we still are—but only with our clothes on.

But he is still looking at me that way.

He smiles, a small, shy smile. Then he puts his hands on my waist and draws me toward him. He bends down and kisses between his fingers and whispers "beautiful" against my stomach.

And I believe him.

He stands and presses his lips to mine, his mouth open, his hands on my bare hips, his thumbs slipping under the top of my jeans. I touch his chest, lean into him, feel his sigh singing in my bones.

"I love you, you know," I say.

"I know," he replies.

With a quirk of his eyebrows, he bends and wraps an arm around my legs, throwing me over his shoulder. A laugh bursts from my mouth, half joy and half nerves, and he carries me across the room, dropping me unceremoniously on the couch.

He lies down next to me, and I run my fingers over the flames wrapping around his rib cage. He is strong, and lithe, and certain.

And he is mine.

I fit my mouth to his.

+++

I was so afraid that we would just keep colliding over and over again if we stayed together, and that eventually the impact would break me. But now I know I am like the blade and he is like the whetstone—

I am too strong to break so easily, and I become better, sharper, every time I touch him.

CHAPTER FORTY-TWO

TOBIAS

THE FIRST THING I see when I wake, still on the couch in the hotel room, are the birds flying over her collarbone. Her shirt, retrieved from the floor in the middle of the night because of the cold, is pulled down on one side from where she's lying on it.

We have slept close to each other before, but this time feels different. Every other time we were there to comfort each other or to protect each other; this time we're here just because we want to be—and because we fell asleep before we could go back to the dormitory.

I stretch out my hand and touch my fingertips to her tattoos, and she opens her eyes.

She wraps an arm around me and pulls herself across

the cushions so she's right up against me, warm and soft and pliable.

"Morning," I say.

"Shh," she says. "If you don't acknowledge it, maybe it will go away."

I draw her toward me, my hand on her hip. Her eyes are wide, alert, despite just having opened. I kiss her cheek, then her jaw, then her throat, lingering there for a few seconds. Her hands tighten around my waist, and she sighs into my ear.

My self-control is about to disappear in five, four, three . . .

"Tobias," she whispers, "I hate to say this, but . . . I think we have just a *few* things to do today."

"They can wait," I say against her shoulder, and I kiss the first tattoo, slowly.

"No, they can't!" she says.

I flop back onto the cushions, and I feel cold without her body parallel to mine. "Yeah. About that—I was thinking your brother could use some target practice. Just in case."

"That might be a good idea," she says quietly. "He's only fired a gun . . . what, once? Twice?"

"I can teach him," I say. "If there's one thing I'm good at, it's aiming. And it might make him feel better to do something."

"Thank you," she says. She sits up and puts her fingers through her hair to comb it. In the morning light its color looks brighter, like it's threaded with gold. "I know you don't like him, but . . ."

"But if you're going to let what he did go," I say, taking her hand, "then I'm going to try to do the same."

She smiles, and kisses my cheek.

+++

I skim the lingering shower water from the back of my neck with my palm. Tris, Caleb, Christina, and I are in the training room in the GD area underground—it's cold and dim and full of equipment, training weapons and mats and helmets and targets, everything we could ever need. I select the right practice gun, the one about the size of a pistol, but bulkier, and offer it to Caleb.

Tris's fingers slide between mine. Everything comes easily this morning, every smile and every laugh, every word and every motion.

If we succeed in what we attempt tonight, tomorrow Chicago will be safe, the Bureau will be forever changed, and Tris and I will be able to build a new life for ourselves somewhere. Maybe it will even be a place where I trade my guns and knives for more productive tools, screwdrivers and nails and shovels. This morning I feel like I could be so fortunate. I could.

"It doesn't shoot real bullets," I say, "but it seems like they designed it so it would be as close as possible to one of the guns you'll be using. It feels real, anyway."

Caleb holds the gun with just his fingertips, like he's afraid it will shatter in his hands.

I laugh. "First lesson: Don't be afraid of it. Grab it. You've held one before, remember? You got us out of the Amity compound with that shot."

"That was just lucky," Caleb says, turning the gun over and over to see it from every angle. His tongue pushes into his cheek like he's solving a problem. "Not the result of skill."

"Lucky is better than unlucky," I say. "We can work on skill now."

I glance at Tris. She grins at me, then leans in to whisper something to Christina.

"Are you here to help or what, Stiff?" I say. I hear myself speaking in the voice I cultivated as an initiation instructor, but this time I use it in jest. "You could use some practice with that right arm, if I recall correctly. You too, Christina."

Tris makes a face at me, then she and Christina cross the room to get their own weapons.

"Okay, now face the target and turn the safety off," I say. There is a target across the room, more sophisticated than the wooden-board target in the Dauntless training rooms. It has three rings in three different colors, green, yellow, and red, so it's easier to tell where the bullets hit. "Let me see how you would naturally shoot."

He lifts up the gun with one hand, squares off his feet and shoulders to the target like he's about to lift something heavy, and fires. The gun jerks back and up, firing the bullet near the ceiling. I cover my mouth with my hand to disguise my smile.

"There's no need to *giggle*," Caleb says irritably.

"Book learning doesn't teach you everything, does it?" Christina says. "You have to hold it with *both* hands. It doesn't look as cool, but neither does attacking the ceiling."

"I wasn't trying to look cool!"

Christina stands, her legs slightly uneven, and lifts both arms. She stares at the target for a moment, then fires. The training bullet hits the outer circle of the target and bounces off, rolling on the floor. It leaves a circle of light on the target, marking the impact site. I wish I'd had this technology during initiation training.

"Oh, good," I say. "You hit the air around your target's body. How useful."

"I'm a little rusty," Christina admits, grinning.

"I think the easiest way for you to learn would be to

mimic me," I say to Caleb. I stand the way I always stand, easy, natural, and lift both my arms, squeezing the gun with one hand and steadying it with the other.

Caleb tries to match me, beginning with his feet and moving up with the rest of him. As eager as Christina was to tease him, it's his ability to analyze that makes him successful—I can see him changing angles and distances and tension and release as he looks me over, trying to get everything right.

"Good," I say when he's finished. "Now focus on what you're trying to hit, and nothing else."

I stare at the center of the target and try to let it swallow me. The distance doesn't trouble me—the bullet will travel straight, just like it would if I was closer. I inhale and brace myself, exhale and fire, and the bullet goes right where I meant to put it: in the red circle, in the center of the target.

I step back to watch Caleb try it. He has the right way of standing, the right way of holding the gun, but he is rigid there, a statue with a gun in hand. He sucks in a breath and holds it as he fires. This time the kickback doesn't startle him as much, and the bullet nicks the top of the target.

"Good," I say again. "I think what you mostly need is to get comfortable with it. You're very tense."

"Can you blame me?" he says. His voice trembles, but just at the end of each word. He has the look of someone who is trapping terror inside. I watched two classes of initiates with that expression, but none of them was ever facing what Caleb is facing now.

I shake my head and say quietly, "Of course not. But you have to realize that if you can't let that tension go tonight, you might not make it to the Weapons Lab, and what good would that do anyone?"

He sighs.

"The physical technique is important," I say. "But it's mostly a mental game, which is lucky for you, because you know how to play those. You don't just practice the shooting, you also practice the focus. And then, when you're in a situation where you're fighting for your life, the focus will be so ingrained that it will happen naturally."

"I didn't know the Dauntless were so interested in training the brain," Caleb says. "Can I see you try it, Tris? I don't think I've ever really seen you shoot something without a bullet wound in your shoulder."

Tris smiles a little and faces the target. When I first saw her shoot during Dauntless training, she looked awkward, birdlike. But her thin, fragile form has become slim but muscular, and when she holds the gun, it looks easy. She squints one eye a little, shifts her weight, and fires. Her bullet strays from the target's center, but only by inches. Obviously impressed, Caleb raises his eyebrows.

"Don't look so surprised!" Tris says.

"Sorry," he says. "I just . . . you used to be so clumsy, remember? I don't know how I missed that you weren't like that anymore."

Tris shrugs, but when she looks away, her cheeks are flushed and she looks pleased. Christina shoots again, and this time hits the target closer to the middle.

I step back to let Caleb practice, and watch Tris fire again, watch the straight lines of her body as she lifts the gun, and how steady she is when it goes off. I touch her shoulder and lean in close to her ear. "Remember during training, how the gun almost hit you in the face?"

She nods, smirking.

"Remember during training, when I did *this*?" I say, and I reach around her to press my hand to her stomach. She sucks in a breath.

"I'm not likely to forget that anytime soon," she mutters.

She twists around and draws my face toward hers, her fingertips on my chin. We kiss, and I hear Christina say something about it, but for the first time, I don't care at all.

+++

There isn't much to do after target practice but wait. Tris and Christina get the explosives from Reggie and teach Caleb how to use them. Then Matthew and Cara pore over a map, examining different routes to get through the compound to the Weapons Lab. Christina and I meet with Amar, George, and Peter to go over the route we're going to take through the city that evening. Tris is called to a last-minute council meeting. Matthew inoculates people against the memory serum all throughout the day, Cara and Caleb and Tris and Nita and Reggie and himself.

There isn't enough time to think about the significance of what we're going to try to do: stop a revolution, save the experiments, change the Bureau forever.

While Tris is gone, I go to the hospital to see Uriah one last time before I bring his family back to him.

When I get there, I can't go in. From here, through the glass, I can pretend that he is just asleep, and that if I touched him, he would wake up and smile and make a joke. In there, I would be able to see how lifeless he is now, how the shock to his brain took the last parts of him that were Uriah.

I squeeze my hands into fists to disguise their shaking.

Matthew approaches from the end of the hallway, his hands in the pockets of his dark blue uniform. His gait is relaxed, his footsteps heavy. "Hey."

"Hi," I say.

"I was just inoculating Nita," he says. "She's in better spirits today."

"Good."

Matthew taps the glass with his knuckles. "So . . . you're going to go get his family later? That's what Tris told me."

I nod. "His brother and his mom."

I've met Zeke and Uriah's mother before. She is a small woman with power in her bearing, and one of the rare Dauntless who goes about things quietly and without ceremony. I liked her and I was afraid of her at the same time.

"No dad?" Matthew says.

"Died when they were young. Not surprising, among the Dauntless."

"Right."

We stand in silence for a little while, and I'm grateful for his presence, which keeps me from being overwhelmed by grief. I know that Cara was right yesterday to tell me that I didn't kill Uriah, not really, but it still *feels* like I did, and maybe it always will.

"I've been meaning to ask you," I say after a while. "Why are you helping us with this? It seems like a big risk for someone who isn't personally invested in the outcome."

"I am, though," Matthew says. "It's sort of a long story."

He crosses his arms, then tugs at the string around

his throat with his thumb.

"There was this girl," he says. "She was genetically damaged, and that meant I wasn't supposed to go out with her, right? We're supposed to make sure that we match ourselves with 'optimal' partners, so we produce genetically superior offspring, or something. Well I was feeling rebellious, and there was something appealing about how forbidden it was, so she and I started dating. I never meant for it to become anything serious, but . . ."

"But it did," I supply.

He nods. "It did. She, more than anything else, convinced me that the compound's position on genetic damage was twisted. She was a better person than I was, than I'll ever be. And then she got attacked. A bunch of GPs beat her up. She had kind of a smart mouth, she was never content to just stay where she was—I think that had something to do with it, or maybe nothing did, maybe people just do things like that out of nowhere, and trying to find a reason just frustrates the mind."

I look closely at the string he's toying with. I always thought it was black, but when I look closely, I see that it's actually green—the color of the support staff uniforms.

"Anyway, she was injured pretty badly, but one of the GPs was a council member's kid. He claimed the attack was provoked, and that was the excuse they used when they let him and the other GPs off with some community service, but I knew better." He starts nodding along with his own words. "I knew that they let them off because they thought of her as something less than them. Like if the GPs had beat up an animal."

A shiver starts at the top of my spine and travels down my back. "What . . ."

"What happened to her?" Matthew glances at me. "She died a year later during a surgical procedure to fix some of the damage. It was a fluke—an infection." He drops his hands. "The day she died was the day I started helping Nita. I didn't think her recent plan was a good one, though, which is why I didn't help out with it. But then, I also didn't try that hard to stop her."

I cycle through the things you're supposed to say at times like these, the apologies and the sympathy, and I don't find a single phrase that feels right to me. Instead I just let the silence stretch out between us. It's the only adequate response to what he just told me, the only thing that does the tragedy justice instead of patching it up hastily and moving on.

"I know it doesn't seem like it," Matthew says, "but I hate them."

The muscles in his jaw stand at attention. He has never struck me as a warm person, but he's never been cold, either. That is what he's like now, a man encased in ice, his eyes hard and his voice like a frosty exhale.

"And I would have volunteered to die instead of Caleb . . . if not for the fact that I really want to see them suffer the repercussions. I want to watch them fumble around under the memory serum, not knowing who they are anymore, because that's what happened to me when she died."

"That sounds like an adequate punishment," I say.

"More adequate than killing them would be," Matthew says. "And besides, I'm not a murderer."

I feel uneasy. It's not often you encounter the real person behind a good-natured mask, the darkest parts of someone. It's not comfortable when you do.

"I'm sorry for what happened to Uriah," Matthew says. "I'll leave you with him."

He puts his hands back in his pockets and continues down the hallway, his lips puckered in a whistle.

CHAPTER FORTY-THREE

TRIS

THE EMERGENCY COUNCIL meeting is more of the same: confirmation that the viruses will be dropped over the cities this evening, discussions about what planes will be used and at what times. David and I exchange friendly words when the meeting is over, and then I slip out while the others are still sipping coffee and walk back to the hotel.

Tobias takes me to the atrium near the hotel dormitory, and we spend some time there, talking and kissing and pointing out the strangest plants. It feels like something that normal people do—go on dates, talk about small things, laugh. We have had so few of those moments. Most of our time together has been spent running from one threat or another, or running toward one threat or another. But I can see a time on the horizon when that won't need to happen anymore. We will reset the people in the compound, and work to rebuild this place together. Maybe then we can find out if we do as well with the quiet moments as we have with the loud ones.

I am looking forward to it.

Finally the time comes for Tobias to leave. I stand on the higher step in the atrium and he stands on the lower one, so we're on the same plane.

"I don't like that I can't be with you tonight," he says. "It doesn't feel right to leave you alone with something this huge."

"What, you don't think I can handle it?" I say, a little defensive.

"Obviously that is not what I think." He touches his hands to my face and leans his forehead against mine. "I just don't want you to have to bear it alone."

"I don't want you to have to bear Uriah's family alone," I say softly. "But I think these are things we have to do separately. I'm glad I'll get to be with Caleb before . . . you know. It'll be nice not having to worry about you at the same time."

"Yeah." He closes his eyes. "I can't wait until tomorrow, when I'm back and you've done what you set out to do and we can decide what comes next."

"I can tell you it will involve a lot of this," I say, and I press my lips to his.

His hands shift from my cheeks to my shoulders and then slide painstakingly down my back. His fingers find the hem of my shirt, then slip under it, warm and insistent.

I feel aware of everything at once, of the pressure of his mouth and the taste of our kiss and the texture of his skin and the orange light glowing against my closed eyelids and the smell of green things, growing things, in the air. When I pull away, and he opens his eyes, I see everything about them, the dart of light blue in his left eye, the dark blue that makes me feel like I am safe inside it, like I am dreaming.

"I love you," I say.

"I love you, too," he says. "I'll see you soon."

He kisses me again, softly, and then leaves the atrium. I stand in that shaft of sunlight until the sun disappears.

It's time to be with my brother now.

CHAPTER FORTY-FOUR

TOBIAS

I CHECK THE screens before I go to meet Amar and George. Evelyn is holed up in Erudite headquarters with her factionless supporters, leaning over a map of the city. Marcus and Johanna are in a building on Michigan Avenue, north of the Hancock building, conducting a meeting.

I hope that's where they both are in a few hours when I decide which of my parents to reset. Amar gave us a little over an hour to find and inoculate Uriah's family and get back to the compound unnoticed, so I only have time for one of them.

+++

Snow swirls over the pavement outside, floating on the wind. George offers me a gun.

"It's dangerous in there right now," he says. "With all that Allegiant stuff going on."

I take the gun without even looking at it.

"You are all familiar with the plan?" George says. "I'm going to be monitoring you from here, from the small control room. We'll see how useful I am tonight, though, with all this snow obscuring the cameras."

"And where will the other security people be?"

"Drinking?" George shrugs. "I told them to take the night off. No one will notice the truck is gone. It'll be fine, I promise."

Amar grins. "All right, let's pile in."

George squeezes Amar's arm and waves at the rest of us. As the others follow Amar to the parked truck outside, I grab George and hold him back. He gives me a strange look.

"Don't ask me any questions about this, because I won't answer them," I say. "But inoculate yourself against the memory serum, okay? As soon as possible. Matthew can help you."

He frowns at me.

"Just do it," I say, and I go out to the truck.

Snowflakes cling to my hair, and vapor curls around my mouth with each breath. Christina bumps into me on our way to the truck and slips something into my pocket. A vial.

I see Peter's eyes on us as I get in the passenger's seat. I'm still not sure why he was so eager to come with us, but I know I need to be wary of him.

The inside of the truck is warm, and soon we are all covered with beads of water instead of snow.

"Lucky you," Amar says. He hands me a glass screen with bright lines tangled across it like veins. I look closer and see that they are streets, and the brightest line traces our path through them. "You get to man the map."

"You need a map?" I raise my eyebrows. "Has it not occurred to you to just . . . aim for the giant buildings?"

Amar makes a face at me. "We aren't just driving straight into the city, we're taking a stealth route. Now shut up and man the map."

I find a blue dot on the map that marks our position. Amar urges the truck into the snow, which falls so fast I can only see a few feet in front of us.

The buildings we drive past look like dark figures peeking through a white shroud. Amar drives fast, trusting the weight of the truck to keep us steady. Between snowflakes, I see the city lights up ahead. I had forgotten how close we were to it, because everything is so different just outside its limits.

"I can't believe we're going back," Peter says quietly, like he doesn't expect a response.

"Me either," I say, because it's true.

The distance the Bureau has kept from the rest of the world is an evil separate from the war they intend to wage against our memories—more subtle, but, in its way, just as sinister. They had the capacity to help us, languishing in our factions, but instead they let us fall apart. Let us die. Let us kill one another. Only now that we are about to destroy more than an acceptable level of genetic material are they deciding to intervene.

We bounce back and forth in the truck as Amar drives over the railroad tracks, staying close to the high cement wall on our right.

I look at Christina in the rearview mirror. Her right knee bounces fast.

+++

I still don't know whose memory I'm going to take: Marcus's, or Evelyn's?

Usually I would try to decide what the most selfless choice would be, but in this case either choice feels selfish. Resetting Marcus would mean erasing the man I hate and fear from the world. It would mean my freedom from his influence.

Resetting Evelyn would mean making her into a new mother—one who wouldn't abandon me, or make decisions out of a desire for revenge, or control everyone in an effort not to have to trust them.

Either way, with either parent gone, I am better off. But what would help the city most?

I no longer know.

+++

I hold my hands over the air vents to warm them as Amar continues to drive, over the railroad tracks and past the abandoned train car we saw on our way in, reflecting the headlights in its silver panels. We reach the place where the outside world ends and the experiment begins, as abrupt a shift as if someone had drawn a line in the ground.

Amar drives over that line like it isn't there. For him, I suppose, it has faded with time, as he grows more and more used to his new world. For me, it feels like driving from truth into a lie, from adulthood into childhood. I watch the land of pavement and glass and metal turn into an empty field. The snow is falling softly now, and I can faintly see the city's skyline up ahead, the buildings just a shade darker than the clouds.

"Where should we go to find Zeke?" Amar says.

"Zeke and his mother joined up with the revolt," I say. "So wherever most of them are is my best bet."

"Control room people said most of them have taken up

residence north of the river, near the Hancock building," Amar says. "Feel like going zip lining?"

"Absolutely not," I say.

Amar laughs.

It takes us another hour to get close. Only when I see the Hancock building in the distance do I start to feel nervous.

"Um . . . Amar?" Christina says from the back. "I hate to say this, but I really need to stop. And . . . you know. Pee."

"Right now?" Amar says.

"Yeah. It came on all of a sudden."

He sighs, but pulls the truck over to the side of the road.

"You guys stay here, and don't look!" Christina says as she gets out.

I watch her silhouette move to the back of the truck, and wait. All I feel when she slashes the tires is a slight bounce in the truck, so small I'm sure I only felt it because I was waiting for it. When Christina gets back in, brushing snowflakes from her jacket, she wears a small smile.

Sometimes, all it takes to save people from a terrible fate is one person willing to do something about it. Even if that "something" is a fake bathroom break.

Amar drives for a few more minutes before anything happens. Then the truck shudders and starts to bounce like we're going over bumps.

"Shit," Amar says, scowling at the speedometer. "I can't believe this."

"Flat?" I say.

"Yeah." He sighs, and eases on the brakes so the car slips to a stop by the side of the road.

"I'll check it," I say. I jump down from the passenger's seat and walk to the back of the truck. The back tires are completely flat, flayed by the knife Christina brought with her. I peer through the back windows to make sure there's only one spare tire, then return to my open door to give the news.

"Both back tires are flat and we only have one spare," I say. "We're going to have to abandon the truck and get a new one."

"Shit!" Amar smacks the steering wheel. "We don't have time for this. We have to make sure Zeke and his mother and Christina's family are all inoculated before the memory serum is released, or they'll be useless."

"Calm down," I say. "I know where we can find another vehicle. Why don't you guys keep going on foot and I'll go find something to drive?"

Amar's expression brightens. "Good idea."

Before moving away from the truck I make sure that there are bullets in my gun, even though I'm not sure if I'll need them. Everyone piles out of the truck, Amar shivering in the cold and bouncing on his toes.

I check my watch. "So you need to inoculate them by what time?"

"George's schedule says we've got an hour before we reset the city," Amar says, checking his watch too, to make sure. "If you want us to spare Zeke and his mother the grief and let them get reset, I wouldn't blame you. I'll do it if you need me to."

I shake my head. "Couldn't do that. They wouldn't be in pain, but it wouldn't be real."

"As I've always said," Amar says, smiling, "once a Stiff, always a Stiff."

"Can you . . . not tell them what happened? Just until I get there," I say. "Just inoculate them? I want to be the one who tells them."

Amar's smile shrinks a little. "Sure. Of course."

My shoes are already soaked through from checking the tires, and my feet ache when they touch the cold ground again. I'm about to walk away from the truck when Peter speaks up.

"I'm coming with you," he says.

"What? Why?" I glare at him.

"You might need help finding a truck," he says. "It's a big city."

I look at Amar, who shrugs. "Man's got a point."

Peter leans in closer and speaks quietly, so only I can

hear. "And if you don't want me to tell him you're planning something, you won't object."

His eyes drift to my jacket pocket, where the memory serum is.

I sigh. "Fine. But you do what I say."

I watch Amar and Christina walk away without us, heading toward the Hancock building. Once they're too far away to see us, I take a few steps back, slipping my hand into my pocket to protect the vial.

"I'm not going to look for a truck," I say. "You might as well know that now. Are you going to help me with what I'm doing, or do I have to shoot you?"

"Depends what you're doing."

It's hard to come up with an answer when I'm not even sure. I stand facing the Hancock building. To my right are the factionless, Evelyn, and her collection of death serum. To my left are the Allegiant, Marcus, and the insurrection plan.

Where do I have the greatest influence? Where can I make the biggest difference? Those are the questions I should be asking myself. Instead I am asking myself whose destruction I am more desperate for.

"I'm going to stop a revolution," I say.

I turn right, and Peter follows me.

CHAPTER FORTY-FIVE

TRIS

MY BROTHER STANDS behind the microscope, his eye pressed to the eyepiece. The light in the microscope platform casts strange shadows on his face, making him look years older.

"This is definitely it," he says. "The attack simulation serum, I mean. No question."

"It's always good to have another person verify," Matthew says.

I am standing with my brother in the hours before he dies. And he is analyzing serums. It's so stupid.

I know why Caleb wanted to come here: to make sure that he was giving his life for a good reason. I don't blame him. There are no second chances after you've died for something, at least as far as I know.

"Tell me the activation code again," Matthew says. The activation code will enable the memory serum weapon, and another button will deploy it instantly. Matthew has made Caleb repeat them both every few minutes since we got here.

"I have no trouble memorizing sequences of numbers!" Caleb says.

"I don't doubt that. But we don't know what state of mind you'll be in when the death serum begins to take its course, and these codes need to be deeply ingrained."

Caleb flinches at the words "death serum." I stare at my shoes.

"080712," Caleb says. "And then I press the green button."

Right now Cara is spending some time with the people in the control room so she can spike their beverages with peace serum and shut off the lights in the compound while they're too drunk to notice, just like Nita and Tobias did a few weeks ago. When she does that, we'll run for the Weapons Lab, unseen by the cameras in the dark.

Sitting across from me on the lab table are the explosives Reggie gave us. They look so ordinary—inside a black box with metal claws on the edges and a remote detonator. The claws will attach the box to the second set of laboratory doors. The first set still hasn't been repaired since the attack.

"I think that's it," Matthew says. "Now all we have to do is wait for a little while."

"Matthew," I say. "Do you think you could leave us alone for a bit?"

"Of course." Matthew smiles. "I'll come back when it's time."

He closes the door behind him. Caleb runs his hands over the clean suit, the explosives, the backpack they go in. He puts them all in a straight line, fixing this corner and that one.

"I keep thinking about when we were young and we played 'Candor,'" he says. "How I used to sit you down in a chair in the living room and ask you questions? Remember?"

"Yes," I say. I lean my hips into the lab table. "You used to find the pulse in my wrist and tell me that if I lied, you would be able to tell, because the Candor can always tell when other people are lying. It wasn't very nice."

Caleb laughs. "That one time, you confessed to stealing a book from the school library just as Mom came home—"

"And I had to go to the librarian and apologize!" I laugh too. "That librarian was awful. She always called everyone 'young lady' or 'young man.'"

"Oh, she loved me, though. Did you know that when I was a library volunteer and was supposed to be shelving books during my lunch hour, I was really just standing in the aisles and reading? She caught me a few times and never said anything about it."

"Really?" I feel a twinge in my chest. "I didn't know that."

"There was a lot we didn't know about each other, I guess." He taps his fingers on the table. "I wish we had been able to be more honest with each other."

"Me too."

"And it's too late now, isn't it." He looks up.

"Not for everything." I pull out a chair from the lab table and sit in it. "Let's play Candor. I'll answer a question and then you have to answer a question. Honestly, obviously."

He looks a little exasperated, but he plays along. "Okay. What did you really do to break those glasses in the kitchen when you claimed that you were taking them out to clean water spots off them?"

I roll my eyes. "That's the one question you want an honest answer to? Come on, Caleb."

"Okay, fine." He clears his throat, and his green eyes fix on mine, serious. "Have you really forgiven me, or are you just saying that you have because I'm about to die?"

I stare at my hands, which rest in my lap. I have been able to be kind and pleasant to him because every time I think of what happened in Erudite headquarters, I immediately push the thought aside. But that can't be forgiveness—if I had forgiven him, I would be able to think of what happened without that hatred I can feel in my gut, right?

Or maybe forgiveness is just the continual pushing aside of bitter memories, until time dulls the hurt and the anger, and the wrong is forgotten.

For Caleb's sake, I choose to believe the latter.

"Yes, I have," I say. I pause. "Or at least, I desperately want to, and I think that might be the same thing."

He looks relieved. I step aside so he can take my place in the chair. I know what I want to ask him, and have since he volunteered to make this sacrifice.

"What is the biggest reason that you're doing this?" I say. "The most important one?"

"Don't ask me that, Beatrice."

"It's not a trap," I say. "It won't make me un-forgive you. I just need to know."

Between us are the clean suit, the explosives, and the backpack, arranged in a line on the brushed steel. They are the instruments of his going and not coming back.

"I guess I feel like it's the only way I can escape the guilt for all the things I've done," he says. "I've never wanted anything more than I want to be rid of it."

His words ache inside me. I was afraid he would say that. I knew he would say that all along. I wish he hadn't said it.

A voice speaks through the intercom in the corner. "Attention all compound residents. Commence emergency lockdown procedure, effective until five o'clock a.m. I repeat, commence emergency lockdown procedure, effective until five o'clock a.m."

Caleb and I exchange an alarmed look. Matthew shoves the door open.

"Shit," he says. And then, louder: "Shit!"

"Emergency lockdown?" I say. "Is that the same as an attack drill?"

"Basically. It means we have to go *now,* while there's still chaos in the hallways and before they increase security," Matthew says.

"Why would they do this?" Caleb says.

"Could be they just want to increase security before releasing the viruses," Matthew says. "Or it could be that they figured out we're going to try something—only, if they knew that, they probably would have come to arrest us."

I look at Caleb. The minutes I had left with him fall away like dead leaves pulled from branches.

I cross the room and retrieve our guns from the counter, but itching at the back of my mind is what Tobias said yesterday—that the Abnegation say you should only let someone sacrifice himself for you if it's the ultimate way for them to show they love you.

And for Caleb, that's not what this is.

CHAPTER FORTY-SIX

TOBIAS

MY FEET SLIP on the snowy pavement.

"You didn't inoculate yourself yesterday," I say to Peter.

"No, I didn't," Peter says.

"Why not?"

"Why should I tell you?"

I run my thumb over the vial and say, "You came with me because you know I have the memory serum, right? If you want me to give it to you, it couldn't hurt to give me a reason."

He looks at my pocket again, like he did earlier. He must have seen Christina give it to me. He says, "I'd rather just *take* it from you."

"Please." I lift my eyes up, to watch the snow spilling over the edges of the buildings. It's dark, but the moon provides just enough light to see by. "You might think you're pretty good at fighting, but you aren't good enough to beat me, I promise you."

Without warning he shoves me, hard, and I slip on the snowy ground and fall. My gun clatters to the ground, half buried in the snow. *That'll teach me to get cocky,* I think, and I scramble to my feet. He grabs my collar and yanks me forward so I slide again, only this time I keep my balance and elbow him in the stomach. He kicks me hard in the leg, making it go numb, and grabs the front of my jacket to pull me toward him.

His hand fumbles for my pocket, where the serum is. I try to push him away, but his footing is too sure and my leg is still too numb. With a groan of frustration, I bring my free arm back by my face and slam my elbow into his mouth. Pain spreads through my arm—it hurts to hit someone in the teeth—but it was worth it. He yells, sliding back onto the street, his face clutched in both hands.

"You know why you won fights as an initiate?" I say as I get to my feet. "Because you're cruel. Because you like to hurt people. And you think you're special, you think everyone around you is a bunch of sissies who can't make the tough choices like you can."

He starts to get up, and I kick him in the side so he goes sprawling again. Then I press my foot to his chest, right under his throat, and our eyes meet, his wide and innocent and nothing like what's inside him.

"You are not special," I say. "I like to hurt people too. I can make the cruelest choice. The difference is, sometimes I don't, and you always do, and that makes you evil."

I step over him and start down Michigan Avenue again. But before I take more than a few steps, I hear his voice.

"That's why I want it," he says, his voice shaking.

I stop. I don't turn around. I don't want to see his face right now.

"I want the serum because I'm sick of being this way," he says. "I'm sick of doing bad things and liking it and then wondering what's wrong with me. I want it to be over. I want to start again."

"And you don't think that's the coward's way out?" I say over my shoulder.

"I think I don't care if it is or not," Peter says.

I feel the anger that was swelling within me deflate as I turn the vial over in my fingers, inside my pocket. I hear him get to his feet and brush the snow from his clothes.

"Don't try to mess with me again," I say, "and I promise I'll let you reset yourself, when all this is said and done. I have no reason not to."

He nods, and we continue through the unmarked snow to the building where I last saw my mother.

CHAPTER FORTY-SEVEN

TRIS

THERE IS A nervous kind of quiet in the hallway, though there are people everywhere. One woman bumps me with her shoulder and then mutters an apology, and I move closer to Caleb so I don't lose sight of him. Sometimes all I want is to be a few inches taller so the world does not look like a dense collection of torsos.

We move quickly, but not too quickly. The more security guards I see, the more pressure I feel building inside me. Caleb's backpack, with the clean suit and explosives inside it, bounces against his lower back as we walk. People are moving in all different directions, but soon, we will reach a hallway that no one has any reason to walk down.

"I think something must have happened to Cara," Matthew says. "The lights were supposed to be off by now."

I nod. I feel the gun digging into my back, disguised by my baggy shirt. I had hoped that I wouldn't have to use it, but it seems that I will, and even then it might not be enough to get us to the Weapons Lab.

I touch Caleb's arm, and Matthew's, stopping all three of us in the middle of the hallway.

"I have an idea," I say. "We split up. Caleb and I will run to the lab, and Matthew, cause some kind of diversion."

"A diversion?"

"You have a gun, don't you?" I say. "Fire into the air."

He hesitates.

"Do it," I say through gritted teeth.

Matthew takes his gun out. I grab Caleb's elbow and steer him down the hallway. Over my shoulder I watch Matthew lift the gun over his head and fire straight up, at one of the glass panels above him. At the sharp bang, I burst into a run, dragging Caleb with me. Screams and shattering glass fill the air, and security guards run past us without noticing that we are running away from the dormitories, running toward a place we should not be.

It's a strange thing to feel my instincts and Dauntless training kick in. My breathing becomes deeper, more even, as we follow the route we determined this morning.

My mind feels sharper, clearer. I look at Caleb, expecting to see the same thing happening to him, but all the blood seems to have drained from his face, and he is gasping. I keep my hand firm on his elbow to steady him.

We round a corner, shoes squeaking on the tile, and an empty hallway with a mirrored ceiling stretches out in front of us. I feel a surge of triumph. I know this place. We aren't far now. We're going to make it.

"Stop!" a voice shouts from behind me.

The security guards. They found us.

"Stop or we'll shoot!"

Caleb shudders and lifts his hands. I lift mine, too, and look at him.

I feel everything slowing down inside me, my racing thoughts and the pounding of my heart.

When I look at him, I don't see the cowardly young man who sold me out to Jeanine Matthews, and I don't hear the excuses he gave afterward.

When I look at him, I see the boy who held my hand in the hospital when our mother broke her wrist and told me it would be all right. I see the brother who told me to make my own choices, the night before the Choosing Ceremony. I think of all the remarkable things he is—smart and enthusiastic and observant, quiet and earnest and kind.

He is a part of me, always will be, and I am a part of him, too. I don't belong to Abnegation, or Dauntless, or even the Divergent. I don't belong to the Bureau or the experiment or the fringe. I belong to the people I love, and they belong to me—they, and the love and loyalty I give them, form my identity far more than any word or group ever could.

I love my brother. I love him, and he is quaking with terror at the thought of death. I love him and all I can think, all I can hear in my mind, are the words I said to him a few days ago: *I would never deliver you to your own execution.*

"Caleb," I say. "Give me the backpack."

"What?" he says.

I slip my hand under the back of my shirt and grab my gun. I point it at him. "Give me the backpack."

"Tris, no." He shakes his head. "No, I won't let you do that."

"Put down your weapon!" the guard screams at the end of the hallway. "Put down your weapon or we will fire!"

"I might survive the death serum," I say. "I'm good at fighting off serums. There's a chance I'll survive. There's no chance you would survive. Give me the backpack or I'll shoot you in the leg and take it from you."

Then I raise my voice so the guards can hear me. "He's my hostage! Come any closer and I'll kill him!"

In that moment he reminds me of our father. His eyes are tired and sad. There's a shadow of a beard on his chin. His hands shake as he pulls the backpack to the front of his body and offers it to me.

I take it and swing it over my shoulder. I keep my gun pointed at him and shift so he's blocking my view of the soldiers at the end of the hallway.

"Caleb," I say, "I love you."

His eyes gleam with tears as he says, "I love you, too, Beatrice."

"Get down on the floor!" I yell, for the benefit of the guards.

Caleb sinks to his knees.

"If I don't survive," I say, "tell Tobias I didn't want to leave him."

I back up, aiming over Caleb's shoulder at one of the security guards. I inhale and steady my hand. I exhale and fire. I hear a pained yell, and sprint in the other direction with the sound of gunfire in my ears. I run a crooked path so it's harder to hit me, and then dive around the corner. A bullet hits the wall right behind me, putting a hole in it.

As I run, I swing the backpack around my body and open the zipper. I take out the explosives and the detonator. There are shouts and running footsteps behind me. I don't have any time. I don't have any time.

I run harder, faster than I thought I could. The impact of each footstep shudders through me and I turn the next corner, where there are two guards standing by the doors Nita and the invaders broke. Clutching the explosives and detonator to my chest with my free hand, I shoot one guard in the leg and the other in the chest.

The one I shot in the leg reaches for his gun, and I fire again, closing my eyes after I aim. He doesn't move again.

I run past the broken doors and into the hallway between them. I slam the explosives against the metal bar where the two doors join, and clamp down the claws around the edge of the bar so it will stay. Then I run back to the end of the hallway and around the corner and crouch, my back to the doors, as I press the detonation button and shield my ears with my palms.

The noise vibrates in my bones as the small bomb detonates, and the force of the blast throws me sideways, my gun sliding across the floor. Pieces of glass and metal spray through the air, falling to the floor where I lie, stunned. Even though I sealed off my ears with my hands, I still hear ringing when I take them away, and I feel unsteady on my feet.

At the end of the hallway, the guards have caught up with me. They fire, and a bullet hits me in the fleshy part of my arm. I scream, clapping my hand over the wound, and my vision goes spotty at the edges as I throw myself around the corner again, half walking and half stumbling to the blasted-open doors.

Beyond them is a small vestibule with a set of sealed, lockless doors at the other end. Through the windows in those doors I see the Weapons Lab, the even rows of machinery and dark devices and serum vials, lit from beneath like they're on display. I hear a spraying sound and know that the death serum is floating through the air, but the guards are behind me, and I don't have time to put on the suit that will delay its effects.

I also know, I just know, that I can survive this.

I step into the vestibule.

CHAPTER FORTY-EIGHT

TOBIAS

FACTIONLESS HEADQUARTERS—BUT this building will always be Erudite headquarters to me, no matter what happens—stands silent in the snow, with nothing but glowing windows to signal that there are people inside. I stop in front of the doors and make a disgruntled sound in my throat.

"What?" Peter says.

"I hate it here," I say.

He pushes his hair, soaked from the snow, out of his eyes. "So what are we going to do, break a window? Look for a back door?"

"I'm just going to walk in," I say. "I'm her son."

"You also betrayed her and left the city when she

forbade anyone from doing that," he says, "and she sent people after you to stop you. People with guns."

"You can stay here if you want," I say.

"Where the serum goes, I go," he says. "But if you get shot at, I'm going to grab it and run."

"I don't expect anything more."

He is a strange sort of person.

I walk into the lobby, where someone reassembled the portrait of Jeanine Matthews, but they drew an X over each of her eyes in red paint and wrote "Faction scum" across the bottom.

Several people wearing factionless armbands advance on us with guns held high. Some of them I recognize from across the factionless warehouse campfires, or from the time I spent at Evelyn's side as a Dauntless leader. Others are complete strangers, reminding me that the factionless population is larger than any of us suspected.

I put up my hands. "I'm here to see Evelyn."

"Sure," one of them says. "Because we just let anyone in who wants to see her."

"I have a message from the people outside," I say. "One I'm sure she would like to hear."

"Tobias?" a factionless woman says. I recognize her, but not from a factionless warehouse—from the Abnegation sector. She was my neighbor. Grace is her name.

"Hello, Grace," I say. "I just want to talk to my mom."

She bites the inside of her cheek and considers me. Her grip on her pistol falters. "Well, we're still not supposed to let anyone in."

"For God's sake," Peter says. "Go tell her we're here and see what she says, then! We can wait."

Grace backs up into the crowd that gathered as we were talking, then lowers her gun and jogs down a nearby hallway.

We stand for what feels like a long time, until my shoulders ache from supporting my arms. Then Grace returns and beckons to us. I lower my hands as the others lower their guns, and walk into the foyer, passing through the center of the crowd like a piece of thread through the eye of a needle. She leads us into an elevator.

"What are you doing holding a gun, Grace?" I say. I've never known an Abnegation to pick up a weapon.

"No faction customs anymore," she says. "Now I get to defend myself. I get to have a sense of self-preservation."

"Good," I say, and I mean it. Abnegation was just as broken as the other factions, but its evils were less obvious, cloaked as they were in the guise of selflessness. But requiring a person to disappear, to fade into the background wherever they go, is no better than encouraging them to punch one another.

We go up to the floor where Jeanine's administrative office was—but that's not where Grace takes us. Instead she leads us to a large meeting room with tables, couches, and chairs arranged in strict squares. Huge windows along the back wall let in the moonlight. Evelyn sits at a table on the right, staring out the window.

"You can go, Grace," Evelyn says. "You have a message for me, Tobias?"

She doesn't look at me. Her thick hair is tied back in a knot, and she wears a gray shirt with a factionless armband over it. She looks exhausted.

"Mind waiting in the hallway?" I say to Peter, and to my surprise, he doesn't argue. He just walks out, closing the door behind him.

My mother and I are alone.

"The people outside have no messages for us," I say, moving closer to her. "They wanted to take away the memories of everyone in this city. They believe there is no reasoning with us, no appealing to our better natures. They decided it would be easier to erase us than to speak with us."

"Maybe they're right," Evelyn says. Finally she turns to me, resting her cheekbone against her clasped hands. She has an empty circle tattooed on one of her fingers like a wedding band. "What is it you came here to do, then?"

I hesitate, my hand on the vial in my pocket. I look at her, and I can see the way time has worn through her like an old piece of cloth, the fibers exposed and fraying. And I can see the woman I knew as a child, too, the mouth that stretched into a smile, the eyes that sparkled with joy. But the longer I look at her, the more convinced I am that that happy woman never existed. That woman is just a pale version of my real mother, viewed through the self-centered eyes of a child.

I sit down across from her at the table and put the vial of memory serum between us.

"I came to make you drink this," I say.

She looks at the vial, and I think I see tears in her eyes, but it could just be the light.

"I thought it was the only way to prevent total destruction," I say. "I know that Marcus and Johanna and their people are going to attack, and I know that you will do whatever it takes to stop them, including using that death serum you possess to its best advantage." I tilt my head. "Am I wrong?"

"No," she says. "The factions are evil. They cannot be restored. I would sooner see us all destroyed."

Her hand squeezes the edge of the table, the knuckles pale.

"The reason the factions were evil is because there

was no way out of them," I say. "They gave us the illusion of choice without actually giving us a choice. That's the same thing you're doing here, by abolishing them. You're saying, go make choices. But make sure they aren't factions or I'll grind you to bits!"

"If you thought that, why didn't you tell me?" she says, her voice louder and her eyes avoiding mine, avoiding me. "Tell me, instead of *betraying* me?"

"Because I'm afraid of you!" The words burst out, and I regret them but I'm also glad they're there, glad that before I ask her to give up her identity, I can at least be honest with her. "You . . . you remind me of *him*!"

"Don't you dare." She clenches her hands into fists and almost spits at me, "Don't you *dare*."

"I don't care if you don't want to hear it," I say, coming to my feet. "He was a tyrant in our house and now you're a tyrant in this city, and you can't even see that it's the same!"

"So that's why you brought this," she says, and she wraps her hand around the vial, holding it up to look at it. "Because you think this is the only way to mend things."

"I . . ." I am about to say that it's the easiest way, the best way, maybe the only way that I can trust her.

If I erase her memories, I can create for myself a new mother, but.

But she is more than my mother. She is a person in her

own right, and she does not belong to me.

I do not get to choose what she becomes just because I can't deal with who she is.

"No," I say. "No, I came to give you a choice."

I feel suddenly terrified, my hands numb, my heart beating fast—

"I thought about going to see Marcus tonight, but I didn't." I swallow hard. "I came to see you instead because . . . because I think there's a hope of reconciliation between us. Not now, not soon, but someday. And with him there's no hope, there's no reconciliation possible."

She stares at me, her eyes fierce but welling up with tears.

"It's not fair for me to give you this choice," I say. "But I have to. You can lead the factionless, you can fight the Allegiant, but you'll have to do it without me, forever. Or you can let this crusade go, and . . . and you'll have your son back."

It's a feeble offer and I know it, which is why I'm afraid—afraid that she will refuse to choose, that she will choose power over me, that she will call me a ridiculous child, which is what I am. I am a child. I am two feet tall and asking her how much she loves me.

Evelyn's eyes, dark as wet earth, search mine for a long time.

Then she reaches across the table and pulls me fiercely

into her arms, which form a wire cage around me, surprisingly strong.

"Let them have the city and everything in it," she says into my hair.

I can't move, can't speak. She chose me. She chose me.

CHAPTER FORTY-NINE

TRIS

THE DEATH SERUM smells like smoke and spice, and my lungs reject it with the first breath I take. I cough and splutter, and I am swallowed by darkness.

I crumple to my knees. My body feels like someone has replaced my blood with molasses, and my bones with lead. An invisible thread tugs me toward sleep, but I want to be awake. It is important that I want to be awake. I imagine that wanting, that desire, burning in my chest like a flame.

The thread tugs harder, and I stoke the flame with names. Tobias. Caleb. Christina. Matthew. Cara. Zeke. Uriah.

But I can't bear up under the serum's weight. My body

falls to the side, and my wounded arm presses to the cold ground. I am drifting. . . .

It would be nice to float away, a voice in my head says. *To see where I will go . . .*

But the fire, the fire.

The desire to live.

I am not done yet, I am not.

I feel like I am digging through my own mind. It is difficult to remember why I came here and why I care about unburdening myself from this beautiful weight. But then my scratching hands find it, the memory of my mother's face, and the strange angles of her limbs on the pavement, and the blood seeping from my father's body.

But they are dead, the voice says. *You could join them.*

They died for me, I answer. And now I have something to do, in return. I have to stop other people from losing everything. I have to save the city and the people my mother and father loved.

If I go to join my parents, I want to carry with me a good *reason*, not this—this senseless collapsing at the threshold.

The fire, the fire. It rages within, a campfire and then an inferno, and my body is its fuel. I feel it racing through me, eating away at the weight. There is nothing that can kill me now; I am powerful and invincible and eternal.

I feel the serum clinging to my skin like oil, but the darkness recedes. I slap a heavy hand over the floor and push myself up.

Bent at the waist, I shove my shoulder into the double doors, and they squeak across the floor as their seal breaks. I breathe clean air and stand up straighter. I am there, I am *there*.

But I am not alone.

"Don't move," David says, raising his gun. "Hello, Tris."

CHAPTER FIFTY

TRIS

"HOW DID YOU inoculate yourself against the death serum?" he asks me. He's still sitting in his wheelchair, but you don't need to be able to walk to fire a gun.

I blink at him, still dazed.

"I didn't," I say.

"Don't be stupid," David says. "You can't survive the death serum without an inoculation, and I'm the only person in the compound who possesses that substance."

I just stare at him, not sure what to say. I didn't inoculate myself. The fact that I'm still standing upright is impossible. There's nothing more to add.

"I suppose it no longer matters," he says. "We're here now."

"What are you doing here?" I mumble. My lips feel awkwardly large, hard to talk around. I still feel that oily heaviness on my skin, like death is clinging to me even though I have defeated it.

I am dimly aware that I left my own gun in the hallway behind me, sure I wouldn't need it if I made it this far.

"I knew something was going on," David says. "You've been running around with genetically damaged people all week, Tris, did you think I wouldn't notice?" He shakes his head. "And then your friend Cara was caught trying to manipulate the lights, but she very wisely knocked herself out before she could tell us anything. So I came here, just in case. I'm sad to say I'm not surprised to see you."

"You came here alone?" I say. "Not very smart, are you?"

His bright eyes squint a little. "Well, you see, I have death serum resistance and a weapon, and you have no way to fight me. There's no way you can steal four virus devices while I have you at gunpoint. I'm afraid you've come all this way for no reason, and it will be at the expense of your life. The death serum may not have killed you, but I am going to. I'm sure you understand—officially we don't allow capital punishment, but I can't have you surviving this."

He thinks I'm here to steal the weapons that will reset the experiments, not deploy one of them. Of course he does.

I try to guard my expression, though I'm sure it's still slack. I sweep my eyes across the room, searching for the device that will release the memory serum virus. I was there when Matthew described it to Caleb in painstaking detail earlier: a black box with a silver keypad, marked with a strip of blue tape with a model number written on it. It is one of the only items on the counter along the left wall, just a few feet away from me. But I can't move, or else he'll kill me.

I'll have to wait for the right moment, and do it fast.

"I know what you did," I say. I start to back up, hoping that the accusation will distract him. "I know you designed the attack simulation. I know you're responsible for my parents' deaths—for my *mother's* death. I know."

"I am not responsible for her death!" David says, the words bursting from him, too loud and too sudden. "I *told* her what was coming just before the attack began, so she had enough time to escort her loved ones to a safe house. If she had stayed put, she would have lived. But she was a foolish woman who didn't understand making sacrifices for the greater good, and it *killed* her!"

I frown at him. There's something about his reaction—about the glassiness of his eyes—something that he mumbled when Nita shot him with the fear serum—something about *her*.

"Did you love her?" I say. "All those years she was sending you correspondence . . . the reason you never wanted her to stay there . . . the reason you told her you couldn't read her updates anymore, after she married my father . . ."

David sits still, like a statue, like a man of stone.

"I did," he says. "But that time is past."

That must be why he welcomed me into his circle of trust, why he gave me so many opportunities. Because I am a piece of her, wearing her hair and speaking with her voice. Because he has spent his life grasping at her and coming up with nothing.

I hear footsteps in the hallway outside. The soldiers are coming. Good—I need them to. I need them to be exposed to the airborne serum, to pass it on to the rest of the compound. I hope they wait until the air is clear of death serum.

"My mother wasn't a fool," I say. "She just understood something you didn't. That it's not sacrifice if it's someone *else's* life you're giving away, it's just evil."

I back up another step and say, "She taught me all about real sacrifice. That it should be done from love, not misplaced disgust for another person's genetics. That it should be done from necessity, not without exhausting all other options. That it should be done for people who need your strength because they don't have enough of their own. That's why I need to stop you from 'sacrificing' all those people and their memories. Why I need to rid the world of you once and for all."

I shake my head.

"I didn't come here to steal anything, David."

I twist and lunge toward the device. The gun goes off and pain races through my body. I don't even know where the bullet hit me.

I can still hear Caleb repeating the code for Matthew. With a quaking hand I type in the numbers on the keypad.

The gun goes off again.

More pain, and black edges on my vision, but I hear Caleb's voice speaking again. *The green button.*

So much pain.

But how, when my body feels so numb?

I start to fall, and slam my hand into the keypad on my way down. A light turns on behind the green button.

I hear a beep, and a churning sound.

I slide to the floor. I feel something warm on my neck, and under my cheek. Red. Blood is a strange color. Dark.

From the corner of my eye, I see David slumped over in his chair.

And my *mother* walking out from behind him.

She is dressed in the same clothes she wore the last

time I saw her, Abnegation gray, stained with her blood, with bare arms to show her tattoo. There are still bullet holes in her shirt; through them I can see her wounded skin, red but no longer bleeding, like she's frozen in time. Her dull blond hair is tied back in a knot, but a few loose strands frame her face in gold.

I know she can't be alive, but I don't know if I'm seeing her now because I'm delirious from the blood loss or if the death serum has addled my thoughts or if she is here in some other way.

She kneels next to me and touches a cool hand to my cheek.

"Hello, Beatrice," she says, and she smiles.

"Am I done yet?" I say, and I'm not sure if I actually say it or if I just think it and she hears it.

"Yes," she says, her eyes bright with tears. "My dear child, you've done so well."

"What about the others?" I choke on a sob as the image of Tobias comes into my mind, of how dark and how still his eyes were, how strong and warm his hand was, when we first stood face-to-face. "Tobias, Caleb, my friends?"

"They'll care for each other," she says. "That's what people do."

I smile and close my eyes.

I feel a thread tugging me again, but this time I know that it isn't some sinister force dragging me toward death.

This time I know it's my mother's hand, drawing me into her arms.

And I go gladly into her embrace.

+++

Can I be forgiven for all I've done to get here?

I want to be.

I can.

I believe it.

CHAPTER FIFTY-ONE

TOBIAS

EVELYN BRUSHES THE tears from her eyes with her thumb. We stand by the windows, shoulder to shoulder, watching the snow swirl past. Some of the flakes gather on the windowsill outside, piling at the corners.

The feeling has returned to my hands. As I stare out at the world, dusted in white, I feel like everything has begun again, and it will be better this time.

"I think I can get in touch with Marcus over the radio to negotiate a peace agreement," Evelyn says. "He'll be listening in; he'd be stupid not to."

"Before you do that, I made a promise I have to keep," I say. I touch Evelyn's shoulder. I expected to see strain at the edges of her smile, but I don't.

I feel a twinge of guilt. I didn't come here to ask her to lay down arms for me, to trade in everything she's worked for just to get me back. But then again, I didn't come here to give her any choice at all. I guess Tris was right—when you have to choose between two bad options, you pick the one that saves the people you love. I wouldn't have been saving Evelyn by giving her that serum. I would have been destroying her.

Peter sits with his back to the wall in the hallway. He looks up at me when I lean over him, his dark hair stuck to his forehead from the melted snow.

"Did you reset her?" he says.

"No," I say.

"Didn't think you would have the nerve."

"It's not about nerve. You know what? Whatever." I shake my head and hold up the vial of memory serum. "Are you still set on this?"

He nods.

"You could just do the work, you know," I say. "You could make better decisions, make a better life."

"Yeah, I could," he says. "But I won't. We both know that."

I do know that. I know that change is difficult, and comes slowly, and that it is the work of many days strung together in a long line until the origin of them is forgotten. He is afraid that he will not be able to put in that work, that he will squander those days, and that they will leave him worse off than he is now. And I understand that feeling—I understand being afraid of yourself.

So I have him sit on one of the couches, and I ask him what he wants me to tell him about himself, after his memories disappear like smoke. He just shakes his head. Nothing. He wants to retain nothing.

Peter takes the vial with a shaking hand and twists off the cap. The liquid trembles inside it, almost spilling over the lip. He holds it under his nose to smell it.

"How much should I drink?" he says, and I think I hear his teeth chattering.

"I don't think it makes a difference," I say.

"Okay. Well . . . here goes." He lifts the vial up to the light like he is toasting me.

When he touches it to his mouth, I say, "Be brave."

Then he swallows.

And I watch Peter disappear.

+++

The air outside tastes like ice.

"Hey! Peter!" I shout, my breaths turning to vapor.

Peter stands by the doorway to Erudite headquarters, looking clueless. At the sound of his name—which I have told him at least ten times since he drank the serum—he raises his eyebrows, pointing to his chest. Matthew told us people would be disoriented for a while after drinking the memory serum, but I didn't think "disoriented" meant "stupid" until now.

I sigh. "Yes, that's you! For the eleventh time! Come on, let's go."

I thought that when I looked at him after he drank the serum, I would still see the initiate who shoved a butter knife into Edward's eye, and the boy who tried to kill my girlfriend, and all the other things he has done, stretching backward for as long as I've known him. But it's easier than I thought to see that he has no idea who he is anymore. His eyes still have that wide, innocent look, but this time, I believe it.

Evelyn and I walk side by side, with Peter trotting behind us. The snow has stopped falling now, but enough has collected on the ground that it squeaks under my shoes.

We walk to Millennium Park, where the mammoth bean sculpture reflects the moonlight, and then down a set of stairs. As we descend, Evelyn wraps her hand around my elbow to keep her balance, and we exchange a look. I wonder if she is as nervous as I am to face my father again. I wonder if she is nervous every time.

At the bottom of the steps is a pavilion with two glass blocks, each one at least three times as tall as I am, at either end. This is where we told Marcus and Johanna we would meet them—both parties armed, to be realistic but even.

They are already there. Johanna isn't holding a gun, but Marcus is, and he has it trained on Evelyn. I point the gun Evelyn gave me at him, just to be safe. I notice the planes of his skull, showing through his shaved hair, and the jagged path his crooked nose carves down his face.

"Tobias!" Johanna says. She wears a coat in Amity red, dusted with snowflakes. "What are you doing here?"

"Trying to keep you all from killing each other," I say. "I'm surprised you're carrying a gun."

I nod to the bulge in her coat pocket, the unmistakable contours of a weapon.

"Sometimes you have to take difficult measures to ensure peace," Johanna says. "I believe you agree with that, as a principle."

"We're not here to chat," Marcus says, looking at Evelyn. "You said you wanted to talk about a treaty."

The past few weeks have taken something from him. I can see it in the turned-down corners of his mouth, in the purple skin under his eyes. I see my own eyes set into his skull, and I think of my reflection in the fear landscape, how terrified I was, watching his skin spread over mine like a rash. I am still nervous that I will become him, even now, standing at odds with him with my mother at my side, like I always dreamed I would when I was a child.

But I don't think that I'm still afraid.

"Yes," Evelyn says. "I have some terms for us both to agree to. I think you will find them fair. If you agree to them, I will step down and surrender whatever weapons I have that my people are not using for personal protection. I will leave the city and not return."

Marcus laughs. I'm not sure if it's a mocking laugh or a disbelieving one. He's equally capable of either sentiment, an arrogant and deeply suspicious man.

"Let her finish," Johanna says quietly, tucking her hands into her sleeves.

"In return," Evelyn says, "you will not attack or try to seize control of the city. You will allow those people who wish to leave and seek a new life elsewhere to do so. You will allow those who choose to stay to *vote* on new leaders and a new social system. And most importantly, *you*, Marcus, will not be eligible to lead them."

It is the only purely selfish term of the peace agreement. She told me she couldn't stand the thought of Marcus duping more people into following him, and I didn't argue with her.

Johanna raises her eyebrows. I notice that she has pulled her hair back on both sides, to reveal the scar in its entirety. She looks better that way—stronger, when she is not hiding behind a curtain of hair, hiding who she is.

"No deal," Marcus says. "I am the leader of these people."

"Marcus," Johanna says.

He ignores her. "*You* don't get to decide whether I lead them or not because you have a grudge against me, Evelyn!"

"Excuse me," Johanna says loudly. "Marcus, what she is offering is too good to be true—we get everything we want without all the violence! How can you possibly say no?"

"Because I am the rightful leader of these people!" Marcus says. "I am the leader of the Allegiant! I—"

"No, you are not," Johanna says calmly. "*I* am the leader of the Allegiant. And you are going to agree to this treaty, or I am going to tell them that you had a chance to end this conflict without bloodshed if you sacrificed your pride, and you said no."

Marcus's passive mask is gone, revealing the malicious face beneath it. But even he can't argue with Johanna, whose perfect calm and perfect threat have mastered him. He shakes his head but doesn't argue again.

"I agree to your terms," Johanna says, and she holds out

her hand, her footsteps squeaking in the snow.

Evelyn removes her glove fingertip by fingertip, reaches across the gap, and shakes.

"In the morning we should gather everyone together and tell them the new plan," Johanna says. "Can you guarantee a safe gathering?"

"I'll do my best," Evelyn says.

I check my watch. An hour has passed since Amar and Christina separated from us near the Hancock building, which means he probably knows that the serum virus didn't work. Or maybe he doesn't. Either way, I have to do what I came here to do—I have to find Zeke and his mother and tell them what happened to Uriah.

"I should go," I say to Evelyn. "I have something else to take care of. But I'll pick you up from the city limits tomorrow afternoon?"

"That sounds good," Evelyn says, and she rubs my arm briskly with a gloved hand, like she used to when I came in from the cold as a child.

"You won't be back, I assume?" Johanna says to me. "You've found a life for yourself on the outside?"

"I have," I say. "Good luck in here. The people outside—they're going to try to shut the city down. You should be ready for them."

Johanna smiles. "I'm sure we can negotiate with them."

She offers me her hand, and I shake it. I feel Marcus's eyes on me like an oppressive weight threatening to crush me. I force myself to look at him.

"Good-bye," I say to him, and I mean it.

+++

Hana, Zeke's mother, has small feet that don't touch the ground when she sits in the easy chair in their living room. She is wearing a ragged black bathrobe and slippers, but the air she has, with her hands folded in her lap and her eyebrows raised, is so dignified that I feel like I am standing in front of a world leader. I glance at Zeke, who is rubbing his face with his fists to wake up.

Amar and Christina found them, not among the other revolutionaries near the Hancock building, but in their family apartment in the Pire, above Dauntless headquarters. I only found them because Christina thought to leave Peter and me a note with their location on the useless truck. Peter is waiting in the new van Evelyn found for us to drive to the Bureau.

"I'm sorry," I say. "I don't know where to start."

"You might begin with the worst," Hana says. "Like what exactly happened to my son."

"He was seriously injured during an attack," I say. "There was an explosion, and he was very close to it."

"Oh God," Zeke says, and he rocks back and forth like

his body wants to be a child again, soothed by motion as a child is.

But Hana just bends her head, hiding her face from me.

Their living room smells like garlic and onion, maybe remnants from that night's dinner. I lean my shoulder into the white wall by the doorway. Hanging crookedly next to me is a picture of the family—Zeke as a toddler, Uriah as a baby, balancing on his mother's lap. Their father's face is pierced in several places, nose and ear and lip, but his wide, bright smile and dark complexion are more familiar to me, because he passed them both to his sons.

"He has been in a coma since then," I say. "And . . ."

"And he isn't going to wake up," Hana says, her voice strained. "That is what you came to tell us, right?"

"Yes," I say. "I came to collect you so that you can make a decision on his behalf."

"A decision?" Zeke says. "You mean, to *unplug* him or not?"

"Zeke," Hana says, and she shakes her head. He sinks back into the couch. The cushions seem to wrap around him.

"Of course we don't want to keep him alive that way," Hana says. "He would want to move on. But we would like to go see him."

I nod. "Of course. But there's something else I should

say. The attack . . . it was a kind of uprising that involved some of the people from the place where we were staying. And I participated in it."

I stare at the crack in the floorboards right in front of me, at the dust that has gathered there over time, and wait for a reaction, any reaction. What greets me is only silence.

"I didn't do what you asked me," I say to Zeke. "I didn't watch out for him the way I should have. And I'm sorry."

I chance a look at him, and he is just sitting still, staring at the empty vase on the coffee table. It is painted with faded pink roses.

"I think we need some time with this," Hana says. She clears her throat, but it doesn't help her tremulous voice.

"I wish I could give it to you," I say. "But we're going back to the compound very soon, and you have to come with us."

"All right," Hana says. "If you can wait outside, we will be there in five minutes."

+++

The ride back to the compound is slow and dark. I watch the moon disappear and reappear behind the clouds as we bump over the ground. When we reach the outer limits of the city, it begins to snow again, large, light flakes that swirl in front of the headlights. I wonder if Tris is watching it sweep across the pavement and gather in piles by the airplanes. I wonder if she is living in a better world than the one I left, among people who no longer remember what it is to have pure genes.

Christina leans forward to whisper into my ear. "So you did it? It worked?"

I nod. In the rearview mirror I see her touch her face with both hands, grinning into her palms. I know how she feels: safe. We are all safe.

"Did you inoculate your family?" I say.

"Yep. We found them with the Allegiant, in the Hancock building," she says. "But the time for the reset has passed—it looks like Tris and Caleb stopped it."

Hana and Zeke murmur to each other on the way, marveling at the strange, dark world we move through. Amar gives the basic explanation as we go, looking back at them instead of the road far too often for my comfort. I try to ignore my surges of panic as he almost veers into streetlights or road barriers, and focus instead on the snow.

I have always hated the emptiness that winter brings, the blank landscape and the stark difference between sky and ground, the way it transforms trees into skeletons and the city into a wasteland. Maybe this winter I can be persuaded otherwise.

We drive past the fences and stop by the front doors,

which are no longer manned by guards. We get out, and Zeke seizes his mother's hand to steady her as she shuffles through the snow. As we walk into the compound, I know for a fact that Caleb succeeded, because there is no one in sight. That can only mean that they have been reset, their memories forever altered.

"Where is everyone?" Amar says.

We walk through the abandoned security checkpoint without stopping. On the other side, I see Cara. The side of her face is badly bruised, and there's a bandage on her head, but that's not what concerns me. What concerns me is the troubled look on her face.

"What is it?" I say.

Cara shakes her head.

"Where's Tris?" I say.

"I'm sorry, Tobias."

"Sorry about what?" Christina says roughly. "Tell us what *happened*!"

"Tris went into the Weapons Lab instead of Caleb," Cara says. "She survived the death serum, and set off the memory serum, but she . . . she was shot. And she didn't survive. I'm so sorry."

Most of the time I can tell when people are lying, and this must be a lie, because Tris is still alive, her eyes bright and her cheeks flushed and her small body full of power and strength, standing in a shaft of light in the atrium. Tris is still alive, she wouldn't leave me here alone, she wouldn't go to the Weapons Lab instead of Caleb.

"No," Christina says, shaking her head. "No way. There has to be some mistake."

Cara's eyes well up with tears.

It's then that I realize: Of course Tris would go into the Weapons Lab instead of Caleb.

Of course she would.

Christina yells something, but to me her voice sounds muffled, like I have submerged my head underwater. The details of Cara's face have also become difficult to see, the world smearing together into dull colors.

All I can do is stand still—I feel like if I just stand still, I can stop it from being true, I can pretend that everything is all right. Christina hunches over, unable to support her own grief, and Cara embraces her, and

all I'm doing is standing still.

CHAPTER FIFTY-TWO

TOBIAS

WHEN HER BODY first hit the net, all I registered was a gray blur. I pulled her across it and her hand was small, but warm, and then she stood before me, short and thin and plain and in all ways unremarkable—except that she had jumped first. The Stiff had jumped first.

Even I didn't jump first.

Her eyes were so stern, so insistent.

Beautiful.

CHAPTER FIFTY-THREE

TOBIAS

BUT THAT WASN'T the first time I ever saw her. I saw her in the hallways at school, and at my mother's false funeral, and walking the sidewalks in the Abnegation sector. I saw her, but I didn't see her; no one saw her the way she truly was until she jumped.

I suppose a fire that burns that bright is not meant to last.

CHAPTER FIFTY-FOUR

TOBIAS

I GO TO see her body . . . sometime. I don't know how long it is after Cara tells me what happened. Christina and I walk shoulder to shoulder; we walk in Cara's footsteps. I don't remember the journey from the entrance to the morgue, really, just a few smeared images and whatever sound I can make out through the barrier that has gone up inside my head.

She lies on a table, and for a moment I think she's just sleeping, and when I touch her, she will wake up and smile at me and press a kiss to my mouth. But when I touch her she is cold, her body stiff and unyielding.

Christina sniffles and sobs. I squeeze Tris's hand, praying that if I do it hard enough, I will send life back into her body and she will flush with color and wake up.

I don't know how long it takes for me to realize that isn't going to happen, that she is gone. But when I do I feel all the strength go out of me, and I fall to my knees beside the table and I think I cry, then, or at least I want to, and everything inside me screams for just one more kiss, one more word, one more glance, one more.

CHAPTER FIFTY-FIVE

IN THE DAYS that follow, it's movement, not stillness, that helps to keep the grief at bay, so I walk the compound halls instead of sleeping. I watch everyone else recover from the memory serum that altered them permanently as if from a great distance.

Those lost in the memory serum haze are gathered into groups and given the truth: that human nature is complex, that all our genes are different, but neither damaged nor pure. They are also given the lie: that their memories were erased because of a freak accident, and that they were on the verge of lobbying the government for equality for GDs.

I keep finding myself stifled by the company of others

and then crippled by loneliness when I leave them. I am terrified and I don't even know of what, because I have lost everything already. My hands shake as I stop by the control room to watch the city on the screens. Johanna is arranging transportation for those who want to leave the city. They will come here to learn the truth. I don't know what will happen to those who remain in Chicago, and I'm not sure I care.

I shove my hands into my pockets and watch for a few minutes, then walk away again, trying to match my footsteps to my heartbeat, or to avoid the cracks between the tiles. When I walk past the entrance, I see a small group of people gathered by the stone sculpture, one of them in a wheelchair—Nita.

I walk past the useless security barrier and stand at a distance, watching them. Reggie steps on the stone slab and opens a valve in the bottom of the water tank. The drops turn into a stream of water, and soon water gushes out of the tank, splattering all over the slab, soaking the bottom of Reggie's pants.

"Tobias?"

I shudder a little. It's Caleb. I turn away from the voice, searching for an escape route.

"Wait. Please," he says.

I don't want to look at him, to measure how much, or

how little, he grieves for her. And I don't want to think about how she died for such a miserable coward, about how he wasn't worth her life.

Still, I do look at him, wondering if I can see some of her in his face, still hungry for her even now that I know she's gone.

His hair is unwashed and unkempt, his green eyes bloodshot, his mouth twitching into a frown.

He does not look like her.

"I don't mean to bother you," he says. "But I have something to tell you. Something . . . *she* told me to tell you, before . . ."

"Just get on with it," I say, before he tries to finish the sentence.

"She told me that if she didn't survive, I should tell you . . ." Caleb chokes, then pulls himself up straight, fighting off tears. "That she didn't want to leave you."

I should feel something, hearing her last words to me, shouldn't I? I feel nothing. I feel farther away than ever.

"Yeah?" I say harshly. "Then why did she? Why didn't she let you die?"

"You think I'm not asking myself that question?" Caleb says. "She loved me. Enough to hold me at gunpoint so she could die for me. I have no idea why, but that's just the way it is."

He walks away without letting me respond, and it's probably better that way, because I can't think of anything to say that is equal to my anger. I blink away tears and sit down on the ground, right in the middle of the lobby.

I know why she wanted to tell me that she didn't want to leave me. She wanted me to know that this was not another Erudite headquarters, not a lie told to make me sleep while she went to die, not an act of unnecessary self-sacrifice. I grind the heels of my hands into my eyes like I can push my tears back into my skull. *No crying,* I chastise myself. If I let a little of the emotion out, all of it will come out, and it will never end.

Sometime later I hear voices nearby—Cara and Peter.

"This sculpture was a symbol of change," she says to him. "Gradual change, but now they're taking it down."

"Oh, really?" Peter sounds eager. "Why?"

"Um . . . I'll explain later, if that's okay," Cara says. "Do you remember how to get back to the dormitory?"

"Yep."

"Then . . . go back there for a while. Someone will be there to help you."

Cara walks over to me, and I cringe in anticipation of her voice. But all she does is sit next to me on the ground, her hands folded in her lap, her back straight. Alert but relaxed, she watches the sculpture where Reggie stands under the gushing water.

"You don't have to stay here," I say.

"I don't have anywhere to be," she says. "And the quiet is nice."

So we sit side by side, staring at the water, in silence.

+++

"There you are," Christina says, jogging toward us. Her face is swollen and her voice is listless, like a heavy sigh. "Come on, it's time. They're unplugging him."

I shudder at the word, but push myself to my feet anyway. Hana and Zeke have been hovering over Uriah's body since we got here, their fingers finding his, their eyes searching for life. But there is no life left, just the machine beating his heart.

Cara walks behind Christina and me as we go toward the hospital. I haven't slept in days but I don't feel tired, not in the way I normally do, though my body aches as I walk. Christina and I don't speak, but I know our thoughts are the same, fixed on Uriah, on his last breaths.

We make it to the observation window outside Uriah's room, and Evelyn is there—Amar picked her up in my stead, a few days ago. She tries to touch my shoulder and I yank it away, not wanting to be comforted.

Inside the room, Zeke and Hana stand on either side of Uriah. Hana is holding one of his hands, and Zeke is holding the other. A doctor stands near the heart monitor, a clipboard outstretched, held out not to Hana or Zeke but to *David*. Sitting in his wheelchair. Hunched and dazed, like all the others who have lost their memories.

"What is *he* doing there?" I feel like all my muscles and bones and nerves are on fire.

"He's still technically the leader of the Bureau, at least until they replace him," Cara says from behind me. "Tobias, he doesn't remember anything. The man you knew doesn't exist anymore; he's as good as dead. *That* man doesn't remember kill—"

"Shut up!" I snap. David signs the clipboard and turns around, pushing himself toward the door. It opens, and I can't stop myself—I lunge toward him, and only Evelyn's wiry frame stops me from wrapping my hands around his throat. He gives me a strange look and pushes himself down the hallway as I press against my mother's arm, which feels like a bar across my shoulders.

"Tobias," Evelyn says. "Calm. Down."

"Why didn't someone lock him up?" I demand, and my eyes are too blurry to see out of.

"Because he still works for the government," Cara says. "Just because they've declared it an unfortunate accident doesn't mean they've fired everyone. And the government isn't going to lock him up just because he killed a rebel under duress."

"A rebel," I repeat. "That's all she is now?"

"Was," Cara says softly. "And no, of course not, but that's what the government sees her as."

I'm about to respond, but Christina interrupts. "Guys, they're doing it."

In Uriah's room, Zeke and Hana join their free hands over Uriah's body. I see Hana's lips moving, but I can't tell what she's saying—do the Dauntless have prayers for the dying? The Abnegation react to death with silence and service, not words. I find my anger ebbing away, and I'm lost in muffled grief again, this time not just for Tris, but for Uriah, whose smile is burned into my memory. My friend's brother, and then my friend, too, though not for long enough to let his humor work its way into me, not for long enough.

The doctor flips some switches, his clipboard clutched to his stomach, and the machines stop breathing for Uriah. Zeke's shoulders shake, and Hana squeezes his hand tightly, until her knuckles go white.

Then she says something, and her hands spring open, and she steps back from Uriah's body. Letting him go.

I move away from the window, walking at first, and then running, pushing my way through the hallways, careless, blind, empty.

CHAPTER FIFTY-SIX

THE NEXT DAY I take a truck from the compound. The people there are still recovering from their memory loss, so no one tries to stop me. I drive over the railroad tracks toward the city, my eyes wandering over the skyline but not really taking it in.

When I reach the fields that separate the city from the outside world, I press down the accelerator. The truck crushes dying grass and snow beneath its tires, and soon the ground turns to the pavement in the Abnegation sector, and I barely feel the passage of time. The streets are all the same, but my hands and feet know where to go, even if my mind doesn't bother to guide them. I pull up to the house near the stop sign, with the cracked front walk.

My house.

I walk through the front door and up the stairs, still with that muffled feeling in my ears, like I am drifting far away from the world. People talk about the pain of grief, but I don't know what they mean. To me, grief is a devastating numbness, every sensation dulled.

I press my palm to the panel covering the mirror upstairs, and push it aside. Though the light of sunset is orange, creeping across the floor and illuminating my face from below, I have never looked paler; the circles under my eyes have never been more pronounced. I have spent the past few days somewhere between sleeping and waking, not quite able to manage either extreme.

I plug the hair clippers into the outlet near the mirror. The right guard is already in place, so all I have to do is run it through my hair, bending my ears down to protect them from the blade, turning my head to check the back of my neck for places I might have missed. The shorn hair falls on my feet and shoulders, itching whatever bare skin it finds. I run my hand over my head to make sure it's even, but I don't need to check, not really. I learned to do this myself when I was young.

I spend a lot of time brushing it from my shoulders and feet, then sweeping it into a dustpan. When I finish, I stand in front of the mirror again, and I can see the edges of my tattoo, the Dauntless flame.

I take the vial of memory serum from my pocket. I know that one vial will erase most of my life, but it will target memories, not facts. I will still know how to write, how to speak, how to put together a computer, because that data was stored in different parts of my brain. But I won't remember anything else.

The experiment is over. Johanna successfully negotiated with the government—David's superiors—to allow the former faction members to stay in the city, provided they are self-sufficient, submit to the government's authority, and allow outsiders to come in and join them, making Chicago just another metropolitan area, like Milwaukee. The Bureau, once in charge of the experiment, will now keep order in Chicago's city limits.

It will be the only metropolitan area in the country governed by people who don't believe in genetic damage. A kind of paradise. Matthew told me he hopes people from the fringe will trickle in to fill all the empty spaces, and find there a life more prosperous than the one they left.

All that I want is to become someone new. In this case, Tobias Johnson, son of Evelyn Johnson. Tobias Johnson may have lived a dull and empty life, but he is at least a whole person, not this fragment of a person that I am, too damaged by pain to become anything useful.

"Matthew told me you stole some of the memory serum and a truck," says a voice at the end of the hallway. Christina's. "I have to say, I didn't really believe him."

I must not have heard her enter the house through the muffle. Even her voice sounds like it is traveling through water to reach my ears, and it takes me a few seconds to make sense of what she says. When I do, I look at her and say, "Then why did you come, if you didn't believe him?"

"Just in case," she says, starting toward me. "Plus, I wanted to see the city one more time before it all changes. Give me that vial, Tobias."

"No." I fold my fingers over it to protect it from her. "This is my decision, not yours."

Her dark eyes widen, and her face is radiant with sunlight. It makes every strand of her thick, dark hair gleam orange like it's on fire.

"This is *not* your decision," she says. "This is the decision of a coward, and you're a lot of things, Four, but not a coward. Never."

"Maybe I am now," I answer passively. "Things have changed. I'm all right with it."

"No, you're not."

I feel so exhausted all I can do is roll my eyes.

"You can't become a person she would hate," Christina says, quietly this time. "And she would have hated this."

Anger stampedes through me, hot and lively, and the muffled feeling around my ears falls away, making even this quiet Abnegation street sound loud. I shudder with the force of it.

"Shut up!" I yell. "Shut up! You don't know what she would hate; you didn't know her, you—"

"I know enough!" she snaps. "I know she wouldn't want you to erase her from your memory like she didn't even matter to you!"

I lunge toward her, pinning her shoulder to the wall, and lean closer to her face.

"If you *dare* suggest that again," I say, "I'll—"

"You'll what?" Christina shoves me back, hard. "Hurt me? You know, there's a word for big, strong men who attack women, and it's *coward*."

I remember my father's screams filling the house, and his hand around my mother's throat, slamming her into walls and doors. I remember watching from my doorway, my hand wrapped around the door frame. And I remember hearing quiet sobs through her bedroom door, how she locked it so I couldn't get in.

I step back and slump against the wall, letting my body collapse into it.

"I'm sorry," I say.

"I know," she answers.

We stand still for a few seconds, just looking at each other. I remember hating her the first time I met her, because she was a Candor, because words just dribbled out of her mouth unchecked, careless. But over time she showed me who she really was, a forgiving friend, faithful to the truth, brave enough to take action. I can't help but like her now, can't help but see what Tris saw in her.

"I know how it feels to want to forget everything," she says. "I also know how it feels for someone you love to get killed for no reason, and to want to trade all your memories of them for just a moment's peace."

She wraps her hand around mine, which is wrapped around the vial.

"I didn't know Will long," she says, "but he changed my life. He changed *me*. And I know Tris changed you even more."

The hard expression she wore a moment ago melts away, and she touches my shoulders, lightly.

"The person you became with her is worth being," she says. "If you swallow that serum, you'll never be able to find your way back to him."

The tears come again, like when I saw Tris's body, and this time, pain comes with them, hot and sharp in my chest. I clutch the vial in my fist, desperate for the relief it offers, the protection from the pain of every memory clawing inside me like an animal.

Christina puts her arms around my shoulders, and her embrace only makes the pain worse, because it reminds me of every time Tris's thin arms slipped around me, uncertain at first but then stronger, more confident, more sure of herself and of me. It reminds me that no embrace will ever feel the same again, because no one will ever be like her again, because she's gone.

She's gone, and crying feels so useless, so stupid, but it's all I can do. Christina holds me upright and doesn't say a word for a long time.

Eventually I pull away, but her hands stay on my shoulders, warm and rough with calluses. Maybe just as skin on a hand grows tougher after pain in repetition, a person does too. But I don't want to become a calloused man.

There are other kinds of people in this world. There is the kind like Tris, who, after suffering and betrayal, could still find enough love to lay down her life instead of her brother's. Or the kind like Cara, who could still forgive the person who shot her brother in the head. Or Christina, who lost friend after friend but still decided to stay open, to make new ones. Appearing in front of me is another choice, brighter and stronger than the ones I gave myself.

My eyes opening, I offer the vial to her. She takes it and pockets it.

“I know Zeke’s still weird around you,” she says, slinging an arm across my shoulders. “But I can be your friend in the meantime. We can even exchange bracelets if you want, like the Amity girls used to.”

“I don’t think that will be necessary.”

We walk down the stairs and out to the street together. The sun has slipped behind the buildings of Chicago, and in the distance I hear a train rushing over the rails, but we are moving away from this place and all that it has meant to us, and that is all right.

+++

There are so many ways to be brave in this world. Sometimes bravery involves laying down your life for something bigger than yourself, or for someone else. Sometimes it involves giving up everything you have ever known, or everyone you have ever loved, for the sake of something greater.

But sometimes it doesn’t.

Sometimes it is nothing more than gritting your teeth through pain, and the work of every day, the slow walk toward a better life.

That is the sort of bravery I must have now.

EPILOGUE

Two and a Half Years Later

Evelyn stands at the place where two worlds meet. Tire tracks are worn into the ground now, from the frequent coming and going of people from the fringe moving in and out, or people from the former Bureau compound commuting back and forth. Her bag rests against her leg, in one of the wells in the earth. She lifts a hand to greet me when I'm close.

When she gets into the truck, she kisses my cheek, and I let her. I feel a smile creep across my face, and I let it stay there.

"Welcome back," I say.

The agreement, when I offered it to her more than two years ago, and when she made it again with Johanna shortly after, was that she would leave the city. Now, so much has changed in Chicago that I don't see the harm in her coming back, and neither does she. Though two years have passed, she looks younger, her face fuller and her smile wider. The time away has done her good.

"How are you?" she says.

"I'm . . . okay," I say. "We're scattering her ashes today."

I glance at the urn perched on the backseat like another passenger. For a long time I left Tris's ashes in the Bureau morgue, not sure what kind of funeral she would want, and not sure I could make it through one. But today would be Choosing Day, if we still had factions, and it's time to take a step forward, even if it's a small one.

Evelyn puts a hand on my shoulder and looks out at the fields. The crops that were once isolated to the areas around Amity headquarters have spread, and continue to spread through all the grassy spaces around the city. Sometimes I miss the desolate, empty land. But right now I don't mind driving through the rows and rows of corn or wheat. I see people among the plants, checking the soil with handheld devices designed by former Bureau scientists. They wear red and blue and green and purple.

"What's it like, living without factions?" Evelyn says.

"It's very ordinary," I say. I smile at her. "You'll love it."

+++

I take Evelyn to my apartment just north of the river. It's on one of the lower floors, but through the abundant windows I can see a wide stretch of buildings. I was one of the first settlers in the new Chicago, so I got to choose where I lived. Zeke, Shauna, Christina, Amar, and George opted to live in the higher floors of the Hancock building, and Caleb and Cara both moved back to the apartments near Millennium Park, but I came here because it was beautiful, and because it was nowhere near either of my old homes.

"My neighbor is a history expert, he came from the fringe," I say as I search my pockets for my keys. "He calls Chicago 'the fourth city'—because it was destroyed by fire, ages ago, and then again by the Purity War, and now we're on the fourth attempt at settlement here."

"The fourth city," Evelyn says as I push the door open. "I like it."

There's hardly any furniture inside, just a couch and a table, some chairs, a kitchen. Sunlight winks in the windows of the building across the marshy river. Some of the former Bureau scientists are trying to restore the river and the lake to their former glory, but it will be a while. Change, like healing, takes time.

Evelyn drops her bag on the couch. "Thank you for letting me stay with you for a little while. I promise I'll find another place soon."

"No problem," I say. I feel nervous about her being here, poking through my meager possessions, shuffling down my hallways, but we can't stay distant forever. Not when I promised her that I would try to bridge this gap between us.

"George says he needs some help training a police force," Evelyn says. "You didn't offer?"

"No," I say. "I told you, I'm done with guns."

"That's right. You're using your *words* now," Evelyn says, wrinkling her nose. "I don't trust politicians, you know."

"You'll trust me, because I'm your son," I say. "Anyway, I'm not a politician. Not yet, anyway. Just an assistant."

She sits at the table and looks around, twitchy and spry, like a cat.

"Do you know where your father is?" she says.

I shrug. "Someone told me he left. I didn't ask where he went."

She rests her chin on her hand. "There's nothing you wanted to say to him? Nothing at all?"

"No," I say. I twirl my keys around my finger. "I just wanted to leave him behind me, where he belongs."

Two years ago, when I stood across from him in the park with the snow falling all around us, I realized that just as attacking him in front of the Dauntless in the Merciless Mart didn't make me feel better about the pain he caused me, yelling at him or insulting him wouldn't either. There was only one option left, and it was letting go.

Evelyn gives me a strange, searching look, then crosses the room and opens the bag she left on the couch. She takes out an object made of blue glass. It looks like falling water, suspended in time.

I remember when she gave it to me. I was young, but not too young to realize that it was a forbidden object in the Abnegation faction, a useless and therefore a self-indulgent one. I asked her what purpose it served, and she told me, *It doesn't do anything obvious. But it might be able to do something in here.* Then she touched her hand to her heart. *Beautiful things sometimes do.*

For years it was a symbol of my quiet defiance, my small refusal to be an obedient, deferent Abnegation child, and a symbol of my mother's defiance too, even though I believed she was dead. I hid it under my bed, and the day I decided to leave Abnegation, I put it on my desk so my father could see it, see my strength, and hers.

"When you were gone, this reminded me of you," she says, clutching the glass to her stomach. "Reminded me of how brave you were, always have been." She smiles a little. "I thought you might keep it here. I intended it for you, after all."

I wouldn't trust my voice to remain steady if I spoke, so I just smile back, and nod.

+++

The spring air is cold but I leave the windows open in the truck, so I can feel it in my chest, so it stings my fingertips, a reminder of the lingering winter. I stop by the train platform near the Merciless Mart and take the urn out of the backseat. It's silver and simple, no engravings. I didn't choose it; Christina did.

I walk down the platform toward the group that has already gathered. Christina stands with Zeke and Shauna, who sits in the wheelchair with a blanket over her lap. She has a better wheelchair now, one without handles on the back, so she can maneuver it more easily. Matthew stands on the platform with his toes over the edge.

"Hi," I say, standing at Shauna's shoulder.

Christina smiles at me, and Zeke claps me on the shoulder.

Uriah died only days after Tris, but Zeke and Hana said their good-byes just weeks afterward, scattering his ashes in the chasm, amid the clatter of all their friends and family. We screamed his name into the echo chamber of the Pit. Still, I know that Zeke is remembering him today, just as the rest of us are, even though this last act of Dauntless bravery is for Tris.

"Got something to show you," Shauna says, and she tosses the blanket aside, revealing complicated metal braces on her legs. They go all the way up to her hips and wrap around her belly like a cage. She smiles at me, and with a gear-grinding sound, her feet shift to the ground in front of the chair, and in fits and starts, she stands.

Despite the serious occasion, I smile.

"Well, look at that," I say. "I'd forgotten how tall you are."

"Caleb and his lab buddies made them for me," she says. "Still getting the hang of it, but they say I might be able to run someday."

"Nice," I say. "Where is he, anyway?"

"He and Amar will meet us at the end of the line," she says. "Someone has to be there to catch the first person."

"He's still sort of a pansycake," Zeke says. "But I'm coming around to him."

"Hm," I say, not committing. The truth is, I've made my peace with Caleb, but I still can't be around him for long. His gestures, his inflections, his manner, they are hers. They make him into just a whisper of her, and that is not enough of her, but it is also far too much.

I would say more, but the train is coming. It charges toward us on the polished rails, then squeals as it slows to a stop in front of the platform. A head leans out the window of the first car, where the controls are—it's Cara, her hair in a tight braid.

"Get on!" she says.

Shauna sits in the chair again and pushes herself through the doorway. Matthew, Christina, and Zeke follow. I get on last, offering the urn to Shauna to hold, and stand in the doorway, my hand clutching the handle. The train starts again, building speed with each second, and I hear it churning over the tracks and whistling over the rails, and I feel the power of it rising inside me. The air whips across my face and presses my clothes to my body, and I watch the city sprawl out in front of me, the buildings lit by the sun.

It's not the same as it used to be, but I got over that a long time ago. All of us have found new places. Cara and Caleb work in the laboratories at the compound, which are now a small segment of the Department of Agriculture that works to make agriculture more efficient, capable of feeding more people. Matthew works in psychiatric research somewhere in the city—the last time I asked him, he was studying something about memory. Christina works in an office that relocates people from the fringe who want to move into the city. Zeke and Amar are policemen, and George trains the police force—Dauntless jobs, I call them. And I'm assistant to one of our city's representatives in government: Johanna Reyes.

I stretch my arm out to grasp the other handle and lean out of the car as it turns, almost dangling over the street two stories below me. I feel a thrill in my stomach, the fear-thrill the true Dauntless love.

"Hey," Christina says, standing beside me. "How's your mother?"

"Fine," I say. "We'll see, I guess."

"Are you going to zip line?"

I watch the track dip down in front of us, going all the way to street level.

"Yes," I say. "I think Tris would want me to try it at least once."

Saying her name still gives me a little twinge of pain, a pinch that lets me know her memory is still dear to me.

Christina watches the rails ahead of us and leans her shoulder into mine, just for a few seconds. "I think you're right."

My memories of Tris, some of the most powerful memories I have, have dulled with time, as memories do, and they no longer sting as they used to. Sometimes I actually enjoy going over them in my mind, though not often. Sometimes I go over them with Christina, and she listens better than I expected her to, Candor smart-mouth that she is.

Cara guides the train to a stop, and I hop onto the platform. At the top of the stairs Shauna gets out of the chair and works her way down the steps with the braces, one at a time. Matthew and I carry her empty chair after her, which is cumbersome and heavy, but not impossible to manage.

"Any updates from Peter?" I ask Matthew as we reach the bottom of the stairs.

After Peter emerged from the memory serum haze, some of the sharper, harsher aspects of his personality returned, though not all of them. I lost touch with him after that. I don't hate him anymore, but that doesn't mean I have to like him.

"He's in Milwaukee," Matthew says. "I don't know what he's doing, though."

"He's working in an office somewhere," Cara says from the bottom of the stairs. She has the urn cradled in her arms, taken from Shauna's lap on the way off the train. "I think it's good for him."

"I always thought he would go join the GD rebels in the fringe," Zeke says. "Shows you what I know."

"He's different now," Cara says with a shrug.

There are still GD rebels in the fringe who believe that another war is the only way to get the change we want. I fall more on the side that wants to work for change without violence. I've had enough violence to last me a lifetime, and I bear it still, not in scars on my skin but in the memories that rise up in my mind when I least want them to, my father's fist colliding with my jaw, my gun raised to execute Eric, the Abnegation bodies sprawled across the streets of my old home.

We walk the streets to the zip line. The factions are gone, but this part of the city has more Dauntless than any other, recognizable still by their pierced faces and tattooed skin, though no longer by the colors they wear, which are sometimes garish. Some wander the sidewalks with us, but most are at work—everyone in Chicago is required to work if they're able.

Ahead of me I see the Hancock building bending into the sky, its base wider than its top. The black girders chase one another up to the roof, crossing, tightening, and expanding. I haven't been this close in a long time.

We enter the lobby, with its gleaming, polished floors and its walls smeared with bright Dauntless graffiti, left here by the building's residents as a kind of relic. This is a Dauntless place, because they are the ones who embraced it, for its height and, a part of me also suspects, for its loneliness. The Dauntless liked to fill empty spaces with their noise. It's something I liked about them.

Zeke jabs the elevator button with his index finger. We pile in, and Cara presses number 99.

I close my eyes as the elevator surges upward. I can almost see the space opening up beneath my feet, a shaft of darkness, and only a foot of solid ground between me and the sinking, dropping, plummeting. The elevator shudders as it stops, and I cling to the wall to steady myself as the doors open.

Zeke touches my shoulder. "Don't worry, man. We did this all the time, remember?"

I nod. Air rushes through the gap in the ceiling, and above me is the sky, bright blue. I shuffle with the others toward the ladder, too numb with fear to make my feet move any faster.

I find the ladder with my fingertips and focus on one rung at a time. Above me, Shauna maneuvers awkwardly up the ladder, using mostly the strength of her arms.

I asked Tori once, while I was getting the symbols tattooed on my back, if she thought we were the last people left in the world. *Maybe,* was all she said. I don't think she liked to think about it. But up here, on the roof, it is possible to believe that we are the last people left anywhere.

I stare at the buildings along the marsh front, and my chest tightens, squeezes, like it's about to collapse into itself.

Zeke runs across the roof to the zip line and attaches one of the man-sized slings to the steel cable. He locks it so it won't slide down, and looks at the group of us expectantly.

"Christina," he says. "It's all you."

Christina stands near the sling, tapping her chin with a finger.

"What do you think? Face-up or backward?"

"Backward," Matthew says. "I wanted to go face-up so I don't wet my pants, and I don't want you copying me."

"Going face-up will only make that more likely to happen, you know," Christina says. "So go ahead and do it so I can start calling you Wetpants."

Christina gets in the sling feet-first, belly down, so she'll watch the building get smaller as she travels. I shudder.

I can't watch. I close my eyes as Christina travels farther and farther away, and even as Matthew, and then Shauna, do the same thing. I can hear their cries of joy, like birdcalls, on the wind.

"Your turn, Four," says Zeke.

I shake my head.

"Come on," Cara says. "Better to get it over with, right?"

"No," I say. "You go. Please."

She offers me the urn, then takes a deep breath. I hold the urn against my stomach. The metal is warm from where so many people have touched it. Cara climbs into the sling, unsteady, and Zeke straps her in. She crosses her arms over her chest, and he sends her out, over Lake Shore Drive, over the city. I don't hear anything from her, not even a gasp.

Then it's just Zeke and me left, staring at each other.

"I don't think I can do it," I say, and though my voice is steady, my body is shaking.

"Of course you can," he says. "You're *Four*, Dauntless legend! You can face anything."

I cross my arms and inch closer to the edge of the roof. Even though I'm several feet away, I feel my body pitching over the edge, and I shake my head again, and again, and again.

"Hey." Zeke puts his hands on my shoulders. "This isn't about you, remember? It's about her. Doing something she would have liked to do, something she would have been proud of you for doing. Right?"

That's it. I can't avoid this, I can't back out now, not when I still remember her smile as she climbed the Ferris wheel with me, or the hard set of her jaw as she faced fear after fear in the simulations.

"How did she get in?"

"Face-first," Zeke says.

"All right." I hand him the urn. "Put this behind me, okay? And open up the top."

I climb into the sling, my hands shaking so much I can barely grip the sides. Zeke tightens the straps across my back and legs, then wedges the urn behind me, facing out, so the ashes will spread. I stare down Lake Shore Drive, swallowing bile, and start to slide.

Suddenly I want to take it back, but it's too late, I am already diving toward the ground. I'm screaming so loud, I want to cover my own ears. I feel the scream living inside me, filling my chest, throat, and head.

The wind stings my eyes but I force them open, and in my moment of blind panic I understand why she did it this way, face-first—it was because it made her feel like she was flying, like she was a bird.

I can still feel the emptiness beneath me, and it is like the emptiness inside me, like a mouth about to swallow me.

I realize, then, that I have stopped moving. The last bits of ash float on the wind like gray snowflakes, and then disappear.

The ground is only a few feet below me, close enough to jump down. The others have gathered there in a circle, their arms clasped to form a net of bone and muscle to catch me in. I press my face to the sling and laugh.

I toss the empty urn down to them, then twist my arms behind my back to undo the straps holding me in. I drop into my friends' arms like a stone. They catch me, their bones pinching at my back and legs, and lower me to the ground.

There is an awkward silence as I stare at the Hancock building in wonder, and no one knows what to say. Caleb smiles at me, cautious.

Christina blinks tears from her eyes and says, "Oh! Zeke's on his way."

Zeke is hurtling toward us in a black sling. At first it looks like a dot, then a blob, and then a person swathed in black. He crows with joy as he eases to a stop, and I reach across to grab Amar's forearm. On my other side, I grasp a pale arm that belongs to Cara. She smiles at me, and there is some sadness in her smile.

Zeke's shoulder hits our arms, hard, and he smiles wildly as he lets us cradle him like a child.

"That was nice. Want to go again, Four?" he says.

I don't hesitate before answering. "Absolutely not."

+++

We walk back to the train in a loose cluster. Shauna walks with her braces, Zeke pushing the empty wheelchair, and exchanges small talk with Amar. Matthew, Cara, and Caleb walk together, talking about something that has them all excited, kindred spirits that they are. Christina sidles up next to me and puts a hand on my shoulder.

"Happy Choosing Day," she says. "I'm going to ask you how you really are. And you're going to give me an honest answer."

We talk like this sometimes, giving each other orders. Somehow she has become one of the best friends I have, despite our frequent bickering.

"I'm all right," I say. "It's hard. It always will be."

"I know," she says.

We walk at the back of the group, past the still-abandoned buildings with their dark windows, over the bridge that spans the river-marsh.

"Yeah, sometimes life really sucks," she says. "But you know what I'm holding on for?"

I raise my eyebrows.

She raises hers, too, mimicking me.

"The moments that don't suck," she says. "The trick is to notice them when they come around."

Then she smiles, and I smile back, and we climb the stairs to the train platform side by side.

+++

Since I was young, I have always known this: Life damages us, every one. We can't escape that damage.

But now, I am also learning this: We can be mended. We mend each other.

ACKNOWLEDGMENTS

To me, the acknowledgments page is a place for me to say, as sincerely as possible, that I don't prosper, in life or in books, because of my own strength or skill alone. This series may have only one author, but this author wouldn't have been able to do much of anything without the following people. So with that in mind: Thank you, God, for giving me the people who mend me.

Here they are—

Thank you to: my husband, for not only loving me in an extraordinary way but for some difficult brainstorming sessions, for reading *all* the drafts of this book, and for dealing with Neurotic Author Wife with the utmost patience.

Joanna Volpe, for handling everything LIKE A BOSS, as they say, with honesty and kindness. Katherine Tegen, for excellent notes and for continually showing me the compassionate candy center inside the publishing badass. (I won't tell anyone. Wait, I just did.) Molly O'Neill, for all your time and work and for the eye that spotted *Divergent* from what I'm sure was a giant stack of manuscripts. Casey McIntyre, for some major publicity prowess and for showing me astounding kindness (and dance moves).

Joel Tippie, as well as Amy Ryan and Barb Fitzsimmons,

for making these books so gorgeous Every. Single. Time. The amazing Brenna Franzitta, Josh Weiss, Mark Rifkin, Valerie Shea, Christine Cox, and Joan Giurdanella, for taking such good care of my words. Lauren Flower, Alison Lisnow, Sandee Roston, Diane Naughton, Colleen O'Connell, Aubry Parks-Fried, Margot Wood, Patty Rosati, Molly Thomas, Megan Sugrue, Onalee Smith, and Brett Rachlin, for all your marketing and publicity efforts, which are far too substantial to name. Andrea Pappenheimer, Kerry Moynagh, Kathy Faber, Liz Frew, Heather Doss, Jenny Sheridan, Fran Olson, Deb Murphy, Jessica Abel, Samantha Hagerbaumer, Andrea Rosen, and David Wolfson, sales experts, for your enthusiasm and support. Jean McGinley, Alpha Wong, and Sheala Howley, for getting my words on so many shelves across the globe. For that matter, all my foreign publishers, for believing in these stories. Shayna Ramos and Ruiko Tokunaga, production whizzes; Caitlin Garing, Beth Ives, Karen Dziekonski, and Sean McManus, who make fantastic audiobooks; and Randy Rosema and Pam Moore of finance—for all your hard work and talent. Kate Jackson, Susan Katz, and Brian Murray, for steering this Harper ship so well. I have an enthusiastic and supportive publisher from top to bottom, and that means so much to me.

Pouya Shahbazian, for finding *Divergent* such a good

movie home, and for all your hard work, patience, friendship, and horrifying bug-related pranks. Danielle Barthel, for your organized and patient mind. Everyone else at New Leaf Literary, for being wonderful people who do equally wonderful work. Steve Younger, for always looking out for me in work and in life. Everyone involved in "movie stuff"—particularly Neil Burger, Doug Wick, Lucy Fisher, Gillian Bohrer, and Erik Feig—for handling my work with such care and respect.

Mom, Frank, Ingrid, Karl, Frank Jr., Candice, McCall, Beth, Roger, Tyler, Trevor, Darby, Rachel, Billie, Fred, Granny, the Johnsons (both Romanian and Missourian), the Krausses, the Paquettes, the Fitches, and the Rydzes—for all your love. (I would never choose my faction before you. Ever.)

All the past-present-future members of YA Highway and Write Night, for being such thoughtful, understanding writer buddies. All the more experienced authors who have included me and helped me for the past few years. All the writers who have reached out to me on Twitter or e-mail for camaraderie. Writing can be a lonely job, but not for me, because I have you. I wish I could list you all. Mary Katherine Howell, Alice Kovacik, Carly Maletich, Danielle Bristow, and all my other non-writer friends, for helping me keep my head on straight.

All the Divergent fansites, for crazy-awesome internet (and real-life) enthusiasm.

My readers, for reading and thinking and squealing and tweeting and talking and lending and, above all, for teaching me so many valuable lessons about writing and life.

All of the people listed above have made this series what it is, and knowing you all has changed my life. I am so lucky.

I'll say it one last time: Be brave.

SPECIAL THANKS

In the spring of 2012, fifty blogs helped spread their love for the **DIVERGENT** series by supporting the release of **INSURGENT** in a faction-based online campaign. Every participant was integral to the success of this series! Thank you to:

ABNEGATION: Amanda Bell (faction leader), Katie Bartow, Heidi Bennett, Katie Butler, Asma Faizal, Hafsah Faizal, Ana Grilo, Kathy Habel, Thea James, Julie Jones, and HD Tolson

AMITY: Meg Caristi, Kassiah Faul, and Sherry Atwell (faction leaders), Kristin Aragon, Emily Ellsworth, Cindy Hand, Melissa Helmers, Abigail J., Sarah Pitre, Lisa Reeves, Stephanie Su, and Amanda Welling

CANDOR: Kristi Diehm (faction leader), Jaime Arnold, Harmony Beaufort, Damaris Cardinali, Kris Chen, Sara Gundell, Bailey Hewlett, John Jacobson, Hannah McBride, and Aeicha Matteson

DAUNTLESS: Alison Genet (faction leader), Lena Ainsworth, Stacey Canova and Amber Clark, April Conant, Lindsay Cummings, Jessica Estep, Ashley Gonzales, Anna Heinemann, Tram Hoang, Nancy Sanchez, and Yara Santos

ERUDITE: Pam van Hylckama Vlieg (faction leader), James Booth, Mary Brebner, Andrea Chapman, Amy Green, Jen Hamflett, Brittany Howard, O'Dell Hutchison, Benji Kenworthy, Lyndsey Lore, Jennifer McCoy, Lisa Parkin, and Lisa Roecker

ALLEGIANT

BONUS MATERIALS

BONUS MATERIALS

NATALIE'S JOURNALS

WEEK 49
THURSDAY NIGHT

I'M PRETTY SURE David won't be interested in hearing about this, so I'm going to put it in my private journal instead of the official record.

Today I stayed after school to tutor Andrew, like I have been for the past few weeks as we get ready for our psychology exam. We were going over the evidence for and against biological explanations for personality traits as opposed to experiential explanations, such as parenting, history, and so on. I remember that because I was arguing for the latter and he was arguing for the former—it's just like an Erudite to get all caught up in biology, really—and I was really close to spilling the secret, *the* secret.

I asked him if he thought the faction system could just be a way to condition people to have certain personality traits—like behavioral modification. He said the factions were more likely to be a way of grouping people with similar genetic material—that our personalities are determined by our genes more than what we're taught. He kept using words like "thus" and "therefore," and every time he did I made a face at him. It took a few times for him to know that he should laugh. Anyway, then I trapped him, and I asked him why, if personalities are genetically determined, children of the same parents have different personalities. He stared at me, and he started to get that creeping red blotch on his cheeks that he always gets when he's sort of embarrassed. I watched him scramble for an answer, and his hair fell out of its slick style and over his forehead, and strangely, I felt like I had to stop myself from pushing it back. Like I almost had to grab my own hand to keep myself from doing it.

He came up with an answer—something about how if children can inherit different eye colors from their parents, they can also inherit different personality traits. But I wasn't really listening. I was just staring at his hair and wondering when it happened, when I started to want to touch him.

WEEK 49
FRIDAY NIGHT

WE STAYED AFTER school for tutoring again today, even though the exam was this morning. We brought our books even though there wasn't anything to do. I think we still felt like we needed an excuse. People don't just mingle outside their factions for no good reason.

I felt this itch in my fingers to do something, and the sun was reflecting off his glasses so I couldn't see his eyes. On an impulse I reached forward and took them off his face. I guess I'd never noticed before how blue they were, bright like the shirt he was wearing. He just stared at me, but not like he thought I was crazy, more like he was just curious.

He asked me why I had spoken so passionately the day before about parents and how personalities are determined. I hadn't realized that I had been "passionate," but it felt strange, realizing that he had noticed something about me. That maybe he had been watching me as carefully as I watched him.

I told him that my parents had been violent people, but I didn't turn out that way. He seemed confused—I'm Dauntless, after all, and we tend to be a violent bunch. But we aren't all the same, and I told him that, too. I remember what he said in response:

"Still, if you didn't turn out that way, you neither learned from their behavior nor inherited their genetic predisposition toward violence. Which means you've confounded both theories."

I smiled a little, but I didn't feel much like smiling. I

felt like every muscle in my body was coiled up tight.

Then he said—how could I forget it?—"I'm not surprised. You confound me all the time."

He touched my face, running his index finger over the piercings in my ear, and pushed his hand into my hair. Then he leaned in close and kissed me.

The Dauntless are all about taking action, but I swear, in that moment I couldn't move a muscle. All I could do was run through the sensations in my mind to seal them in my memory. How gentle and curious his fingers were as they danced over my ear. How his hands smelled like apple-scented soap and ink. How orange-red-yellow the light in the room was, because the sun was setting.

When I finally opened my eyes, I felt like I had made the moment permanent in my mind.

He started to get blotchy again, so I told him not to overthink it. He just laughed.

WEEK 50
MONDAY NIGHT

TODAY, WHEN ANDREW and I were on our way out of the school, he looked around to make sure no one was watching, then hooked his index finger around mine as we walked to the train tracks. Then, when the train horn sounded in the distance, he kissed me again, and stood back as I jumped on.

He's not the first boy I've kissed. But it's like everything is new, like I'm a new person here.

It's just a few weeks until the Choosing, and I'm supposed to pick Erudite anyway, according to David's instructions. Maybe it'll be all right, if Andrew is there. Maybe I can make it through initiation if I have his help.

I feel stupid even saying this, but that's why I'm going to say it here, in this private spot where no one else can hear it:

I feel like I'm in love.

WEEK 52
TUESDAY NIGHT

I DON'T KNOW what to do.

Andrew came to me yesterday in a panic, wild-eyed like I'd never seen him before. He wasn't even wearing his glasses. He told me that he had seen something terrible—one of his peers was doing some kind of cruel experiment under the supervision of an Erudite leader, her mentor. His mentor.

"I can't choose Erudite," is what he kept saying, and he kept shaking his head, too, like it was on a swivel.

"I know," is all I could think to say. "But where can you go?"

There were only three options, as far as he was concerned: Amity, Abnegation, or Candor.

"You can't be Candor, you're too private," is what I told him. "And you can't be Amity, either, because you care too much about taking action."

He looked startled. I guess I would have been startled too, if some girl I'd only known for a few months, only kissed a few times, assessed me like that. Like it's easy to label a person. Smart, private, handsome.

That left Abnegation. Narrowing it down to that faction seemed to steady him a little.

I got so sad, looking at him, like the little balloon that had begun to inflate inside me since he had kissed me was deflating. Or like I was a flower, wilting. I am supposed to join Erudite. To sidle up to whoever is killing the Divergent. To stop them.

That means that if I follow my mission, Andrew and I will be separated by the walls that divide the factions.

He must have seen my sadness in my face, because his wild look went away, and he took my hands in his. He told me he shouldn't even say it, but that I could join

Abnegation with him, that we would be safe there. Happy. A second later he took it back, reminded me that I had to make my own choice, that I shouldn't think of him.

But I can't help it.

WEEK 52
LATER TUESDAY NIGHT

HE SAID WE could be safe in Abnegation. My whole life I've wanted to be safe. I did things I shouldn't have in an attempt to make myself safe, but safety had eluded me anyway.

I've always watched the Abnegation every morning at school, how they slipped along the sides of the halls and sat quietly at lunch, how a small group of them sat on the steps every morning to help one another with homework. The Dauntless around me called them dull, but to me they always looked like they were floating on clouds. I guess having a distinct sense of purpose can do that to you, whereas the Dauntless are just restless, prone to bursts of restless action.

I would choose Abnegation, if I could, even if Andrew wasn't choosing it too. But I have a mission. I can't lose sight of it.

And now it's three in the morning and I can't sleep. I told myself when I came here that I wouldn't be taken in by the faction system. That I ought to maintain my distance from it. But I can feel the magic of it here, the options laid out in front of me, not so many that I feel overwhelmed, not so few that I feel stifled. And worse are the people who believe in those options, believe they are a way not just to live but to thrive.

I could thrive in Abnegation. And I've never been able to choose safety for myself. Now I'm not allowed to even when it's right in front of me. Even though this life is mine and I'm the only one who has to live it.

It's a lot to think about.

WEEK 52
FRIDAY AFTERNOON

MY DAUNTLESS MOTHER sat me down at the kitchen table today, and she was doing that thing she always does when she's nervous, flipping her septum piercing up into her nostrils and then down again.

She told me she saw my preliminary simulation results. She said she knew I was Divergent, and that in Dauntless, the Divergent tended to die without warning. She said that if I wanted to stay safe, I should choose another faction.

There's that word again, "safe." The truth is, I wouldn't be any safer in Erudite as a Divergent than I would be in Dauntless. That leaves me with the same choices Andrew had: Amity, Abnegation, or Candor.

Is it cowardly to choose safety over my mission? To choose love over my mission?

Or is it brave, to choose the life I want instead of the life I feel obligated to live?

WEEK 53
SUNDAY MORNING

YESTERDAY I CHOSE Abnegation. David isn't happy; no one over there is. But I am. I'm happy.

We waited for everyone else to walk out of the Choosing Ceremony and then we cleaned up after them, emptied all the bowls, careful of the broken glass in the Candor bowl and the hot coals in the Dauntless one. Then all the initiates had a meal together, each one serving the person on his left. I gave Andrew extra butter on his bread.

Then there was the foot-washing. I thought it would be awkward and gross, having a stranger touch my feet. But there were lit candles all around, so the room glowed orange, and everything was quiet except for the splashing of water and the humming of the woman in front of me.

And no, it wasn't the most comfortable thing I've ever done, but I just focused on the ritual of it. Hundreds of Abnegation had done that exact same thing at that exact same stage in their lives. Someday, I knew, if I lasted that long, I would do it for some initiates myself. Maybe even for my children. And it felt weighty, when I thought about it that way, and important, like something holy.

They told us to expect thirty days of service. Serving the poor, serving the rich, serving our elders, serving one another. Then they taught us the Abnegation manifesto, modest and brief as it is, and I had it memorized by the second run-through. We all chanted it, quietly, so the room was full of whispers. Then the girls went to a dormitory in Abnegation headquarters and the boys went to another.

The girls there stared openly at my tattoos when I changed into my gray Abnegation shirt. Most of them are Abnegation, and they've never seen a Dauntless up close. Some are Amity, too. But there was one Erudite girl, and she asked me about it as I took out my lip piercing for good.

"You transferred from Dauntless? That's rare," she said. I had already decided I liked her right away, just because of the way her limbs seemed to smack into everything when she walked, and because of her wild hair. Evelyn was her name.

"I know," I said. "So is transferring from Erudite."

She asked me what I thought so far. I told her everything seemed good, because the other girls were listening and I didn't want to say all the things I was thinking—that yes, Abnegation's way of life was peaceful and beautiful, but I was nervous about it. Afraid, not of danger or death, but of boredom.

Maybe she understood what I was thinking, because she leaned in close so she could keep her voice down and said, "Not so exciting, is it? But we didn't choose this for the constant thrills, right?"

I nodded. She smiled and started to braid her hair. I lay back in bed. The window next to my bed was open, so I fell asleep to the feeling of the cool air rushing over my toes.

Evelyn is right. I didn't choose Abnegation for the constant thrills. I chose it because it was the only guarantee of living a good life. And because I missed out on the opportunity to help other people once—I won't do it again.

This morning at breakfast Andrew smiled at me from across the table, and all my fears about Abnegation dissolved.

I didn't really expect to love it here. But I think I might. Now I just have to figure out a way to help the Divergent from inside the wrong faction.

YEAR 29, WEEK 18
SATURDAY MORNING

THE HOUSE FEELS so empty with the children gone. Last night Andrew came home from the Choosing Ceremony and shut himself in the bedroom for hours. I kept standing by the door with my fist raised to knock, and then losing my nerve. Even after all these years, sometimes it's difficult to know how to show him that I love him.

I went into Caleb's room and peeked under his bed and found a stack of library books there, gathering dust. They're in a box near the back door now, so I can return them to the school. It appears he was very interested in neuroscience. I always knew that my Caleb was bright—how could either of my children escape that, with their father's genes?—but I was never sure what he would make of it. I'm still not.

Beatrice, however, was a mystery. There was nothing in her room to suggest to me that she might choose Dauntless. I suppose her choice might have been an answer to the age-old question: safety or freedom? You can have both, but not always in equal measure. I chose the former, and she chose the latter.

I wish I had been able to be more open with both of them. Not to change their choices, but to make sure they are prepared for what they will find in their new factions. For Beatrice, in Dauntless, there will be danger; for Caleb, in Erudite, the threat of corruption. But I didn't succeed in warning either of them.

It's so quiet here, and Andrew looks worn. And I'm just sitting here with my failure.

I suppose there's always Visiting Day.

YEAR 29, WEEK 21
FRIDAY AFTERNOON

David,

I got your message, and I appreciate the warning. I will try to protect my family, as you suggested, but you know as well as I do that I'm not going to leave it at that.

If this is the last message I send you . . . well, let's just say I hope you burn for this.

Sincerely,

Natalie

DELETED SCENE FROM ALLEGIANT

FEAR NUMBER TATTOOS

This scene originally appeared right before Tris, Tobias, and the others leave the city for the outside world. It takes place at the now-abandoned Dauntless compound, where the former Dauntless are gathering to defy the factionless and their strict curfew policies. I cut it to resolve some pacing issues, but originally I wrote it because it establishes so many characters and dynamics and emotions in such a short space, and it's the last hurrah of Dauntless, sort of bookending the series. You may recognize bits of it—some of the information in this passage is now sprinkled throughout ALLEGIANT.—Veronica Roth

TRIS

TORI, WHO IS carrying a small cardboard box, sets it down and climbs onto one of the tables. Then she holds up a hand for silence. It comes in bits and pieces.

"I called this meeting partly to stick it to Evelyn Johnson—" Cheering. "And partly for another reason."

She reaches into the box at her feet and takes out a tattoo needle.

"To create something that binds us all together." She holds the needle in both hands, as gently as she would hold a child. "No matter what ridiculous system the factionless come up with for everyone, we will always be the people who know their fears and choose to face them rather than ignore them. So I think we should always wear them on our skin."

She rolls up one of her sleeves, revealing a large number 12 on her upper arm.

"I have twelve fears," she says. "And I've faced them all."

I expect the Dauntless to whoop, or scream, or stomp their feet, but this time, they don't. Instead, several of them start to line up in front of Tori's table, rolling up their own sleeves.

My chest aches. This might be the last thing we ever do as a faction. The last night of being Dauntless, not just for those of us who are leaving the city but for everyone who ever spilled his or her blood on the coals. I hear the sizzle in my ears, the moment after I chose, and my vision goes blurry.

I know it's time to leave the factions behind, whether I agree with Evelyn or not. But for some reason it's still hard to let them go.

Tobias crosses the room and sits beside me. I bump my shoulder against his. His hair—still short, but longer than it was when I first met him—is tousled, and he smells like air, like wind, like sweat.

Across the room, Tori is already drawing a number on a woman's arm, and one of the other Dauntless sits down with Tori's partner, Bud, who has more ink than skin—it creeps up his throat and over his jaw and cradles his skull with images.

"I'd better get in Bud's line," I say, holding up my wrist. The outline of Tori's teeth still marks my skin in scabs. It's a souvenir of our fight in Erudite headquarters, when she wanted to kill Jeanine and I wanted to force her to reveal the Edith Prior video. "Tori would probably rather stab me than tattoo me right now."

"You should just punch her," Uriah says, pointing lazily at me. "Anyone who resorts to *biting* needs a good punch, in my opinion."

I frown at him. "Are you *drunk*?"

"Absolutely not."

"I'm not an idiot," I say. "But clearly *you* are. Remember what tonight is?"

"I'll be fine," Uriah says.

"He's my responsibility, anyway," says Tobias. "According to Zeke, if anything happens to him on our little mission, my head will be mounted on a stick somewhere outside Dauntless headquarters."

"I believe I said it would be mounted on a fork, because a stick is too tough-looking. But yeah. That's right," says Zeke. "I may be smaller than you, but I'm much cleverer."

Uriah makes a face at Zeke and follows Christina to the tattoo lines.

The Dauntless cycle through the lines quickly. Time wears on, and as it does, I become more and more aware of what we are going to do tonight. Leave the city. Break the law. Maybe never return. Find the world outside. Hear the answers to all our questions.

Are we really just an experiment? How long have you been out there? Have you been watching us? What do you want from us?

And for me, the most important one: *Who is Edith Prior*?

Christina returns from the tattoo line with a number 13 on her arm. I notice a few tiny shapes floating over the 3, and she gives me a wicked smile.

"Moths," she explains. "Tough as cotton balls, right?"

I laugh, and then I wonder if it's all right to laugh, because that's what Will said to her when he found out she was afraid of moths. But I guess that, after someone dies, what's all right to feel is whatever you do feel. And Christina is still smiling.

"Feels good to think about it," she says as she sits on my other side. "You know?"

I nod, and even though I'm a Stiff and I don't do this sort of thing, I grab her hand and squeeze it.

Uriah approaches the table not long after her, his right sleeve rolled up to reveal a clear bandage. Through the bandage I see the dark outline of the number 10.

He doesn't sit down. His hands are shaking, and as I watch, a tear drops straight from his eye and onto the table.

"What is it?" says Zeke.

"Had her add an extra one," said Uriah. "Because of Mar."

He means Marlene, Uriah's girlfriend, my friend, who walked straight off the roof of the Pire under a simulation. She is the reason Uriah is falling apart.

Christina gets up and puts an arm around Uriah's waist. She's almost as tall as he is, and she meets his eyes steadily. "Come on, Uri. We can talk it out by the chasm."

She helps him turn around and walk toward the doors. Their path wavers with Uriah's footsteps, but Christina is patient with him; she just guides him, her head bent close to his. Zeke watches them until they disappear into the Pit, then says, "We should get going."

Tobias and I stand in Bud's line, and Shauna maneuvers her wheelchair to Tori's line, ahead of Zeke. I check my watch. We only have a few hours until we set our escape plan in motion—I didn't intend to spend those hours waiting for a tattoo, but maybe that's just the way it's going to be.

"I'm really going to miss this place," I say.

"Really?" He shrugs. "My thoughts are more like, 'Good riddance.'"

"There's *nothing* you'll miss? No good memories?" I elbow him.

"Fine. There are a few." He smiles.

"Any that don't involve me?" I say. "That sounds really self-centered. You know what I mean."

"Sure. I guess." Tobias shrugs. "I mean, I got to have a different life here, a different name, even. Here I was always Four, thanks to my initiation instructor. He came up with the nickname."

"The legendary Four," I say with a flourish of my hand.

"Indeed." He spreads his arms wide. "And how fortunate you are to bask in my presence."

I jab him in the ribs with my elbow.

"Why haven't I met this initiation instructor?"

"Because he's dead." Tobias says "dead" like it's just another word, but his eyes find mine and I can tell this is anything but a casual topic. "Amar was Divergent."

I touch his arm, lightly, but there isn't much to say. He shifts like he's uncomfortable.

"See?" he says. "Too many bad memories here. I'm ready to leave."

We are quiet for a while, and it feels comfortable, which is a strange thing for me. Usually silence is charged with all the words a person isn't saying, or can't find a way to say, but with him, I feel like my presence is enough, like his presence is enough.

We move closer and closer to the tattoo needles, and when we're a few feet away, Tori says without lifting her head, "You two, get in my line instead."

I feel nervous, but I don't want her to know that I'm afraid of her, so I do what she says.

I go before Tobias, and when Tori finishes with the Dauntless woman in front of me, she curls her finger at me. "You're up."

She is switching out the old needle for a new one and preparing a new batch of ink. Her hands are bare and small, steadier than any hands I've ever seen. They almost seem to rest on top of the air like it's a table, motionless.

I sit in front of her.

"You can come closer, you know," she says. "I won't bite." She tilts her head. "Oh, wait. I have done that, haven't I?"

I scoot closer.

"I know your upper arm is already taken, so you can choose a different place," she says, and her voice is unexpectedly soft. Her eyes, which curve gently down at the edges, find mine.

"Okay," I say.

"Your number?" she says. "Or your best approximation of it?"

My fear number, when I went through my fear landscape during initiation, was seven. But am I afraid of the same things now that I was when I was an initiate? Am I still afraid of being responsible for my family's deaths when they're already gone? Am I still afraid of being with Tobias, in *that* way?

"If you're having trouble, think of the tattoo as a memory of your fears as a Dauntless initiate," Tori says. "The number can change, but the memory will always be the same, and that's what you're recording, not your fear count."

That makes it easier. "My number was seven."

I offer my arm to her, and she cleans my forearm with antiseptic, then touches the needle to my skin. I am used to the prick of the needle and the stinging pain that makes my eyes water. I don't even have to look away this time. I just watch the needle move, and her hand wiping the excess ink, and my skin turning red around it. I still don't like the buzzing sound it makes—it's like a swarm of bees.

"Apparently you didn't need Jeanine to be alive after all," Tori says quietly. "You didn't need her to be alive in order to get the video shown."

"I didn't know that at the time."

"Or a part of you didn't want to know. Wanted to keep her alive."

"I'm glad she's dead."

"Hmm."

"Hey," I say harshly, so she pauses, lifts the needle. "I hated her. I'm glad she's dead. You're not the only one she stole people from, so stop acting like it."

She doesn't answer. Instead she goes back to the tattoo, tracing each line, filling in the space between them. When she finishes, the skin around the number 7 is bright red, but it doesn't hurt that much. She bandages it, and I realize that the room has gone quiet. Bud is putting away his supplies, and Tobias, standing behind me, is the last one in line. The silence is for him.

+++

"WE ALL KNOW *your* number, Tobias Eaton," Tori says.

I still feel a prickle of fear whenever someone says my name out loud, like it's a forbidden word. For a long time it belonged only to me, until I gave it to Tris, but then the Candor wrenched it from me with their truth serum, and now it belongs to everyone.

My shirt has long sleeves that are tight around the wrist, so I pull one up as far as it will go—to my elbow—and sit, offering my blank skin for her to mark. I am already warm with embarrassment, standing in this room that shouldn't be silent but is. She raises an eyebrow at me.

"I don't remember putting a tattoo on your arm," she says, slapping my upper arm lightly. "Come on, let them all see the fine work I did on your back."

She asked me, once, why I got so many tattoos if I was always going to keep them covered, even in the heat of summer when most Dauntless wear as little clothing as possible. I didn't give her a reason, but I still remember it—I wanted the tattoos to cover all the places he hurt me, the back that bore the belt and the side that bore the fist.

A lot of people hate scars, but before I joined Dauntless, I had always wished that I had some. I wanted to have some kind of reminder that while wounds heal, they don't disappear forever—we carry them everywhere, always, and that is the way of things, the way of scars. So I got the tattoos instead.

And I hid them, because I didn't want these people to see those wounds, even if they wouldn't know what they were looking at.

I curl my fingers around the hem of my shirt and pull it over my head. I sit up straight, my back to the room, the flames on my side expanding and contracting with my hurried breaths. Tori cleans the skin on my arm, and I feel like their stares are the flames, and my skin heats up more for every second they spend looking at me.

They are silent while she draws the number, and at first I feel like their silence is cruel, like it scrutinizes me. But as she draws the last lines on me, I realize that the Dauntless shout when they feel camaraderie, and they are silent when they feel respectful. To them I am still the man with only four fears.

I stare down at the 4 as she covers it with a bandage, and I realize that this, unlike the other tattoos, is something I am proud to carry everywhere, proud even to carry outside the fence, to whatever will come next.

#VOTEALLEGIANT WINNING SCENE

STRIKE FIRST, STRIKE HARD

It was really difficult to cut this scene from ALLEGIANT. *I originally had an entire section where Tris, Tobias, and the others reunite with the rest of Dauntless—a kind of quiet rebellion in which they assert their choice to stay a faction no matter what the factionless say. And this moment that Tris has with Peter was a part of it. It showed some of Peter's vulnerability as well as how much Tris has changed since he first tormented her in this dormitory. She is stronger, now, but harder too; not all of the lessons she has learned are good ones. But I cut the Dauntless section because it slowed down the plot when I needed it to speed up, and with it went Tris and Peter.*

TRIS

THE TRAINS AREN'T running, so I walk to Dauntless headquarters. Alone. That seems about right—the first time

I went to Dauntless headquarters I was also alone, but in a crowd, standing on the edge of the roof in just my Abnegation shirt, about to throw myself into a life I knew nothing about.

The streets are cracked and worn, and all the buildings look the same to me except the Pire, piercing the sky in the distance, much smaller than the Hub but still the largest building around here. But I am not looking for the Pire; I am looking for the hole I jumped into, once to become Dauntless, and once to save my family.

I know it is south of the Pire, and close to the train tracks—close enough to leap from the tracks to a rooftop—so I follow them, higher here than anywhere else in the city, suspended above me by a complex system of latticed wood and metal. I see the place where they curve around a rooftop, and then I spot the hole in the space between two brick-and-glass buildings.

It seems much smaller here than it did from the roof. Maybe it's just that I feel larger now, because so much has happened since I last saw it—I feel like more of a person, more of myself, now that I have made difficult decisions and lost people and then almost lost myself, but not quite.

I walk right up to the edge, just to make sure there is still a net at the bottom. Then I back up, run a few steps, and launch into emptiness. My stomach drops and the darkness engulfs me, like the Dauntless compound is a creature and this is its mouth. I hit the net and it doesn't sting like it did when I jumped from the roof; it just cradles me, and I hook my fingers in the spaces to pull myself to the edge.

I remember Tobias's hand stretching toward me, guiding me to the wood platform when I first made this jump. I remember dropping to the platform and seeing him for the first time, his eyes dark and familiar, his mouth asking for my name.

Tris, I said, for the first time.

I walk down the hallway to the Pit. The doors are already open, and it occurs to me that I might not be the only one who came here early. I take my knife from my back pocket. There is rust at the end of the blade, but it feels solid in my hands, stronger than the damage time can do.

The chasm roars, the water crashing against the rocks. I search the Pit walls for movement and, seeing none, I walk to the railing. I wonder now, and should have wondered before, where this water comes from, and where it leads. But the world felt so small to me, before, and my greatest worries involved the Choosing Ceremony and the Erudite hatred of Abnegation. Since then my worries have been growing, expanding to include not just the whole city but the space that lies beyond it, and I have no idea how much space that is.

I see bits of paper at the bottom of the chasm, and aluminum cans, their labels worn off by the river. I remember dangling over it with a hand on my throat, my vision going dark at the edges, and I back away, air hissing between my teeth.

I came here for nostalgia. But a lot of bad things happened here, and though the bad things that came next quickly exceeded them, I still bear the marks of the old wrongs, like little fingerprints all over my body.

I walk toward the faction transfer dormitory, finding my way by the emergency lights, which will be on for as long as the city has electricity. The door to the dormitory, like the doors to the Pit, is already open.

I enter cautiously, one foot at a time. I'm not sure who I expect to be here—Peter? Drew? Edward?

I don't see anyone, so I walk to my bunk. The covers are still curled back in the shape of a body, but it's not my body—the Dauntless stayed here briefly before the Erudite attack, and I'm sure every bed was occupied. I open the drawers under the mattress, and laugh out loud.

I find my gray sneakers, gray shirt, and gray pants. A black dress. A watch. Black boots. All the possessions I managed to acquire before Jeanine Matthews changed the world.

With another look around, I pull my red shirt over my head and put on the gray one instead. I replace the new

Abnegation watch with the old one, though they're nearly identical. I take off my sneakers and pull on the black boots instead.

I am just tying the laces when I hear a noise—footsteps. I grab my knife, ignoring the tightness in my throat, and point it at the doorway.

"Stop," I say when a shape appears in the hallway just outside.

"A little touchy, Stiff?"

Peter. Of course.

"What are you doing here?" I say.

"I heard there's a Dauntless gathering tonight. You mean you didn't know about it? Can't say I'm not surprised."

"Of course I know about it. That's why I'm here too."

He sighs and runs his fingers along one of the bed-frames. "What a shame."

He sits on one of the mattresses—his old one, if I remember right. He flicks his hair—still unnaturally shiny—from his eyes. "There's really no need to keep pointing that knife at me."

"Are you kidding?" I say. "As far as I'm concerned, you're going to be at knifepoint until everyone else gets here. And maybe even then."

"Whatever." He opens the drawer beneath his bed and

rummages through a stack of papers inside. One of my shoelaces is still untied, but I can't finish tying it without putting the knife down, so I just sit on my old bed and watch him.

"What are those?" I say, nodding to the papers in his hands. "A record of your evil deeds?"

"Yes. Right here I talk about how easy it was to dangle you over the chasm. Because you're so very small."

Anger burns through my curiosity, and my hands shake with it. "It was pretty easy to put a bullet in your arm, too. Want me to reopen that wound, for old times' sake?"

He is not provoked. He flips the page in his hand, and this time I can read the words on the back of it. Written in a lazy scrawl: "public humiliation, abandonment, loss of control, failure, betrayal, death . . ." The list continues, but it's too dark for me to see. They're his fears. He kept a record of them.

"How many did you have?"

He looks up, then crumples the piece of paper into his fist, packing it tighter and tighter until the ball is the size of a nut.

"Why, so you can lord over me how you have only eight, or whatever your number was?" he says, and it's one of the first times I've ever heard him sound defensive. "No thanks. I'm good."

"I had seven," I say. "And I conquered one."

"I don't care."

"I bet you had a lot," I say. "I bet you have more now than you ever did before. Someone as pathetic as you has a lot to be afraid of."

He lunges toward me, and I hold the knife next to my face like I am about to throw it. He freezes.

"Bet you wouldn't be so brave without that knife."

"Bet I'm not stupid enough to put it down just to prove to you how brave I am."

He stares at me for a few seconds, his fingers splayed, taut, at his sides. Then he leaves.

I release the breath I was holding, and lean my arms into my knees, the dagger dangling between my legs. For a moment I think I should feel bad for insulting him and provoking him after he took a huge risk in saving my life. But then I remember how he almost ended it too, and how he beat me senseless in training, and how he cut out Edward's eye, and all my guilt dissipates like an exhale.

Besides, I have learned an important lesson since I first walked into this room: Strike first, and strike hard, and you might have a shot at survival.

Turn the page to read
favorite quotes from

ALLEGIANT

illustrated by fellow Initiates

Risa Rodil

Danemar Kristine Calise

Maria Veronica F. Parajes

Sulla Montes

I wonder if fears ever really go away or if they just lose their power over us.

—TRIS

I'M DAUNTLESS

I'm A GOOD Shot and I PROVIDE much-needed EYE CANDY.

-URIAH

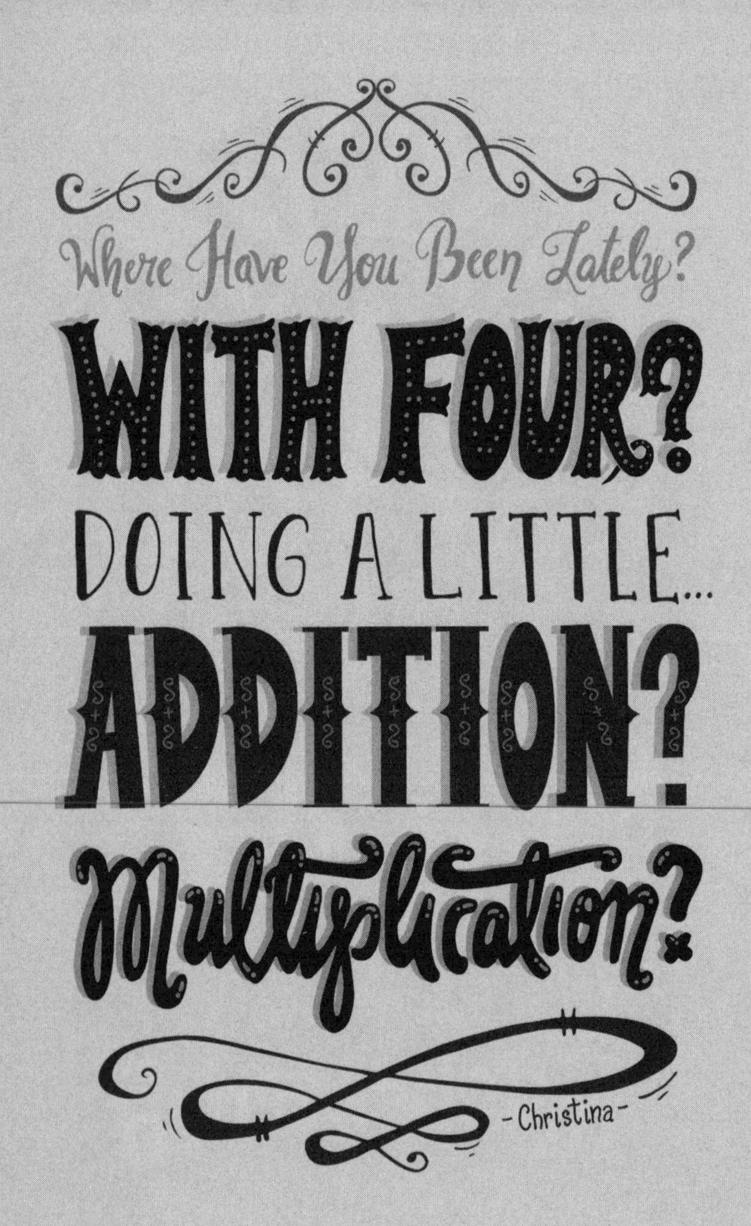
Where Have You Been Lately?
WITH FOUR?
DOING A LITTLE...
ADDITION?
Multiplication?
-Christina-

To Be Such a COMPLICATED, Mysterious PIECE OF BIOLOGICAL MACHINERY! THAT IS A SPECIAL thing, Unprecedented in all of EVOLUTIONARY HISTORY. Our Ability to Know About OURSELVES AND THE WORLD IS WHAT MAKES Us human.

— Caleb —

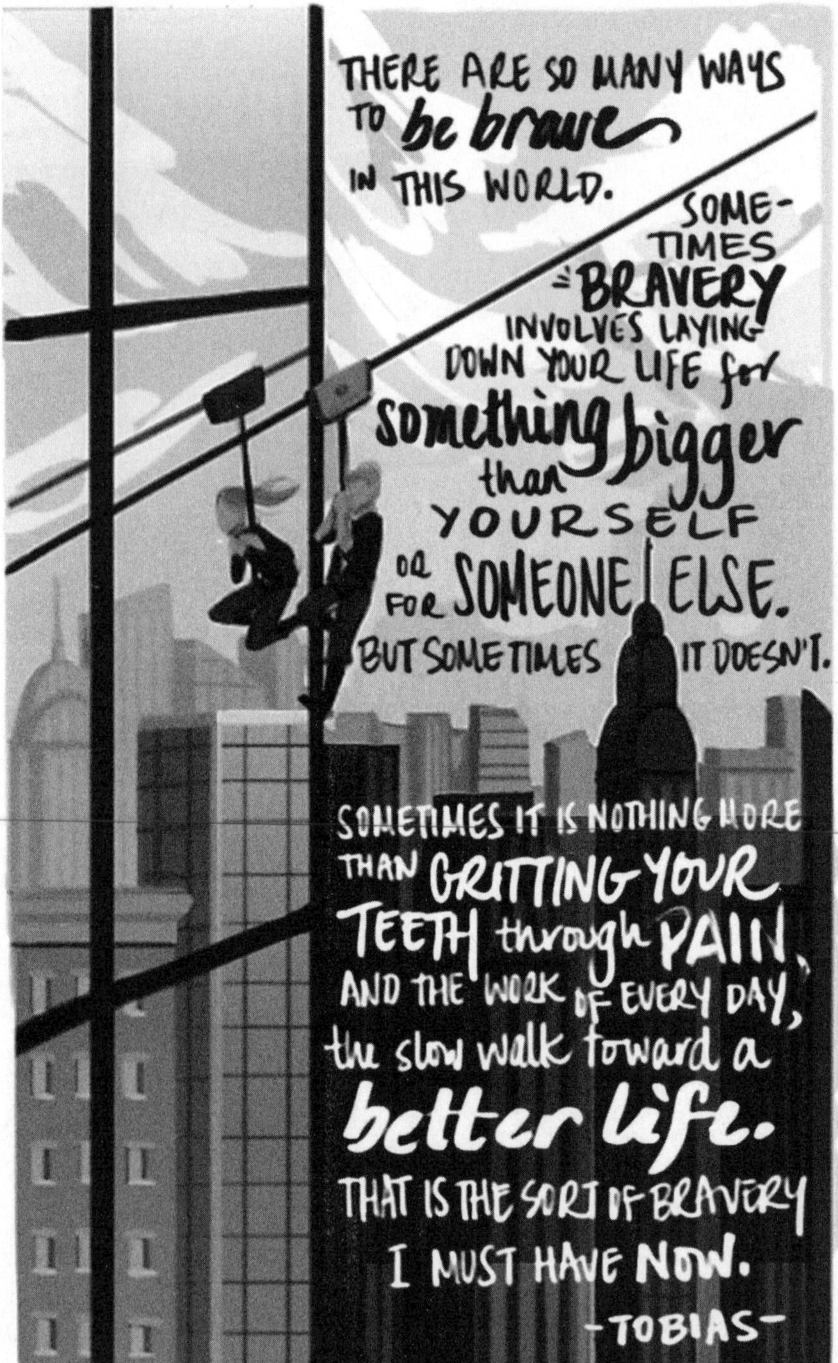

THERE ARE SO MANY WAYS
TO be brave
IN THIS WORLD.
SOME-
TIMES
BRAVERY
INVOLVES LAYING
DOWN YOUR LIFE for
something bigger
than
YOURSELF
OR
FOR SOMEONE ELSE.
BUT SOMETIMES IT DOESN'T.

SOMETIMES IT IS NOTHING MORE
THAN GRITTING YOUR
TEETH through PAIN,
AND THE WORK OF EVERY DAY,
the slow walk toward a
better life.
THAT IS THE SORT OF BRAVERY
I MUST HAVE NOW.

-TOBIAS-

SHE TAUGHT ME ALL ABOUT REAL
sacrifice
THAT IT SHOULD BE DONE
FROM love...
FROM NECESSITY,
NOT WITHOUT EXHAUSTING
ALL OTHER OPTIONS. THAT
IT SHOULD BE DONE FOR THE
people WHO NEED YOUR
strength
BECAUSE THEY DON'T HAVE
ENOUGH OF THEIR OWN.
-TRIS-

I AM

BRAVE

RESPECTED

LOVED

AND

WORTH LOVING

Tris

I DON'T JUST STAY WITH HIM BY DEFAULT.

I CHOOSE TO.

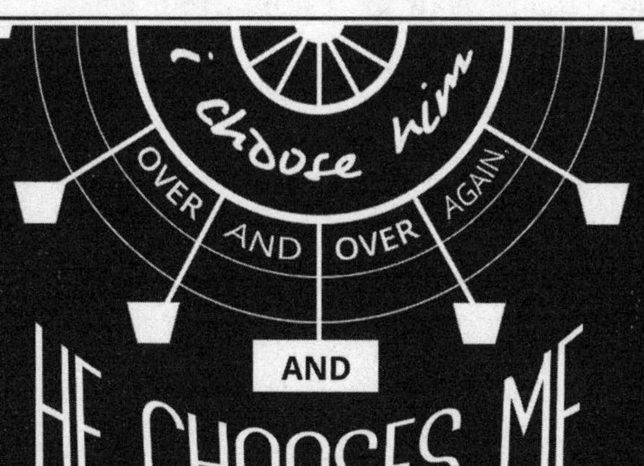

HE CHOOSES ME.

Tris

ALLEGIANT DISCUSSION QUESTIONS

1. The third book in the DIVERGENT series opens with Tris being held prisoner by Evelyn, Tobias's mother. Describe the circumstances surrounding her imprisonment. What can you infer from the text about her situation? Explain how Tobias comes to her rescue.

2. Why is Tris angry with Caleb, her brother, and why does Tobias plan his escape from prison? Is Tris's anger justified? Why or why not?

3. Who are the Allegiants and what is their mission? How do Tris and Tobias become involved in their movement? Why does Cara choose Tris and Tobias as part of her team?

4. Describe Tobias's relationship with his parents. Who are they and why does his mother tell him about the Allegiants?

5. Why do Tris and Tobias want to go "outside the fence"? Describe the world of the compound and the work of the Bureau. How does this world differ from the lives Tris and Tobias have known? What parallels, if any, can you draw with modern society and class systems?

6. Who is David and why does he want Tris to train to be a member of the council? Why is Tris interested in this role? What does she learn about her mother while living at the compound and how does this information affect her beliefs?

7. Both Tris and Tobias undergo genetic testing. What does Tobias learn about himself and how does this information affect his self-image?

8. Both Tobias and Tris visit the fringe. Characterize this community. How does it differ from their city? How does it differ from the compound? Why do they go there and what effect does it have on them?

9. Tobias asks Cara how she can forgive Tris for killing her brother. What answer does she give? What does her response say about her character?

10. Who is Nita and what role does she play in the story? Is she a likeable character? Why or why not?

11. What do Tobias and Tris learn about the work of the Bureau and why do they plot to secure the memory serum?

12. How does Tris save the Bureau? Are her actions characteristic of her personality? How is her brother affected by her choice?

13. Tobias has an unstable relationship with both of his parents. After watching video of both parents he says, "I feel like what I have become is halfway between my mother and my father, violent and impulsive and desperate and afraid." Explain his thinking. Would you agree or not?

14. At the end of the story, Tobias says, "There are so many ways to be brave in this world. Sometimes bravery involves laying down your life for something bigger than yourself, or for someone else. . . . Sometimes it is nothing more than gritting your teeth through pain, and the work of every day, the slow walk toward a better life." Why does Tobias make this statement? What examples in your life or in the lives of those around you support this belief?

15. The freedom to choose is one recurring theme in the story. Use evidence from the text to discuss this theme.